METROPOLIS

METROPOLIS

a novel

B. A. Shapiro

ALGONQUIN BOOKS OF
CHAPEL HILL 2022

Published by
Algonquin Books of Chapel Hill
Post Office Box 2225
Chapel Hill, North Carolina 27515-2225

a division of
Workman Publishing
225 Varick Street
New York, New York 10014

LIBRARY OF CONGRESS CATALOGING-IN-PUBLICATION DATA
Names: Shapiro, Barbara A., [date]– author.
Title: Metropolis : a novel / B.A. Shapiro.
Description: Chapel Hill, North Carolina : Algonquin Books of
Chapel Hill [2022] | Summary: "The interlocking stories of six characters whose
only connection is their units at a storage facility, where a tragic accident will either
tear them apart or help them salvage their own precarious lives"— Provided by publisher.
Identifiers: LCCN 2021057377 | ISBN 9781616209582 (hardcover) |
ISBN 9781643752945 (ebook)
Subjects: LCGFT: Novels.
Classification: LCC PS3569.H3385 M48 2022 | DDC 813/.54—dc23/eng/20211126
LC record available at https://lccn.loc.gov/2021057377

10 9 8 7 6 5 4 3 2 1
First Edition

In loving memory of my parents

An imbalance between rich and poor is the oldest and most fatal ailment of all republics.

Unknown

METROPOLIS

PART ONE

BOSTONGLOBE.COM, JANUARY 7, 2018. Cambridge, MA— Rescue workers were dispatched to the Metropolis Storage Warehouse at Massachusetts Avenue and Vassar Street in response to a 911 call at 11:15 this evening. At least one person was taken to Massachusetts General Hospital with critical injuries after a fall down an elevator shaft. Details are limited, and neither police nor hospital officials identified the victim. Questions were raised about what people were doing at the self-storage facility at that hour, and police are investigating other violations concerning the building. *This is a developing story. It will be updated.*

1

ZACH
May 2018

It's Rose's fault. It's Aetna's fault. It's Otis Elevator's fault. All of the above and none of the above. Zach Davidson hovers at the edge of the crowd, but at six two it's tough to blend into the background. The auctioneer doesn't know Zach is the recipient of the money from the forthcoming sales, and he wants to keep it that way, although he doesn't know why this matters. He isn't even sure why he's come, unless as some perverse form of self-flagellation.

"Most of you know the rules," the auctioneer begins in her booming voice, "but I'm going to go over them quickly. Due to foreclosure of the building, the contents of twenty-two abandoned storage units are up for sale. The minimum bid is one hundred dollars. Cash only. I'll open the door to each unit, and you'll have five minutes to see what's inside, and then I'll start the auction. You may not cross the threshold. You may not touch anything. You may not ask me any questions, because I don't have any answers. You take it all or you leave it all. Then we move on to the next unit. Is this clear?"

There's a murmur of acceptance, which echoes off the concrete walls and floor, the steel-reinforced ceiling. They're standing outside the office that used to belong to Rose, the woman Zach shouldn't have relied on. Every direction he looks pisses him off. Rose's empty desk, the dim bulbs, the peeling paint. He turns his back on the yellow police tape stretched across the elevator.

It's been almost four months since it happened, and still no one knows for sure if it was an accident, attempted murder, or even suicide. Could be any of them, but it doesn't make all that much difference. He's screwed any which way. Damn elevator. Damn Rose. Damn hard luck.

He follows the auctioneer as she marches down a corridor lined with heavy metal doors, each imprinted with a round medallion containing a large *M* intertwined with a smaller *S* and *W*. Metropolis Storage Warehouse. One hundred and twenty-three years old. Six stories high. Ninety feet wide. Four hundred and eighty feet long. Almost four hundred storage units of various sizes and shapes; some even have windows. Zach knows it well.

The potential bidders are a mixed bunch. Two men in ratty clothes smell as if they've been sleeping on the street, which they probably have. Another three look like lawyers or real estate developers, and there's a foursome of gray-hairs who appear to have just stepped off the golf course. A gaggle of middle-aged women in running shoes sends stern glances at a girl clutching a pen and a pad of paper, who seems far too young to be the mother of the children she's yelling at. Male, female, tall, short, fat, slim, white, Black, brown, rich, poor, clever, or not so clever. Like the inner recesses of Metropolis itself, a diverse assemblage that stands in contrast to the archipelago of cultural and economic neighborhoods Boston has become.

Zach has owned Metropolis for ten years, bought at a ridiculously low price in a quasi-legal deal that looked to be the way out of the consequences of his bad choices. Although it still belongs to him, however temporarily, he has no idea what's behind any of the doors. The building had a well-deserved shady reputation when he purchased it, and he concluded he was better off not knowing what people were storing in their units. In retrospect, a little prying might have averted this mess.

The auctioneer, a beefy woman with biceps twice the size of Zach's, takes a key from her backpack and dramatically twists it into the lock. Then she slides the ten-foot-wide fireproof door along its track on the floor to reveal a murky room, lumpy with shadowy objects. She reaches inside and flips on the light.

"Take it all! Leave it all!" she cries. "Five minutes!"

Revealed by naked light bulbs hanging from the eleven-foot ceiling, #114 is decidedly dull. An old refrigerator, an electric stove, a bunch of mismatched chairs, a couple of mattresses, clothes overflowing from open cartons scattered all over the floor. There are at least two dozen sealed boxes lined up against the far wall and a four-foot pile of empty picture frames ready to topple. Everything is coated with what appears to be decades of dust. Zach groans inwardly. He needs every cent he can squeeze out of this auction, and no one's going to bid on any of this junk.

But he's wrong. After the auctioneer starts rippling her tongue in an impenetrable torrent of words, people start raising their hands. When the contents go for $850, Zach is flabbergasted. The other units surely contain more impressive stuff than this and should generate even higher bids.

Some do, some don't, and two are completely empty.

"Take it all! Leave it all! Five minutes!"

When the auctioneer unlocks the door of #357, there's a collective gasp. The interior looks like a stage waiting for the evening performance to commence: a complete upscale office suite, including a desk, bookshelves, and a small conference table surrounded by four chairs. Bizarre. It goes for $3,500.

On the fifth floor is a tiny and perfectly immaculate unit: a neatly made single bed, an intricately carved rolltop desk, a chair, a small bureau. Nothing else. One thousand dollars. In #454, there's another bizarre tableau. Creepy, actually. It appears to belong to a couple of teenagers. Two desks piled with books and trophies, walls covered with movie posters, and corkboards adorned with invitations and photos and newspaper clippings. Did they come here to study? To hide? Zach stretches his neck in as far as he can without the auctioneer cutting it off.

She almost does. "Step back, sir!" she yells, her voice stiletto-sharp.

"This minute!" Everyone looks at him as if he's committed a heinous crime. "Take it all! Leave it all! Five minutes!"

Annoyed, he does as she orders, but he wants to see more, surprised to find himself interested in the lives lived here. This is something he'd never considered before, or to be more correct, he had thought about it, but only as a means to get the bad guys out of the building and clean up his own act. Now the questions surge. Who were these people? Why these particular items? And, most intriguing of all, why did they leave so much behind?

Unit 421 is another stage, but this one is freakish in its attention to detail. It's a double unit with two round windows, and it looks like an upscale studio apartment, perhaps a pied-à-terre. Against one wall, a queen-size bed is covered by a rumpled silk bedspread and an unreasonable number of pillows. A nightstand holding a lamp and a clock sits to its right side; a large abstract painting is centered over the headboard. At the other end of the unit is an overstuffed reading chair, a writing desk, and a sectional couch, also with too many pillows, facing a large-screen television. In the corner, there's a small table, two chairs, and a compact kitchen featuring cabinets, a refrigerator, a microwave, and a fancy hot plate.

"Take it all! Leave it all! Five minutes!"

This time there's no doubt in Zach's mind to whom the unit belongs, or rather, to whom it had belonged. Liddy Haines. He closes his eyes and presses his forefinger to the bridge of his nose in an attempt to make the horrific image go away, which it does not. Six thousand dollars.

Unit 514 was apparently used as a darkroom, and from the looks of it, also as a bedroom. He stares at the sheets pooling at the edge of a cot, at the dirty clothes heaped on the floor. He's seen three beds in three different units over the last hour, and he clenches his fists to contain his anger. If Rose didn't know people were living here, she should have. It was a lawsuit waiting to happen—even if it wasn't the lawsuit now upending his life. An irony he'd appreciate more if he weren't so damn furious.

In contrast to Liddy Haines's unit, there's no expensive furniture here, but there is a lot of high-quality photographic equipment. A long table edges the south side of the room, overflowing with trays, chemicals, jugs, paper, an enlarger, and an assortment of spools, filters, thermometers, and timers. A clothesline with pins attached stretches over the jumble, and there are at least a dozen five-gallon Poland Spring containers, most of them full, along with another dozen warehouse-size cartons of energy bars.

A Rolleiflex camera is perched atop a stack of cartons, its well-worn leather strap dangling. Zach recognizes it because of the nature photography he's been doing lately, his current obsession. Highpointing, climbing the highest peak in every state, was his last one, and that's what got him into taking landscape pictures in the first place. But his interest in mountaineering has been waning—thirty-two states is more than enough—as his new interest in photography has waxed. He's usually only good for one obsession at a time, dropping the previous one when another grabs his fancy. He's an all-in or all-out kind of guy.

The Rolleiflex is a twin-lens reflex, medium format, which hardly anyone uses anymore. But if you know what you're doing, it takes remarkable photos. Zach rented one when he was at Bryce last year, and the first time he looked down into the viewfinder—which is at waist, rather than eye, level—he was blown away.

The vastness of the mountains and the big sky in front of him were perfectly reflected through the lens, without the tunnel vision effect of a standard camera. When he returned to Boston, he kept it a few extra days and experimented with street photography. The cool part is that because you're looking down rather than directly at your subject, no one is aware they're being photographed. Vivian Maier, arguably one of the greatest street photographers ever, used a Rolleiflex.

Zach leans into the unit as far as the fascist will allow, searching for pictures. There are a few lying about, but it's difficult to see them from the hallway. The ones he can see are all square rather than rectangular, a feature of the Rolleiflex. He tilts his head and squints at a photo on the end of the table closest to him: a striking black-and-white with afternoon sunlight cutting a diagonal across the image.

A man is standing in front of an open door with an arched top; the word "Office" can be clearly read behind his head. His shoulder leans against the doorframe, one knee slightly bent. His eyes stare off into the distance. Before Zach understands what he's seeing, his stomach twists. It's a photograph of him.

2

ROSE

Eight Months Earlier: September 2017

The first of the month is the day most of the money comes in. Direct deposit, checks in the mail, and then there's the cash, that nice hard cash. But because of the Labor Day holiday, this month the rent is due on the fifth. Rose waits in her office, which is shabby but big. Way too big. It's three storage units combined, a waste of rentable space as far as she's concerned, but she just works here, so it's Zach Davidson's problem, not hers. And she knows he couldn't care less.

She likes that she has a window facing the street and the door to the hallway has a window, so there's plenty of light, even in the winter. She gets to see who's coming in and going out of the building. It's important for her to keep tabs. She considers this part of her job, even if Zach never really said it was.

She enters the rent data into a spreadsheet and carefully double-checks her work. She's as far from a computer expert as you can get, and she doesn't want to make any mistakes. The nuns hammered this fear of mistakes into her with smacks to the knuckles and by making her spend lots of afternoons sweeping the vestry. But their lessons about honesty and virtue don't seem to have stuck so well. Or maybe they did, and that's why her stomach runs sick on rent day.

Serge steals in around nine thirty. He's a tall man, way too thin, and even though he looks like the Scarecrow in *The Wizard of Oz*, he moves like the Tin Man. He's probably only a couple years older than her, but he looks like he's sixty, what with his skin all pasty and white. Even stranger is that his eyes are a really light green, like no color she's ever seen before, and they don't match his red hair and beard at all.

He's a photographer but not a particularly good one. His pictures are black-and-white, and almost all of them are of ugly or sad people who never smile. Lots of them are just the backs of people and some are just shadows. Serge has no idea she knows any of this. None of the renters have any idea all she knows about them, and the thought of her secret visits to their units always gives her a jolt of forbidden pleasure.

Serge doesn't make eye contact because he never does, but instead of being annoyed Rose feels sorry for him. She can tell he's lonely. Heck, she knows he is, and she wishes she could do something to make him feel better. Even though this isn't her problem any more than Zach Davidson losing money because of her too-big office is her problem, she wants Serge to be happy. Or at least happier.

Serge sends jumpy glances around the room like he's making sure they're alone even though it's obvious they are. Then he slides an envelope across her desk, hiding it under his bony hand until she grabs its edge and puts it in the drawer.

"Thanks, Serge," Rose tells him. "A beautiful day out, don't you think?" She wants to get him to talk to her so she can find out more about him. "I'm looking forward to getting out at lunch, maybe a walk along the river," she lies. She never takes more than a few minutes out of the office and eats at her desk to make sure she doesn't miss anything. Someone is always moving in or moving out or asking about space or complaining about the space they already have. "How about you?"

She waits, and when he doesn't move or say anything, she tries again. "You know, I just can't decide. Across the river to the Esplanade or maybe down Mem Drive to the science museum? What do you think?" Instead of answering, he shakes his head and goes out to the hallway. Soon she hears the creak of the elevator as it takes him up to the fifth floor.

Not long after Serge leaves, Liddy walks in. "Hey," Rose says.

"Hey." Liddy leans against the doorjamb and smiles, but it's not much of one.

Rose still can't figure it out, but somehow she and Liddy have become friends. Sort of. Daytime friends anyway, like a work friend who stops by your desk a couple of times a week to say hello. It's not like Rose would ever invite Liddy to her house or anything. But still, it's quite something. What with Liddy and her Ivy League education and rich husband and kids at a fancy boarding school in Switzerland, and Rose with none of these. But Liddy doesn't seem to notice the differences between them. Or at least pretends she doesn't. She's not stuck-up at all, and even at her age she's knockout gorgeous.

Rose doesn't want Liddy to hang around, because she might get suspicious if Marta comes in. But she senses Liddy has something to share, and because Rose can't resist a good share she asks if Liddy wants a cup of coffee. Liddy hesitates, then asks for tea. Rose rummages around in a cabinet and finds a tea bag and two mugs. She's a coffee drinker herself, and although she tries to keep it down to four cups a day, she always drinks more. This will be her third so far this morning.

Still standing, Liddy asks awkwardly, "How goes the new school year?"

Rose thinks this is a weird question because it's got to be the last thing Liddy wants to talk about, what with this being the first year her kids are away. Liddy told her that it was her husband who made the decision to send the two of them to boarding school and that she didn't like it one bit. So this must be the thing Liddy says before she's ready to say the real thing she wants to say.

Rose wants to hear the real thing, but sometimes you have to wait until the other person is ready to spill the good stuff, so she says, "Charlotte hates her teacher and Emma says none of her friends are in any of her classes, which is something I know isn't true. Michael slinks out of the house every morning without saying a word to anyone. Who knows if he's even going to school?"

"Sorry about Michael, but he's just a kid. He'll come around." Liddy stares into her mug as if there are leaves to read instead of a tea bag floating like a dead goldfish on top of the yellowy water. "The world is so crazy. Oppressive, even. "

"You okay?" The world is crazy, but Rose thinks Liddy must be talking about the husband, the great and terrible W. Garrett Haines the Third. On top of sending the kids away, he sold their house in Weston and made Liddy move into the city with him. Not that Rose would mind living at Millennium Tower—"The Tower," as everyone calls it. But Liddy once said that she'd rather her twins had a home to come back to. And why would she have stashed all their old stuff in her unit unless Garrett wouldn't let her keep it?

Liddy puts her half-empty cup next to the coffee machine and hands Rose her envelope. "I'm fine," she says as she walks out the door. Which Rose doesn't believe for a second.

Fortunately, Liddy is long gone when Marta shows. The young woman steps up to Rose's desk but doesn't sit. "I cannot thank you enough for what you are doing for me," she says in her perfect but fake-sounding English. "If it were not for your many kindnesses—"

Rose raises her hand to stop the girl with the sad puppy-dog eyes because Marta's gratitude makes her feel even worse than she always feels on rent day. Marta is from Venezuela and she's pretty in the way girls from South America are with their dark hair and skin that looks like they're tan all the time. She has the most beautiful smile, which she doesn't use much, and she's really smart and used to be really rich like those people in soap operas with maids and swimming pools and bars in their living rooms.

When Marta was trying to convince Rose that she would be no trouble if Rose let her live at Metropolis, she said she went to some school in France and then to college at Cambridge. The one that's in England not Massachusetts. This must be why she talks like she's stuck-up but she isn't. Just like Liddy isn't. Marta is also brave about facing a whole bunch of really bad stuff that she hasn't told Rose about. But Rose knows enough of Marta's story to get why she's not going to share her problems. "It's okay, Marta. Really," she says. "You don't have to thank me, hon."

Marta hands her an envelope and slips out of the office without another word. Rose puts Marta's envelope on top of Serge's.

WITH CHECKS AND cash in her pocketbook, Rose locks the office door and heads to the ATM. The students are back with all their noise and hustle-bustle. She imagines their summers in Maine or Cape Cod with them riding around in those fast little boats her Vince is always mooning after. She stands at the corner of Mass Ave and Vassar Street, right across from MIT, where all these smarty-pants go, and where she hopes her smarty-pants Emma will go someday—with a full scholarship. The students ignore the light and jaywalk like the cars aren't even there. Like they're the president. And they're everywhere, crowding every sidewalk, and now they're all at the machine where she needs to make her deposit.

Rose crosses the street and goes to the back of a line snaking into the gas station parking lot and presses her pocketbook close, itching to be done with it because she wants to put the whole business behind her for another thirty days. Shifting on her feet, she turns and looks back at Metropolis, a bulky six-story brick building with crazy round windows and castle-like towers sticking up at the top.

It's so different from the rows of garage doors you see on the self-storage places along the highway, and she wonders what they were thinking back in the olden days building it in such a fancy way. A renter who looked up a bunch of facts about the building said it was one of the first storage places in the city, like in the late 1800s. Railroad tracks ran next to it, and men would unload their wares for only short periods of time, just as long as it took them to sell them.

Over the years, electricity and heat were put in so things could be stashed for much longer. And once air-conditioning and Wi-Fi were added, anyone could do anything with their units. Which is exactly what they do. Like Jason Franklin, the lawyer, and the young girl who builds crazy sculptures out of junk. METROPOLIS STORAGE WAREHOUSE is painted in twelve-foot-high white block letters across its sides. FIRE PROOF. The words look funny next to the swanky decorations, but she figures the outside isn't all that much stranger than the people inside.

It's where she's worked for over ten years now, ever since Zach bought it. First she was just the receptionist and Zach was there doing most of the other stuff in the office. Then when Zach got to trust her more, he stopped coming in all that much. It seemed like he lost interest in the whole business and just turned it over to her. Which she's got no problem with.

He's a weird guy, leaving for weeks at a time to do things like scuba diving or mountain climbing or jumping out of airplanes. She has no idea why anyone would want to take those kinds of chances with their life. But he's really nice—charming even—and he laughs a lot so what else he does is another thing that isn't her problem. All that matters is that he promoted her to bookkeeper/receptionist and then to office manager/bookkeeper/receptionist, and she's proud of how well she's done.

It's a good job, and she's got good benefits and good pay. She makes more than Vince does but she never mentions this. It's way more than she could make anywhere else, with her high school education and bare-bones computer skills. And here she is risking it all. But just like everyone else, she's got to do what she's got to do to for her family.

When her turn finally comes, she steps into the suffocating room. She uses the Metropolis card first and feeds in the rent checks. Then she puts in a different card and deposits the cash into her own account. As she stuffs the receipts into her wallet and steps out into the fresh air, someone grabs her arm.

"Making the deposit?" Zach asks.

3

MARTA

It is a very good thing none of this happened until after she had finished collecting her data. It is also a very good thing that her friend Kevin is willing to run her numbers on his computer account, as it is not safe to log into hers. If it were not for Kevin, there would be no possibility of completing her dissertation, and this work is what keeps her mind from somersaulting in devastating directions, of which there are many.

Marta's real name is Mercedes Bustamante, but no one knows this at Metropolis, and the people who know her as Mercedes do not know she is also Marta. Nor do they know where she is. It is the only way to protect herself and to continue her research. She is trying to understand which aspects of childhood social class are the most powerful predictors of adult achievement, and hence, how these factors affect the perpetuation of economic inequality in the hope of alleviating it.

For Marta, finding the answers to these questions has been her passion for the last four years. She has passed her proposal defense, surveyed 102 subjects, analyzed almost all of the data, and written seven of the twelve chapters in her outline. Dr. Ullman, the chair of her dissertation committee, was so impressed with her initial findings he encouraged her to begin applying for teaching jobs. But this was Before. Before all hell broke loose, as the Americans say.

Just this morning, Kevin sent over the results of her latest multiple regressions, which are stunning. She's been poring over the numbers for hours, and now her neck hurts and her lower back is in a knot. She stands and stretches, ready for a run, some air, and vitamin D. Plus it is Monday afternoon, and at three o'clock she makes her weekly call to Dr. Ullman, which she can do only from a public place and in a different location each time.

Spending her days in complete darkness is not a good thing for either her mind or her body, but this was never how she had planned to use this storage unit. It was meant to be a place to keep her files, along with the other detritus of her four years of research. The cartons of raw data, surveys, permissions, articles, printouts, and multiple chapter drafts were beginning to form towers tall enough to create walkways through her apartment. And then there were the dozens and dozens of books.

As planned, it is all here, yet now she is also. Along with a bed, a roll-top desk, and a quarter of a million dollars in cash.

MARTA LOVES THE Esplanade, the park that runs along the Boston bank of the Charles. She used to live in Back Bay, in a high-ceilinged apartment carved out of a nineteenth-century mansion with expansive river views: the footpath wending its way between city and water, the playgrounds and docks, the sailboats and the Hatch Shell, MIT and the Museum of Science on the other side of the river. That apartment is gone, as is so much else, but the Esplanade is still hers. She crosses the Mass Ave Bridge at a warm-up pace.

When she reaches the path, she increases her speed and heads west, toward BU. Although it is September, the sun is warm and the sky is a deep azure. She throws herself into the pleasure of her body's movements as well as the endorphins flooding her. She is light on her feet and feels as if she could run forever. As she falls into a steady rhythm, her mind stills. For a few minutes, her only problem is avoiding the duck droppings scattered all over the path.

Then her watch beeps to remind her it is time to make her call. Marta doesn't want to stop, but she is looking forward to telling Dr. Ullman about her regression results. She slows, stretches, and then sits on an empty bench. She looks around to make certain no one is close enough to overhear and pulls out her prepaid phone.

She cannot afford to have her own cell phone, but this is not because she does not have the money to pay for one. She cannot afford to take the chance, because ICE might use it as a tracking device and discover where she is. She pays cash to buy the least expensive phone with the fewest number of minutes and replaces it often. Burners, Kevin told her the drug dealers call them. He learned this from a television show.

"How are you, my dear?" Dr. Ullman asks instead of saying hello.

He has become like a grandfather to her over the years she has been in Boston. He was first her professor and then her advisor. Although he is still all of these things, now he is also her friend and protector. Many times, he has asked her to call him Al. Her fellow graduate students, Americans all, have no issue with such informality, yet she cannot bring herself to do this. Even Dr. Ullman has no idea where she is living—if she is in the state or not, in the country or not. He asks no questions, as they both understand it is best for him to know as little as possible.

"I am fine. I am more than fine. I received some new regressions this morning, and they are even better than I had hoped. The F-ratio is almost forty, and most of the variables are statistically significant. Some very much so. Zip code and maternal education are, as you say, driving it out of the water."

He chuckles. "Blowing it out of the water." There is silence on his end, and then he clears his throat. "I want to hear all about it, but we have to talk about something first."

Marta leans her head against the back of the bench and stares up into the cloudless sky.

"It was a different agent this time," he says.

"Did he come to your office?"

"To my house. And he was a she."

Marta sits up. To his house? This has never happened before. "I am so sorry to bring you into my problems. I am so sorry to make trouble for you at your home. We must stop—"

"There's no reason to apologize. I want to help you—you know that. Not to mention that you have to get that dissertation finished in order for us to become famous. I'm not quitting on you until I see our names on the lead article of the *American Sociological Review*."

Marta is undeterred by his attempt at lightness. "Do you think she has come to your home because she knows we are in contact with each other?"

"It's possible, but I got the feeling she was fishing. She mentioned twice that Belmont isn't a sanctuary city." He chuckles again. "I told her she was free to search the house for you, but that was clearly not her intention."

"What was her intention?"

"My guess is it was a warning. For me not to be in contact with you. And if we were in touch, for you to know you're still on their radar. But again, I don't think she believes I know where you are. I think she's just covering her butt. How many minutes do you have left on your phone?"

Marta is confused by the non sequitur. "What is it you mean?"

"After that visit, I'm guessing neither my home phone or cell are safe, so I'm going to get myself a prepaid, then I'll call you back on it so you have the number. Do you have enough minutes?"

"Yes, yes I do. Yet I do not feel comfortable with this."

"Mercedes, you're not getting rid of me. I'll call you tomorrow at eleven in the morning. I want to hear all about those numbers."

Two DAYS LATER, the good weather has disappeared. Rain is coming down in sheets, which the wind fractures and blows into wet shards. The leaves whip furiously, as if they are trying to fight off an assailant, and pedestrians scramble with their heads down to wherever they need to go. "Need" is the operative word here, for no one would be out in this weather if they had a choice.

Marta has no access to a window, so she did not realize the weather was this bad. She is standing inside Metropolis's front door, staring at the flooded parking lot and dressed for a run she is not going to be able to take. She has run through rainstorms and snowstorms and on blisteringly hot days, but that was Before. Now she cannot take the risk. Rain is a slippery invitation to break a bone. A visit to the hospital is out of the question.

She turns to the stairwell and begins climbing. Although there are only five floors of storage units, there is an extra flight at the top, leading to a small landing with a doorway blocked by a wrought-iron grill. So this makes five sets of stairs of twenty-four steps or a total of 120 steps. The stairwell is lined by dingy gray cinder block, full of chips and gouges, and there is mold clinging to the corners. It's shadowy and smells like dead mushrooms and gasoline, but Marta pretends not to notice. This is no Esplanade, but at least she can still exercise.

Up and down five times, followed by a sprint along the first-floor corridor lined with closed metal doors: 101, 102, 103, through to 163. She runs back to the stairwell, where she ascends to the second floor and runs down this hallway and returns to the stairwell. Then up and along the third-, fourth-, and fifth-floor corridors, plus a climb to the sixth-floor landing and a race to the bottom again. She does this five times. The punishing routine clears her mind. There is nothing to think about except her footfalls and the stairs and the hallways and the doors rushing past. As she begins to slow down during the last set, the world returns.

She heard on NPR this morning that, according to Veppex, the Organization of Politically Persecuted Venezuelans Abroad, Maduro and his fraudulent national constituent assembly, his so-called "truth commission," are on a new and even more violent rampage, hunting down everyone they believe is working against them. They are imprisoning and executing hundreds, which includes many innocents. Maduro "disappeared" her father, murdered her brother, and forced the rest of her family into hiding. Now the American government wants to send her back there.

4

SERGE

Serge goes outside to take photographs on his up days and stays in his storage unit on his down days. But no matter what, he goes to Brick & Trowel six nights a week, where he washes dishes until two or three o'clock in the morning. He doesn't talk to anyone there and nobody talks to him. But they smile at him a lot.

If the day isn't too down, he develops or prints his pictures. When it's too down, he lies on his cot and lets the hours pass him by. This is why he has so many pictures that he still has to develop and print. He's been down for a while now. Days or weeks, he's lost track. But today is an up day. Out of nowhere, like always. He has no windows to the world outside, but he senses that the sun is shining. Which means there will be sharp shadows. His favorite.

He's lived in Boston for over twenty years but in some ways it feels like he just got here. When he walks the crowded streets of Downtown Crossing he still gets excited at the chatter of different languages and how everyone looks so different from each other and from him. Nothing at all like the lonely farmhouse he ran away from. He wants to know these people but not in the way regular people want to know other people.

He throws on his long coat and gently places his Rolleiflex into a deep pocket he's lined with layers of heavy felt for protection. Then he takes the Red Line to Downtown Crossing. He climbs out of the subway into a place that's always moving. Always changing. Lots of faces. Lots of stories. It's five o'clock, the time of best September light. He pulls the camera from his pocket and hangs it around his neck. Cups it in his hands. Presses it to him. The Rolleiflex is his best friend. A 1958 twin-lens reflex 3.5F, which shields him from the world while letting him into it.

He doesn't have to lift the camera to his face because it's an old-fashioned style where the viewfinder is on the top. He holds it at his waist and just looks down at it like he's minding his own business when he's actually taking pictures. This way no one is aware of what he's doing and they act like their real selves. Once in a while he gets caught, and sometimes people get mad. But that doesn't happen very much. Click. Click.

Shot from the side: an old man's face full of stubble and wrinkles turns away from an even older man who's talking to him. Shot from behind: a line of tired, mostly overweight women stand at a bus stop with huge bags resting at their feet. Shot through a window full of gold letters: a jeweler stares into a small eyepiece. Shot from below: a guy in a suit with a huge and fancy watch marches down the sidewalk like he owns the world.

Not centered. Moving out of or into the frame. Sometimes he holds the camera sideways. Sharply lit. Not pretty pictures. Not meant to be. The truest picture is the one where the person has no idea he's in a photograph, when he's not pretending to be someone else. This makes him known in a way that he will never see or even know himself. A photographer's job is to be a ghost, not appearing in the photos but still there.

Serge has thousands of prints and contact sheets, many more thousands of negatives and rolls of undeveloped film. He's never shown a single photograph to anyone. They are his alone. He ducks into a west-facing alley and casts his shadow at a sharp angle against the brick. He presses the shutter, then does it three more times. He's never taken a picture of his own face but he has lots of photographs of his shadow. This is his truth: he's both here and not here at all.

IT WAS AN especially late night. Brick & Trowel, being the very cool bar/restaurant it is, never closes before the witching hour, two a.m. in Cambridge. Usually Serge gets to leave by two forty-five, no later than three. But last night there was a private party, and when there are private parties the owner doesn't close down the way he's supposed to. The longer people drink, the more money he makes. This doesn't work out so good for Serge. Like this morning, when he didn't get home until after four.

He sleeps late and wakes up groggy, the rumble of the huge dishwasher still stuffing up his ears. He puts a toothbrush and toothpaste into his back pocket and heads for the bathroom. There's one on the fourth floor and one on the second and he switches back and forth between the two every other day so he's not always in the same bathroom or hallway or stairwell. He uses the shower in the janitor's room late at night. He hardly ever runs into another person.

Today there's more going on than usual. On the fifth floor, his floor, a door is wide open. Inside are dozens of doghouses. Most are lined up on shelves, but some are at least four feet tall and stand on the floor. Each one is decorated in a different way. One is covered with dog bones, one with flowers, one with fire hydrants. They have windows and doors, and the insides are painted to match the outsides. Some even have wallpaper. Pictures of dogs on the walls. Dog beds inside. Serge steps away before the man kneeling in front of the largest doghouse notices him.

When he reaches the fourth floor, there's a door pushed halfway open. He takes a step closer and hides behind a pole, cranes his neck to see better. There's nobody inside but it looks like a rich teenager's bedroom. Two teenagers. Two desks are covered with books and notebooks, two bureaus, and two corkboards full of papers and photos. Movie and music posters. Home to a boy and a girl. He notices there aren't any beds. Just a chair and a footstool with a small table next to it. There's something about this that makes him sure it was created by a woman. And then he gets what it is. A shrine. To her children.

Darkness presses down on him, and he shivers from the cold that fills his bones. The children are dead, and the mother is trying to keep them alive in her mind. She sits in her chair and looks at all of their things. She visits them and cries for them. He walks quickly to the bathroom, closes the door behind him, and leans against it, overwhelmed by sadness.

Maybe he's been wrong about taking pictures of people when they're not aware of themselves. Maybe the way to find the truest photo is by taking pictures of what a person can't leave behind. Like the pictures he's been taking of his shadow. Here and not here.

SERGE WORKS ON coming up with the courage to ask Rose to help him. He doesn't like talking to people, and he really doesn't like talking to people if he has to ask them a favor. But he can't get the idea of photographing the insides of the storage units out of his head. He wants it more than he wants to eat. Rose has a master key and she's nosy enough to know when someone is or isn't in the building.

What he's asking for is probably against the law. But it's against the law for him to be living here, and Rose is okay with that as long as he gives her money every month. So he'll offer her money. Offering is different from asking a favor. He doesn't have much money, but he doesn't spend much and he'll pay what he has to.

Soon. He'll do it soon. Maybe even today. He picks up his Rolleiflex and begins shooting his own unit.

5

JASON

A large Black woman stands outside Jason's door. She's wearing a dark dress, a wildly colorful scarf, and a skeptical expression. He's grown used to this expression, has seen it many times over the last nine months. "This a lawyer's office?" she asks.

He pushes his glasses up his nose and comes from behind his walnut desk, bought almost a decade ago for a different time and space. He holds out his hand. "I'm Jason Franklin, and you must be Ms. Bell. And yeah, you're in the right place. May look strange, but I make it work."

She takes him in, along with the bookshelves lined with legal tomes, and four ladder-back chairs circling a small table. "Damnedest thing I've ever seen," she finally says.

"The trade-offs you make to do the work you want." Only partially true.

"You're telling me you'd rather be here than in some big office tower downtown?"

"Crazy, huh?" He leads her inside and pulls out a chair at the table. "Take a load off, Ms. Bell. Want some coffee? Tea? Something cold?"

It's clear she's still not convinced, but she sits and asks for water, watches him closely as he retrieves two bottles from the dorm-room refrigerator, hands her one, and keeps the other for himself. "How do I know you're a real lawyer?" she asks.

Jason points to the framed documents on the wall: undergraduate diploma from the University of Pennsylvania, law school diploma from Harvard, Massachusetts Bar admission certificate.

"You went to Harvard?" she asks.

He doesn't answer, just grabs the handle embedded inside the ten-foot-wide door and pulls the massive piece of steel across the floor, closing them in. The door is heavy, but in the nine months since he moved here he's learned how to brace his legs to make shutting it look easy. This is about as far as he could be from his Seaport office with its thirty-seventh-floor harbor view. But here he stands, inside a windowless yet well-appointed storage unit.

"Got to be one hell of a story." Ms. Bell places her immense purse on the chair next to her and opens her water bottle. She waits a minute to see if he's going to tell it, and when he doesn't, she begins. "You helped my friend Alborz with her visa, and she says you're smart and there's nothing highfalutin about you. Realtor said I need a lawyer, and I figure a Black man would understand better."

He gets a file folder and a legal pad from his desk, then sits down across from her at the table. He opens the file. "You said you've got issues with a developer wanting to buy your property. He strong-arming you?"

"W. G. Haines Companies." Ms. Bell's voice is thick with disdain. "Trying to buy up the whole block. Bought most of it already."

Jason knows all about Haines Companies. Muscular and moneyed and looking to get even more so. "You're not interested?"

Ms. Bell pulls a handful of papers from her purse. One is a map. "I live here." She points to a red circle in the middle of a block in low-rent Roxbury, five blocks west of Boston's fashionable South End, which has been pushing its fashionableness toward its neighbor for the past few years. "Was my grandmama's house," she explains. "Then my mama's, and now it's mine. Because of their hard work and some my own, I don't owe a cent on it. We're a family of hardworking and hard-saving teachers. We're tough and always take care of ourselves."

"Both my parents are teachers." Jason already likes this woman, as well as the idea of helping her, of being able to help her. Not to mention screwing Haines Companies. David vs. Goliath perhaps, but David did win that one. "Also hardworking, hard-saving, tough, and proud of it."

"That's not how Haines sees it. To them, I'm a pain in the ass. Think just because I'm Black and living in Roxbury, they can push me around."

"Then they've clearly got another think coming."

"Except every one of my neighbors saw dollar signs and signed contracts. So maybe Haines's thinking is better than we want to say. Even more messed up is those idiots were so hyped to get their hands on the money, they took what was offered and made my property worth less."

"So you're looking to sell? But it's got to be at the right price?"

"A fair price," she corrects. "My husband died a few years back, and I have three kids. One at UMass Boston and two at the Burke coming up. Got to give them options."

"And Haines is lowballing?"

"The real estate guy said that if my house were on a different block, one Haines hasn't gotten its chops into, I could get at least fifty grand more." She jabs at the map. "Getting over a thousand dollars a square foot in the South End, he says. Around seven hundred in the block next to Mass Ave. And Haines thinks I'm going to jump for joy at a measly three hundred because we're three blocks further in."

"That's the offer?"

"They went up to three fifty but say that's all they're going." She juts out her chin. "So I want to sue them. Or have you pretend to sue them. Scare them into doing what's right."

"Seems workable."

"And there's more going on, but I don't know if you can help me with that part."

Jason tilts his head and waits.

"It's the neighbors. Some of them at least. Haines's deal is no one gets their money till the entire block's bought in."

"You the last holdout?"

"First, wet toilet paper on the bushes. Then, they egged my car. Last week, a bag of dog poop on the front stoop."

"Nasty," he says. "You sure it's the neighbors?"

Her eyes widen. "You saying it could be Haines?"

"Not saying it is or it isn't. Just thinking out loud." He doubts it is Haines. The moves are too unsophisticated. But you never know. That could be the point.

Jason looks at the map. Ms. Bell's property is in the middle of a line of attached row houses, which Haines probably wants to turn into expensive condominiums. It seems that with a little persuasion, the company could be convinced to add another fifty grand to the pot, maybe more. They have an urban gold mine here, and no company looking to develop in Boston wants to be sued for intimidating minority homeowners. "I'm going to check this out and see what Haines is up to, Ms. Bell. But I'm thinking we can make them do a hell of a lot better than that."

She stands, smiles, and holds out her hand. "Kimberlyn."

He shakes it and returns the smile. "Jason."

JASON HAS COME to dread Friday evenings. It's the night he's expected for dinner at his parents' house, along with his two sisters, their husbands, and the three nieces he's nuts for. In his old life, he'd looked forward to Fridays all week, a break from the demands of his job into the warmth and laughter of the house in Jamaica Plain where he was raised. Those days, he often had difficulty getting out of work early enough to join them. Now that's the lie he tells them to stay away.

In his old life, he was an immigration attorney at Spencer Uccello, a rising star in one of the top firms in the city, where no one doubted he was headed toward partnership. He provided strategic advice to large American companies looking to hire foreign nationals and to large foreign companies looking to launch in the US. He brought in a lot of money, and even better than that, he was filling their diversity quota, his photo looking good on their website.

He loved growing up in JP, a section of Boston known for its compatible mingling of race, ethnicity, and wealth, and he'd always imagined raising a family there. Though his family was middle class, he'd been around the one percent a lot, first at Boston Latin, then Penn, then Harvard, and most recently at his fancy-ass white firm. He's a natural at code switching.

But he got carried away by the headiness of his new status, just like Sabrina, his ex-wife, had warned. The first in his family to command a high-six-figure salary. The first in his family to live in a doorman building. Money to burn after all those years of careful budgeting, his student loans disappeared in two years.

Then, The Case happened, and his ass got hauled out of capitalist heaven and dumped into a self-storage unit. It's well past time to tell his family the truth, but he can't face their disappointment. He, the bullied fat boy who made good, proving to his tormentors that his glasses and studiousness didn't make him a loser. They made him a winner.

The family would be devastated, especially Tawney, his oldest niece, who idolizes him and is studying hard to become a big-time lawyer just like her uncle. His sister is thrilled, as not many fifteen-year-old girls in Tawney's set are willing to give up their parties because they want to go to law school.

He checks his phone. Five thirty, and his mother likes them all there by six. He hasn't been to JP in three weeks. It's not as if he's got all that much work to do, and he misses them. He thinks about the suit he'll have to run to his apartment and put on, the cheery lies he'll have to tell, the pride in his father's eyes, the adoration in Tawney's. He punches in the number. "So sorry, Mom," he says. "It's another working weekend."

6

LIDDY

Liddy presses a glass of vodka on the rocks between her palms. She's standing in front of the floor-to-ceiling windows that stretch across the northwest wall of her kitchen, dining room, and living room, and her eyes follow the sweep of Boston spread out fifty floors below her. The multiple bridges crossing the Charles River as it travels to the ocean. The Public Garden, along with the gleaming gold dome of the State House. The Common, where cows grazed in the seventeenth century. From her bedroom, she can see the harbor and its islands, the ocean beyond.

She lives in luxury at The Tower. Her husband owns one of the largest real estate development companies in New England. Her two children are healthy and happy. Her closets and jewelry boxes overflow, and *Boston Globe* photographers are always ready to snap her picture at charity functions for the Names column or Party Lines. She's the epitome of the enviable bold-faced name, a woman of wealth and substance.

Yet some of Liddy's happiest moments are when she's curled up with a novel in her favorite reading chair, which is inside a self-storage unit in Cambridge filled with Robin and Scott's childhood possessions. Possessions Garrett had insisted wouldn't fit in the condo when they moved out of their house in Weston.

"Who needs all that junk?" he'd asked, nuzzling her neck. "The kids have flown the coop, and now it's just you and me. Like it used to be. Like it should be."

Instead of arguing, which she'd learned not to do, she brought the twins' things to Metropolis without his knowledge, certain the kids would want their mementos. And now she can sit in her unit and be as close to them as a mother can be to children who are thousands of miles away.

The doorman rings to tell her that her limousine has arrived. A crazy gesture, the limo, especially as she's going only a quarter mile, across the Common, to the Four Seasons Hotel. But Garrett is fond of such gestures, especially if he believes there will be a media presence, which tonight there certainly will be.

She throws back the rest of her drink, sucks on an ice cube for the last vestiges, and places the glass in the sink. Then she ducks into her bathroom to brush the alcohol from her breath and check herself in the mirror. The dress is a deep purple, her best color. It's cut low, but not plunging, now that she's crossed the great divide over to forty and has since added another four years. It's fitted, amplifying her small waist, but not too tight, the silk floating an inch from her skin. The slit in the dress stops at knee level, but her heels are high and stylish, her hair newly highlighted, and she's wearing Garrett's early Christmas present, an emerald-and-diamond pendant. She takes the elevator down and glides through the marble lobby.

When Liddy arrives at the hotel, the cameras flash, and despite herself, her spirits rise. She's always been a sucker for a good party. Tonight is the annual fundraiser for one of her favorite charities, Boston Partners in Education. She and Garrett are major donors to many local nonprofits. Have been for years. The name W. Garrett Haines III graces buildings on the campuses of Boston-area universities, museums, and hospitals.

Although her name never accompanies his, those in the know recognize she's the impetus behind his generosity, and she's aware they sometimes refer to her as the East Coast Melinda Gates. To be fair, Garrett's desire to help others is sincere, which is one of the reasons she fell for him in the first place. But over the years, this caring has shifted from heartfelt giving into more of a PR event for W. G. Haines Companies.

As soon as she steps into the lobby, Liddy is scooped up by Janie Labott, the current president of the charity. Janie is good at her job, but she has no sense of humor, and really, what kind of name is Janie for a grown woman?

"You look fantastic, as always," Janie fawns, and then draws Liddy close. "Please, here, to the right, the VIP salon."

"Is there a bar?" Liddy deadpans.

Janie looks blank. "But of course," she says primly. "Top-shelf."

Liddy presses her lips together to keep from laughing.

"You don't want top-shelf? I'm sure I can get you whatever kind of beverage you'd prefer."

"Top-shelf is fine."

Janie tips her head, still confused. "Only the best for our major donors."

Liddy goes straight to the bar and orders a vodka, this one straight up. The bartender pours her a shot of Grey Goose VX. She lifts the glass, toasting him and his top shelf, then takes a stiff hit. She supposes some might call her a functioning alcoholic. Perhaps that's what she would call herself. But she's functioning, and if a drink here or there helps her deal, so be it. Plus she's meeting Sandy in half an hour for even stronger reinforcements.

She's soon swallowed by a swirl of local bigwigs, including the mayor, the superintendent of schools, and high-ranking members of almost every educational charity in the state, along with the moneyed do-gooders of her social set. There are handshakes and air-kisses and hugs, compliments and bad breath, not to mention a few too many men "accidentally" brushing her breasts. People want to tell her how thankful they are for her support, how wonderful she is, how lucky the city is to have her—and about their own funding needs. This from the politicians as well as from the charities.

Although Liddy recognizes these maneuverings for what they are, she's enjoying herself. She's comfortable being the center of attention, holds it naturally. But for almost all her life, it was awarded to her for something she did nothing to deserve: beauty. Bestowed on her through no effort of her own. Now she's finally being appreciated for something she's actually done.

Then Garrett is at her elbow, whispering apologies in her ear, kissing her on the lips, holding the kiss for a moment longer than appropriate in a public setting. She smiles at him, and he smiles back. Those who notice the kiss smile also, some a bit snidely. Garrett isn't a handsome man, and he doesn't need to be. He carries himself with an air of casual confidence, has a grin that beams across the room, and exudes enough charisma to dazzle the entire city, which is exactly what he's done. He charmed her the same way.

Liddy's phone dings. "Be right back," she says, and makes her escape. In two minutes, she enters a one-seater bathroom hidden in a corner near the caterer's offices. Sandy is waiting for her. The women hug warmly. They met when their children were in kindergarten and bonded over their mutual dislike for the pretentious Weston mothers. They began drinking wine while the kids played, moved on to smoking pot when the kids were old enough to be on their own, and graduated to cocaine pretty soon thereafter.

Sandy and Gary left Weston for Rockport when their youngest went to boarding school in New Hampshire. They have a lovely bungalow, which Liddy covets, set atop a rocky outcropping with sweeping views of the ocean and a double lighthouse not far from shore. Rockport is an artsy town, small and picturesque, full of painters and writers and nonconformists. There's also a lot of drug use, and Sandy has access to whatever she might want.

Due to the distance, which isn't all that long in miles, but is very long in traffic, Liddy and Sandy don't see each other as much as they used to. But during the fundraiser season, Liddy has Sandy bring her a gram or two of coke when they share a charity event. They both prefer it this way now, meeting in a public place rather than either's home, which prevents them from diving into the gram and finishing it off in one sitting. There's also the thrill of the clandestine, of overtly breaking the law, of doing something no one would ever expect of their respectable middle-aged selves.

Envelopes are exchanged, and Sandy warns, "It's really good. When you do it, take it slow."

Liddy is amused. "Take it slow? This from you, the woman who can't say no?"

"See these bags dripping down into my cheeks?" Sandy points to the slightly bruised areas under her eyes that her concealer doesn't quite cover. "That's from not being able to say no last night. I'm trying to save you from walking around looking like the living dead."

"Will do," Liddy says, although she probably won't be able to. That's the problem with cocaine: once you start, it's almost impossible to stop. She puts the envelope in her purse, pats it affectionately. Garrett is off on a business trip to France in two days. She'll wait until then.

Sandy leaves first, and Liddy waits a few minutes so they don't enter the ballroom together. This is completely unnecessary, but the pseudo-drug-dealer game is fun. When she slides into her chair, she glances across the room at Sandy, who winks at her.

The Haineses are seated at the head table, Janie at Garrett's side and the mayor at Liddy's. Although she's to introduce Janie after the mayor introduces her, Liddy orders another vodka.

7

ZACH

Eight months later: May 2018

At the end of the day, the auctioneer counts the cash and then removes a small stack from the pile. "That's thirteen hundred ninety-five for me, leaving twelve thousand five hundred fifty-five for you." She pauses, a you-can't-put-anything-over-on-me glint in her eye. "You didn't pay me the seven hundred fifty for the photography equipment in unit five fourteen, but you owe me my ten percent on it anyways." She takes out three twenties, a ten, and a five, gives Zach the rest. "Leaving twelve thousand four hundred eighty for you." She didn't like it that, as she'd put it, he'd "spied on her" when he didn't tell her until the auction was over that he owned the building.

The thick wad of cash in his hand floods him with memories he'd rather not contemplate, so instead he argues in his head with the auctioneer. In actuality, he's paying himself the money for #514, or more accurately not paying any money at all, because the contents already belong to him and therefore she's not entitled to her cut. If he'd known what was inside the unit, it wouldn't have been put on the auction list. She has some nerve taking his seventy-five dollars.

"Not a bad haul for two hours' work." She stuffs her thinner wad of cash into her back pocket and whistles tunelessly as she goes out the door.

He can't take the elevator behind the yellow tape, so he climbs the stairs to the fifth floor, still irrationally irked about the seventy-five dollars. He's sure she assumes he's some one-percenter with gobs of money—which is exactly what he is not—but it wouldn't have killed her to let it go. People and their misplaced assumptions. But seeing that photograph of himself was totally unnerving, and he's got more important things to worry about than some woman's glee at ripping him off for a few bucks. Even if he needs every one.

Zach had no choice but to buy #514's contents before anyone else did. From the shirt he's wearing in that photo, it's clear it was taken right after he purchased Metropolis, when half the drug dealers in Boston were storing their stashes in the building. Including Zach. Although this particular picture isn't incriminating, there might be others that are. Incriminating for him and for the many people who wouldn't be happy if photographs of them fell into the wrong hands. Like those of the police or the FBI or the IRS.

He enters the unit and lifts the photo off the table, studies it carefully. Yup, it's him all right. No denying that. He has to destroy it along with all the others. The nights and days after "the elevator incident," as he's come to think of it, Metropolis was swarming with police. They questioned him, Liddy, Rose, and that lawyer named Jason ad nauseum, then crawled over every inch of the elevators and hallways. But as far as Zach knows, with the exception of Liddy's and Jason's, the cops didn't go into any other tenant's unit. He doesn't want to think about what might have happened had they searched Serge's.

As he stares at the younger version of himself, he starts to notice what an extraordinary shot it is, and he wonders if there are more of this quality. He walks along the desk and looks into the open cartons. Indeed, there are many more, along with what looks like hundreds of negatives and almost as many rolls of undeveloped film. He sits down on the wobbly chair in front of the enlarger, picks up the sheaf of prints next to it, and begins to flip through them.

Zach doesn't immediately see another of him or anyone else from his early days at Metropolis, but there are many of the building, both inside and out. There are even more of Downtown Crossing and Methadone Mile, a stretch of cracked sidewalk near Boston Medical Center, where the victims of the opioid crisis live and get high and die. Like his friend Tony. More memories he doesn't want to think about.

From his recent foray into photography, however limited, Zach has no doubt that the photographs are sensational. The play of light across the foreground and background, the clarity of the images, the asymmetrical composition in contrast to the square frames, the calm intensity and gravity of the subjects. The intimate glimpse into lives being lived. Like photos of the great street photographers Vivian Maier and Robert Frank and Diane Arbus. How could work of this caliber have been abandoned inside a self-storage unit?

8

LIDDY

In the limo for their three-minute ride home, Garrett slips his hand under Liddy's dress and up her thigh. She starts to cough, which gives her an excuse to move her leg a few inches. As he's deathly afraid of colds, she hopes it will also give her an excuse to fend off his advances. "What a lovely affair," she says in a gravelly voice, then clears her throat ostentatiously. "Janie thinks it might have brought in close to a million dollars."

"You're a lovely affair," he murmurs. "The belle of the ball."

"I told Janie we'd match ten percent of the take," Liddy prattles away, trying to slow him down. She coughs again, sniffles. "She's going to announce it by the end of the week."

Garrett pulls his hand away, squares his shoulder, and says nothing. Liddy freezes. She never knows what's going to set him off, but she wouldn't have expected a small matching gift could be a trigger; they give tens of millions of dollars away every year. At least if she had to slip, she's glad she slipped with a witness nearby. Making a scene in front of the driver, or anyone else, has never been Garrett's style. He saves his real self for her.

According to an article she read on how to deal with men like Garrett, she's not supposed to engage: no fighting back, no overexplaining, no mollifying, no apologizing. Prickles of sweat dot her collarbone as she takes her time climbing out of the car, thanks the driver profusely. She stops to chat with Theo, the doorman, about his daughter, who just started college and is desperately homesick, hoping this digression will give Garrett time to process his overreaction and take some heat out of his fury.

Garrett clasps Theo by the shoulder. "Don't worry, man. She'll come around."

They all wish each other a good night, and Garrett and Liddy step into the elevator. As soon as the doors close, Garrett's face hardens. "You didn't think to ask my permission before making your promises?"

"I'm sorry," Liddy says. "I had no idea you'd get so upset." She struggles to keep her voice even. "We gave them two million last year, so because this is a lot less, I didn't think you'd mind."

"That's not the point, and you—" The doors open to the fiftieth floor, and the discussion stops. They silently walk down the thickly carpeted hallway to their apartment. Once inside, Garrett resumes. "Just because all those people suck up to you, don't forget the money comes from me. I gave them two million dollars last year, not you."

Liddy turns her back on him and hangs up her coat. She already blew the article's advice, reverting to apologizing and putting the blame on herself, just as she's done for most of their twenty-two years of marriage. It's a difficult habit to break, and after the fight they'd had over the kids going to boarding school in Zurich, it's become even harder. Although he didn't actually hurt her that night, he gave her reason to fear that he might.

The fight began after she begged him, cried, promised anything if he'd let the twins stay at Buckingham Browne & Nichols, their school in Cambridge. But he wouldn't consider it. She threatened divorce if he sent them away, and he jumped to the crazy conclusion that this meant she was having an affair. Mere children would never be enough to cause a woman to forsake a husband as wonderful as he.

When she laughed at this, he gripped her in a headlock and pressed the inside of his elbow so tightly into her throat that she couldn't breathe.

She gasped for air that wasn't there, certain he was going to break her windpipe.

"I'd rather you were dead than with someone else," he said, his voice soft, almost purring. "You're mine, and I'll kill you before I let you leave me."

Then he'd released her, claiming he was joking. But it didn't feel like a joke, and Liddy was truly shaken. For the first time since she met Garrett, she was afraid of him. Not only for her own sake, but for the kids. If Garrett killed her, he'd be their only parent, which she would not allow to happen. Ever. And she'd understood that she had to mollify him at all costs.

Now, Garrett grabs her by the arm and forces her to face him. "You must ask me first," he says. "You can't go around making grand gestures without my permission."

She wiggles free and looks over his shoulder into the distance. "Fine," she says coolly. "I'm going to bed."

Her lack of emotion enrages him. "And when you wake up in the morning, you're going to call your little pal Janie and tell her there isn't going to be any matching donation. That you don't have the authority to make such a decision on your own."

Liddy can't contain herself any longer. She tosses her head and looks him straight in the eye. "If I do that, it'll make you look like a bad guy who doesn't want to help kids. And we know that's not how you want to present yourself to your adoring flock."

"Don't be stupid." His laugh is deep. "I'll just let it be known that my accountants are in the process of reassessing my charitable-giving strategies, so no monies are available at the moment, but that they will be before the end of the year. I'll come out of it looking just fine, but you won't."

"Fuck you!" she screams at him. When she turns to walk to the bedroom, he wrenches her back, crushes her to his chest. Then he pushes her roughly away and punches her in the stomach. She slides down the wall, once again trying to find air.

IN THE MORNING, there's a huge bouquet of red roses on her bureau along with a card that reads *I'm sorry for last night. I love you more than life itself and don't know what came over me. Please tell me you forgive me.* He must have ordered them after she went to sleep. Screw him. Flowers and cheap sentiments can't undo what he did or stop the pain pulsing in her midsection or erase her terror of what might come next.

Garrett punched her. Hard. In the past, she'd waved off his anger and unwarranted jealousy, convincing herself that as long as he didn't physically hurt her, she wasn't being abused. It wasn't abuse when he'd told her she couldn't balance a checkbook, or made fun of her desire to write a novel, or blamed her for forgetting to mail invitations to their New Year's party when it was he who'd forgotten. Yes, he'd pushed her around a little here and there, twisting her wrist until she winced, or "accidentally" stomping on her foot, but now she's contending with a whole different animal. Her stomach is bruised, blooming red and purple. It's hot to the touch and hurts like hell.

If he loved her more than life, he'd bring the kids home. But in his mind, Robin and Scott are his rivals, and now that they're thousands of miles from her, he'll do everything he can to keep them there. Like ignoring their protests that they wanted to spend Christmas at home and signing them up for an archaeological dig in Turkey over holiday break anyway. He did this because then there won't be enough time for them to come back to the United States before school starts.

Garrett claims he and she have moved beyond suburbia and children, when actually he's the one who's moved back to where he always wanted to be: childless. Her pregnancy was the cause of his misery for the past fourteen years. At the time, he'd demanded she get an abortion, but was it her fault that due to her irregular periods she hadn't noticed she was pregnant until it was too late to have the procedure? Perhaps it was.

Liddy knows it's a bad idea to do the coke now. A very bad idea. She should wait until Garrett leaves for Europe, as she'd planned, but she barely slept last night. All those dark hours of fear and rage while she hatched escape schemes. What to do? Where to go? How to pull it off?

She takes Sandy's envelope from where she hid it in her underwear drawer, listens carefully. Garrett left for work hours ago. No one's in the apartment, but she waits, to make sure. Sometimes he just shows up, always with a plausible excuse, but she knows he's checking on her, waiting to catch her in the affair he insists she's having.

Which she isn't. At least not yet. And if she does, it won't be with a man. She's fantasized about making love to a woman, even watched a bit of soft lesbian porn. What a hoot it would be to see Garrett's face if he discovered she was having a lesbian affair, that she preferred a mere woman to the rich-and-famous him.

When Liddy is sure she's alone, she returns to her bathroom, closes and locks the door. From behind an extra set of sheets, she grabs a box that contains a small glass trivet, a short glass straw, and a single-edge razor blade. Then she opens the packet, taps a fat mound of powder onto the trivet, and deftly cuts it into four parallel lines.

A fiery blast up one nostril, then up the other. She inhales sharply through her nose, inhales again. The sweet, icy bitterness drips down the back of her throat, and she revels in the euphoria and energy it will soon bring. In minutes, last night is far away, and it's easier to ignore the pain in her stomach. Sandy wasn't kidding. This is good. When she's dressed, she looks over at the two lines waiting on the trivet. What the hell.

She worries that Garrett will come home to shower after his lunch-time workout. And today he might want to bestow an even larger flower arrangement and probably some guilt-induced jewelry. Or he might want to punch her again, maybe do something even worse. But she won't be here. She sees herself in her storage unit, comforted by her children's possessions, cutting lines on the little table next to her reading chair. She texts the valet for her car.

THERE'S AN ACCIDENT on the Longfellow Bridge, and it takes her an hour to make a trip that normally takes ten minutes. By the time she gets to Metropolis, her high has dissipated. Her mouth feels like a sandpit, and she has that uneasy emptiness inside her bones for which there's only one cure. She hurries to the elevator, pumps the button until it opens. Then she jabs multiple times at the button for the fourth floor, which, obviously, doesn't make the rickety thing go any faster. She paces the tiny box as the elevator lumbers its way upward. "Come on, come on," she mutters.

Finally, she's chopping the coke, just as she'd visualized, although now her hand is shaking. She snorts two hefty lines and waits in relieved anticipation for the rush to come. And it does, slamming into her brain, driving out the emptiness and anxiety. She grabs a bottle of water from the small refrigerator and drinks deeply, then runs her eyes lovingly over all the items enfolding her.

Robin's books and soccer trophies, Scott's movies and drawings and photographs, their desks and bureaus still holding their papers and clothes, the corkboards cluttered with party invitations and photos and postcards. Exactly like their rooms in Weston. She knows this is a bizarre thing to do, that she's acting like a crazy lady. But she misses them so much that she's willing to do anything that allows her to be with even a small part of them.

On top of Robin's bureau is the dollhouse Liddy's uncle made when Robin was little, a replica of their home in Weston. He even crafted tiny couches and beds just like the ones they had, and her daughter's dollhouse bedroom is the same bright yellow Robin's real bedroom was when she was five. Robin loved the dollhouse as a little girl and continued to move the furniture around into middle school. Liddy did this also, especially when she was high on cocaine. She still does.

Liddy goes over to the dollhouse, her fingers itching to freshen the living and family rooms. There's a semicircular black sectional in the living room. What if she switched it with the green leather L-shaped sofa in the family room? She begins to play with the pieces, removing and replacing a rug, a table, a lamp, changing it up.

While she works, she slips back into her life in Weston. Into her expansive home and the gardens she tended so carefully, the sound of the birds in the morning, the silence that fell so softly over the property in the evening. The twins' laughter when the three of them played Legos or cooked or gardened or read together, their "expeditions" to Walden Pond or the sculpture garden at the deCordova Museum. Garrett, always working, never joined them. And even if he'd been available, he wasn't a Legos or sculpture garden kind of father.

His fury at her pregnancy remained after the kids were born, but he appeared to come around when the twins turned into adorable toddlers who were crazy about him. He even agreed to move to Weston to give them all more space. She'd hoped that as the kids got older he would soften even more.

There are four bedrooms and a study on the second floor, and Liddy rearranges these also, swapping beds and bureaus, night tables and desks. In truth, those days she's reliving didn't last all that long, driven away by Garrett's jealousy when he realized that, although the children were older, they still demanded most of her time.

He installed a live-in nanny, but Liddy made excuses so she could take care of the kids herself. She also refused to leave them to accompany him on business trips or go on vacations without them. This did not go over well, and, in retrospect, that's when it all began in earnest. At the time, she'd thought it was her own shortcomings that caused him to treat her so badly. Now she sees that this is exactly what he wanted her to believe.

In the six years before the twins were born, when everything was about the two of them and she was his golden girl, she believed Garrett was the best, the smartest, the most wonderful man ever, and the fact that he'd chosen her constantly amazed her. They had so much in common: travel, skiing, the symphony, not to mention an unwholesome devotion to the Red Sox. Although she wanted children, she agreed not to have any when he told her he couldn't see himself as a father. They had been so madly in love and so hot for each other that nothing else mattered.

Liddy reviews her handiwork in the dollhouse. She doesn't like how Robin's and Scott's rooms look redecorated and returns them to their original configurations. She prefers to remember the bedrooms exactly as they were, for the kids to be exactly as they were. Of course she does.

She's thought about leaving Garrett obviously, but obviously, has never gone through with it. At first, she didn't recognize what was happening, and then as the truth started to dawn on her, she convinced herself the situation wasn't so bad, that if she did everything he wanted he would change back into the man she had married. When this didn't work, she stayed because the children were young, because she couldn't figure out how to go about it, because she didn't have the funds the three of them would need.

But this was before he sent the twins away. Before he almost strangled her. Before he punched her. Liddy gingerly touches her stomach and winces. It's time. He'll never change—and it's more than possible that he'll get worse. The kids are older, half of their friends shuffling between parental homes or in blended families.

When Liddy was a newlywed, her mother advised her to start stashing money in an account Garrett didn't know about, claiming that every woman needed money of her own in case of an emergency. And this is that emergency. Her mother deposited the maximum tax-deductible amount annually, and Liddy added to it regularly herself. The account has grown and should be able to cover her for a while. She cannot stay in this marriage any longer. She will not.

The only thing that makes her hesitate is his threat to kill her. The scheme she devised last night is a first step. It will keep her off his radar and give her time to figure out her next moves. But no matter what, she will never leave her children motherless, never leave them alone with him. And she will do anything and everything necessary to ensure this does not happen.

9

ROSE

Rose doesn't want to go to the ATM, but she's only got three dollars in her wallet so she has to. When two twenties spit out of the machine, she stuffs them in her pocketbook and squints through the plate glass window. Yesterday Zach was standing on the other side and he'd nearly scared her to death when she walked out.

The receipts were still in her hand when he gripped her arm, and it was like they say it is right before you die and you see your whole life as a movie. Or maybe it was the opposite because what she saw was what was going to happen next if Zach figured out what she was doing. Fired, arrested, disgraced and then having to confess her sins to Vince, and him figuring that she did it because he didn't make enough money and being double mad. She also saw her Michael roaming the streets with his bad friends and getting into trouble instead of playing football.

Michael is only fourteen but he'd been hanging out with the wrong crowd all through middle school. Because he's got such a large build, he made the high school football team even though he's just a freshman, and she figured this would be the perfect way for him to make some different friends and stay off the streets. But football costs a lot and Vince would never have agreed to spending the money.

There was the $175 district fee just to be a player, and then $290 more for a week of summer football camp, and all those other extras that no one tells you about. Food and sweatshirts, even special socks. And there's more stuff all the time. But because Serge and Marta pay for it, Vince doesn't know that football is expensive.

In those seconds with Zach, she prayed as hard as she'd ever prayed. And thank you, Jesus, her prayers were answered. Zach knew nothing. He saw her through the window and he's such a friendly guy that he just wanted to say hello. He'd stopped at Metropolis to pick up something from his own storage unit and needed cash so he was waiting in line to use the same machine.

Even though Zach isn't here today and she's not making any secret deposits, Rose feels guilty and mad at the same time. Heck, it's not like any of this is something she wants to do. It's something she has to do. And anyways there're good things about it, like Michael staying out of trouble and where would Marta and Serge live if it weren't for her?

Serge is such an odd duck, quite someone. What he was asking her to do today, well, she could never have even thought of such a thing. She didn't say she'd do it but didn't say she wouldn't. Except that she knows she will because she can't say no to the extra money. But letting him go into someone else's unit when they aren't there is kind of creepy. And Zach would probably be as mad as he'd be if he found out about Serge and Marta. Maybe even more.

Serge promised he wouldn't touch anything and would be inside each unit for a really short time to take his pictures. It's not like she thinks he'd steal anything because she knows about people and he's just not that type. But it's not fair to the renters, who think she's making sure no one messes with their stuff. Or to Zach, who thinks the same thing. On the other hand, it's not like anyone's going to get hurt.

And anyways, she's been going into the units for years with no one finding out. She knows she's nosy—Vince says this all the time—but it's not just about being nosy. It's about her doing her job. She's actually giving added protection to the renters by checking that everything is okay when they're not there. She's got a master key so she can easily do what Serge wants. And then there's that extra money. Michael said Coach was going to give them a list of a bunch more stuff they're going to need when the weather gets colder.

Rose stops at the 7-Eleven and feels bad when she buys an expensive sandwich. It isn't in their budget, but Emma and Charlotte got into a big fight this morning and almost missed their bus, so Rose didn't have time to make anything for her own lunch. On good days, her commute takes less than an hour: Blue Line at Wonderland to Downtown Crossing, then Red Line to Kendall and a ten-minute walk to Metropolis. But you never know when your train is going to stop dead or when there's no train at all. Zach asked her to be at her desk by eight thirty—no later than nine—so that's what she's got to do no matter what kind of fuss her girls make.

When she's back at the office, she rubs her hands together and pops a pod into the Keurig. There are three appointments this afternoon with people who might want to rent a unit. These meetings are her favorite part of the job because she gets to find out about the potential renters. And if she asks a few more questions than she actually has to, no one's the wiser. She also likes to see if any of them might become a friend. Sometimes the job can be boring, and it's good to have people to talk to. Like when Liddy comes around.

Rose knows Liddy is in the building today, because she saw her rush to the elevator. Liddy didn't even wave through the window, which was disappointing. It's not like Liddy stops by every day, but Rose enjoys it when she does. She knows it's weird, but she wants to be with Liddy kind of the way she did when she was a little girl and she and her best friend Mary-Joanne had to be together every minute. Holding hands as they walked to school, squeezing tight next to each other on Mary-Joanne's bed to read the same magazine, begging their mothers to let them have dinner together.

The appointments are all duds. A middle-aged man with a huge beer belly, who huffed when she told him the price of the smallest unit and then slammed his fist on her desk and stormed out. A no-show followed by a girl wearing one of those long scarf-like things—a burka, Rose thinks it's called, but it could also be the one that starts with an *h*. It was all black and covered the girl's hair and neck and went down to her shoulders, but at least it didn't cover her face. She talked so softly that Rose could barely understand her.

The woman did rent a unit, but she's not going to be a friend. Even if it's unchristian of her, Rose doesn't trust those people. It's not that she has anything against immigrants—take Marta, for example, who's the nicest thing—or that she thinks they're all terrorists. It's just that she doesn't like how they're always showing off their differences. When her family came to the United States they did everything to become Americans as fast as they could. They felt lucky and proud to be here and Rose believes everyone should do the same thing.

There's a cheery knock on her open door, and Liddy bounds in. "Hey."

"Hey," Rose says, unable to hold back her grin. "You been hanging out upstairs? I saw you came in earlier."

Liddy raises her arms and turns in a graceful full circle. "I've been playing with the dollhouse."

"The dollhouse?" Rose repeats, confused. Liddy seems happy but also like maybe she's too happy. She's sweaty and her eyes look funny.

"My daughter's old dollhouse. It's quite relaxing. Moving the furniture. Pretending. Leaving your body to go somewhere else. No, that's not it—it's more as if your brain leaves your body and takes up residence in the house." She starts to laugh. "Residence in the house. The way I used to be. But I was a resident, not residence, but close enough. The house is the residence. I was the resident. But not anymore."

Rose wonders if Liddy is drunk. "I was going to have a cup of coffee. Want to join me?"

"Tea sounds stupendous," Liddy says. "I think you should try some tea. Coffee isn't good for you. Not for your nerves or for your stomach. I'm not saying go cold turkey, but what if you had a cup of tea every other time? Coffee at breakfast, tea when you get into the office. Then coffee at lunch but tea in the afternoon. Doesn't that sound good? I think you should definitely try it."

Rose grabs two tea bags and two mugs. She doesn't like tea because it's all watery and doesn't taste like anything, but if Liddy is willing to stay long enough to drink a cup Rose isn't going to say no to that.

"Or you could go half-and-half," Liddy continues. "Half regular and half decaf. Mix them together and then you'll cut out half the caffeine without noticing it. What do you think?"

Rose doesn't know what to think about tea or coffee or the weird way Liddy is acting. "Why don't you take a load off?"

Liddy sits but leaps up after only a few seconds. "Went to a big fund-raiser last night. Boston Partners in Education, tons of big mucky-mucks. Garrett said I was the belle of the ball, so it had to be fantastic, right? And it was, in its own way. Top-shelf liquor, so that's always a plus."

Rose puts Liddy's mug in front of her chair and hopes she'll sit down again, but Liddy ignores the tea and begins to pace the long room. "Is everything okay?" Rose asks.

Liddy comes back with a grin on her face. "As okay as it's ever been." She grabs the mug and takes a big sip. It looks like it burns her tongue, but she takes another sip anyway. Finally she sits, but her eyes dart around the room. She sniffs and takes a tissue from her pocket and presses it to her nose. "So are there any large storage units with a window available? A double unit would be perfect. Maybe one with two windows? The expense doesn't matter. Doesn't matter in the least. It's the space I need."

Rose checks her computer for the list of vacant units. "There's actually one not that far from yours on the fourth floor. You want to switch?"

"No. An additional one. The fourth floor would be perfect. Close to the twins."

"You have more of their stuff?"

"It's for my stuff."

"Cleaning out the condo?"

Liddy shrugs and presses the tissue to her nose again.

"You want to talk about it?" Rose wishes more than anything that Liddy does. Nothing makes two people closer than shared secrets.

Liddy downs the rest of her tea, leans her head on the back of the chair, and sniffs again. "You're a good person, Rose," she says to the ceiling, and then it's like a plug has been pulled and all her energy rushes out of her.

"And so are you," Rose says uncertainly. Suddenly Liddy looks so unhappy and worn. The old saying that money doesn't buy happiness crosses Rose's mind.

Liddy pops up like she was stabbed by a knife. Her pupils are so big they almost block out the blue of her eyes, and her hands are shaking. "I have to go. Back upstairs. Right now."

Rose stands, not knowing what else to do. Liddy rushes to her, hugs her and pulls her tight, hanging on like she's drowning. This shocks Rose, but she wishes they could stay like this forever, that Liddy would stay forever. "Don't go," she whispers before she can stop the words.

Liddy presses her forehead down to Rose's, gives her a quick kiss on the lips, and disappears out the door.

10

MARTA

It is another rainy day, and Marta has just finished her usual work-out: twenty-five times up and down the five sets of stairs and a sprint along each corridor between each set of five. She stretches and goes into her cool-down routine: a stroll through the first-, second-, third-, and fourth-floor corridors on her way home to the fifth floor. As she walks the third floor, she notices an odd thing. Although it is not unusual to see people moving things in or out of the building, it is unusual to see a man seated behind a desk in a storage unit set up like a tasteful office. She has never noticed him before and suspects he's either new or usually keeps his door closed.

The man is engrossed in the pile of papers before him and does not look up. She silently circles back. It appears from the numerous hand-somely bound books on the shelves that he is a professional, probably an attorney, and she immediately intuits he is trustworthy and smart. This intuition is based on more than the fact that his glasses and round face give him a nerdy nice-guy appearance. She recognizes this about him because she knows things. Or more correctly, sometimes she knows things.

A lawyer with an office in a storage unit? This is strange. Yet there is her own situation: a wealthy and privileged woman working on her PhD while living in a storage unit. Perhaps she should introduce herself so they can compare notes.

Instead, she returns to her own unit and grabs a towel along with some clothes, soap, and shampoo. It is after two in the afternoon, which means the custodian is finished for the day and she can take a shower. There is a bathroom in Rose's office, one on the second floor, and one on the fourth, but each contains only a toilet and sink. If it were not for the stall with a showerhead in the custodian's closet, she would not be able to live here. One cannot exercise as hard or as often as she does and wash up in a sink. The shower is cramped and not very clean, but it is enough.

She removes the key hidden under the mat and slips it into the lock. She steps into the closet and locks the door from the inside. Access to this room is included in the additional money she pays Rose so she can live at Metropolis. Marta wonders if the lawyer also gives Rose money on the side. But it's probably not illegal to use a storage unit for whatever purpose you choose during the day. Staying overnight is, as the Americans say, another story. Rose explained that the building is neither zoned nor insured for residential use, so it is against the law for a person to sleep here. Marta avoids breaking the law at all costs, but in this instance she has no choice.

While she showers, she steps around the stack of buckets and mops in the corner of the stall and wonders if the lawyer upstairs might be able to help her. She has the feeling maybe he can. Her grandmother always said Mercedes was *una hija de visión*, a daughter of vision, which is an aptitude passed down through their maternal line. Abuela told stories of female ancestors who became revered saints because of their second sight and of others who were burned at the stake for the same. Many were forced to practice in hiding, some doing good and others doing evil. Mamá told Abuela that she was not to fill Mercedes's head with such nonsense, but her abuela, also *una hija*, would fill her head when Mamá was busy. Abuela said the ability to see into the future often skips a generation.

Marta is a social scientist, enamored of data analysis and statistics, but she is also intrigued by the possibilities of a realm that is not quantifiable. Sometimes she is able to decipher the essence of a person from just a single glance, as was the way she sensed the lawyer's decency, but most of the time she knows nothing. Occasionally she can see cancer lurking within a stranger's body, but more often she is blind to an illness lying in wait.

It would seem that if the lawyer leaves his door open, he has nothing to hide. Yet it is also true that despite the air-conditioning and heat pumped into the units, sometimes a whiff of fresh—or not-so-fresh—air is necessary. She does not open her door often, but as her unit is at the end of the corridor on the fifth floor, where there is little traffic, once in a while she allows herself the luxury.

When Marta discovered there was an outstanding warrant for her arrest, she combined the names of two childhood friends, emptied her bank accounts, and moved into Metropolis, telling no one where she was going. She didn't contact a lawyer, because she was afraid. Lawyers in her country are almost always corrupt. They either work for those in control or they are only concerned with their own interests. Even though Dr. Ullman told her this usually is not the case in America, she is not convinced.

Yet she must do something. She cannot go back to Venezuela. There is nothing for her there except death. She does not know where her mother or sisters are, and although she hopes they were able to leave the country safely, the fact that they might be anywhere plagues her. As does the fear that they are nowhere.

After a long afternoon of writing and crunching numbers, Marta takes a stroll to stretch out the kinks in her back. As she walks along the third floor, she decides that if his door is open, she will stop and say hello. Perhaps she will ask a question or two.

It is closed.

She does the same the next day and then the next. On the fourth day, the door is open. When she passes by, the man lifts his head and smiles at her. It is a nice smile that reaches his eyes, and dimples crease his dark skin. She gives him a curt nod but does not linger. What if Abuela is wrong?

WHEN MARTA NEXT talks to Dr. Ullman, he once again suggests she contact an attorney. The female agent showed up on campus and was asking people in the department if they were aware he was in contact with Mercedes. Everyone denied it, an honest response, as no one is aware, yet Dr. Ullman was bothered by the agent's persistence and the way she framed the question as if it were a statement of fact that just needed verification. "I still don't believe she knows anything," he told her, "but I also have the feeling that she's not ready to give up."

So Marta continues to stroll along the third floor, and one afternoon the door is again open. She knocks tentatively.

When he sees her, he stands and comes toward her. "The runner has decided to slow down and take a break."

"Ah, yes." She shifts on her feet. "I have decided to take a break."

He pushes back his glasses and holds out his hand. "Jason Franklin."

She shakes it, although more weakly than she would have liked. Her friend Kevin is always telling her it is important in America for a woman to have a strong grip. She pumps again with more enthusiasm. "Marta Arvelo."

"Please come into my humble abode, Ms. Arvelo." He gestures to the table. "Make yourself comfortable. Can I get you something to drink? Coffee, tea, water?"

"No, thank you, Mr. Franklin." Marta sits and looks around. What is she doing here?

He takes a seat across from her. "Yes, I'm a real lawyer. And yes, my office is in a storage unit."

She likes his directness and decides to match it with her own. At least partially. "Yes, I am a real graduate student. And yes, my office is also in a storage unit."

Mr. Franklin grins, and although he is not a particularly good-looking man, the warmth in his eyes makes it seem as if he is. "Quieter than your apartment?"

"You are exactly right."

"And all this working out? Is that your procrastination?"

"You are exactly right."

"Maybe I should give it a try."

She does not know what to say. She has never been particularly good around men and has had only one long-term boyfriend, Sam, during her first year in graduate school. After they broke up, she did not miss him and became so engaged in her studies that she never pursued another relationship. She has always liked being with women better, and despite the teachings of the church, she now accepts that this is who she is. Her two female relationships in college were far more fulfilling than hers was with Sam. They were also far more devastating when they ended.

"I prefer to run on the Esplanade," she finally manages. "I only exercise inside when the weather is bad."

He nods solemnly, and an awkward silence persists until he says, "Well, it's nice to meet you, Marta Arvelo."

She springs up. "It is also nice to meet you. I did not mean to disturb you in the middle of your workday."

"Oh, that's not what I meant. I'm not all that busy at the moment."

Marta sits back down. He seems to be a decent man, as she originally felt he was, yet, her abuela's assertions notwithstanding, she knows nothing about him. She cannot just blurt out her legal problems. What if he works for Homeland Security or ICE? What if this is what they call a front, and he is part of a trap set up to catch her? These concerns are most likely nonsensical, yet she cannot be too careful.

"Ms. Arvelo," he says, "is there a reason you decided to knock at my door today?" His eyes crinkle with mischief. "Aside from the obvious fact that you were interested in meeting a man as devastatingly handsome and successful as I am?"

"I, uh . . ." She flushes and twists the gold ring her father gave her for her fifteenth birthday.

"It's okay. Not important. I'm just glad for a little company. Where are you at school? What are you studying?"

Marta is grateful for his tact. "I am a student at Tufts University. I am finishing my dissertation for a degree in sociology. I came to the United States to pursue my studies seven years ago."

"Where did you come from?"

"I am from Venezuela."

Mr. Franklin tries to hide it, but she can see a flash of both understanding and sympathy in his expression. "It's terrible what's going on in your country. And ours isn't making it any better."

Marta looks at her hands. "Do you know anything about immigration law, Mr. Franklin?"

"Jason, please." He hesitates and then says, "As it happens, that's my area. For many years, I was involved on the other end, but lately I've been handling immigration cases for those caught in the system. Unfortunately, it's a booming business these days."

Marta glances at the open door. What does he mean by "the other end?"

Jason follows her gaze. "Do you want me to close it?"

"I do not wish to interfere with your work. I think it is best I come back at some other time."

"You can do that, of course. Anytime. But if you think there's a way I can help you, you're welcome to tell me now. I don't charge anything for the initial exploratory meeting."

"Oh, no. It is not the money. I can pay you. It is that I do not know if . . ."

"If you can trust me?"

Marta is not as happy about his directness as she was earlier. "It is not that I do not believe you are a fine man. I am certain you are. It is—"

"I understand. Of course you're cautious. I'm a complete stranger with an office in a storage unit." He hesitates. "Do you know how attorney-client privilege works in the United States?"

"I understand an attorney is not to speak of anything said by his client. But these rules are easy to break." She is puzzled when Jason appears to wince.

"In this country, it's not a rule," he says quickly. "It's the law. A lawyer can get disbarred—not be allowed to practice law anymore—if it's proven he or she broke attorney-client privilege." For a moment, Jason's mouth twists into a frown, as if what he's saying is distasteful.

"Laws are easy to break, also," she says.

"Yes, but this one hardly ever is."

Marta scrutinizes his face, the thoughtful expression and his honest eyes. Dr. Ullman urged her to do this, but it is so difficult to know what is the right thing. She recognizes that she is a pawn, less than a pawn, in a game orchestrated by egomaniacal men who control all the knights and bishops as well as the king and the queen. Even though it is obvious Jason is neither an egomaniacal nor a powerful man, it is best to be wary. She thanks him for his time, excuses herself, and returns to her studies.

11

JASON

Jason pulls into a parking spot, looks up at the massive brick building, and contemplates the zigs and zags life can take. A few years ago, drinking with work buddies, his friend Han told a story about a cousin who had an office in a self-storage unit somewhere off I-93. Some kind of consultant. It was legal, Han said, and cheap.

At the time, they had laughed at the absurdity of the idea, all of them comfortably situated in their tony offices at Spencer Uccello. But after his forced departure from the firm, Jason realized it wasn't absurd at all: legal and cheap with a month-to-month lease was just what he needed while he figured out what he wanted to do when he grew up.

He punches in the code at the door, waves to Rose as he passes her office, and climbs the stairs to the third floor. He hates that creaky old passenger elevator. Actually, no. It's not hatred; it's fear. He doesn't like constricted spaces, especially ones that rattle when they move. Who knows when it might decide to get stuck between floors or, worse, plummet to the basement? He supposes he could use the freight elevator, which is huge, but that one's even creakier, so maybe it's not claustrophobia at all.

When he gets to his office, he makes himself a cup of coffee and settles down to work. He has more cases than he would have thought when he set up shop less than a year ago. After the new administration came to power and rolled out its sweeping restrictions on immigration, his email and phone filled with pleas for help. He's also taken on a few domestic violence and criminal cases, and now he's added Kimberlyn Bell's battle with a real estate conglomerate. Not a full roster, and many of his clients can't pay much, but he still has some money from his big-paycheck days. And he's able to take on clients Spencer Uccello never would.

Like Kimberlyn's beef with W. G. Haines Companies. After a few well-placed calls, in which he mentioned "injunction" and "protests at city board hearings," Haines Companies is now reconsidering its position vis-à-vis Ms. Bell, and Jason is confident she's going to get a fair price for her house. A feel-good victory, however small. He imagines his ex-colleagues at Spencer Uccello laughing at this thought. And their mockery, despite everything, shames him.

His mind drifts to Marta Arvelo, who he assumes has an immigration problem, although he's learned people harbor all sorts of secrets one would never suspect. His curiosity is piqued not only by this question, but also by the fact that she's beautiful, has a magnetic smile, and is clearly very intelligent.

He's never been much of a ladies' man, to say the least. Never even dated until his junior year in college, after he dropped forty pounds and had the growth spurt his mother had been promising for a decade. But even then, he usually waited until a girl made the first move, his self-image shaped by being that fat, uncoordinated kid who hid in the library.

Until Sabrina, who initially sought him out in law school, but whom he'd ultimately pursued. Once they were together, she so smart and capable and sexy, he couldn't consider himself a loser anymore. Unfortunately, his self-esteem took a hit after Sabrina walked out, and he hasn't dated since.

The divorce devastated him, and had almost equally devastated his mother, but his ambition had been too unfettered to save their marriage, his need to prove himself to his childhood tormentors too strong. Sabrina abhorred Spencer Uccello, said she couldn't stand what it was doing to him, who he was becoming. But he'd denied her accusations, blind to the truth of them, and refused to leave the firm. He was a damn fool.

She moved to San Francisco and is working at a nonprofit victims' assistance organization called Safe Future. Now that he's no longer a "corporate snake," as she once called him, they've been in contact more frequently. She's been friendlier, lighter, and he wonders if there might be a chance to reverse his mistake. But with three thousand miles between them, it's unlikely. Maybe Marta Arvelo could help him stop tripping over Sabrina. But Marta may not come back, and he's not going to start slinking around the building looking for her.

Then one morning, she's standing in the hallway in front of his office. She smiles tentatively, asks if he has a free moment.

"Of course," he says. "Please, come in, sit." He moves from his desk to the table and motions to a chair. "Coffee, tea, water, soda?" he asks. "Can I get you something to drink?" he adds unnecessarily.

"I am fine, thank you." Marta remains standing, obviously uncomfortable, too, looking everywhere but at him.

He doesn't know if this visit is business or pleasure, and he doesn't want to presume, so he leaves the pad of paper on his desk and sits down. She finally lowers herself to the chair, but her back is stiff, and she looks as if she's ready to bolt.

"You're writing your doctoral thesis, right?" he asks. "How's it going?"

"I have good days and bad days," she says. "Do you know anything about sociology?"

"Pretty much all there is to know," he deadpans. "The study of society, right?"

"So then you do not know very much." She starts to visibly relax, her eyes crinkling a bit.

"An undergrad business major followed by law school doesn't leave a lot of room for the more interesting subjects. Tell me about your work. Your research project."

"I am testing which factors given at birth have the most effect on later-life outcomes. The inequities at the starting gate that hold you back or push you forward."

"You mean like IQ?"

"More sociological than biological. We refer to them as 'socioeconomic resources,' and I am looking at indicators that reflect those resources. My hypothesis is partially based on an exercise called The Race of Life."

"Never heard of it." Jason finds both the woman and her research intriguing.

"You can watch the video on YouTube. It is short. A group of people stands at the starting line for a short footrace with a hundred-dollar prize. But before they can begin, they must respond to a series of statements. A 'yes' answer allows them to take two steps forward, a 'no' and they must remain in place."

"Like what?"

"When you were growing up, you never had to worry that your cell phone would be shut off. You had more than fifty books in your home. You went to a private school. You never had to help with the bills. Your mother graduated from college. Things like that."

"And we know who wins."

"It is not about who is winning." Marta leans toward him, her face glowing. "A person in the back can run very fast or a person in the front can stumble and fall. It is to show that the starting line is not the same for everyone. This is because some people are given advantages by accident of birth that they did nothing to achieve. And others have disadvantages because of the same."

"Of course, stupid of me. Race of Life. Sure, I see. And you want to know which of these advantages is the most important?"

"Yes. How they rank in importance and how they interact with each other. It is my hope that someday these insights might help drive policies that will make outcomes more equitable."

"What a fantastic topic. Good for you." He fears he sounds like an overly perky preschool teacher. "It must be hard. And working at Metropolis by yourself has to be too." Not much better. "But cool. Very cool. So, like, what did you work on this morning?" Jesus, now he sounds like a dopey teenager. He's definitely out of practice at flirting. Not that he ever was in practice.

Marta takes on an exaggerated pedagogical pose, folds her finger together on the table. "Today I am working on the chapter discussing the tools I created to measure each of my independent variables. How I developed the items for each. How I determined which had to be eliminated for ambiguity. How I entered the remaining ones into a principal component factor analysis with varimax rotation, and what that analysis revealed." She smiles mischievously. "Blah, blah, blah."

Jason is thoroughly enjoying her. "Does this mean you don't want to tell me more?"

"Maybe I will do this at some other time." She hesitates. "I am interested in this exploratory meeting you mentioned the last time we spoke."

He stands, slides the door shut, and takes the legal pad and a pen from his desk. Obviously, a business meeting. "Please tell me how I might be able to help you."

"I am from Venezuela, as I mentioned before. I have been in this country for seven years, ever since I was issued an F-1 full-time student visa with an I-94 D/S to study here. You are familiar with this?"

"You're saying that you have a visa that allows you to stay in the US until you graduate, as long as you remain a full-time student."

"I *had* a visa. Everything was fine until an admin in my department mistakenly reported to ICE that I was not maintaining my course load. She did not understand that although I had completed my classes, while I am working on my dissertation I remain a full-time student."

"Why didn't they just send you a notice to appear before a judge?"

"They did. This same admin—I think she is what you call a temp?—she did not send the address change I gave her to the Boston ICE office when I moved. ICE sent the notice to my old address, but it was not forwarded in time." Marta looks down. "It is my fault. I know how important it is to do everything with ICE exactly, and I have done this the whole time I have been in the US. I should have checked to make sure the admin did what I had requested."

"Whoops," he says, but it's way more than whoops. After 9/11, the rules were tightened for student visas, and one of the nonnegotiable requirements is that a student must update his or her place of residence through their college, which is then responsible for informing ICE. This means Marta is in violation of yet another federal law.

"I did finally receive the notice months after it was issued," she continues. "I contacted the court and was informed I had 'fallen out of status,' and as I had not appeared at the hearing, my visa had been revoked in absentia."

This kind of bullshit makes him want to spit. "And?"

"I was told I am now in violation of US immigration laws, and I am subject to arrest, imprisonment, and removal from the country." There is no mischievous smile as she relates this. "I hung up the phone, packed up a few things, and left my apartment."

"How long ago was that?"

"Eighty-two days. It is not possible for me to go back to my country. I am not safe there."

"Is anyone in your family a Venezuelan government official?"

"Why do you ask this?"

"It might be important."

"My father worked for Chávez, and then he worked for Maduro until Maduro turned against him. For what, my mother does not know. She said one day, without any warning or suggestion such a thing could occur, Papí did not come home from work."

"This happened while you were here?"

She nods, jaw clenched. "The following week, Maduro had my brother shot, and my mother and sisters went into hiding. They could not tell me where they were going, so I do not know where they are."

Jason takes this in. Chances are they're all dead, and if Marta returns she will be too. "I'm sorry for your many losses, but these aggressions against your family will strengthen your case for asylum after you get beyond the deportation issues." He wants to kick himself for putting it so bluntly.

Marta's stoicism crumbles for a moment, but she quickly realigns her face.

"Does anyone know where you are?" Jason asks.

"No one knows this. I am in contact with a professor, but we use disposable phones, and even he does not know how to find me. ICE agents have spoken with him numerous times. Recently one went to his home, and then she went to Tufts asking many questions of people in my department. My professor thinks she is not going to give up."

What she's describing is a high-priority investigation, which means ICE will be putting in far more effort than they might in a standard case and it's unlikely they will back off. The level of harassment infuriates Jason. There are so many more dangerous people to pursue than a graduate student who's followed all the rules for seven years. Unless she isn't telling him the whole story, which is sometimes the case during exploratory meetings.

"Using disposable phones is smart," he says. "But it would be better not to even use those. Sometimes the government makes deals with the shops that sell them."

Marta doesn't respond, and she doesn't look at him, instead focusing on the law books on the shelf to his right. He guesses she's not going to get rid of her phone. Nor does he blame her. This professor is probably her only contact with the world she once flourished in. How can she let go of that?

"I have to ask, do you have a criminal record? Either here or at home?"

"I have never committed a crime. I have adhered to all regulations regarding my visa. I have presented my paperwork in a timely fashion. I have gone to all required hearings except the last, and I recognize that I am responsible for this lapse."

"It was the admin's mistake, not yours. Don't be so hard on yourself." Easy for him to say. "But what about your father? Your brother? Any records?"

"I am fairly certain they have also committed no crimes. But this does not mean that in my country they do not have a criminal record."

Jason pushes his glasses back on his nose. "Where are you living?"

She doesn't answer.

"Marta, I promise you I won't tell anyone what we discuss here except when it's information necessary to get your visa reinstated or to file for asylum. And under no circumstances will I reveal your location."

"Do you think you can do either of these things?"

At first, he's confused, then he realizes she's not going to tell him where she's living, which is her prerogative. "I can try." Jason moves to his computer. "Let me check the exact wording of the travel ban." He types and then skims the page on the screen. "Was your father in the Ministry of Foreign Affairs or Justice and Peace? How about the Migration and Immigration Administration? The Corps for Scientific, Penal, and Criminal Investigations?"

"I am not sure, but it is possible."

"It says here that it's only the people who worked for those agencies, and their families, who are barred from the US. If your father didn't work at any of them, it may help in the long term. But the first step is to prove that you never purposely violated your status, so there was no reason for the removal order in the first place. After that, you can pursue asylum."

He reads further. A summary states that all Venezuelan citizens holding US visas are open to questioning and that an immigration officer can reduce the time allotted on the visa for anyone he or she deems to be under suspicion. It does not stipulate what the visa holder might be under suspicion of.

"Thank you," Marta is saying. "I would like to hire you to begin immediately. I would also like to pay you for this meeting. My mother was able to wire money before they went into hiding."

"I never charge for the exploratory, so don't worry about it. Just let me do a little investigating. See what I can come up with. I'd like to try to come at this from a variety of directions, if it's possible." He doesn't mention what he just discovered.

"You will try this, and also for political asylum? I think political asylum would be the best for me, and I think I would have many reasons to be a good candidate."

"Have you spoken to a lawyer about this before?"

Again, she doesn't meet his eyes. "I have not."

Jason remembers her comment at their first meeting, questioning the trustworthiness of lawyers. "I'm going to check out all the possibilities. And, yes, you are a good candidate for asylum."

"Thank you."

He pushes the legal pad across the table and hands her his pen. "Can you please write down your father's name, last address, and date of disappearance. Also for your brother. Your mother and your sisters. Your address in Venezuela." He ticks off the items on his fingers. "The name and address of your department at Tufts. The name of the admin who made the mistakes. The address they had on record and the address where you moved. I'll also need your passport and visa. Do you happen to have them with you?"

Marta hesitates.

"I can't help if I don't have this information," he says gently. "You need to think about your next steps if you're not comfortable sharing it with me. Do you want to take a few days to consider?"

"Marta Arvelo is not my real name." She digs into her back pocket, puts her passport and visa on the table. "I am Mercedes Bustamante."

"Good move." Jason takes the documents over to his scanner and makes copies. "I'll keep these materials in my safe, so don't worry about anyone finding them."

Marta nods as she writes down the information he requested.

"Should we set up another meeting?" he asks. "Now that I told you not to use a disposable phone, I'm guessing there's no way to contact you?"

She hands him the pad. "If you tell me when you think you will have enough to discuss, I will come to you."

As Jason takes her documents from the scanner and places them on the table, he calculates. He's got a number of cases he should work on before Marta's, but she clearly needs help. As soon as possible. "How about a week from today? Same time?"

Marta nods again and stands.

He escorts her to the door, opens it, and asks, "Is your living situation safe? Do you have somewhere to sleep? Heat? Locked doors? Access to water? Do you feel secure there?" When she doesn't respond, he says, "If the answer to any of these questions is no, we need to find you somewhere else to live."

"Thank you," Marta says. "I believe I am as safe as I can be."

12

SERGE

Serge can't stop thinking about the mother mourning her children in that storage unit he walked by the other day. In his nightmares her shadow hangs from his back. The little children hover around him. He knows they grew to be teenagers, but they were babies once, and babies they still are in his dreams. "How did you die?" he asks the little girl. "How long has it been?" he asks the little boy.

They don't answer but he knows they can hear him. The mother can too but he can't see her face. He wonders how she's surviving all that grief. He'd like to think she's getting better but her space is so soaked with pain that he knows she isn't. Sorrow, emptiness, loneliness, pressing down on her. He dreams about her every night. The dreams are terrifying because her suffering is his own.

Rose agreed to unlock the doors for fifty dollars apiece, but he hasn't asked her to do this yet, even though he wants very badly to photograph the units. He's afraid of what might be inside. The world is a bad place when even a glimpse into a storage unit creates so much sadness, and he doesn't know how much more sadness he can take.

So he goes to work at night and stays inside the rest of the time. He and his cot. It's better this way. Except when the storage-unit mother comes to him and makes him think about Alice, his own mother, who would never be mourning her children.

Alice had a suppertime rule. Whoever finished their food last had to wash the dishes. So every meal was very fast, and she liked this because she was always saying she had no patience for what she called their "jibber-jabber." His father was hardly ever there, but when he was, the rule didn't apply to him. Or to Alice.

Serge was the oldest and could shovel down his food faster than his brother and sister, who were three and four years younger than him. Anton and Anastasia fought about everything, but they fought the most about supper. He was seventeen the night Anton became so angry when Anastasia finished first that Anton grabbed a steak knife off the table and stabbed her in the hand. Alice was more bothered that Anastasia wouldn't be able to milk the cows for at least a month than that her daughter had been hurt. Serge left the next day and has never gone back.

One morning he wakes up and realizes that he hasn't dreamed about the storage-unit mother and her children in almost a week. This must mean the mother is dead too. This makes him feel better because then she's out of her misery and is with her little boy and girl. His sadness begins to lift and when his energy comes back he's ready to take pictures of what he's begun to think of as storage stage sets.

He's ready to hold his Rolleiflex, to use the viewfinder the way an astronomer uses a telescope to discover unseen life. The inner life of the storage stage sets. Like the astronomer, he'll use dark and light to describe the invisible.

ROSE UNLOCKS THE door of #357. "You can only stay for ten minutes," she tells him. "It looks like he left for the day, but you can't ever be sure. He could come back for something. Or maybe he only went out to grab a cup of coffee." She glances up and down the corridor. "Might even have an appointment coming in."

Serge isn't worried about how long it will take him but he wants Rose to go away. He'll be fast because his photographs are never set up or changed by fake lighting. He takes pictures of what's in front of him. Not what isn't in front of him. She's standing too close, and she keeps trying to look at his eyes.

"I'll be watching the front door," Rose continues jabbering. Jibber-jabber. "If he comes in, I'll think of some way to keep him downstairs, but I can't do it for long. That's why ten minutes. Absolute tops."

"That's fine," he says, and his voice comes out like a frog's. He holds his Rolleiflex at stomach level and stares at the key in her hand.

Finally she unlocks the door, flips the light switch, and then rushes away to cut off whoever the renter is. "Don't forget to turn off the light and lock the door behind you," she calls over her shoulder. "Ten minutes. That's it."

Serge pushes the heavy door along its track, steps inside, and pulls it closed behind him. The renter must be a lawyer because there are law books on the shelves. And a rich one, from the expensive furniture. A rich lawyer with an office in a self-storage unit? Maybe the furniture is stolen, or a lot cheaper than it looks. Maybe he's a con man with a classy looking operation to take advantage of innocent victims. Serge's Rolleiflex will show who this guy really is.

Looking down into the viewfinder, Serge spins around, searching for odd combinations. The shiny finish of the table against the cinder-block walls. The graceful curve of a chair leg against the cracked cement floor. The harsh overhead light vs. the soft leather of the books. The metal computer vs. the gentle swirls in the mahogany desk. He presses the shutter. Click. Click. He presses again and again. The film is gone quickly. Only twelve shots to a roll.

Unloading and loading used to be tricky but now it's a cinch. He easily feeds the film across all the rollers so he won't waste any of it when he advances to the next shot. It also used to be tricky because what you see and photograph is a square, not a rectangle like most cameras. But it turns out that you can do a lot with squares that you can't do with rectangles.

He turns the camera at a twenty-five-degree angle, tilts his head to see into the viewfinder, and presses the shutter. Click. Click. Now everything's off-kilter, more alert. Serge sees the printed images floating up to him from the watery developer tray, gaining substance and giving the lawyer form.

The next day Rose unlocks another unit for him, and he's baffled by what's in front of him. A maze, but not really a maze. Dozens of cartons and jars filled with crazy things that make a crooked and confusing path from the door to the back wall. The Rolleiflex will be his dowsing stick. He looks into the viewfinder and steps between a box of seashells and a box of straws, then between a basket holding balls of aluminum foil and another full of tiny paintbrushes. He stops dead, sucks in his breath. There's a snake on the floor. Many snakes coiled together. Then he realizes they're not moving, not alive, and there are little bits of aluminum foil floating above them.

This is voodoo. Or witchcraft or some kind of sorcery. Nothing good. He should get out of here. Right now. Back out slowly. Instead he turns in a circle, holds the camera stiffly in front of him. It's his shield and his lookout.

His hands drop, and he laughs out loud.

The snake is made of dominos. Glued together. Many colors. Many kinds. Many dots. Flying out in geometric patterns between the ups and downs of the domino roller coaster. He kneels. It looks like child's play, but it isn't. It's wondrous. A work of art that holds him and keeps him and makes him want to weep. With both joy and sorrow. No need to look for odd combinations here.

13

ZACH
Seven months later: May 2018

The day after the auction, Zach packs up the contents of #514, which according to Rose's spreadsheet belonged to a man named Serge Laurent, who always paid his rent on time and in cash, and gave no home address, no bank account, no phone number, no email, no nothing. A man who had materialized out of nowhere and apparently returned there.

Zach scoops up every photograph, contact sheet, negative, and undeveloped roll of film he can find and throws them into the cartons he brought with him, then moves all the furniture and gear to make sure he hasn't missed any photos. He ignores the rickety furnishings, the old clothes, the energy bars, and the photographic equipment, with the exception of the Rolleiflex camera. The leavings will be disposed of by College Hunks Hauling Junk, which will be clearing out the building in preparation for the sale.

Unfortunately, "sale" is a misnomer. Although there will be lots of papers to sign at the time ownership is transferred, there will be no money involved. In exchange for his liability in the elevator incident, Zach is turning over the property without a penny of compensation. No more business. No more investment property. No more income. Yup, no one-percenter.

Metropolis was dropped in his lap at the moment he needed it most, and it fulfilled its function many times over. The early years were demanding, but he toughed them out, turned Metropolis legit, and got himself out of the marijuana business, which had been his objective from the start—that and using the purchase to launder his drug money.

The drug stuff had started as a lark, dealing small amounts of pot out of his dorm room at Yale, but it became a monster in six short years. Even though he'd never sold anything but pot, he'd gone big-time, and was soon hanging out with guys who cared little about the disastrous effects of what they were doing as long as they were getting high and jet-setting around the world.

Admittedly, Zach had enjoyed this too, but when his childhood friend Tony died, along with a dozen others, due to a bad batch of heroin that Nick, a business associate of Zach's, had sold them, Zach wanted out. He was devastated by Tony's death and shamed by his part in what he'd considered a game—but clearly was not. So when Nick needed fast cash to get out of the country before the cops caught him, he'd offered Zach Metropolis at a ridiculously low price, and Zach grabbed it.

The building was a money machine. Three hundred eighty-four units, almost always continually rented, provided him with all the cash he needed to support his rather indulgent lifestyle. Owning Metropolis transformed him into a respectable, tax-paying businessman, if one with wild, risk-taking hobbies, a reinvention he was quite proud of. And one he assumed would continue as long as he wanted it to. Which isn't quite the way things turned out. Not for him, and not for everyone else whose world was destroyed by a broken elevator.

A single moment causing such widespread damage. Financial ruin, heartbreak, pain, incapacitation. And why did it happen? It's been months, and still no one knows for sure. Was it an accident, suicide, murder? No one knows this either. The media is rife with speculation, but so far that's all it's been, and the questions remain.

Zach has always been a much better spender than saver, and although he's got some money in the bank, there's not that much of it. It might last him nine months, a year if he sticks to a strict budget, which is unlikely. So here he is at thirty-seven, nearly broke and scurrying around to hide transgressions he believed he'd put behind him long ago.

As he gathers the photographs, he notices one of the creepy kids' room he saw at the auction. He looks at it in awe. An amazing shot, black-and-white, as all of Laurent's photos appear to be. An image of inanimate desks and books and drawings without a single person in it, yet full of angst and questions. A beam of light separates the armchair from the children's lives, allowing the chair itself to appear to be observing from afar, a distance that somehow feels vast. What's the story here? Who are these absent kids? Who's watching them from the empty chair? And most of all, why?

He thinks about the other abandoned units he saw that day: Liddy Haines's pied-à-terre, the fancy office, the small, neat monk's retreat. Are there exceptional photos of these places too? Brilliant shots of other units, once full and now cleaned out? So many mysteries inside a building he'd always considered lifeless.

There are a mind-boggling number of undeveloped film canisters. His guess of many hundreds can't be all that far off the mark. He plunges his hands into a batch, rolls the small plastic tubes around in his fingers, tosses some in the air, watches them fall. A potential trove just waiting to be discovered. Perhaps a gold mine as well. And there's nothing he needs right now more than a gold mine.

Zach's original plan was to destroy all the photographs, contact sheets, negatives, and undeveloped canisters, fearing they might reveal his crimes as well as those of his early tenants. But how can he do this now that he's aware of their potential value artistically and financially? He scans the equipment scattered on the table, and then it hits him: he'll develop the film himself. He'll get rid of anything incriminating, and if the other photos are as good as he suspects, entire new possibilities will open to him.

Most of the gear he needs is right here for the taking. Actually, it's already his. And there's a decent-size extra bathroom in his condo that could easily be converted into a darkroom. He's never developed a photograph in his life, but before he started scuba diving or hang gliding or competitive skijoring, he hadn't known anything about them either. Same with highpointing and nature photography. He catches on quickly, and he's pretty resourceful. Excitement rises within him. Time for another reinvention.

He runs down the stairs and retrieves the flattened cartons he'd left in his trunk wedged under Rose's computer and files. Rose, who can't be all that much older than he is but seems older than his own mother. Rose, who appeared competent, but clearly wasn't. Rose, who begged him to forgive the unforgivable. Damn her to hell.

When Zach returns to #514, sweaty from his exertion on this unseasonably warm May afternoon, he packs up the darkroom tools and chemicals. It's an unwieldy mix, some of it large and bulky, and the rest small and fragile. The enlarger weighs a ton. It takes three trips down the long, desolate corridor to load up the freight elevator at the back of the building. The smaller elevator, closer to #514, is crisscrossed with yellow police tape, presumably out of order forever.

Once he manages to squeeze it all into his Prius, Zach looks up at Metropolis, rising at least seventy feet above the sidewalk. Such a majestic building for such a mundane purpose. The crenellated, corbeled cornices. The square corner tower, two others atop the entrances. The round punched-brick window cutouts. Evocative of a medieval castle, and now just as ominous.

14

ROSE

Rose relives Liddy's hug and kiss as she hangs on to the strap in the packed Red Line subway car. Liddy held her really tight, like she was leaning on her. This must mean that they are really friends, maybe even special friends. The kiss on the lips was kind of weird but maybe that's what some people do with their friends. Rose has never kissed a friend like that but she knows other people do things differently than she does. Like how Europeans kiss on both cheeks.

When she switches to the Blue Line she still has to stand but is grateful it isn't as crowded as the Red Line. And the people in this car look a lot more like her than the ones in the last one. No Cambridge types here, with their cool glasses and fake-ripped expensive clothes, but her Revere folks. Down to earth and not afraid to say what they think.

It's not that she doesn't like people who are different from her. She likes Marta and Jason Franklin and there are lots of others. Like Liddy, who has lots of money. It's just that she feels more comfortable with her own. Doesn't everyone? Except that in the ten years she's been making this trip, even the Blue Line has become more different from her than it used to be.

A boy with a backpack gets on the train and smashes her in the shoulder with it. He doesn't apologize even though he knows he did it, and Rose supposes Michael wouldn't apologize either. Her sweet little boy has been gobbled up by some large, smelly man-child who isn't sweet at all. But even Michael, who's always on her mind and is her biggest concern, can't push away Liddy. Rose wonders what that whole thing about her wanting another unit is about and frowns. Somehow it seems like it must be something bad.

She feels a squeeze of thankfulness when she walks through the front door of her familiar apartment. It isn't big, but it's more than enough for the five of them. It's the same as her mother's and as her brother's downstairs. The exact same layout of rooms she's always lived in.

The entrance is through the small sunroom facing the street, then the living room and the dining room and the kitchen after that. There are three bedrooms to the left of the other rooms, with one bathroom. It would be nice to have two bathrooms, but there are dark hardwood floors and wide moldings and a pretty built-in china cabinet. Rose wonders if one of her children will live here someday. Then she and Vince will take over her parents' apartment on the first floor and babysit for the grandkids.

Emma and Charlotte are doing their homework at the dining room table. Emma, who's the little boss at eleven even though she's only one year older than Charlotte, is making sure her sister is doing her math problems right. "One-quarter is the same as point two five," Emma says, her voice a perfect imitation of a teacher disappointed by a slow student. "They mean exactly the same thing."

Charlotte doesn't raise her head. "That's stupid."

"It's not stupid. It's math. You're stupid if you don't understand that."

"I am not stupid!" Charlotte cries. "Math is stupid if it needs two ways to say the same thing. And you're stupid if you don't understand that!"

"Don't call each other stupid," Rose says. "Emma, do your own homework and let your sister do hers."

"But she's doing it all wrong, and I was just trying to—"

"Emma." Rose points to the history book open in front of her older daughter. "Your homework." She goes into the kitchen and checks the cabinets and refrigerator to figure out what to make for supper. She actually agrees with Charlotte because what's the point in making math any more complicated than it already is?

There's enough leftover lasagna for tonight if she bakes up a lot of garlic bread—and serves Michael last, because he could probably eat all the lasagna by himself. She'll make a salad for herself and Emma, green beans for Vince and Charlotte because it's the only vegetable they'll eat. Michael refuses to eat anything green. As she pulls things from the refrigerator, she calls out for Michael. She gets no answer so she calls again. He should be home from football practice by now, and if he isn't that's a bad sign. She marches out of the kitchen and bangs on his door. No answer.

"Michael's not here," Emma tells her in a singsongy voice that shows how happy she is to know something her mother doesn't.

"Where is he then?"

"Haven't seen him." Emma grins. "Probably should check your phone, Mom."

It's annoying the way the kids are always making snide comments about her lack of computer skills but she does as Emma suggests. There's a text from Michael telling her that he's going to have dinner at Reggie's. He doesn't ask. He just says. He's been having dinner at Reggie's an awful lot lately. Reggie is one of the boys Rose doesn't like from Michael's middle school days, and Reggie doesn't play football. She should call his mother to make sure Michael is there, but she doesn't know the mother and doesn't want to admit that she doesn't know where her own kid is. At least now she doesn't have to worry about not having enough lasagna.

Rose goes back into the kitchen and softly presses her tongue to the exact spot where Liddy kissed her. She likes the feeling and likes the memory. Warmth spreads up her cheeks, and she smiles again. When she finishes dinner preparations, she shoos the girls from the table so she can set it. She should make them do it, but they always make such a fuss that it's easier just to do it herself. Vince will be here in a few minutes and he likes his dinner on the table as soon as he gets home. Her Vince is a good man. A hardworking man, a good husband and father, and he doesn't drink too much. She's lucky to have him. Much luckier than her friend Katherine, whose Rick makes Liddy's Garrett look like a pussycat.

Vince comes through the door and calls out his usual, "Daddy's home!"

Emma and Charlotte go running. They push at each other to get to him first. "Daddy! Daddy!" they cry in unison.

He winces as he picks each girl up, but twirls her around and kisses her on the head before setting her down again. "Princess One and Princess Two! How are my two beauties tonight?"

"Dinner will be ready in five minutes," Rose calls.

He comes into the kitchen, pecks her cheek, and grabs a Bud Light. "I'm beat."

She doesn't tell him she's beat too. He works in a Home Depot warehouse, which is a hard job that's sometimes backbreaking and made worse by the bad injuries he got in Afghanistan. While she gets to sit in a comfortable office all day mostly just drinking coffee and sometimes hanging out with Liddy. Rose presses her tongue to her lip again. It's been a long time since Vince kissed her on the lips. Even longer since they had relations.

She counts back and realizes it might be a year. It's not that she doesn't love him, because she does with all her heart and has ever since they were kids. It's just that sometimes it feels more like they're brother and sister. But after being married for so many years she supposes this isn't such a bad thing. She waves her good, hardworking husband toward the dining room. "Take a load off, hon. I'll bring dinner right in."

15

LIDDY

It takes two days for Liddy to fully recover from the cocaine. As she knew she would, she snorted the entire gram that afternoon, then took sleeping pills to avoid the crash and climbed into bed. Although the pills took care of the first wave of punishing withdrawal, they did nothing for the morning after. Or the morning after that. The days either. There was the stomach distress, the dry mouth, the light sensitivity, and the aching teeth, but the worst part was the pervasive sensation of unease, edging into dread. It was housed in her chest and billowed outward with every breath.

In her Weston days, the recovery was much quicker. Two aspirin and a strong cup of coffee the morning after, and she was good to go. Not so anymore. Aging will do that to a person. The high isn't worth this extended recuperation, forty-eight hours of misery vs. six hours of exhilaration, and she vows her coke days are over. But as with so many promises she's made to herself to quit whichever substance she was currently overindulging in, this one, too, will be broken.

By the third morning, she's sipping tea at the kitchen table, breathing fully and deeply. Garrett is in Europe on his business trip. He told her he'd be gone four or five days, but it could be more. Or less. He likes to keep her guessing.

It's her day to tutor at the Burke, a low-income high school that's so overcrowded they hold classes on Saturday mornings, but she has a little time before she has to leave. Nonetheless, she stands and puts her mug into the dishwasher. Then she hesitates, reconsiders, and takes the mug out. She pours herself another cup and sighs. If she can't decide whether or not to have a second cup of tea, how the hell is she going to decide whether to end her marriage?

When she was in the throes of fury and pain, not to mention high on cocaine, her decision to leave him was clear-cut. But now she's beginning to waver. Not in her hatred of him or her desire to be free of his clutches, just a rethinking of the logistical, financial, and familial difficulties involved, the myriad ways she could fail. But there's still the punch. And his relentless and growing need to control her.

There's no denying Garrett was controlling from the beginning. He questioned her endlessly about where she'd been and who she'd been with, what her plans were for the next day, sometimes suggesting she not do that particular thing, not see that particular person. At the time, she'd viewed these as signs of his concern for her happiness, his interest in her activities, an expression of how much he loved her. And maybe it was. But it's difficult to believe it still is.

Heading for the Burke, Liddy pulls onto Washington Street in the heart of the recently branded Midtown, which has always been known as Downtown Crossing. It's an area hardly anyone lived in twenty years ago, when it was filled with empty storefronts and garbage. Now the neighborhood boasts some of the most expensive residences in the city, along with a slew of trendy restaurants, overpriced furniture stores, and a high-end Roche Brothers supermarket.

Dipping along the edge of Chinatown and past Bay Village's narrow streets and handsome brick row houses, she drives over the Mass Pike and into an area of the South End that only recently was home to warehouses, parking lots, and the *Boston Herald*'s production facilities. Now it's called the Ink Block, another newly named district, this one created expressly for the young techies flooding into the area. Here, it's Whole Foods that feeds the highly paid residents.

Then everything begins to shift from chic to shabby. At first slowly, as some gentrification has pushed into Dorchester, and then more rapidly. No more gleaming towers. No more historic brownstones. No more well-dressed people walking their designer dogs or pushing expensive baby strollers. Warren Street. Blue Hill Ave.

Tree roots heave themselves through sidewalks, roads crumble at their edges, and the people appear to be crumbling along with them. These folks move more slowly, smile less frequently, walk less erect, as if carrying burdens too heavy for their shoulders. Car repair shops, check cashers, bodegas, and broken windows. Inconsistent garbage collection, and not a supermarket to be seen. She's barely traveled two miles.

This transition is always troubling. Heartbreaking, actually. She consoles herself with the thought that she's doing what she can to help, or at least trying, both personally and financially. But she feels the weight and the guilt of her privilege.

When she gets to the Burke, classes are changing and the halls are chaotic. Lockers slam. Students strut and shove and kiss and laugh, calling to each other as if shouting across a football field. It's heartening to know that no matter how rich or poor, teenagers act like teenagers. And high schools smell like they do everywhere: a mixture of shampoo, sweat, dust, Pine-Sol, and chalkboards, although no one uses chalk and erasers anymore.

She steps into the library, which also sounds and smells like all libraries, but there the similarity ends. Books line the shelves, but they, like the buildings she just passed, are well-worn, in some cases falling apart. A couple dozen computers sit atop a line of desks, but they, too, are outdated. Some even sport bulky cathode-ray monitors, their rear ends jutting out at least a foot. More than a few screens have a yellow sticky note in the middle of their blank faces: out of order.

Liddy settles herself in an alcove holding a battered table that looks as if it came from someone's grandmother's dining room. This is where the tutors work. She's here to help seniors with their college essays. It's a PEN/ New England program, and she's been a volunteer since its inception.

She joined PEN, a national writers' organization, decades ago, when she intended to be a writer.

Well, she actually was a writer then. Of a sort. At least six short stories and a similar number of essays published, although, as Garrett later pointed out, nowhere particularly prestigious. The first draft of a novel completed, now stuffed in the back of her closet, full of characters she thinks of as old friends, who are waiting for her to come back and set them straight. Garrett called it her "little story," and teased that her MFA was from a "hick university," not acknowledging that the University of Iowa has one of the best creative writing programs in the country.

"You Liddy?" a thin girl with earrings hanging to her shoulders asks.

"I am." Liddy grins, probably too broadly, points to the chair next to her. "You must be Kennedy."

Kennedy sits grudgingly, inspects her fingernails. "I'm a shitty writer."

"That's what everyone says. I bet you're a lot better than you think."

AFTER WORKING WITH three students, Liddy heads home, tired and depleted but feeling that at least she accomplished something. She grabs her usual lunch of yogurt and crackers and settles herself back at the kitchen table, just as indecisive as she was earlier. Garrett.

She thinks back to the afternoon her mother told her that she had lost all her assets in Bernie Madoff's Ponzi scheme. Neither she nor her mom actually understood the ins and outs of what had happened, but it was clear to Liddy that her seven-figure inheritance was gone. She immediately called Garrett, and even though it was the middle of the day, he came right home. When he walked in the door, she and her mother were holding each other, confused and devastated.

Liddy jumped up and threw herself in his arms. "It can't be what her financial advisor told her. How could this be possible when the government is overseeing—"

"Shh" he murmured. Then he gently loosened Liddy's grasp, led her to the couch, and knelt next to his mother-in-law. "It's going to be fine, Harriet. I'll take care of everything."

Over the following months, Garrett worked with the lawyers and accountants, bought her mother's house so she could remain in it, and wrestled enough money out of Madoff's remaining assets to provide a small income. And when her mom developed dementia, he paid, without complaint, for the pricey nursing home. How proud Liddy had been of him, how much she'd loved him for his kindness and generosity.

He was equally generous with her household account, depositing more than she needed into the checkbook every month, encouraging her to use what was left over to buy little luxuries, to indulge herself and the children. Of course, the better decked out and pampered they were, the better he looked. Whatever his motive, this and her mother's generosity had allowed her to stash over $200,000 in an offshore account. Not a tax dodge, a safety net, set up for a circumstance just like this.

She looks out over Boston into Cambridge, imagines she can see Metropolis, and thinks about the time stretching forward. Forty, perhaps fifty more years with Garrett, her puppeteer. He sent her children away. He took her house away. He scorned her dream of becoming a novelist. He belittled and controlled her. He threatened to kill her. He tried to strangle her. And then he punched her. She finishes her tea and places the cup in the dishwasher. There is nothing to rethink.

Obviously, she never told Garrett she'd moved the twins' belongings to Metropolis, and as she's always paid Rose in cash, there's no way to connect her with the building. It's against the law for anyone to live in a storage unit, so it won't occur to him to look for her there. She's willing to pay Rose handsomely and is sure Rose will let her move in. The woman is always so happy to see her, always wants her to stay longer, sulks if Liddy doesn't come by for a few days. And Liddy is well aware that Rose would love to know more about her life, for them to share confidences, to be friends.

Rose's interest has always made Liddy uncomfortable, but Rose is a good soul, and she's clearly bored and lonely. It costs Liddy nothing to pop into her office once in a while. But it's almost as if Rose lives in a different world, in an older and simpler time, with absolute rights and wrongs. She married just out of high school and lives in the same triple-decker where she grew up, in the scrappy town of Revere. A serious Catholic. Liddy can't imagine how Rose interpreted her cocaine-induced antics last week, or what might be going through Rose's mind in the wake of her kiss.

What a colossal mistake. What the hell was she thinking? She'd been flying too high, hadn't been thinking at all. In that moment, she'd been overwhelmed by gratitude for Rose's kindness and concern, but hugging and then kissing her? Stupid, stupid, stupid. Yet another reason to stop doing cocaine.

She has to clear the air. But what explanation can she give? She can't tell Rose about the coke, because Rose would be horrified that she's using drugs. In another universe, Liddy could just move her belongings to a different storage site. But that isn't going to happen. She can't leave Garrett without Rose's help.

16

ROSE

Rose has been waiting since last Thursday for Liddy to come by the office. It's been five days so far, including the weekend, since she saw her, since the kiss. Both last week and today, Rose has tried to keep busy with paperwork and phone calls and interviews. But there's still been lots of empty hours to drink too much coffee and wonder where Liddy might be. If the fact that she hasn't been in for so long means she's trying to avoid her.

Then three reports of possessions going missing from storage units came in and distracted her. It happens every once in a while, but it's never happened all together like this. It almost always turns out that the renter misplaced their things or brought them somewhere else, but Mr. Peters and Angie Holladay and Linda Shields all say they would remember if that was the case. Not enough time has gone by to tell for sure, but it was all expensive stuff, which is suspicious. The only thing Rose can do is hope it was forgetfulness so there'll be no reason to tell Zach. Or even worse, to tell the police. That would make her look bad.

And then there was the whole weekend trying to keep Vince from beating up on Michael after he didn't come home all night without telling them. Michael has Vince's temper and he's got at least two inches and thirty pounds on his father. Plus his new football skills. It was all she could do to keep them from bashing each other's heads in. More likely it would have been Michael bashing Vince's head in. Michael usually comes home after practice but he's been staying out late at Reggie's more and more. If it weren't for the football, she'd be really worried. Because he's got to keep fit and can't do any drugs in order not to get kicked off the squad. She tried to reach Reggie's mom a couple of times but just got the answering machine. Then the machine stopped picking up and there's been no call back.

Finally, late Monday afternoon Liddy steps into the office looking guilty and uncomfortable. She sits on the edge of a chair and covers her face, then peers through her fingers at Rose. "I was in here, in your office, on Wednesday afternoon, wasn't I?"

"Yes . . . ," Rose says, and tries to keep her voice normal. Of course Liddy was here Wednesday afternoon.

"I'm so embarrassed," Liddy says. "I have this vague memory of being in here, but I was so drunk I didn't know if I was or I wasn't. I never drink during the day, but I was so upset about, about . . . well, Garrett . . ."

Heat climbs Rose's neck. After she's been stewing about the kiss, is Liddy saying she doesn't remember it? That she was so drunk she had a blackout? Rose has seen lots of blackout drunks, and was even one herself once or twice in her younger days, but Liddy didn't act like any drunk she'd seen before. Liddy was walking back and forth across the office and her balance was fine. She wasn't slurring her words either.

"I, I remember being in my unit," Liddy continues. "And I definitely remember playing with Robin's dollhouse, but then it all gets blurry . . ."

Rose tries to match up Liddy's words with what happened. She knows there are lots of kinds of drunks: the crying ones, the mean ones, the dopey ones, the quiet ones. So maybe she's got it wrong. Maybe Liddy was drinking tequila or one of those other kinds of alcohol her Vince says makes you a different kind of drunk.

"You came down here after that, told me about the dollhouse," Rose says. "I, uh, I kind of thought you might be drunk. You were acting weird."

"Was I? How awful. Did I do anything terrible?" Liddy looks at Rose for a second, then her eyes slide away.

There's something in Liddy's voice that makes Rose think she's lying. That this is a made-up story so they can pretend the kiss never happened. That Liddy had never said what a good person Rose was. It would be an easy way out. An easy way to make it all go away. "It was just me and you," Rose says quickly to hide her disappointment and shame. "You were a bit silly actually, but nothing terrible at all."

"Well, that's a huge relief," Liddy says. "So you forgive me?"

"There's nothing to forgive," Rose says, but she kind of thinks there is. Like that Liddy was sort of leading her on about how close friends they were and might be lying about it to her now. "Except that you should never have gotten behind the wheel in that condition."

"I know. It was dumb. I promise I won't do it again."

"I'm not your mother." Rose is suddenly afraid Liddy might be lying about this too. "You don't need to promise me anything. You need to promise yourself." But then she remembers that it's probably all fake and Liddy wasn't drunk at all. Or was she?

"Okay, Mom," Liddy says, and flashes her a grin.

Rose struggles to return it. "You, uh, you never came in after that. And then it was the weekend. Is everything all right? You said you were upset about Garrett. Did he, uh, do something bad?"

"Actually I'm more than all right. And I have a proposition for you."

Rose's heart jumps. "What kind of proposition?"

"I have a favor to ask you, and it's a big one." Liddy hesitates. "I have to leave Garrett, and I have to go somewhere, at least for a while, where he can't find me . . ."

"Is this about the double unit you were asking about the other day? There's no problem with that. It's not a favor."

"The favor part is that I don't just want the unit—I want to move in there." Then she explains how and why she wants to do this.

LIDDY TOLD ROSE enough bad things about Garrett for her to be glad Liddy is going to leave him. What a horrible, horrible man. But she worries that hiding at Metropolis is a bad idea. If Garrett is as smart as

Liddy says, it seems like he'd be able to find her. Then again, it also seems weird that he'd spend tons of money and time to try to find someone he doesn't love. But when she asked about it, Liddy explained that it isn't so much that he doesn't love her. She said it's that in his own screwed-up way he loves her too much. Which Rose gets because her sister-in-law Maggie had a boyfriend like that.

Although the whole kiss thing still kind of bothers her, she's happy Liddy is around more. She's paying twice as much as Marta and Serge combined, and over the last couple of weeks Rose has been helping with the move. This means she gets to hang out with Liddy way more than when Liddy only had one unit.

The new one is very nice, as storage units go, with two round windows and way more light than any of the others. All the furniture Liddy buys makes it even nicer. Every day, FedEx and UPS and lots of other trucks show up with packages addressed to #421, and there are as many different names on the address labels as there are packages. That Liddy is a clever one.

Rose brings in things that Liddy forgets to buy or doesn't think she needs. Rose's parents' apartment is so crowded with stuff her mother saved over the years that you can barely walk through the rooms. And the basement is crammed full. Mama would happily give Rose's friend enough to furnish an entire house. But Liddy doesn't need a full set of silverware or glasses or dishes, so Rose takes a handful of each to #421. She even found a new toaster oven in the basement that was still in its box.

And then there are the little presents Rose picks up just because. Some pretty throw pillows to brighten up the couch and bed, and two hand-painted teacups from a fancy gift shop she passes on her way to work. The cups were pricey and she feels terribly guilty, but every time Liddy drinks from one Rose knows that she'll think about her. Liddy is excited and nervous and always moving fast, but Rose sees how much she appreciates her help. Together they unpack boxes and move furniture around and hang posters and lay down rugs. It's almost like two girlfriends setting up their first apartment.

She worries that even with all these nice things Liddy will be lonely and maybe scared when she's alone at night and on the weekends. It occurs to Rose that when Liddy moves in she should introduce her to Marta. It's not like they'd be close friends or anything. They're as different as different can be, way more than she and Liddy are. Skin color, nationality, and Marta is a lot younger than Liddy. But wouldn't it make both of them feel better to know there's another girl in the building? If she were Liddy or Marta, she'd sleep a lot easier.

17

LIDDY

Liddy googles "how to disappear." No credit cards. No phone calls. No internet. No car. Delete social media accounts. Destroy photos, amass cash. Dye hair, buy new clothes, get a hat. Quit job, concoct an excuse for friends. Go far away, plant false leads, construct a new history, etc., etc., etc. Some of the advice isn't relevant, as she's not trying to disappear forever. But much of it is, because Garrett is sure to hire a detective to find her.

She continues to give Garrett the cold shoulder, and he's growing tired of playing the repentant apologizer. He presents Boston Partners in Education with the gift she promised, in an attempt to prove his good intentions, but the other day she caught him reading her texts. He claimed he was looking for the time of a dinner date, but then why didn't he check her calendar? He insists they share all their passwords and gets angry and carries on if she doesn't inform him when she changes one.

She tells her friends and the Burke that she's going to a writers' retreat for a few months to work on her novel. She tells the twins the same and explains that there's no cell service but she'll have access to a landline and will call them. She returns her leased car to the dealer so the addresses in the GPS will be wiped clean, drops her cell into a storm drain, clears her computer's history, and donates it to the Burke. Then she cleans out her secret bank account. Two hundred thousand dollars in cash should be more than enough to hold her until she figures out her final exit strategy.

She buys a bed, bureau, couch, desk, chairs, tables, lamps, television, refrigerator, kitchen supplies, dozens of books she's always wanted to read, even a few inexpensive paintings and rugs. She ships them all to Metropolis under a variety of false names, a different name for each purchase, procured from a diverse group of stores, always with cash. When she shops, sometimes she wears a long dark wig, sometimes a short blond one. Sometimes glasses, sometimes not. Sometimes in heavy makeup, sometimes clean-faced. Hats.

She gets the same kick out of this probably unnecessary subterfuge that she gets out of copping cocaine from Sandy in a hotel bathroom, and she takes a quick trip up to Rockport to do just that. She orders a case of cabernet and a few bottles of vodka. She buys a computer and a printer and a box of paper. She retrieves her old manuscript from the back of the closet.

Every time she leaves the condo, she brings a few items of clothing with her—nothing obvious, nothing bulky, just enough to fill a couple of shopping bags. She doesn't want to take so much that Garrett will notice her closet appears emptier than usual. Nor is it necessary to have everything in place when she moves in. At first, Garrett's detective will be searching for her at writers' retreats, not looking for her at Metropolis, or in Cambridge, for that matter, so she'll be free to pick up whatever else she might need. Just to be safe, she'll stay in the unit most of the time. Hence, the books and the manuscript she's planning to rewrite. When she ventures out, she'll wear one of her disguises.

Rose has been helpful with the logistics, particularly in directing the many delivery people to #421 no matter what name is on the order, and helping her set up the unit. She's paid her for her time, of course, but Liddy feels uneasy with Rose's willingness to drop everything if she thinks Liddy needs her, and even more uncomfortable with what seems to be Rose's desire to be close friends. Part of this is because in order to make her plan work, Liddy was forced to confide in Rose more than she would have in ordinary circumstances. A few days ago, Rose showed up with a box of her mother's dishes, silverware, and glasses—even a toaster oven. Yesterday, she shyly presented Liddy with a pair of hand-painted teacups as a "housewarming present."

ON A LATE September morning, Liddy leaves a note informing Garrett she's going to a writers' retreat, that he won't be able to reach her, and she doesn't know when she'll return. She casually exits The Tower, walks to Tremont Street, and hails a cab to Cambridge. She's jittery and scared. She's also thrumming with adrenaline.

This is it. She's finally doing it. She isn't going to be that obsequious little patsy anymore, purring while caged within Garrett's golden bars. She's going to reclaim herself, the self he tried to destroy, almost did destroy. She's going to write that novel he ridiculed. She's going to figure out how to get away from him for good. She's going to be happy.

But happiness doesn't come as easily as she'd hoped. Once she's settled in the unit, her pied-à-terre as she tries to think of it, happy is not what she feels. As confidence in her vanishing act deserts her, vulnerability and fear sweep in. She flinches at every sound, certain it's Garrett come to claim her, punish her, humiliate her, maybe even kill her for leaving him. He's sneakier, crueler, and more persistent than she'll ever be, and he has the resources to get what he wants. And what he wants is for her to be back in her place, under his control. His detective is most likely already hot on her trail. Men like Garrett refuse to lose.

When she calls Robin from Rose's cell, her daughter is upset. "Dad texted me and Scott last night and asked if we knew where you were."

"Scott and me," Liddy corrects automatically.

"Mom," Robin whines.

"He knows where I am."

"About the writers' retreat, yeah, but he doesn't know where it is, and he sounded kind of mad. Where is it, anyway?"

Liddy sighs loudly and gives the answer she's prepared. "I'm afraid he'll come here and try to convince me to come home. Now that you kids are away at school, I need to find out if I have what it takes to be a writer."

Robin pauses, as if she understands more than Liddy is telling. "Okay, but you should tell him anyway."

"I'll think about it," Liddy says.

As homey as she tries to make the space, there's no hiding the cinder-block walls and the concrete floor, even after she and Rose put down a couple of rugs. And it feels claustrophobic, despite the two round windows and the high ceiling. She understands now that her plan to stroll through Cambridge in a wig and sunglasses was naïve, and she huddles inside her unit. *He sounded kind of mad.* She's afraid to go out, to expose herself to the detective. The days are endless, the nights even longer.

In the evenings, Liddy stretches out on the couch, her feet on the coffee table, a throw pillow Rose gave her scrunched at her back, and watches sitcoms. Tonight, the show is predictable, but she has trouble following it. She hasn't been able to read a book, not even a magazine, and she lacks the focus to work on her novel.

Along with the numbing fear, unanswerable questions swirl through her mind. Will he find her, hurt her, kill her? Where will she go next? What will she do when her money runs out? What's the long-term plan? What about the twins? It all seemed easier when she was scheming, packing, buying, checking items off her list. She was moving forward then. Now she's moving nowhere, staring at an idiotic TV family worried about a rabbit in the garden.

18

MARTA

Marta is concerned about what Jason Franklin might be doing on her behalf and to whom he might be speaking. What if his questions give ICE more ammunition against her or, worse, reveal her location? What if he discovers her chances for reinstatement and asylum are poor? She wishes she had reminded him not to tell anyone he is from Boston. She wishes she had not given him her real name. She wishes she had never walked into his office.

Her worrying stirs up questions about her mother and sisters. Where are they? How are they surviving? Have they survived? Her brother is dead, and she is certain her father is also, but what of the others? Marta tries to see into the future, but she sees no one. If she is truly *una hija de visión*, why is there only blankness?

She runs every morning and sometimes in the late afternoon, stopping at Anna's Taqueria and Area Four and the Saté Grill truck, where she eats voluminous amounts of food. When it rains, she runs up and down the stairs and along the corridors of Metropolis. She avoids Jason's floor.

She throws herself into completing a chapter on her measurement tools. Although explaining the intricacies of multivariate statistics would bore most people to death, Marta enjoys the task. She loves finding ways to succinctly describe the graceful mathematics underlying her calculations. It is like taking apart a piece of machinery and putting it together in a simpler and more elegant way.

She thinks of how amused Jason was when she explained it to him, and how he appreciated her tongue-in-cheek hyperjargon. He is a good man. She was right about that, and she can tell he is a good attorney. It is also a positive sign that he specializes in immigration law. He knows what he is doing, and he will not give anything away to ICE. What is done is done, and she will just have to trust him.

MARTA ARRIVES AT Jason's door at the time and day she promised. She has been dreading this moment but becomes less concerned when he seems truly happy to see her. Perhaps the news is not as bad as she imagined.

"How goes the dissertation?" Jason asks when they are seated at his table.

"It is going very well, thank you. I finished the chapter I was telling you about the last time. And now I am writing up a description of each hypothesis and the data I collected to sustain or refute it."

"The results of your varimax rotation?"

Marta laughs. "Not in this chapter, no."

"But your data is showing that your variables affect later-life outcomes?"

"I believe it does, and I also believe you must have been a very good student to remember this." She is pleased with this additional evidence of his intelligence.

"School always came easy to me." He shrugs. "Not so much life."

Marta would like to ask him more about his life and about his unconventional work situation. But despite all the years she has been in America, her reserve holds her back. Instead she asks, "Do you have any information for me?"

He opens his laptop, slides his finger along the touch pad, and taps a few keys. Then he turns the computer so they can both see it. "Let's take a look."

Marta flinches when she sees the logo on the top of the screen: an eagle encircled by the words "U.S. Department of Homeland Security."

Underneath, it reads "U.S. Citizenship and Immigration Services." She pushes her chair back a few inches and concentrates on Jason's diplomas.

"The procedures are complicated and convoluted, and, in many ways, frustrating," Jason is saying. "But let me walk you through them, and then we can do some brainstorming before we make any decisions."

Her eyes snap back to the screen at his words. "I am very sorry, but as I know nothing of American law, I am afraid I will be of no help in the decision-making."

"This is a collaboration, Marta. We need to work together to determine which steps you want to take. It's a tortuous process, and there are lots of different ways we can go. We'll do whatever you want to do."

Marta despairs at his words. "How am I to know what I want to do?"

"I'll break down all this legalese and we'll work our way through it until you do." Jason smiles. "Okay?"

Marta hesitates. "Okay."

"As we discussed last week," Jason begins, "I still plan to determine if your father, and therefore your family, falls within one of the groups specified by the administration for deportation. But whatever we find, we're still going to need to apply for defensive asylum."

"This is the same thing as political asylum?"

"It's a form of political asylum. But you're defending yourself against an existing deportation order. Which is different than if you'd just arrived in the US and wanted to stay because you're afraid of persecution or torture in your home country."

"I am afraid of persecution and torture in my home country."

"That's part of this too. But because you're currently in violation of your immigration status, this is where we have to start."

Marta stares at the cinder-block walls, the cement ceiling, and the huge steel door sealing them in. She tries to speak. No sound emerges.

"The two processes are similar," Jason says. "In both, you have to convince the Executive Office for Immigration Review that your fears are credible. It's just that you'll appear before an immigration judge instead of an asylum officer."

"This is worse than if I appeared before an officer?"

"I'm not going to sugarcoat this for you." Jason looks her directly in the eye. "You didn't comply with a deportation order, whether you did so knowingly or not. So you've been placed in removal proceedings for immigration violations, which, as you know, is why ICE is searching for you. The bottom line is that you've broken United States law. Therefore, in order to ask to stay in the country, you must go before a judge to explain why you broke this law and why there's reason to reconsider the order. And, yes, it's somewhat worse. It's more adversarial."

Once again, Marta appreciates his directness, but coils of fear begin to snake their way through her. Her mouth is dry, and although a water bottle is within reach, her hands are trembling, and she does not want Jason to see this. "But if I am able to convince the immigration judge that I will be killed if I return to Venezuela, he will be able to grant me asylum, yes?"

"Yes. It's called 'credible fear,' which you certainly have. And if the judge doesn't approve the request, there's an appeals process."

"But if our request is rejected," she says slowly, realizing what Jason is not telling her, "because I broke the law, I will go to jail while it is being reconsidered?"

"If that happens, I'll try to persuade the court to release you on your own recognizance while the appeal is pending." Jason pauses. "But I have to tell you, given the current political climate, it's likely you'll be placed in detention."

The coils squeeze. "As I have broken the law by remaining in the country, is it possible they will put me in jail as soon as I enter the courtroom?"

"Again, if that happens, I'll try to persuade the judge to release you."

"But given the current political climate," she says, "it is likely the court will not be persuaded."

To this, Jason has no response.

Marta stumbles upstairs, locks the door, and collapses on her bed. There is a saying in Spanish, *entre la espada y la pared,* "between a sword and a wall," which is analogous to the English "between a rock and a hard place." And this is exactly where she finds herself. She cannot go before the judge. She cannot go home. She cannot spend her life in a self-storage unit.

THE FOLLOWING MORNING, as she's walking out the front door for her run, Rose calls her name. Marta does not want to respond, but politeness is inbred, and she turns. "Good morning, Rose."

"Come on in for a sec, hon," Rose says. "There's something I want to talk to you about."

Marta freezes and fears she appears like that proverbial deer in the car lights. She does not have the strength to bear any more bad news.

Rose steps closer. "Are you all right?" She takes Marta's arm and gently guides her toward the open office door. "I've got some muffins. Made them myself just last night. Apple, right off the tree. The kids love them, my Vince too. You look like you could use a bit of fattening up."

Marta allows herself to be led, accepts coffee and a muffin, and falls into being mothered. It's soothing to be taken care of. It has been a long time. The coffee is delicious, and the muffin even better. Marta relaxes as Rose chats about the weather and the best way to keep a muffin moist. There is no reason to assume whatever Rose has to tell her is negative.

"Want to split another one with me?" Rose holds up a muffin.

It will not be good to run on a full stomach, but Marta nods. Then she agrees to another cup of coffee. She inhales the rich, dark aroma and wishes she could stay in this moment, secure in the knowledge that her bed and her desk are upstairs and will remain there. As will she.

"There's something I want to tell you," Rose begins tentatively.

Marta reluctantly lifts her nose from the mug. "Yes?"

"I went back and forth, but then I decided it would be better for both of you to know."

Marta braces herself. *For both of you to know.* She has no idea what this means, but she prays Rose's knife will be quick.

"There's another girl living here."

This isn't at all what Marta expected, and for a moment she does not understand. "Another girl is living here . . . ," she repeats slowly. "She is also in a storage unit?"

"Yes!" Rose cries as if bestowing a gift. "Just one floor down from you."

Marta wonders how she is expected to respond to the information. "This is very nice. Thank you for telling me."

"Would you like to meet her? Her name is Liddy. She's wonderful. Beautiful and smart and lots of fun."

Marta can only stare at Rose. Why would a beautiful, smart woman be living at Metropolis? But then why is Jason's office here? Why is she?

"You'd be good for each other, and you'd both know someone else is around in case you need something . . ." Rose's eyes grow moist. "I bet it can get very lonely. Scary, even."

Marta leans over to tie a shoelace that does not need tying. Rose might be too nosy, but the woman has a kind heart. It would be good to have someone else to talk to, but how would she explain to this Liddy who she is and why she is here? It is too risky. Marta shakes her head.

"No one's going to ask any questions," Rose says. "Privacy is very important at Metropolis. As you know."

Marta has always been aware that Rose would like to be taken into her confidence. In fairness, Rose has never asked any questions. She collects Marta's money and lets her be. But Rose is right. It is lonely. And sometimes scary. This Liddy must want to hold her secrets as tightly as Marta does, so maybe the risk is less than she supposes. "Well . . ."

"How about right now?" Rose jumps from her chair. "I can just go up and get her."

"Now?" This is too fast. "I, uh, I do not think it is possible. I was just on my way out for a run, and—"

"You'll love her," Rose says, and flings open the office door. "Your run can wait a few minutes. You stay put, and we'll be back down in a sec."

After Rose leaves, Marta glances out the window at the cars and the trucks and the pedestrians going past. She looks longingly after the runners. Rose has maneuvered her into the situation, but again, manners preclude her from leaving. She hopes this is not a mistake.

When Rose returns with Liddy, who is indeed a beautiful woman, not a girl, Marta recognizes immediately that there has been no mistake. When their eyes meet, Marta understands Liddy recognizes this also. They take each other in, and Marta is filled with amazement and gratitude, along with a calm contentment.

"Liddy Haines," Rose says happily. "Meet Marta Arvelo."

Liddy reaches out to shake Marta's hand. But instead of the ritual greeting, Marta gently takes it and presses it between both of hers. Liddy does not move, and neither does Marta. No words pass between them, but Marta knows, as only *una hija* can know, that she and Liddy are inexorably linked and intertwined far into the future. For both good and, chillingly, for ill.

PART TWO

19

ZACH

Seven months later: May 2018

After leaving Metropolis with Serge Laurent's photos and equipment, Zach pulls up to the Court Square Press building in South Boston, where he's lived in an industrial loft for the last thirteen years. It suits him: big and open, with polished concrete floors, high ceilings, and tons of exposed brick, beams, and ductwork. Perfect for the large parties he likes to throw and the friends who crash with him afterward.

A few months after he moved in, his parents discovered he'd bought the condo—he suspects his cousin Ian—and insisted on visiting. They hadn't completely forgiven him for leaving college halfway through his senior year, and he was pretty sure if they saw the place, the little absolution they had recently begun to grant him would disappear.

Just as he'd figured, when they did eventually show up, they were more than a little suspicious about how their twenty-four-year-old dropout could afford such grand digs. But they didn't ask. And he didn't tell. They haven't returned, and when he goes to Lexington to visit, they never mention it.

Aside from its other highlights, right now the apartment's best feature is that he doesn't have a mortgage. That and the oversize bathroom off the third bedroom. As Zach takes the cartons from the Prius, which he also owns free and clear, he supposes that if things get really bad he could sell both the car and the condo. But he's got a gold mine to unearth before he even considers such a thing.

It turns out that the bathroom is going to make an even better darkroom than he thought. There's a long vanity that looks as if it were originally designed for two sinks but only holds one. Plenty of room for the enlarger and the trays, and the soaking tub is more than big enough for all the chemicals. He can store the photos, negatives, and undeveloped film in the empty linen closet. Best of all, no windows.

Zach has no idea what else he'll need, but that's what the internet is for. And he's sure Katrina, an ex-girlfriend he's remained friends with, will be happy to help. She worked as a photographer before she "got a real job," as she puts it, and now is a graphic designer for a multinational advertising firm.

He empties about half the cartons and then gets distracted by the photos. He's sitting on the edge of the tub leafing through piles of them when he hears Lori calling for him. Lori is his current girlfriend. They've been together for ten months, which is a record for him, although he's thinking they're probably not going to make it to the year mark. She owns a house in Cambridge, but as she sells real estate in both Boston and Cambridge, she sleeps at Court Square almost as often as she sleeps at her own place.

"I'm in here!" Zach calls back.

When she enters the bathroom, her high heels clicking on the floor, he takes note of how hot she looks in her short realtor skirt and jean jacket. Lori kisses him, then looks around at the equipment and piles of photos. "Another new hobby?" she asks with a sarcastic smile. Sarcasm is her strong suit.

"Funny," Zach says. "And, no, it's not a new hobby, just an extension of an old one." He sweeps his arm around the room. "It's going to be a darkroom. Looks almost as if someone planned it for this purpose."

"You know how to develop film?"

"I can learn." He hands her the Rolleiflex. "Look at this cool camera. It's a really good one, a classic. And check out all this great stuff. I found it all in an abandoned unit at Metropolis."

Lori weighs the camera in her hand and, obviously unimpressed, puts it down. She walks along the vanity, eyes the tub. She's a scion of early British and German settlers who came to America in the seventeenth century, a handsome woman, tall and lean, with shiny dark hair.

"What got you into this?"

Zach riffles through his pile of photographs and hands her the one of himself. "This started it."

She stares at the picture, then at him, then back to the picture. "You look so young."

"I was."

"You didn't know it was being taken?" When he shakes his head, she adds, "Or who took it?"

"Not at the time."

"That's creepy. Someone you didn't know taking pictures of you when you had no idea he was doing it?" She gives an exaggerated shiver. "But I still don't get the developing part."

"The photo is from when I first bought Metropolis."

"Ah." Lori knows the story of Metropolis's sordid past, as well as its current circumstances. "Are there pictures of anyone else? Anything illegal?"

"Not so far, but I haven't been through all the photos—and then there's the contact sheets and negatives." Zach points to the cartons full of film canisters. "And these are all undeveloped."

She furrows her brow. "So you're going to develop them all to make sure there's nothing incriminating in them?"

"Yup."

She contemplates this, then asks, "So who took them?"

"According to the records, his name is Serge Laurent, but there's no other info. No address, no phone number. All I know is that he seems to have walked away from what appears to be a lifetime of work. Really good work."

"Weird."

"These are amazing pictures. He's got a real talent." Zach thrusts a few photos at her: a grimy man in a jacket two sizes too small, reading a newspaper, shot from above; a queue of overworked women of color waiting for a bus, shot from behind; a man cleaning his son's shoe as the boy glares straight into the camera; the retreating back of a striding businessman, his Rolex flashing in the sun, shot from below.

Lori glances through them, hands the photos back, shrugs. "They're interesting, I guess, but they don't do much for me." This is one of the things about Lori that Zach isn't particularly fond of: her lack of curiosity.

"Look at how he's captured the essence of the city through the people who live there," he tries anyway. "The contrast between this rich guy and these people on the margins. The detail, the camera angles, the shadows, the asymmetry. It's the revelation of the private moment that's so spectacular." He struggles to express how the photos touch him, how good they are. "It's the truth of it."

"But I thought you just wanted to make sure there's no proof of the criminal doings that went on at Metropolis back in the day? Why don't you throw them all away?"

Zach flips open two of the cartons filled with film canisters. "I want to see what else this guy's done."

"Then wouldn't it be a lot easier to get them developed at a drugstore?"

"If there are incriminating photos, someone might see them."

"I still don't get why you don't just junk them. Wouldn't that be the safest thing?"

He hesitates, wonders whether to tell her about his plan, as she probably won't get that either, then says, "It might be a way to get my hands on some cash. To recoup some of my losses."

"You mean, like sell them to make money?" Lori asks, clearly incredulous. "You think people will want to buy these old black-and-whites?"

Zach figures he'll call Katrina when he finishes unpacking. Katrina will get it.

20

SERGE

In the month or so since Rose started unlocking units for him, Serge hasn't taken any outside photographs. He prefers to shoot his subjects in the building. Hundreds of violins and doghouses and stuffed birds and bicycles and who knows what else. If he didn't have to go to Brick & Trowel, he'd stay inside Metropolis all the time, shooting, developing, printing, sleeping, being by himself.

He doesn't like nature or weather much after having too much of both of them growing up. And even though he used to like shooting photographs of the city he doesn't like to be seen. And he definitely doesn't like anyone to touch him or look in his eyes. There's a fiery pain if he brushes someone's arm, and he doesn't understand why everyone is always trying to gouge his eyes out with their own. But today he has a strong urge to go outside, so strong that he has to put on his coat. He carefully places the camera in his pocket and leaves his dark and familiar cave.

It's late October, and if he were going to like weather this would be it. Sunny and mild with a crisp wind. If he liked nature he'd be taking pictures of New England's famous fall foliage. But that's what everyone sees. He photographs what they don't see. He thinks about going to Methadone Mile but decides no. It's his first day out in a long time so he goes to Downtown Crossing. There's more variety here and it's not nearly as sad. He heads down Washington Street, then Avery to Tremont and over to Boylston, searching for what others can't see. But nothing catches his eye, so he wanders to the Common.

There's a group of about six or seven homeless people he's noticed before. Seven. There are seven today. Seven is a good number. He's always liked seven. He's heard most people like three. But for him it's always been seven. Some days there are a dozen or more of them. One day there was only a woman sitting on a lawn chair sunning herself like she was at the beach. Except her body was covered by a long red poncho and the hood was pulled down over her face.

Watching them, he gets a weird empty feeling in his feet and up into his legs. They remind him of him. Like he used to be. Like he will never be again. Sleeping on a cot surrounded by them. Eating at a table next to them. Waiting in line with them. Using the bathroom with them. Maybe even having to talk to them. Metropolis is his rescuer, his home, why his hands are raw and blistered from the hot dishes. Worth everything he has to do to stay there. Click. Click.

The woman in the red poncho is in her lawn chair, laughing and talking real loud with another woman sitting in a lawn chair next to her. Red Poncho's legs push out farther than a man's. The other one's legs are short and stumpy. The rest of their bodies are the same as their legs. Click. Click. Everyone else are guys, mostly old, or just old-looking. Two are fast asleep with their heads on piles of leaves and newspapers over their faces. Serge likes shooting people with newspapers. There aren't as many around as there used to be. Click. Click. A third man throws back his head and pours an airplane bottle of scotch down his throat. Click. Click.

"Hey, scarecrow cameraman!" Red Poncho shouts. "What the fuck you think you're doing?"

Serge freezes. He hardly ever gets caught shooting. He can't remember if he ever has and also remembers it's happened before. Nothing specific comes to him but it tickles in his brain the way a cough does in his throat.

Red Poncho leaps up from her chair. She's even taller than he thought, and she's coming at him like she wants to trample him. "You can't go around taking pictures of people without their permission. There's a law against that!" She's standing so close he can feel the heat of her and smell her smell of dirt and vanilla. She's trying to gouge his eyes out with hers.

He steps back, grips tight to the camera, looks beyond her left shoulder. Is there a law against it? He doesn't think so. But what does he know? No matter what the law says or doesn't say, she can't take his Rolleiflex. He'll never let anyone take it from him. Never. If she tries, he'll kick her. He will. Even if he's never kicked anyone in his life. He can feel the angry force of her and then he feels it going away. He looks down at where her feet were, hoping she went back to her chair, but the feet are still there.

"You poor schmuck," she says in a nicer tone.

Serge doesn't look at her face and wills her to go away. She doesn't, and he feels her checking him out.

"Want to come sit with us?" She holds out her hand to shake. "Hang out for a while? We won't eat you. Name's Diamond. What's yours?"

Serge steps back again to avoid both her hand and her eyes, but he says, "No, thank you," before he flees.

21

LIDDY

Mario Puzo called it "the thunderbolt" in *The Godfather*, Rodgers and Hammerstein extolled it in "Some Enchanted Evening," and for the first time in her life, Liddy is experiencing it. While there was plenty of passion in her early years with Garrett, and quite a bit with various boys in high school and college, none of that felt anything like this. There's no crowded room, but Liddy knows, just as the characters in that book and musical knew, something incredible is occurring.

Marta presses Liddy's hand between both of hers, and they look into each other's eyes. *I know you,* is what Liddy hears inside her head, what she feels running through her veins. *And you know me.* Liddy is a woman without a spiritual bone in her body, and yet here it is. Heat rushes through her, and a flush spreads across her skin.

"Hello," Marta says, her light Spanish inflection delicious. "It is delightful to meet you."

"And, and," Liddy stutters, "it's delightful to meet you too."

"It is delightful!" Rose cries. "I knew this was a good idea. Now it'll be so much better. A comfort to both of you. To know the other is in the building—especially at night."

Liddy slides her hand from Marta's, but continues to stare into the deep-brown eyes flecked with gold. Marta nods, clearly more comfortable than Liddy is with the emotions racing between them. It's almost as if

Marta expected this to happen. Or it's happened before. Or maybe Marta isn't responding because she doesn't feel the emotions at all.

"Marta is in five-oh-three," Rose is saying, "and Liddy is in four fifty-four—also four twenty-one." She giggles. "So now you know where to find each other."

"Thanks, Rose," Liddy says more sharply than she intends. "Nice to meet you, Marta. I've, uh, I've got a bunch of work to do upstairs, so I've got to run." She scans Marta's workout clothes. "And I guess you do too. Or did." Then she steps out of Rose's office and takes the stairs two at a time so she won't have to wait for the elevator, where either one of them might waylay her.

When Liddy gets to her unit, she chastises herself for jumping to conclusions. What a fool. Marta is lovely and at least fifteen years her junior, and there's no reason she would have any interest in a broken middle-aged woman like herself. Rose seemed to be unaware there was something brewing between them, so maybe it was only a thunderbolt on her end. The cocaine calls from her underwear drawer. She doesn't answer.

She sits down at her desk, grabs a pen, and pulls her manuscript forward. She's going to read it through, take notes on the changes she wants to make, directions she might want to go in. But she does none of these things. The title page taunts her, and the coke's song grows more insistent. She wishes she hadn't made that trip to Sandy's before moving into Metropolis. Finally, she grabs the gram, cuts some lines, and snorts them.

It's as if her brain has been switched on, which she supposes it has, and she's able to totally engage with Clementine, whose life she created so long ago. An old friend she left behind due to Garrett's derision, her own insecurity, and, admittedly, the demands of motherhood. It's exhilarating to hang out with Clementine again, to jump in where they left off, as if no time has passed.

She sketches a bubble chart to assess the relationships between all the characters and begins to graph out a workable three-act structure. She devises a series of obstacles and complications to put in Clementine's way. These may not seem nearly as brilliant tomorrow, but, hey, she's completely enjoying herself, and she's sure that some of the ideas are solid. A novelist, her childhood dream, what her professors at Iowa encouraged her to become, and now she's doing it. Sure, she's forty-four, but many writers don't publish until they're older. When they have something to say.

Liddy snorts and scribbles and has a terrific time until she has to snort more and more to achieve less and less. Her mind skitters to the two other grams in her bureau, but even facing the impending crash, she knows this is a disastrous idea. She takes two sleeping pills, snorts the last two lines, and drinks three glasses of water.

IN THE MORNING, it feels as bad as the last time she did too much coke. Maybe worse. With the exception of an afternoon visit to the shower—horrible, with its grit and odor of scouring power that made her lust for her clean, spacious bathroom at home—she spends the day lying on the couch, berating herself for her lack of restraint. She's willing to give herself a partial pass, though, because she's pleased she finally worked on her novel.

The following day, as the light streams through her windows, Liddy knows she can't stay in the room for another minute. She's nervous about leaving the building, but there's little chance Garrett's detective would be looking for her in Cambridge. Until she stashed the twins' belongings at Metropolis, she'd never had any connection to this city, preferring the faster pace on the other side of the river. And anyway, the PI will be busy checking all the writers' retreats in the country, after determining her passport hasn't been used.

Her head hurts, her mouth is dry, and she feels both unstable and nauseous. But she dons one of her disguises: a dark wig and a pair of overly large sunglasses—the kind she would never wear, as the internet suggested. She exits through the rear door of the building to avoid Rose, whose eager devotion makes her uneasy. As does the episode with Marta Arvelo, which she knows Rose will want to discuss.

Liddy strides purposefully toward Mem Drive. Was it a thunderbolt, or was it a menopause moment? Hot flashes bring on flushes and high emotion. Or she could be losing her mind. While she's fantasized about being with a woman, this doesn't mean she's a lesbian. It's just as likely that she has a strong libido but can't stomach the idea of being with a man.

The sun is strong and, although there's a breeze off the river, the wig doesn't breathe and her scalp is sweaty and itchy. She doesn't like the weight of the sunglasses on her nose either. Who knew a disguise could be so unpleasant? On television, they make it look like such a lark. Liddy scoffs at herself and heads west, toward Harvard Square.

She doesn't get far. Her legs are wobbly, her head pounds, and her bones feel as if they're hollow inside. She drops to a bench, stares unseeing across the Charles at Boston rising on the other bank. She misses her apartment, the light and the views, the shower and the hardwood floors and the thick rugs, all of which she took for granted. She misses the freedom of her old life, to come and go as she pleased, even as she acknowledges this wasn't actually the case. Her coke-fueled optimism is long gone, and the thought of returning to Metropolis is demoralizing. But there's nowhere else to go.

THE WORK SHE did on her manuscript when she was high isn't half-bad. Most of it sucks, and her notes and graphs predictably ramble on into a lot of nonsense, but many of her insights into the characters' backstories are rather good. As is her decision to turn it into a historical novel set in the midnineties, which is when she wrote it, rather than give it an update. This last wouldn't be feasible anyway, as ubiquitous cell phones make a current story impossible. *Leaving Vermont* is the working title.

It's a coming-of-age tale, as she was when she started it, yearning to know who she was, who she would become, and many of the details are autobiographical. Clementine, the protagonist, spends part of the summer after she graduates from college driving around Vermont in her old VW van, which is just like the one Liddy had at the time. Clementine calls it HoJo, because it's blue and orange, like Howard Johnson's restaurants, just as Liddy had. Clementine grew up in Burlington, Vermont, her father a successful attorney who bought up blocks of real estate before it turned into the upscale city it is now. He also served as mayor for twenty years. Her mother loved nothing more than being the First Lady, as she called herself, flaunting their wealth when and wherever she could.

Clementine meanders her way along the lakes and forests of the Green Mountains, listening to AM radio because it's the only band the car can pick up. But even if the radio were more sophisticated, there just wasn't that much FM in northern New England at the time. She dreams of becoming a novelist, but her parents won't hear of it.

Her mother, who started Clementine in beauty pageants when she was three, wants her to find a husband of "equivalent wealth and class," and doesn't believe she's going to be able to do that in a creative writing program in the "boonies of some godforsaken state no one's heard of." Her father wants her to do something "productive," and if she doesn't land in a place where this can happen, there will be no more monthly allowance. Clementine gets herself into all kinds of messes until . . . Well, that's the problem with the manuscript. Liddy was never able to get it to end in a satisfying way. But that's exactly what she's going to do now.

Writing invigorates her, gives her a reason to get up in the morning, gobbles up the hours, the days, the weeks. Still, loneliness is a constant. Robin and Scott are often in her dreams, and she wants them to be with her for real. Garrett haunts her nightmares, and as much as she wants to be free of him, she's been unable to come up with a viable long-term plan. It all seems beyond her at the moment, and it's so much easier to solve Clementine's problems rather than her own.

Liddy starts spending more time out of Metropolis, switching up wigs and coats and glasses. It's well into October, and the weather is cooler, so the wigs aren't quite as onerous, which is good, as the disguises are more necessary. It's been two weeks since she disappeared, and the detective must have determined that she never went to a writers' retreat. Which means that now he'll most likely begin searching the Boston area.

Rose has been showing up at all hours, offering a home-baked muffin or presenting yet another "little gift" to "spruce up the joint." Liddy finally had to explain to her that now that she's working seriously on her novel, she doesn't have much time to hang out. It's not that Liddy doesn't like Rose—she does, and Rose means well—but she finds the attentiveness embarrassing and feels guilty about not returning Rose's feelings. These days Liddy always goes out the rear door to avoid her.

Sometimes she finds herself fantasizing about Marta, about what it would be like to be lovers, and she tries to stop herself from going there. She steers clear of the fifth floor, Marta's floor, and uses the bathroom on the second so she doesn't run into her in the one on the fourth. But this doesn't keep her from reliving their meeting and the thunderbolt that apparently went nowhere.

22

ROSE

Rose is fast asleep and Vince is snoring loudly when her phone vibrates under the pillow. It's four o'clock in the morning. She rushes into the living room so it doesn't wake Vince. He's been in a lot of pain lately and needs whatever sleep he can get. She looks at the screen and sees the call is from the Revere Police Department.

"Is this Mrs. Gentilini?" a man's voice asks. "Michael Gentilini's mother?"

She glances as Michael's closed door. "Yes, yes, it is."

"This is Officer Paul DeVito, Revere Police. Your son's been arrested, and we have him here at the station."

"My son's asleep in his bed," she says, but she knows as soon as she says it that he isn't.

"Why don't you check and make sure," he suggests.

Rose opens Michael's door. The streetlight outside his window streaks light across his messy bed. It's empty.

"Mrs. Gentilini?

It's like her mind isn't working. "I, I don't understand," she finally manages. "Is he okay?"

"I guess you could say he's okay, but he's in a lot of trouble and pretty zonked-out."

"I'm on my way." Rose hangs up the phone and begins to shake. Michael is arrested and zonked out and in trouble. She didn't even ask what he was arrested for. This is exactly what Vince said would happen and that her being too easy on Michael was going to make it worse. Rose hurries into their bedroom, shakes Vince awake, and tells him what she knows.

He jerks up and cries out at the sudden movement. "I'm going to beat the crap out of him!" he shouts. "I should have done it long ago. When I get my hands on him, he's—"

"Shh—you'll wake the girls," she says as she pulls on some clothes.

He throws himself out of bed and immediately falls back into it, and she can't tell if his grimace is because he's angry or because he's in pain. "Damn it all to hell!"

"It's probably some kind of mistake." She touches his shoulder. "I'll go down and check."

"I'm not letting you go out alone in the middle of the night. It's too dangerous and—"

"It's only a few miles away." The last thing she wants is an angry Vince at the police station. "You need to stay with Emma and Charlotte."

Vince winces and eases himself down on the pillow. "Okay, but call as soon as you know what's what."

When Rose climbs into their battered Accord, her fingers don't want to work and it takes way too long to get the key in the ignition. Vince always drives. She holds her hands at ten and two and heads down streets she's known her whole life toward the police station, where she's never been. When she was in high school, she didn't even know the kids who got arrested.

She pulls into the parking lot and rests her head on the steering wheel, steeling herself for what's to come. She forces herself out of the car, but when she opens the station door and searches for Michael, the only person there is a cop behind a tall counter. He looks Italian, which gives her courage, and she walks over. "I'm, I'm, uh, Rose Gentilini. Someone called and said my son Michael is here. Michael Gentilini. But maybe it isn't him."

"That would've been me." Officer DeVito slowly scans his computer as if there were a hundred boys arrested tonight. "Michael Gentilini," he mutters. "Back in lockup. Illegal trespass, theft, and burglary."

"That's impossible," she says. "He wouldn't do anything like that. It's got to be the wrong person." But Michael wasn't in his bed.

"Was a gang-hunting situation."

"A what?"

"It's when feuding gangs search out members of the rival gang and try to kill them."

"No, no, you've got it all wrong," she tells him. "That can't be right. Michael isn't in a gang. And anyway, what kind of gangs are there in Revere? This isn't Boston."

The officer looks at her like what she said was funny. "A security camera caught him and his gangbangers breaking into a building that was 'owned' by another gang. A squad car happened to be in the area and managed to get there before anyone got hurt."

Rose is starting to get mad that the cop isn't listening to her. "Like I just told you before, he's not in a gang," she says. "It's some kind of a big mix-up. He's too young."

Officer DeVito gives her that same look. "Fortunately for your son, unlike his two buddies, who are older, he didn't have a gun. Or we didn't find one on him. Could have ditched it."

Why is he being so stubborn? It's clearly not Michael. "Can I see this person you're talking about?" she asks. "Prove to you it's not him."

"You got a picture?"

Rose never uses the camera on her phone and the last picture they took was the whole family at Christmas about five years ago. "What does this boy look like?" she demands. "Mine's about five nine with, uh, dark hair cut short and dark eyes. I guess he looks Italian. I bet the boy you've got back there doesn't look like that."

"Actually, he does."

"Lots of kids in Revere look like that."

DeVito hits a few keys and turns his screen so that it faces her. There's a picture of Michael. A mug shot. Sweet Jesus. Five ten, with a giant bruise on the left side of his face. His eyes are like slits. He looks way older than he is. "No," she moans, and grabs the edge of the desk.

"I'm sorry, ma'am, but he was also caught with a stolen laptop shoved down the back of his jeans. High on some kind of opioid." He pauses. "I'm sure I don't have to tell you how dangerous that stuff is. It kills. See it every day."

Tears run down her face. "Can I . . . ," she croaks. "Can I take him home now?"

"We're going to have to keep him in custody and refer the case to juvenile court in the morning. Gang hunting is serious business."

"But, but he can't stay here overnight," she says through her sobs. "He's only fourteen, and he's never been arrested before. Please let me take him with me. He's just a baby."

"Babies are home in the middle of the night sucking their thumbs," DeVito says. "Your baby was hanging out on the streets with some very bad actors. He's lucky it wasn't worse."

"Can I at least see him?" she begs. "Talk to him? Let him know I'm here?"

"Not going to matter"—he glances down at the paper in his hand— "Mrs. Gentilini. He's out cold, so he's not going to know you're there anyway. And I'm guessing he's not going to have a whole lot to say."

The cop didn't tell her she couldn't see Michael, but Rose doesn't want to make him angry by insisting. Instead, she presses her arms to her stomach and hunches over. Her boy is high on drugs and sleeping it off in a jail cell.

Then DeVito softens. "They'll be bringing him down there in the morning. Stoughton Juvenile Court. You know where that is?" He scribbles down an address and hands the paper to her. "If you can find yourself a half-decent lawyer, they'll probably be able to get him off."

ROSE DRIVES BACK to the house, changes clothes, and goes to Metropolis to wait for Jason Franklin. Sometimes he gets in early. Officer DeVito said she's got to get a lawyer that isn't one of those guys who work for the city and have way too many cases. Vince is against a lawyer and says they should let Michael deal with the consequences of what he did, that this is the only way he'll learn his lesson. But no matter what Vince says, she's not doing that.

Jason always waves when he comes past her door, and a couple of times she's struck up a conversation with him. From her snooping, she knows he went to Harvard and that he must have at least a little money, given the quality of his furniture, but it's quite something that his office is in a storage unit. When she tried to get him to tell her why, he changed the subject. She's seen the people who come to talk to him, and none of them look like they have any money, so she hopes he won't charge too much.

As soon as she gets to the building, she sees his car in the lot. *Thank you, Jesus.* When she knocks on his half-open door, he says hello like there's nothing surprising about her showing up at six o'clock in the morning, and asks if she wants a cup of coffee. Which she most certainly does. While he's fixing it, she looks around his unit pretending like she's never seen it before. "Pretty fancy," she says.

"Bet it's the nicest lawyer's office in a storage unit you've ever seen," he says with a smile.

She tries to return it, but she can't make her mouth work that way.

"So what's up?" He places the mugs on the table, and they sit down. "I'm guessing you didn't come by this early in the morning for the coffee."

When she finishes telling him about Michael, even though she tries not to, she starts to cry. "I didn't even know there were gangs in Revere so how could I know he was in one of them?"

Jason pushes a box of tissues toward her. "It's not easy being a kid these days. Or a parent. There's so much crazy stuff going on. So many temptations."

"And, and the drugs," she wails, pressing a tissue to her face. "What kind of mother doesn't know that her own son is on drugs?"

"Probably the vast majority of them," Jason says. "But first, we've got to take care of his legal problems."

"I, uh, we, we don't have a lot of money, but I'll pay you for this. I promise. Would it be okay if maybe we did it like on an installment plan?"

"Not a problem. I charge on a sliding scale, so we'll figure it out."

"Thank you, thank you, thank you so much." Rose hands him the paper with the court's address. "Thank you."

He glances at his watch and stands, grabs a jacket and tie from the coatrack behind the desk, and Rose sucks in her breath. That's it? That's all the time he's giving her? He's off on another case?

"We better get going," Jason says. "It's rush hour."

Now she's thoroughly confused. "Get going?"

He holds out his hand to help her up from the chair. "To the courthouse. Michael is just a kid. He didn't have a gun, has no record and no gang affiliation that the cops know for certain. So let's see what we can do to get your boy home."

23

JASON

Stoughton Juvenile Court is in a smallish brick-and-concrete building, much less intimidating than the Boston courts Jason usually works in, although Rose is clearly intimidated. And scared. He opens the door and steps aside so she can go before him. As she enters, she looks up at him, her eyes wary and bloodshot, and nods her thanks.

They make their way through the metal detector, and the guard scowls at them as if they're the criminals. Jason is more than aware that being an asshole is an occupational hazard, and the poor guy can't quit or he'll lose his pension, but really? They step into the lobby, which looks like a movie set for a 1980s courtroom drama.

"I'm going to find out who's handling Michael's case," Jason tells Rose. "Don't worry, we're not going into a courtroom. No judge or anything official like that. Most likely just talking to a court officer." He hopes this is the case, but it could also be a prosecutor.

"I'll just stay here?" Her statement is a question.

"Grab a chair, and I'll be right back," he says as encouragingly as he can.

He discovers that Michael is due to meet with a court officer at eleven o'clock and heads back to Rose. As he moves through the attorneys and clients, Jason hears his name. It's Richard Gorham, his once-fellow associate at Spencer Uccello.

The two of them shake hands, step back, and size each other up. "How's it going, man?" Richard asks. "Guess you got yourself a new job if you're here. Good for you. I heard Bill the Kill agreed to give you a recommendation. Big of him, I've got to say."

The fact that Bill the Kill, aka Bill Stern, a senior partner, was willing to give Jason a recommendation was pretty big of him, and reflected his unvoiced opinion that he understood and perhaps even partially approved of Jason's stance.

Even though Richard doesn't know any of the details of Jason's departure, he clearly senses it has to be something dodgy, and it's a dick move on his part to mention it. Typical.

"I've got my own firm now," Jason says. "Office in Cambridge, near MIT. Busy. Doing a lot of different kinds of work. It's good. Better than good."

"No one to answer to but yourself. Lucky bastard." Richard's wink indicates the opposite.

"Thanks, man. Lucky is exactly how I feel."

"Also terrific for someone who likes to go his own way." Translation: not a team player.

Jason wants to push his ass down the stairs, but instead he leans in as if sharing a confidence. "It's got its pluses and minuses, but between you and me, I've got to tell you, it's almost all on the plus side." The only way to get Richard to shut up is to act as if his antics don't faze you, then he'll go off and try to rattle someone else.

"Glad you found your sweet spot, man." Another wink. "Good for you."

"I have," Jason agrees. "But what about you? Juvenile court isn't Spencer Uccello's usual stomping grounds."

Richard smirks. "A bigwig's kid got herself into a mess of trouble. SNE Worldwide, so you know I've got to get her off ASAP. You know me, keeping those big clients happy is priority number one."

Again, Jason considers throwing Richard down the stairs. Instead, he excuses himself and goes to find Rose. She's staring into her phone, and her posture indicates that she's not seeing anything on the screen. "We're on for eleven," he tells her.

Unfortunately, because the police identified Michael's actions as gang hunting, the officer decides to file formal charges. Although the officer is aware Michael is only fourteen, the boy appears closer to eighteen, with his large build and a five-o'clock shadow at eleven in the morning. Then there's the part where he looks busted, smells like shit, and is clearly strung out.

A juvenile court judge is available, and Michael is arraigned that afternoon, which avoids a return to the jail. The judge decides not to hold an adjudicatory hearing, similar to a criminal trial, and rules that Michael must perform forty hours of community service, pass weekly drug tests, and stay out of trouble for the next six months, after which the charges will be dropped. Then he lets Rose take the boy home.

Rose and Michael are relieved and appreciative. Or at least Rose is. But Jason doesn't have a good feeling about this. If Michael is hooked on opioids, as Rose suspects and the police seem certain of, he's probably going to fail his drug tests. And if Michael is in a gang, there's a good chance he'll get caught up in some kind of criminal activity between now and the end of April. If either of these occurs, the court will reinstate formal charges and the kid will be off to juvenile detention. All bets are off after that.

It's NOT JUST Michael's case Jason is struggling with; it's Marta's also. Although he's an immigration attorney by training, his work at Spencer Uccello was primarily institutional: providing strategic advice to corporations, hospitals, universities, sports teams, and the like, that hired foreign nationals who needed visas and green cards. Few of his clients back then were individuals with personal cases. But he's a quick study. As he delves deeper into the specifics of Marta's situation, he doesn't need to be an expert on individual immigration to understand that she's in deeper trouble than either one of them thought.

Not only was Marta's father in the Ministry of Foreign Affairs in

Venezuela, he also ran the Criminal Investigations Corps for almost a year. According to current US law, officials of both agencies and their immediate families are banned from entering the country, and the visas of those in residence are to be revoked. Which means, even given the Tufts admin's mistakes, there's just cause for withdrawing Marta's visa, and therefore her fall from status is lawful, making her refusal to leave the country a serious crime.

24

ZACH
Seven months later: June 2018

While he's searching for drug-dealing photos, Zach takes an online course on darkroom procedures and techniques. He's motivated, and he completes the class in a few days. Then he starts in on developing Laurent's film. He's almost finished with his fifth roll, and he refills the tank with a wetting agent, lets it sit for a minute, takes the reels from the tank, and uses clips to hang the negatives to dry on the clothesline he's stretched across the bathtub. Soon he'll start a class to learn how to print.

He proudly watches the filmstrips as they gently sway from the breeze of the fan. He hasn't been this hyped about a project since he took up highpointing. His curiosity is at full wattage, and he wants to know everything about everything. He's going to learn a new skill, make a shitload of money, and he's going to give the world the gift of Serge Laurent.

Zach is fascinated by both the transformative nature of the process as well as the chemistry behind it—chemistry was his major in college, his parents hoping this meant he was headed for medical school—and he can't wait to start printing. More transformation, more chemistry, and more magic. Developing is like taking anesthesia for a medical procedure: He's gone for hours inside it, and when he comes back to reality it's as if no time has passed. In the zone.

Nothing is better than the zone, which, as another ex-girlfriend, Suzanne, explained when she broke up with him, his love of the zone is why he's addicted to the high-risk adventures that allow him to step away from commitments whenever they feel too constraining. But developing photographs carries no risk, so maybe he's becoming more mature. Somehow he doesn't think Suzanne would agree.

Another ex, Katrina, the photographer turned graphic designer, may not believe he's any more mature than Suzanne does, but she does believe developing the photos and selling them is a great idea. Katrina stopped by last week to check out Serge's work and was as impressed as Zach with their quality—and she actually knows what she's talking about.

She suggested he try to find Laurent, pointing out that the pictures belong to him. When Zach corrected her, explaining that the photos were his as they were left in an abandoned storage unit that he owned, she looked at him skeptically. "They're his intellectual property," she said with some reprimand in her voice.

She's right, of course, but Zach is not going to look for Laurent. What if Laurent demands the photos back? Although they legally belong to Zach, what if Laurent sues? And even if Zach did decide to reach out to the man, he can't do it until he's developed all the film, to make sure there isn't anything that might further destroy his already destroyed life.

He closely examines the photos Laurent printed, searching for more of himself and of his early tenants' illicit activities. He doesn't see any of him, but he finds some of Nick and his cronies. Zach burns the first one, but it smells so bad that he cuts the rest into tiny pieces and further demolishes them in the garbage disposal. He's sure there must be more.

This undertaking is particularly difficult because the pictures are out of chronological order and were haphazardly thrown into cartons or left in piles around the storage unit. Zach finds this sloppiness strange for a man who spent so much time methodically picking his shots and just as fastidiously developing and printing many of them. It seems likely that Serge has issues, possibly serious ones. But aren't extremely talented people supposed to be a bit off?

Zach turns his full attention to his search-and-destroy mission. The negatives and photos taken at Metropolis right after he bought it in 2008 are his focus, and he starts by separating them by time, then location and subject. But he's drawn to others that fall outside these parameters—particularly the ones of the storage units and those of the tenants themselves.

From the old cars in some of the shots, Zach guesses that the photos span at least twenty-five years. He remembers the messy cot in #514 and wonders if Laurent could have been living illegally in that unit all those years. Was he taking pictures the whole time? Developing and printing them by himself in that grim space? Where was he trained, and who else has seen his work? Where did he go? And, most mystifying, why did he leave it all behind?

As Zach makes his way through the photos, he sees that each one contains a remarkable amount of detail, partly because of the particularities of the Rolleiflex and its film, but mostly because of Laurent's eye for composition. A half-dressed headless mannequin resting against a cluster of garbage cans, a ladder with a broken step rising above her head. A line of men climbing out of a prison van in front of a courthouse, all with heads bowed except for one, who points his middle finger at the camera.

It's almost as if each photograph is telling a story, or is bringing the viewer into a story in progress, a still life hinting at secrets. Zach thinks of his own nature photos and laughs out loud. Anyone can take a picture of a landscape, but taking one that makes the viewer want to understand an unknown person's life, now that's a rare talent.

Zach finds himself obsessively researching the work of the best street photographers. He goes online to study them. He scours the Boston Public Library for art books and biographies. He uses money he shouldn't to fly to LA to see a Vivian Maier retrospective. The more he learns, the more convinced he becomes that Laurent is as good, if not better, than many of these masters. Although his current endeavor was originally about saving his ass and making some money, he now finds himself intrigued by the photographer himself.

He googles Serge Laurent, combs the internet and Facebook and Instagram for similar pictures. He shows a few to a friend of a friend, who's a photography professor at BU. He even posts some on photography message boards, asking if anyone is familiar with the images. There are many compliments but nothing more. It's as if the man never existed, although his photos are testimony that he most certainly did. It strikes Zach that Serge might not be alive. What else but death would cause an artist to abandon his life's work?

But Laurent could also be in a hospital. He could be in jail. He could be lost. He could be mentally ill or an undocumented immigrant picked up by ICE. Zach realizes that postponing his search for Serge is a mistake. If he can determine that the man is dead or not cognizant, or was arrested or deported, then it will be unlikely he would contest ownership of the photos. No worries of possible lawsuits, which means all the proceeds would be his.

The last thing Zach needs right now is another suit, as he just signed off on the last one a week ago: Metropolis is no longer his. He knew this was coming in January, as soon as he discovered what Rose had done, and she cemented it with her deposition in March. Still, the finality of it is a bitter pill. He puts his developing aside and starts seriously trying to find out what happened to Serge.

He strikes out at the hospitals, police stations, homeless shelters, morgues, and ICE offices in and around Boston. He considers giving up, but he's consumed by the desire to put himself in the clear. Serge clearly hung out at Downtown Crossing, so maybe there's someone there who might know his fate. This would be far easier if Zach could find a self-portrait, but there don't seem to be any, although there are plenty of pictures that appear to be Serge's shadow.

He looks tall and thin, which might be the case or just be the nature of shadows. Slightly hunched, always wearing a long, shapeless coat. Zach thinks about asking Rose, who might know what the man looks like, but his anger at her still burns out of control. He can't speak to her, not even text. It's been over five months, and he hasn't been able to let go of what she did to him, of the lives her error destroyed

25

SERGE

Serge dreams of his brother and sister, but in the dream they're dogs. Big dogs who fight each other, wrestling and nipping and growling on the floor. But the dogs never fight with him. He sits in his chair and each dog places its heavy head on one of his thighs. He rubs Anton and Anastasia between their eyes with his thumbs. They purr like cats. Then they are cats. Cats that grow into tigers and begin to roar.

Their sound fills the shadowy space of his dream. Coming at him like the howling ocean. He tries to make himself as small as possible so the tigers won't get him. Then he looks down. His legs have been chewed off.

He bolts awake. There are no tigers. His legs are attached to his body. But the dream doesn't leave him. It keeps sneaking up on him all that day. And the next day and the next and the next. The tigers' roars follow him to Brick & Trowel, louder than the thunder of the dishwasher or the shouts of the chef. When he photographs a storage stage set filled with doghouses, there are hundreds of great cats living inside or on top of them. Growling at him, ready to pounce.

He's afraid he'll go crazy. That he's already crazy. That he'll be ripped apart by the sharp teeth of the sound before he has the chance to take pictures of all the storage sets. There isn't much time left. He pays Rose to let him into one or two or sometimes three units in a single day. Click. Click.

Racks of women's clothing. Thousands of bottles of wine. Rows of locked file cabinets. Collections of elephant statues and CDs and campaign buttons and baseball caps and children's toys. Toilet seats, rotted wood planks, broken chairs, moldy books, battered suitcases, stained mattresses, shoes. So many shoes.

He doesn't question what he's seeing, doesn't wonder why these particular things or this particular place. Click. Click. It's only about dark and light. Composition. Angles. Contrasts. Connections. The three-dimensional turned two-dimensional to reveal the secrets stored inside.

Serge doesn't have time to do any developing because the most important thing is to take all the pictures before he's gone. Which is going to be soon. He has hundreds of other rolls of film that he hasn't developed from before he started on the storage stage sets. He's pretty sure he has a rule that he can only develop the pictures in the order that he took them. Except he thinks that he might remember breaking it. Maybe the one with those poor dead children.

Then everything changes. The roaring of the cats goes quiet when he's at Metropolis but starts up even louder than before as soon as he steps outside. Like it's making up for all the noise it can't get rid of when he's inside. When he comes home from his shift, he rushes into the quiet of his unit. But he's nauseous from the hours of noise and then even more sickened by the weight of the quiet.

Sometimes Rose can't let him into any units. So he has to take pictures of the people in the corridors. Anything so he doesn't have to leave Metropolis. This feels wrong, like an animal spoiling its den, but he has no choice because the roaring outside in the world is eating him alive. People moving in. Moving out. Talking on cell phones. Talking to each other. Replacing light bulbs. Mopping floors. Fixing elevators. Click. Click.

THE NIGHT COMES when he can't go to Brick & Trowel. He can't bear to hear the roaring. Or to be eaten by the roaring. Or to be eaten by the tigers. Or the terrible cold outside. He huddles under his cot and presses his cheek to the dusty floor so he can't hear anything. He loves the silence and loves the safety of the silence. He doesn't want to move. And then he can't.

He sleeps underneath the cot that night and stays there during the next day, stays there the next night and day and the next. He's hiding from the tigers. Even though they can't get at him right now, this is the spot where they began. And like salmon, they could return to the place of their birth to spawn. Then there will be so many more of them. And they will make so much noise. If that happens, he'll put his head into a howling mouth to kill the noise for good.

26

LIDDY

One morning, there's a white envelope in the hallway outside Liddy's door. She guesses it's from Rose, and she's filled with self-reproach because Rose felt she had to resort to leaving a note. Liddy promises herself she'll go down for a cup of tea this afternoon.

But the note isn't from Rose. It's from Marta. *I would very much like to speak with you,* it reads. *May I come by at ten o'clock tomorrow morning? If this is not something you would like to do, please leave me a message at #503 and I will honor that wish.*

Liddy doesn't leave a message, but she does drive herself into a frenzy. It's been two weeks since the morning Rose introduced them, so if Marta had feelings for her, wouldn't she have reached out sooner? What does she want to talk about? Rose? Their shared situation? Fears about the building? Or maybe, just maybe, could she have been hit by that thunderbolt too?

The next morning, Liddy wakes early, although she isn't sure she actually slept. She has her usual breakfast of toast with cottage cheese and two cups of tea, heads downstairs to wash up. Then she goes to #454. She sits down at Robin's desk, touches her books and soccer trophies, switches to Scott's and picks up a notebook full of pencil drawings of little men climbing into and out of fantastical and complicated structures in both two and three dimensions. She pushes her nose into a drawer full of Robin's pajamas, imagines she can still catch her daughter's scent.

Liddy has been using Rose's phone to call the twins, but they're always in a hurry to get off and do whatever it is they're doing, which is a good thing. Sometimes Robin asks how her writing is going, but most of the time Liddy can almost see their eyes roll when she tries to prolong the conversations. Neither of them mentions Garrett, but she can tell it weighs on them.

When she leaves #454, she tries to work on *Leaving* and is unsurprised when the effort goes nowhere. Seven thirty. It occurs to her that she could just go up to #503 now, but that would be rude. Marta initiated this encounter, and it needs to progress on her terms. So Liddy putters around, shuffles the papers on her desk, thinks about which scarf to wear. Eight fifteen.

There's a knock on the door, stronger than Liddy would have expected, and she jumps from the chair where she's been pretending to read. She pushes the heavy door open and smiles at Marta, motions for her to enter. She doesn't look at Marta directly, doesn't trust her voice not to tremble. "Please, please," she finally says, her voice steady, if an octave lower than usual. "Please come in. Sit down. Please make yourself comfortable," she adds, like some robotic servant programed to be polite.

Marta takes in the room. "It is as if I am standing in an apartment in a magazine. I cannot believe you were able to make it look like this."

"I had a lot of decorating experience in my previous life," Liddy says dryly.

"You are an interior designer?"

Liddy laughs. "No, nothing like that, but please, please come join me on the couch." She groans inwardly. Again, robotic. And idiotic.

"Thank you." Marta sits but keeps looking around. "I am sorry if I am staring, but I am finding this so extraordinary, and I do not know how to stop myself. It is as if I have been transported to another world."

The praise makes Liddy uneasy, as does Marta's close proximity. "Can I get you something to drink? Coffee, tea, water?"

"I would love some tea, thank you," Marta says, and their eyes lock.

Liddy forgets about the tea, drops to the couch, and lightly places her hand on Marta's arm. "Do we know each other from somewhere? You seem so, so . . . so familiar."

"I sense this also, but I do not think we know each other from Boston. And I doubt we met in Venezuela."

"So where is this coming from?"

Marta's smile is full, lighting every plane of her face. "Perhaps it is coming from the future."

OVER THE NEXT month, they become lovers. Although Liddy wants this desperately, she's also nervous, having never been with a woman. She's fantasized about it, sure, watched that lesbian soft porn, but actually making love to a woman is a whole other being. Marta is gentle, and knowledgeable, waits to make sure Liddy wants what she has to offer, and Liddy's apprehensions are quickly erased.

Marta's body is soft and full, her runner's tautness stretching just beneath her incredibly smooth mocha skin. Far different from Garrett, from any man—more welcoming, more exciting, exquisite. Then there's Marta's tongue, finding places no man has ever found, turning her inside out with pleasure. And there's Liddy's own tongue, searching Marta's body and learning to bring her the same.

Marta is older than Liddy thought, but there are still twelve years between them, and at first this troubled her. But Marta brushed her concern aside, claiming that their connection is far more powerful than time. "I have a sense about such things," Marta told her. "This is how we are supposed to be."

They tell each other their secrets, both striving to evade those who stalk them, both hoping to someday walk free. The speed at which they've come together amazes Liddy, but Marta just smiled when she mentioned it. "I have found this is often the way with women," Marta said. "We do not have the same fear of commitment as some men do."

They laugh uproariously when they discover they have both hidden bundles of cash in their respective units, and encourage each other to move forward in pursuit of her dreams. During the day they write in their own spaces, but at night they come together in Liddy's.

"Maybe you should think about telling that lawyer you want to keep going," Liddy suggests to Marta one evening. "You shouldn't stop because you're afraid the worst will happen. What if it doesn't and there's a way to make it all go away?"

"Maybe you should think about meeting with him also," Marta suggests to Liddy. "Jason Franklin is a good man, and perhaps he will have ideas about how you can get away from Garrett for good."

One night as they lay coiled together in Liddy's bed, Liddy says, "I don't think our initial connection came from the future at all. I think it was more straightforward than that: pure, unadulterated chemistry. It struck us, and we knew there was no choice but to be together."

Marta doesn't disagree, but she doesn't abandon her original position. "When I do not try to make you think like me," she says, "and you do not try to make me think like you, we can enjoy each other's thinking, and we will be stronger separately and together because of it."

After all those years of Garrett orchestrating her performance as the perfect wife, directing her to listen to this music, buy this dress, befriend that woman, suck up to this man at that dinner party, now she's with someone who just wants her to be herself. Accepts her as she is. No instructions necessary.

27

ROSE

Daylight savings time ended two Sundays ago, and Rose still hasn't gotten used to it. She can't stand the cold and when it turns into night at four in the afternoon, but mostly she can't stand the thought of the dark months lined up in front of her like a row of rotten teeth. On the other hand, it's been three weeks since Michael's arrest and he's been coming home on time and doing his community service on Saturdays at the Shelter for Humanity. So maybe the whole thing will turn out to be good in the end. Like those people who have heart attacks in their forties and then start taking care of themselves.

But he got kicked off the football team and has been hanging with Reggie almost all of the time. Plus he always looks like he's got the flu. She's pretty sure it's drugs even if he's been passing his drug tests. Someone told her about a mother who used her five-year-old daughter's urine so her tests would come up clean.

Vince didn't beat Michael up like he said he would, but he won't talk to him and that makes it tricky for everyone in the house. And Vince said she couldn't tell any of her family or friends what's going on because it's their problem and no one else's business. She had hoped to confide in Liddy because Vince doesn't know her, but Liddy hardly comes around anymore.

How long can a person sit in a room all by themselves and just write?

You'd think that at least once in a while she'd want to get out of there and have a cup of tea and talk to another human being. Every day when Rose leaves work, she looks up at the light from inside Liddy's windows. Today her eyes fill with tears. Even though it turns out that they weren't really friends, she misses the friend she thought she had.

When Rose gets home, Vince is already there. He never comes home this early and he doesn't look good. She rushes over to him and puts her wrist to his forehead. "Are you sick?"

Vince gives her a tight smile. "We have to talk." He tilts his head toward the girls, who are supposedly doing their homework at the dining room table but are bickering instead. "Alone."

Rose doesn't like the sound of this but doesn't ask any questions. She checks Michael's door and sees that it's closed, which hopefully means he's inside, and tells Emma and Charlotte to stop fooling around and get back to work or no dessert. Then she follows Vince into their bedroom and shuts the door. "Is it Michael?" she asks.

He sits down on the bed, rubs his temples, looks into his lap. "I got laid off."

It's like every bone in Rose's body is filled with ice that freezes her in place. She blinks and tries to understand what he's telling her. "But they love you there," she says. When Vince doesn't answer, she adds, "You've been there for over fifteen years, and you always work so hard." She shakes her head. "This doesn't make any sense."

Vince raises his eyes.

She drops to the bed next to him and takes his hand. "It does make sense?"

"I didn't want to worry you." He lifts his knee and grimaces. After 9/11, he enlisted in the army and went to Afghanistan. He was in Kandahar when his tank hit an IED and his right knee and hip got busted up. After seven operations and years of painful rehab, he's mostly wired back together. But doctors can't perform miracles.

"It's bad again?"

"Damien's been covering for me."

There's a buzzing in her ears that makes it hard to hear him. "He's not anymore?"

"It's not Damien's fault. He took a vacation, and the guy they hired to replace him complained to Peter. Said he wasn't going to do the work of two men on a paycheck for one. Can't say I blame him."

"And Peter took some stranger's word over yours?"

"I couldn't say the guy was lying, because he wasn't, so I told Peter about the pain. And when he asked, I had to tell him how I guessed it wasn't going to change much for the better."

"Why would you tell him something like that?" she demands before she can stop herself.

"Because it's the truth."

Rose stands and goes to the window, stares down at the street below. Vince and his black-and-white way of looking at everything makes her so mad. Why couldn't he have just let it be? Wait for Damien to come back? But she doesn't dare ask these questions because the last thing he needs right now is to think that she believes it's his fault. Even if it sort of is.

The people on the sidewalk are all moving fast because of the cold. They rush into the shadows and then pop back out when they get under a streetlight. Rose adds and subtracts in her head, trying to figure what this is going to do to their budget. Even with the extra money from Metropolis, they're in big trouble.

"Damn Taliban may not have won the war," Vince mumbles. "But they sure beat the shit out of me. I'm done for."

"You're not done for!" She sounds angrier then she should and tries again. "It's just one job, Vinnie. There are lots of other ones. You'll be fine."

"Maybe it'll feel better after some rest," Vince says, but it sounds like he doesn't really believe it and is only telling her this to try to make her feel better. Maybe himself too.

"There's lots of work you can do with a bum knee." She sits on the bed again and puts her arms around him and lays her cheek on his chest. "Like work in an office."

Vince kisses the top of her head. "You know I'm not a sit-at-a-desk person."

"You'll figure something out. There's lots of other stuff. Work with your hands. A job in a store. You're good with people, so maybe customer service or something like that." Rose tries to sound like she's not upset.

"Peter was good," Vince says. "I said I'd quit, but he lay me off instead. Said he thought I'd be able to collect unemployment for at least eighteen weeks. Then he said he was sorry that he could only give me one month's severance."

Rose pats his back. "Well, at least there's that."

VINCE SAYS THERE'S no point in looking for a job with the holidays coming. Rose says there should be more jobs because of the holidays and he could pick up hours at a store or a restaurant that needs an extra set of hands or maybe drive for FedEx. But Vince isn't having it. He says he can't stand long enough to work in a store or restaurant, that it'll be too hard for him to lift heavy packages, and what if there are stairs and he has to carry boxes up three flights? He doesn't say that he'd rather sit in his chair with his knee up so he can watch television and mope around all day, but she thinks that's what it's really about.

Rose worries about the bills and about Michael and about Vince's silence and the fact that he's started drinking during the day. His severance will be used up soon and although unemployment will kick in right after that it's only going to be half of what his salary was. Which wasn't all that much to begin with.

The rent they pay her parents is low compared to most rents in Revere but it's still a big chunk of their income. And now it'll be an even bigger chunk. There's no way to cut back on this because her parents need the money to pay the taxes. Rose already buys almost everything from discount and secondhand stores and hasn't gotten anything new for herself in years. Christmas will be here before she knows it.

She starts thinking about raising the extra rent Liddy, Marta, and Serge pay her. None of them will be able to say no because they don't have anywhere else to go. It's still a good deal even at a higher price, but in the end she can't do it. It's not their fault that Vince lost his job or that they've got to live at Metropolis. There's the mean husband and the mean immigration guys, and she's pretty sure someone or something has been very mean to Serge. How can she dump more on these poor souls?

Liddy did stop by a couple of times recently, but she only stayed for one cup of tea, and even though she tried to act all friendly, there was something really standoffish about her. Rose didn't say anything about Michael or about Vince's job. She can't go against her husband's wishes. But it's not just because of Vince. It feels like Liddy is hiding something from her, so Rose can't just start gabbing about her own problems to someone who's not willing to share hers.

ROSE HAS BEEN trying to be cheerful around the kids and not nag Vince about all the stuff he's not doing. But it's hard to be cheerful when fear is filling up your stomach. Sometimes his drinking makes him quiet and sleepy, but other times he gets angry and kind of nasty. Once, he cried for an hour. How's she going to get him not to drink too much at Thanksgiving when there's going to be tons of beer and whiskey?

On Thanksgiving Day, with both their families together at her mother's, Rose keeps a close watch and tries to keep track of the number of shots of Jim Beam Vince has had. But he's cagey and keeps going out to the back porch with his brothers, where she knows there's got to be another bottle they're trying to keep hidden from the wives. He gets through most of dinner okay, but then Vince and his brother Tom get into one of their sports fights. Vince starts in on how it was all Chris Sale's fault because he lost two games to the Astros and killed the Sox's World Series chances.

"You can't blame it all on him," Tom argues. "What about Pomeranz? He lost a game too, and then there was—"

"Bullshit!" Vince yells, slurring the word. "None of that makes a bit of difference." He flings an arm out toward his brother and pushes a half-full dessert platter off the table. It lands upside down, and pumpkin pie oozes all over the dining room rug. At first, he laughs way too loud and insists that's he's the only one who can clean up the mess. But when he's doing it he gets all choked up and rushes upstairs and never comes down again.

Rose tells the family that his knee and hip are acting up again, and that quiets the questions. He doesn't come to lunch or dinner on Friday, and she uses the same excuse. But on Saturday her mother drags her downstairs and forces her to sit at her kitchen table. "What's wrong with you and Vinnie?" she demands.

Rose tries to laugh, but it sticks in her throat. "Nothing, Ma. Nothing."

"It's something." Her mother pours her a cup of coffee and puts a bombolone in front of her. She crosses her arms and stares at her daughter. Then her face softens. "Tell me, *il mio bambino*."

The endearment hits Rose in the gut. She bursts into tears and spills the whole sad story about Michael and then Vince, including her worries about the drinking. Her mother is soothing and sympathetic and says this is just a blip. Vince will snap out of it and get himself a job before Rose knows it. Michael is a kid who made a mistake and has learned his lesson.

When Rose comes upstairs with red eyes, Vince gets suspicious and she has to tell him that she told her mother. He loses it and starts screaming that she disrespected him and broke her promise, and then he gets ugly drunk. He won't speak to her for the rest of the weekend and doesn't even say goodbye when she leaves for work Monday morning. He just clicks the remote, ready for another day of beer and television.

When she gets to Metropolis, she does everything she can to keep from crying but nothing works. She can't just sit here and cry, because someone could come in and that would be very unprofessional. So she goes into the bathroom and throws cold water on her face and decides she needs to talk to Liddy. Even if they haven't seen each other that often lately, when Liddy hears what's going on she'll be glad Rose confided in her.

Rose takes the elevator to the fourth floor and knocks on Liddy's door. "Liddy!" she calls. "It's Rose. I really need to talk to you." She thinks she hears whispering inside that must be the television, which is good because it means she's not interrupting Liddy when she's writing.

The steel door moves slightly on its track. Liddy is standing in the narrow opening, wearing a terry-cloth bathrobe and slippers. At the sight of her, Rose throws herself into Liddy's arms. "Oh, Liddy!" she wails.

Liddy pushes the door open wider with her shoulder, pulls Rose inside and holds her close. "What is it? Is everyone okay? What happened? Are you all right?"

The sympathy and concern in Liddy's voice makes Rose cry harder.

"Come," Liddy says. "Sit down. I'll make you some coffee."

Rose lets Liddy settle her in a chair. She takes the tissue Liddy hands her, bats at her tears, and blows her nose. When she lifts her head, she sees Marta is also sitting at the table, and she's wearing a bathrobe too, but hers is a silky one that doesn't hide the lace nightgown underneath. She has a half-empty coffee cup in front of her, and her feet are bare. There's a kind of embarrassed look on her face.

Rose turns to Liddy, who looks embarrassed too, and then she looks back and forth between them. She's the one who introduced them and hoped they'd be able to help each other, so it doesn't make any sense that they'd look guilty about having a cup of coffee together. Then she notices the tangled sheets and the blanket falling off the side of the bed.

There's that icy feeling inside her bones and that buzzing in her ears. Just like what happened when Vince told her he lost his job. She closes her eyes, hoping that if she doesn't see Liddy and Marta it won't be true. But this doesn't change anything, so she stands up and without telling Liddy why she came she goes back to her office.

28

LIDDY

Liddy starts taking longer and more frequent walks. Marta encourages her to get outside, to stretch her muscles, to get stronger, to breathe fresh air. But none of these is her motivation, or they aren't the main motivation. Liddy is forty-four, and Marta is thirty-two. Enough said.

Now that it's colder and the light thinner, she usually heads out midday when the sun is as strong as it's going to get. She wraps herself in scarves and hats and bulky coats, sometimes wears a wig, sometimes not. The wind off the river is usually too cutting and bitter, so she walks to Harvard Square through neighborhoods of closely packed wood-frame houses that once belonged to blue collar workers and now are worth millions of dollars.

It's a sunny day, although crisp. It's not as cold as it's been, and Liddy strides toward the square, feeling more positive than she has in a long time. She had forgotten how much she enjoys writing, the all-encompassing-ness of it, the way it absorbs her whole brain and the way Clementine is always running around in the back of her mind. There's nothing like the pleasure she gets after a good day of writing. Except being with Marta.

Liddy has been editing some of Marta's chapters, and she's blown away by the sophistication of the research Marta is doing, stunned by the quality and insight of the work and by the fact that a woman this brilliant could be in love with her. The whole idea that privilege, bestowed at birth through no effort of your own, has such a strong effect on your life chances is something Liddy had never considered before, and she's shamed by this.

She thinks about her students at the Burke, grappling with poverty and prejudice and parents so stressed they can't be there for their kids. About the article in the *Globe* describing how the valedictorians of various inner-city schools struggle in college. About Rose and her Michael. Such a huge gulf between these situations and the lives her own children enjoy. And according to Marta's research, this same gap will be there when they're adults. Liddy decides that when things get sorted out, she'll double her time at the Burke and double her contributions. But this plan shames her too. It's her privilege that allows her so-called generosity, however sincere.

Her thoughts return to Marta, a child of privilege herself, who's back at Metropolis crunching her numbers and coming up with ways her results can be turned into progress, and Liddy is warmed by Marta's passion and purpose.

It would be laughable if it weren't so astonishing: she's in love. Whole hog in love, like a besotted teenager, exhilarated and scared and horny as hell. Love in a self-storage unit. Who knew?

Liddy imagines Garrett finding out about Marta. She sees his bicep coming at her throat and remembers his words. *I'd rather you were dead than with someone else. You're mine, and I'll kill you before I let you leave me.*

She looks around, notes the open porches and leafless trees, the empty driveways, how exposed she is, vulnerable. What if Garrett has found out where she is? What if he knows about Marta? What if he's tracked her down and is waiting for his moment to pounce? The only person she sees on the street is a woman in a wool hat walking her dog. The woman reminds Liddy of Rose.

As Liddy tries to tame the surge of panic rising within her, she thinks about the last time she saw Rose. When she went to the office to comfort Rose after the Marta-in-her-bathrobe episode, it had been a fiasco. Rose told her about Michael and Vince with an eerie calm, then snapped, accusing Liddy of "dropping her" and not being there when she needed her the most. Which was partially true and filled Liddy with guilt, but in her own defense, she'd had no idea what was going on in Rose's life. She and Rose didn't discuss Marta, but Marta was clearly part of their conversation. Liddy offered to lend Rose some money to help tide her over, which only made Rose angrier.

As she walks, reflecting on the ebb and flow of her life, of Rose's and Marta's, she spots a man in a shabby green parka whom she's seen before. He's on the sidewalk on the other side of the street, three or four yards ahead of her. She stops, pretends to be checking her phone, watches as he moves away from her.

It's not what she thinks. Can't be. How can he be following her if he's in front of her? He's nondescript, early middle age, average height, brown hair, slightly balding, and she's surprised she even noticed him. The perfect cover for a PI. There's also something in the way he carries himself, how he looks casually to the right and then to the left, signaling a heightened awareness of his surroundings. Not the behavior of a man strolling through his own neighborhood. The behavior of a predator. Stalking her.

Liddy cuts a sharp right onto a cross street, hurries to the next block. Takes another right in the opposite direction of Harvard Square. She steps into a driveway, crouches behind an evergreen tree already strung with Christmas lights. If he's who she thinks he is, he'll come looking for her.

She waits. Nothing. It's just a guy from the neighborhood who takes walks along the same streets at the same time she does. As Liddy starts back toward the sidewalk feeling foolish, he suddenly reappears at her corner. She freezes. He's only a few feet away, on the other side of her tree.

The man hesitates, glances both ways. Takes a left. She peeks between the branches. He's walking more slowly than before, more uncertainly, stops when he reaches Mass Ave. Instead of turning toward the square, he turns the other way. To circle the block one more time. To find the prey he's lost sight of.

She shouldn't follow him. It's too dangerous. But she does. She rushes to Mass Ave and takes a left. Hides behind a garage and clasps her hands together. The man turns left again. Onto the street where she first encountered him. It's Garrett's detective. She's sure of it.

Garrett knows where she is. Knows about Metropolis. Must know about Marta. He'll be coming for her soon. Of this she has no doubt. And she's going to be ready when he does. Prepared to do whatever is necessary to protect herself and her children.

29

JASON

Jason listens thoughtfully as Liddy Haines describes her predicament. Obviously, he knows of W. Garrett Haines III, ironically
of W. G. Haines Companies, the Goliath to his David in Kimberlyn
Bell's housing case. A case that Jason's David actually won, to Kimberlyn's
delight and also his own.

Pretty much everyone in New England knows Garrett Haines, as
his name is on everything from a cancer center to a charity golf tour-
nament to the intensive care unit at Mass General. So Jason isn't particularly surprised by Liddy's story. Men as successful as Garrett Haines
are often bullies, some more so than others. It's difficult to reach that
pinnacle of success without having some bullying in your DNA. But
death threats and punching your wife in the stomach are far beyond
"some bullying."

Liddy's response to her husband's abuse—moving into a storage
unit—indicates a certain level of both desperation and inspiration. She
appears edgy, hyperaware, and he senses that she's leaving some of the
details out. He's guessing something happened recently that made her
seek him out at this particular moment, something that clearly terrifies
her, perhaps so much so that she's not able to talk about it. But no matter
what she's withholding, she needs a high-powered divorce attorney with
decades of experience and the balls of a bull. Which is not him.

"I'm an immigration lawyer," he explains. "We're talking green cards and work visas. Not only am I not qualified to handle divorce cases, but fighting a man like your husband is way out of my league. You need one of the big boys or big girls."

"I can't go to anyone like that." Her eyes dart around the room as if searching for bugs. "Garrett will find out in a nanosecond. His reach is far."

"I have a friend who has a boutique firm in Lexington, Erickson Hamilton. They specialize in family law, and she's one of the best, tough as nails. Well respected, very discreet."

"Lexington is well within Garrett's reach." Liddy runs a finger inside the collar of her blouse. "I need to know my options. How to protect myself."

"Abby Erickson knows a lot more about your options than I do."

Liddy shakes her head. "I can't take the chance."

"There's this thing called attorney-client privilege," he points out, trying not to grimace.

"Not when you're W. Garrett Haines the Third there isn't. His web of spiders is wide and far-flung."

"If you pursue this, won't he find out at some point?"

"That's why I need to do this now. As soon as possible."

Jason looks at the frightened woman across from him. "I'm really sorry, Liddy, but I can't represent you in a divorce suit. I'd only be able to offer you general legal advice, some of the things you might be able to do to make sure you're safe and—"

"That's fine. Safety is my main concern right now."

They make a pact that if she promises to call Abby or find another qualified attorney, he'll do a little preliminary digging. So now he's going to be spending hours researching restraining orders and the intricacies of family law, which he briefly studied years ago.

Yet another case outside his area of expertise: criminal law for Michael Gentilini, real estate law for Kimberlyn Bell. What kind of help is he to these people when he doesn't have the skills they need and deserve? Except neither Rose nor Kimberlyn nor most of his other clients can afford to hire a more experienced lawyer. All they can hope for is an over-worked private attorney or public defender, who has hundreds of needy clients and is able to give them only half an hour of his or her time. What Jason is able to offer has to be better than that. He can't say the same for Liddy, as she can hire anyone she wants, but she appears to be in such pain that he couldn't say no.

There's some good news on the Marta front, and he wishes he knew where she was living or how to contact her. It's been about six weeks since their last conversation, and although he understands her concerns, it's frustrating. He assumes she avoids his floor when she runs, and although he could ask Rose or skulk around the building trying to find her, he's not about to infringe on her privacy.

Fortunately for Marta, she chose to go to graduate school in Massachusetts—Boston, in particular—rather than in Texas or some other conservative state. Federal agents in the commonwealth have stopped arresting undocumented immigrants when they come to government offices seeking asylum. And judges in Boston are blasting ICE's enforcement tactics, especially those related to the arrest and detainment of noncriminal plaintiffs, often releasing people who they feel don't deserve such harsh treatment. These changes bode well for Marta, and he wants to tell her about them.

Then late one frigid afternoon, he looks up from his desk and she's standing tentatively in front of his open door. "Marta," he says, delighted. "Please come in."

"Thank you."

He pulls the door closed behind her and says, "I'm glad to see you." Even in yoga pants and a sweatshirt to ward off the cold, she's incredibly sexy. He'd tell her this if he said things like that. "I hope your multiple regressions are regressing well," he says, because he does say things like this.

"They are, thank you. Very well. May I sit, please?"

"Of course," he says, and pulls out one of the chairs from the table.

"I am sorry it has been so many weeks since I have come to see you."

Jason takes her file out of his drawer and sits across from her. "You weren't very happy when you left here the last time."

"No, I was not. I was discouraged by our conversation."

"Understandable. But I'm glad you stopped by, because I have some new information that will make you feel better."

She brightens, places her hands on the table, leans toward him. "You do?"

"It's nothing specific, just a general change in the local climate."

"So this will only make me feel a little better?" She sits back in her chair and folds her hands in her lap.

"No," he says. "It's good."

When he finishes explaining, Marta asks, "This means we can now go to the court? I will not be detained?"

"It seems like that should be the situation. I assume it's on a case-by-case basis."

Marta eyes him warily. "So you are saying I might still be detained." It's not a question.

"It's possible, yes, and we have to factor this into any decision we might make. But judges' attitudes are changing. Recently, one compared a group of Christians from Indonesia seeking religious asylum to Jewish refugees during World War Two. And another ordered the release of a Syrian national who was in jail for a year after he went to a federal court to try to change his legal status."

"But the man was in jail for a year."

"Last year," he reminds her, pushing his glasses up on his nose. "And I found another way into your case. The reason the officials and their families in Venezuela have been blacklisted is because the US claims the Venezuelan government isn't doing its due diligence to ensure visa holders aren't a threat to national security." He checks his file. "Or public safety."

"I do not understand how this can help us. The government in my country is incompetent and corrupt, and I am sure they are not doing their due diligence in many areas."

"That's not the point," Jason says. "Sure, the country is a mess, but any thinking judge will understand that you, on a student visa and living in the US for seven years, have no complicity whatsoever in what the Venezuelan government is or isn't doing. We can argue that these restrictions don't apply to you."

"You are saying these judges in Boston are now able to be more sympathetic to my argument?"

"That's my hope."

Marta stands, and Jason does also. "Thank you," she says, smiling and holding out her hand. "I cannot thank you enough for pursuing this when I have not followed up on our previous conversations."

He shakes it and would like to pull her toward him, lift her chin, and kiss her, but he does nothing of the sort. "There's still a lot between here and there. Lots more work, lots more questions."

She takes a step back. "Will you have more news for me in a week? I can return then."

"Next week is Christmas, so nothing's going to happen anywhere until after New Year's. But this will give me time to do some research, some prep. So, yes, come back in a week and we'll discuss our next steps."

"I will see you then."

"Remember, there are no guarantees," he says as he pulls the door open, not wanting to give her false hope. When her face falls, he adds, "But I believe that now we've got a fighting chance."

30

ZACH
Six months later: June 2018

Zach is holding a strip of negatives up to the strong June sun and inspecting each shot through his jeweler's loupe. Even reversed and at this tiny size, it's easy to see that there are some exceptional shots here. As always, now that he's mastered a task, in this case developing, he's impatient for the next one. Four of his five printing classes are behind him, and although there are hundreds of rolls still inside their canisters, he's itching to get going on turning some of the negatives into the real thing.

Sometimes he gets so lost in Serge's work that he actually forgets his search-and-destroy mission. He's been through all of Serge's prints and contact sheets multiple times, and although he's happy he hasn't found any more of himself or Nick, he's even more pleased with what appears to be the treasure trove in his bathroom. It's been so all-consuming that he hasn't had a chance to go out and look for Serge, although Katrina keeps bugging him to do so. Which he's now seriously considering.

His latest plan is that if he finds Serge, and the man wants his work back, rather than messing with a potential lawsuit, he'll offer to become his agent. This way he can handle all the details, and Serge will be free to take and print more photos, something Zach is guessing Serge would prefer over the business end.

A 15 or even 20 percent commission is nothing compared to the 100 percent he would get if he sold the photos directly, but if Serge is actively producing more product, and printing it himself, there will be a much larger and higher quality base for his percentage cut. Then he'll go out and grow a stable of other artists, and he'll start a new venture as a talent manager. Even if he discovers that Serge is dead or otherwise incapacitated, he may do it anyway. This career path appeals to him, and it fits with his skill set.

If there's one thing he knows how to do, it's selling. Sales are sales—it's less about the object you're trying to sell than it is about reading your customer and fine-tuning your pitch to their needs and vulnerabilities. He figured out how to convince people to rent storage units, which he was completely ignorant about before he bought Metropolis. But that's probably not the best analogy.

He hangs the negative strip on the line and starts in on the next batch. When his phone rings, he's reluctant to stop, but when he sees who it is, he takes the call. "Yo, Sheldon," he says. "How goes it?"

"Good as gold. Business is booming, and the family is healthy, knock on wood. So who's to complain?" Sheldon pauses. "Listen, there's something we need to talk about. We should have had this conversation earlier, but because you had so many other problems I didn't want to lay anything else on you before you'd absorbed the first round."

A discussion with his accountant is about the last thing Zach wants about now. In 2010, after he stopped dealing and kicked the drug dealers and the other disreputable types out of Metropolis, he needed a clean accountant. Sheldon, the older brother of an ex-girlfriend, has a solo practice in Arlington and is as straight as straight can be. Which was exactly what Zach was looking for. Sheldon knows nothing about Metropolis's past reputation nor how Zach came to own it, and he follows the letter of the law when filing returns.

"Now that the Metropolis sa—the closing—is complete, we need to figure out the best way to handle the taxes on the funds. A tough nut to crack."

"What funds?" Zach asks more sharply than he intends. He appreciates

Sheldon's reluctance to use the word "sale," but there were no funds exchanged. "I don't understand," he adds more evenly.

Sheldon sighs. "Even though you didn't receive any money in the transaction, as far as the IRS is concerned, you did. It's called 'phantom income.'"

"That doesn't make any sense," Zach objects, even as it dawns on him that it actually does.

"According to my records, you bought Metropolis in 2008 for two million dollars, right?"

"Yes . . ."

"And it was appraised earlier in the year for about five million."

"But I wasn't paid that five million."

"Technically that's true, but the way the IRS figures it, you actually did receive the money for the property, and then you paid it to Haines to cover the remainder of the liability your insurance didn't."

"Are you saying that I owe taxes on three million dollars I never got?"

"Not that much," Sheldon says quickly. "According to my calculations, because of the money you spent on upgrades over the years and a few other tax loopholes, you'll owe on roughly two million. It's a capital gain, only fifteen percent, which should run you about three hundred thousand. Plus another five percent for the state, another hundred thousand. So roughly four hundred K."

This is far more money than Zach has in the bank, and he begins to go through a mental list of the things he could sell, followed by the people he might be able to borrow from. The condo. The car. His guitar collection. It wouldn't be difficult to track down some of his old cronies, who'd be more than happy to make a bit of interest on the drug money they're sitting on that they can't invest, but he'd rather not do that. There's always his parents, who'd surely bail him out, but this is no more appealing.

"The IRS is pretty good about setting up installment payment plans," Sheldon is saying. "We can work with them. Try and get it manageable. If you can't beat them, join them."

"Manageable?" Zach starts laughing a bit wildly. This is far worse than Sheldon knows. If the IRS, or even the law-abiding Sheldon, discovers he bought Metropolis from a fugitive drug dealer with his own laundered drug money, his current troubles will look like a day on Maui.

By the time they hang up, Zach has stopped laughing. He paces around his great room, which is indeed great, at least fifteen hundred square feet with an eighteen-foot ceiling. But after a few loops around the circumference, he feels as confined physically as he does mentally. When he'd asked Sheldon about the chances the IRS would look into his tax records for the ten years he owned the property or into its purchase, Sheldon told him this was unlikely. But when Zach pressed, the accountant had to concede that if anything suspicious turned up, they might.

"But you're clean as a whistle," Sheldon assured him, always one for a useful cliché. "I've been your accountant for ten years, so I should know. Dotted all those *t*'s and crossed all those *i*'s. I can tell you there's nothing to worry about."

Clean as a whistle. Right.

A FEW DAYS later, he still hasn't contacted anyone about a potential loan or looked into selling any of his property. He's betting on Sheldon negotiating a reasonable deal, and Zach figures he can use some of his own cash for the first couple of payments if he cuts down on expenses. It's not an appealing prospect, but he's faced unappealing prospects before and come out on top. He'll survive this too.

As long as no one starts snooping into his purchase of Metropolis, he should be okay. It's quite possible the IRS will have no interest in the purchase as long as he pays his installments. If that doesn't happen and they investigate, maybe he'll catch a break because the source of his initial capital is now a completely legal business in Massachusetts. The former clearly more likely than the latter.

It's an exceptional early summer day: cobalt-blue skies with whiffs of clouds pushed by a fresh ocean breeze, about seventy-five degrees. No time to be inside. Why not a trip to Downtown Crossing to search for

Serge? He learned recently that the area has been rebranded as Midtown. Boston is always trying to catch up with New York City. And always failing. He much prefers Boston, and believes the city should just enjoy what it is.

Zach has lived in the Boston area for most of his life, but when he gets to Downtown Crossing, he's amazed at the transformation—and at the realization that he hasn't been here since the Great Recession, a decade ago. It seems as if, over the intervening years, new blocks have been dropped down on the old, smashing them into submission. Gleaming towers, renovated theaters, fancy people, and even fancier cars. Clearly Midtown. He remembers streets with the sad aura of yesteryear about them, lined by parking lots and storefronts with soaped windows, a smattering of cheap restaurants and liquor stores, a deep hole the size of a city block where Filene's used to be.

Now he strains his neck to see the top of a glass-sided building spearing the sky. Millennium Tower, The Tower, home to the most powerful of the powerful, the richest of the rich. It's as different from the structures that populated the old Downtown Crossing as any building could be. He might have seen this evolution in Serge's photographs, but Serge's focus was always on the people on the margins, his dash of the upscale only a contrast to plumb his subjects more deeply.

The Rolleiflex is secure around his neck, but Zach palms it at the bottom so it's a prominent feature as he meanders through the web of streets, hunting for Serge's preferred backdrops: the bus stop on Washington Street; the Green Line station, a squat stone structure on the corner of Tremont and Boylston; the grassy knoll in the corner of the Common not far from the State House.

Zach is hoping someone who's familiar with Serge, if not Serge himself, will see the camera and approach. It's an unusual object and clearly one of Serge's most salient identifiers, so it's logical it would be associated with him. But no one has even looked at it curiously, let alone with recognition.

He stops to ask a couple of kids watching a touch football game if they've ever heard of Serge Laurent or seen a camera like this before. The answer is no. He approaches three elderly women waiting at a crosswalk, but they step back when he comes near, apparently afraid of him, so he says nothing. A man sitting on a bench wearing a Celtics hat doesn't answer his questions, just asks for money. Zach takes a few shots of summer life on the Common, but he knows his own photos will be nothing like Serge's.

A cluster of people wearing tattered clothes, presumably homeless, bunch around three short-legged beach chairs set on the sloping grass. Two of the women are arguing loudly. Zach walks around behind them. Serge has many photographs of similar groups, maybe even this one, often close-ups, so it's possible they know him and his camera.

"That's the damn truth!" the shorter of the two women shouts.

The other one, wearing a fire-red cape and almost six feet tall, leaps from her chair and juts her forefinger up in the air. "You wouldn't know the truth if it was a bird in the sky!" Then she marches toward Charles Street, her cape sledding behind her.

He looks down and snaps a photo, then thinks of how Serge would shoot her. As a story. Zach steps backward, focuses on the short woman as she glares at the retreating figure, and clicks the shutter. Then he takes another, focusing on the red cape fleeing off into the right-hand corner of the shot.

When he turns back to the group, no one else seems to have registered the woman's departure. But then a man with a raggedy mass of red hair and an even redder beard, rises from the ground on one elbow. He follows the cape, then drops back to the grass and closes his eyes. Zach walks around to face the group, the camera preceding him. The short woman and the four men stare at him with hostility; the guy with the red beard appears to be asleep or, more likely, passed-out drunk.

"Any of you know a man named Serge Laurent?" Zach asks, smiling and turning on the charm.

They all silently scowl at him, clearly unaffected by his charm offensive. One of the men sucks down an airplane bottle of vodka and heaves it toward a trash barrel, missing by at least two feet. "Never heard of 'im. And if I did, I sure as hell wouldn't tell you about it."

Zach thanks them for nothing and heads to the Public Garden, frustrated. At least he'll be able to tell Katrina he looked for Serge. And he can always try again.

There are six shots left in the camera, and he selects carefully. Not the swan boats, but the long weeping willow strands skimming the duck pond. Not the whole tree with its thirty-foot wingspan, but the gnarled roots at its base. Not the facade of the Taj Hotel, but the valet inspecting his shoes. He wonders what Serge would think of his choices.

31

SERGE

A drill is boring into Serge's head. Aiming for his right eye. His vision blurs and the world beings to spin. Faster and faster. Spinning all around. Everything is spinning. Tipping. Thick stripes of black. All black.

And then he's wandering in the cold. In a city. He's wearing his coat but it doesn't keep him warm. He thinks he used to be inside, but now he's outside. He thinks he used to have a job but now he doesn't. He thinks he used to live somewhere but now he can't remember.

He tries to remember. A bed. Yes. He had a bed. And a bulky machine that sat on a bench. Or was it a desk? He reaches for the place that used to be his, but it hides behind a blank wall. It doesn't matter. He wouldn't know how to get there anyway.

It must be Christmastime. There are black coals of snow at the edge of the sidewalks and too many lights. He likes the tiny white bulbs. The colored ones give him a headache.

Anton and Anastasia always cried when it was Christmas. He didn't cry because he was the oldest and hoped if he showed them that he didn't care about the holiday then they wouldn't either. It didn't work. Their parents believed in an almighty and vengeful God who created a world that didn't include celebrations. There's no mention of Christmas or Santa Claus in the Bible.

"December twenty-fifth isn't Jesus's birthday!" Alice would rage when

Anton or Anastasia complained that everyone else got presents and got to eat good food. "Our Lord condemns the worship of pagan gods, and December twenty-fifth is a pagan holiday in honor of a pagan god!"

Serge stumbles into a big open space. There are crisscrossing sidewalks and there are people, but not nearly as many as there were when he was here before. When it wasn't so cold. There's a bench and he sits down on it. It reminds him of the bed he once had. He slept under it to stay safe from the tigers. Or were they lions? He doesn't remember why the bed kept him safe, but he does remember it worked. He climbs under the bench and pulls his coat around him, rests his cheek against the ground. It's warmer here. Safer.

WHEN HE WAKES up there's a woman crouched down next to him with her eyes inches from his own. He doesn't like her looking at him this close, so he backs up and smashes his head on the bench. He registers the searing pain but scrambles to the other side and stumbles to his feet.

"It's the scarecrow cameraman!" she cries. "I thought I recognized you!"

He takes a step backward. He has no idea what she's talking about.

"Where's your weird camera?"

He looks down at his hands. They feel empty, like there's something that should be there. Did he have a camera? He doesn't think so.

"Don't you remember me?" Her voice is sharp and loud, and it hurts his ears. She's almost as tall as he is, and is wearing a long red poncho with a big hood flapping on her back. Little Red Riding Hood. He looks around, scared. Where's the Big Bad Wolf?

"Diamond! Remember? Just a couple of months ago. In the fall."

He tries to think how to get away from her.

"Yes, you do! I caught you taking pictures of us. Me and Angela. I called you out!"

Called him out? It's as if she's speaking a foreign language and speaking it too loud. Angela? He wants to walk away from her but doesn't know which direction to go in.

She digs into the pocket of her poncho, pulls out a crumbled waxy bag, waves it at him. "Want a bagel? You look like you could use some food, Scarecrow."

He likes bagels. A lot. And he's hungry.

She pushes it into his hand. "Take it."

There are seeds on the outside, and inside there's cream cheese with green flecks. His stomach rumbles, but he doesn't like the green stuff.

"Don't look at it—eat it!" she yells. "You're a fucking skeleton."

He takes a bite because then maybe she'll stop yelling and maybe even go away. It's hard to bite into but tastes better than he thought it would. He thinks it might have been a long time since he ate.

She does stop yelling, but she doesn't go away. "You poor schmuck," she says when he finishes the bagel.

Something about this sounds familiar, but he has no idea why. "Thank you."

She crosses her arms over her chest and stares at him again. "It's fucking Christmas, and the once-a-year do-gooders are handing out food everywhere. Come with me. We'll get you more to eat."

He wants more to eat so he follows her.

32

MARTA

It's a Sunday evening in early January, and Marta spoons herself into Liddy's warm body as their heartbeats slow. It seems impossible that they have found each other and equally impossible that they would have not. Liddy may be older than she is in years, but Liddy has such a young, optimistic soul—what Marta thinks of as quintessentially American—that it feels as if she, Marta, is the elder. Or this is the way it has seemed until recently. Over the last few weeks, Liddy has been troubled, anxious and frightened, far more so than before, and Marta senses a darkness ahead. "There is something you are not telling me," she says.

Liddy pulls her closer. "I tell you everything," she murmurs into Marta's hair, deflecting.

"It is a difficult time, but we, as you say, are here for each other."

Liddy kisses the back of her neck. "Lucky us." But she does not sound as if she believes she is lucky.

Marta's unease mounts. *Una hija* on high alert. She wraps her arms more tightly around Liddy, hoping that this will protect her from what awaits, knowing that it will not. "Do you want to watch a movie? It would be nice to see something funny."

"Funny's always good." Liddy untangles herself and sits up. "How about some pot and popcorn too?" she asks a bit too brightly.

"Those are also always good."

They climb out of bed and throw on their bathrobes. Liddy puts popcorn in the microwave while Marta fills the vape pen. Usually a few tokes soothes her nerves and takes the edge off the world, but she's afraid that tonight this will not be the case. They sit together on the couch, the bowl of popcorn between them, their legs up on the coffee table, and pass the pen back and forth. After a few minutes, Marta feels Liddy's body begin to relax, but as she feared, her own does not.

"Did you notice there's something wrong with the elevator door on this floor?" Liddy asks.

Elevator. Marta's heart jerks in the way it does when she intuits approaching menace.

"Looks like one of the doors is off its track at the bottom," Liddy continues, her eyes focused on the television. "I took it yesterday and it seemed fine, but this afternoon it was off-kilter."

Marta grabs Liddy's arm. "Do not ride in it."

Liddy does not move or look at her. "Not to worry," she says with an easy dismissiveness that troubles Marta. "I'll take the stairs."

"You cannot ride in it. Promise me. First thing in the morning, we will tell Rose and she will call the—"

A loud banging on the door. Liddy stiffens, then pales.

"What is it?" Marta whispers. "Who is it?"

Liddy stands, pulls the belt of her bathrobe tighter. She squares her shoulders and seems to nod to herself. "Got to be Rose. Coming!" she calls.

It is not Rose, Marta knows. It is danger. Liddy pushes the door open, and indeed it is not Rose. It is a man with an awkward smile on his face. Although Marta has never seen this man before, she recognizes him immediately.

"Garrett." Liddy presses her hand to her chest, but she doesn't sound surprised to see him.

Garrett's smile widens with what seems like real pleasure. "Liddy," he says with a touch of question in the word.

"What are you doing here?"

"I just want to talk." He holds his hands in the air with his palms forward, as if to prove he does not have a weapon. "May I come in?"

Liddy does not move.

Garrett steps around her into the room. He inspects the décor with an astonished expression. "Remarkable. But you always were good at this." When he sees Marta, he holds out his hand. His eyes are warm and his smile is generous. "Mercedes Bustamante, I presume."

Marta backs toward the refrigerator. She'd imagined Garrett would be handsome, taller, bigger. Yet he has something more powerful and probably more useful to a bully. Even after he used her real name and all that implies, she finds herself responding to the pull of him. She almost wants to like him and, worse, for him to like her. *El carisma.*

"Please, Lidia, can we sit down?" he asks. "There's nothing to worry about. I just want to talk. Nothing else. I'm sorry to disturb your"—he pauses, runs his eyes over the vape pen, the popcorn, the unmade bed, then takes a deep breath—"your evening. But it's been a long time, and I miss you so much. I can't go on like this. We can't go on like this."

"I don't want to talk to you."

Marta starts toward the door, but Liddy's eyes beg her to stay.

"I want you to come home, to come back to me." Garrett swallows hard. "Please."

Liddy shakes her head vigorously. "It's over."

"Don't say that. We can do this. I can do this. I'll change."

"You punched me," Liddy says through her teeth.

"Never, never again."

He takes a step forward, but Liddy steps back and pulls Marta with her.

"I was wrong, have been about so many things," he says. "You've never left before. I never realized how much I need you. How much I love you. Remember Santorini? The Serengeti? Our apartment in SoHo? We can get back what we had. Make it even better."

Garrett looks sincere, and Marta fears that he is. He and Liddy have been together for decades. And there are the children. The history. Despite his actions to the contrary, Marta feels he does love Liddy, deeply. And in some ways, Liddy must love him too.

"I'm not coming back." Liddy's voice is tight and low. "Ever."

Liddy's words swamp Marta with relief, but then she catches a shift in Garrett's demeanor. A hardening around his chin and in his eyes. About his shoulders. This is clearly a man who does not like to be crossed. Who will not be crossed. This is the real Garrett vs. the fake Garrett who entered the unit. She grabs Liddy's hand.

Garrett follows the movement. "I'm thinking pretty little Mercedes here should excuse herself, give us some time alone."

Liddy holds Marta's hand so tightly it hurts, and Marta says, "I am staying."

Garrett laughs. "According to ICE, you, Ms. Mercedes Bustamante, are in violation of a deportation order. Have been for months. So unless you're willing to leave and allow me to speak in private to my wife, I believe the only place you'll be staying is in a federal detention center."

Liddy drops Marta's hand, walks up to Garrett, and pushes her face into his. They are almost the same height, and Liddy glares at him. "Don't you dare bring her into this, you brute. She's got nothing to do with us."

"I beg to differ. I daresay she's smack-dab in the middle of us." Another laugh. "The only thing you ever had going for you were your looks, and now that they're fading, you can only attract another man-hater. What will our children say? They'll be devastated that you're willing to destroy their family for you own selfish reasons. They'll turn on you, because it's clear you only care about yourself, that you're a terrible mother."

Garrett's words turn Marta's panic into fury. She crosses her arms over her chest and stands in front of him. "Do not talk to her this way. She cares about her children more than anything. Apparently more than you do."

Garrett flips his hand as if to swat away a fly. "You are so very wrong, little lady," he says imperiously. "She abandoned them. Disappeared from their world to live in this, this—"

"You self-righteous son of a bitch," Liddy spits. "How can I abandon children you sent thousands of miles away?"

Marta wants to protect Liddy, or to at least bear witness, but these are marital arguments, and it is not her place to hear this. Nor does she want to. But she stands her ground.

"I've got a compromise," Garrett offers. "Mercedes, if you're not going to leave, then stay here, take another toke, eat some popcorn, and Liddy and I will go outside to continue our discussion."

"Fine," Liddy says, and then turns to Marta. "We'll just be outside the door."

"But—"

"Let me talk to him. I'm not going to allow him to do this to you."

"This is not what is important at the—"

"You'll be right here if there's a problem," Liddy says, then glowers at Garrett. "I can yell very loud."

"Thank you, Mercedes," Garrett says, reverting to his pseudo-good-guy persona. He tries to take Liddy's arm, but she yanks it away. They walk into the hallway, and Garrett slides the door closed behind them.

Marta presses her ear to the door, but she can only hear their voices, not what they are saying. Flares of anger. Sharp words. More yelling. He could hurt her. He could kill her. Marta pulls the door open an inch, but Liddy and Garrett are standing in front of the elevator, so she's at the wrong angle to see them. *Elevator.* Marta moans softly. Please, God, no.

"Damn it, Liddy!" Garrett shouts. "That's not going to happen, and you know it!"

"Don't be so sure!" Liddy snaps back. "I don't care about your money or your fancy condo. I'll live in a homeless shelter before I live with you!"

"And what about your precious Mercedes? Arc you willing to sacrifice her?"

"Fuck you! Fuck you! Fuck you!" Liddy roars.

Then there's a thump. A grunt. A growl. A scream.

Marta rushes into the hallway. Liddy is standing with her hands covering her mouth. Her eyes are wild. Marta turns just in time to see Garrett's flailing arms disappear under the tilting bottom of the unhinged elevator door. Like a dog's door. He fell through the dog's door.

PART THREE

33

ROSE

Now Rose understands why things have been going missing from the storage units. As she steps silently up Metropolis's rear stairway, she thinks back to last July, when Michael spent a few days at Metropolis with her because he was grounded and she didn't trust that he'd stay in the apartment if no one was there to make him. And then there was this past Christmas vacation, when the same thing happened. This time it was because he was too much for her mother to handle, what with Emma and Charlotte at her apartment all day.

When Michael was in her office, she'd gone nuts with him slouched on the floor in the far corner, sleeping or staring at his phone, rattling her key ring so loud she had to grab it away from him so she could hear herself think. Even more annoying were the tons of questions he asked about the renters and what was in their units. She explained that their personal information was confidential and she had hardly ever seen the inside of anyone's unit. Michael smirked in disbelief when she said this.

He was keeping her from the work she had to do, so she let him roam around the building just to get him out of her hair. She made him come back every fifteen minutes so he couldn't go far and it surprised her when he actually followed this rule. She had hoped this meant he was finally starting to wise up. Foolish, foolish woman. He must have run out and made a copy of the master key during one of his fifteen-minute excursions.

It's ten o'clock on a freezing Sunday night and she told Vince she was visiting with her friend Deb from bingo, who's fighting breast cancer. Vince doesn't know Deb so all Rose has to do is be home by eleven and there won't be any trouble. As long as she doesn't run into anyone she knows. Especially Serge. Rose is pretty sure he isn't here because he works every night at a restaurant in Cambridge, and she hasn't seen him around since sometime before Christmas when he paid her for January. He hasn't asked her to open any units for him since then either. This is disappointing, given their money troubles, and his absence has been worrying her a little. But in the case of tonight it's a plus.

When she was searching Michael's closet for drugs yesterday, she turned up a bunch of electronics, along with most of the items the renters had reported missing. She wishes she could return it all, or at least give back what he stole from Metropolis, especially Angie Holladay's jewelry and Linda Shields's laptop. But it would be suspicious if everything suddenly turned up at the same time, and she's not about to call the police because then she'd have to explain where she got all the stuff, and how can she do that?

But Serge's camera is different. His pictures might be strange, but the camera is special to him. And, the Lord knows, poor Serge hasn't got much. Michael probably thought it was worth a lot of money and tried to fence it, but even she can tell an old camera like this isn't worth anything.

Rose wore her sneakers on purpose so she wouldn't make any noise on the concrete floors, but the sneakers squeak and she has to step extra carefully. None of the hallways are all that bright, but the fifth floor is the worst because so many of the bulbs are out. Which now makes it the best. She's sweaty from nerves and shame, and kind of out of breath. She stays inside the shadows as much as she can.

She makes her way down the long corridor to Serge's unit without a hitch. Relief number one. A quiet knock, and then another only a little bit louder. When there's no answer she twists the master key and steps inside. It's dark and there are no windows and it smells like chemicals and dirty sheets, but Serge isn't here. Relief number two.

She flicks on the light and is glad to see all of Serge's pictures and equipment are still here because that means Michael didn't steal anything else. She puts the camera on the table and, just as fast as she entered, she leaves. The hallway is dark and quiet, but when she passes the stairwell next to the passenger elevator on the fifth floor she hears yelling from the landing below. Nosy as always, she climbs halfway down and cranes her neck.

It's Liddy and she's yelling at a man who has to be Garrett, which means he figured out where she's hiding, just like Liddy said he would. After the way Liddy has been ignoring her, Rose doesn't want to care what Liddy does anymore. But that doesn't mean she doesn't want to know what's going on.

"Goddamn it!" Garrett shouts. "That's not going to happen, and you know it!"

"Don't be so sure!" Liddy yells back. "I don't care about your money or your fancy condo. I'll live in a homeless shelter before I live with you!"

Rose doesn't move. They're both really mad, and Liddy doesn't even look pretty with her face all red. Garrett is much smaller than Rose figured and he's not good-looking at all.

"And what about your precious Mercedes? Are you willing to sacrifice her?" he screams.

"Fuck you! Fuck you! Fuck you!" Liddy screams back.

Rose wonders who Mercedes is—Garrett said "her" so he's not talking about a car, and why would anyone sacrifice a car anyways? But it would be stupid to stick around to find out because either one of them could come up the stairs at any moment. She starts to turn, but then there's a loud thump followed by a grunt. Rose peeks down again, and there's Garrett with his back against the elevator door. He's trying to catch his balance, but he can't. Out of nowhere, the bottom of the door swings inward, and he falls straight down. Liddy screams, and Rose sprints back up to the fifth floor.

Dear Jesus. No one can know she was here or what she was doing, so Rose runs to the far end of the building as quietly as she can. Then she races down to the ground floor and flings herself out the rear door near the railroad tracks. Garrett has to be dead. Even though it's unchristian of her, the first thing she thinks is that it isn't such a bad thing. Unless Liddy pushed him. And if she did it on purpose that would mean she murdered him. Dear Jesus. He could have somehow fallen backward on his own. But that doesn't make any more sense than what the elevator door just did.

34

JASON

Even though it's late Sunday night, Jason is still at his desk at Metropolis. As tight and claustrophobic as this office is, his Allston apartment is worse on both fronts. Plus, the apartment is more depressing. He's got all his big-paycheck furniture there—leather sectional, king-size bed, and sixty-inch television—crammed into three tiny rooms. They had looked great in his wide-open, high-ceilinged, walls-of-glass apartment at the Ink Block in the South End, but in his current abode, not so much. And although his Metropolis setup has similar big-paycheck furniture against a similarly shabby backdrop, at least the office here is roughly the same size as the study in his old apartment, so it doesn't look nearly as sad.

He's working on Marta's case, filling out the ridiculous number of forms the government demands of immigrants seeking asylum. It's astounding that anyone is ever able to get into the country given the restrictive laws, the new administration's enforcement techniques, and this onerous and mostly unnecessary paperwork.

He hears what sounds like scuffling upstairs. People move things in and out at the most unexpected hours, and he often wonders what they're up to. But he's probably better off not knowing. Then there's a loud thud from above, followed by a piercing, high-pitched shriek that sounds as if it's right outside his door.

Jason rushes into the hallway, sees nothing, takes the stairs two at a time. When he reaches the fourth-floor landing, he skids to a stop, blinks, uncomprehending. Liddy is sitting on the floor across from the elevator, wailing, while Marta rocks her. Both women are wearing bathrobes, and their faces are ashen.

When Marta sees him, she cries, "Call nine-one-one! There is a man in the elevator!"

He turns to the elevator. The doors are closed, and it looks the same as it always looks. "A man in the elevator?" Then he sees that one of the doors is slightly askew, that it's tipped inward and hangs out of its track, at a slight angle, and uneven with the other door.

He presses the button. Both women scream.

Liddy raises her head. Her eyes are open so wide that white surrounds her irises. "It's Garrett," she says in a strangled voice. "He fell in." Then she collapses back into Marta.

Liddy doesn't look or sound like herself, and for a moment Jason wonders if he's mistaken, that it's not Liddy Haines at all. But of course it is. "Garrett, your husband? Fell in?" he asks.

What was Garrett Haines doing here? For that matter, what's Marta doing here? But then he understands. Like Liddy, Marta lives at Metropolis, and he feels stupid for not having figured this out earlier.

"Nine-one-one," Marta pleads. "Please."

Jason dashes down to his office, grabs his cell, and dials 911. He's not entirely sure what to tell the dispatcher, but he manages to impart that there's a major emergency. Then he scribbles down his address, grabs his house key and a twenty-dollar bill, dashes back up again.

He presses the items into Marta's hand. "Take a cab to my apartment. Right now. This place is going to be swarming with police in a minute."

Marta shakes her head. "I am not leaving Liddy."

"Yes, you are," Liddy says, snapping back into herself. "Go. Now! I can't have you on my conscience too."

"I'll stay with her," Jason says, helping Marta up from the floor. "You don't have a choice."

"But—"

"It's in Allston. Make yourself at home. Sleep in my bed. I'll be there as soon as I can."

Liddy struggles to her feet. "Please." She pulls Marta into a tight hug, and then pushes her away. "Go!"

With a stricken look over her shoulder, Marta enters the stairwell and disappears. The detached elevator door hangs like a loose tooth. The car is empty.

Liddy bursts into new tears, and Jason tries to comfort her. "He's dead," she sobs inconsolably.

Horrified, Jason realizes Garrett must be lying on the top of the elevator car. That he somehow fell through that hanging door, which must have become unhinged at the bottom somehow. That, as Liddy believes, he's most likely dead. When Jason hears sirens, he tells Liddy to get dressed and that he'll be right back. Then he goes down to meet the EMTs.

As HE DRIVES home hours later, Jason is still not completely sure he understands what happened. There was some kind of bizarre elevator mishap in which the door got off its bottom track. Liddy told the police that she and Garrett were having an argument in front of the elevator, and when Garrett tried to grab her, she sidestepped him, and his momentum hurled him into the door. The force caused it to swing inward, and he fell through the gap, landing two floors below on top of the elevator car.

According to one of the detectives, a similar accident occurred in Fenway Park four years ago. In that case, a twenty-two-year-old woman was horsing around and bumped into one of the closed elevator doors. The bottom of the door swung inward when she struck it, and she fell into the empty shaft and onto the car that was three flights below. Miraculously, she didn't die, but her injuries destroyed any chance for the kind of life she had expected to live. She had been at a Red Sox game with her family, celebrating her graduation from BU.

When the cops first arrived at Metropolis, they focused on Liddy, questioning her over and over until she fell apart so completely that they gave up and allowed her to go in the ambulance with Garrett, promising follow-up in the morning. Then they turned their interest to Jason, clearly suspecting he must have been involved in the incident. What else would a Black man be doing in a self-storage building late at night if he wasn't up to no good? They checked his ID multiple times and repeatedly asked him the same questions. Then they made him take them to his office to prove it existed, scanned their handhelds searching for his rap sheet. Jason was the only one who wasn't surprised when he came up clean.

Garrett isn't dead, although his injuries appear to be as severe as those suffered by the girl at Fenway. The forty-five minutes it took to extract him from the shaft didn't help. He's now in surgery. Liddy spoke with her children in Switzerland, and the headmaster is putting them on a plane first thing in the morning. What a shit show.

As Jason expected, there are no parking spots on his block, and his circles grow wider and wider until he finally finds one about half a mile away. He trudges toward his building, his coat buttoned high against the cruel January wind. Marta buzzes him in.

She's standing in the open doorway when he arrives. "How is Liddy? Where is she?"

"She's fine," he says, leading her back into the apartment and quickly closing the door. "At Mass General with Garrett. She promised to call when she knows more."

"Garrett is not dead?"

"Not yet anyway."

"This is good news." Marta drops her face into her hands. "Thank you for letting me come to your apartment." She raises her head and gives him a slight smile. "Thank you for making me come to your apartment."

"You're welcome," he says as a wave of exhaustion washes over him. "I don't know about you, but I'm beat. I've got to be at the police station at nine o'clock for an interview. As if I haven't been interviewed enough tonight."

What he doesn't tell Marta is that he's placed himself in serious jeopardy by not telling the police Marta was with Liddy. This omission is equivalent to filing a false police report, which, given that he's an officer of the court, is a felony. He knew it was risky, but what were his choices? This isn't the first time he's done something illegal for what he believed was the greater good. Unfortunately, the last time it didn't work out well.

But if he'd revealed Marta's presence, she, an innocent victim of a crazed world, would have been arrested, deported, and most likely murdered when she was returned to Venezuela. He would not, could not, be a party to that. It's not as if her testimony will provide any additional evidence, as she had seen no more than he had. His instinct to protect her overcame his instinct for self-preservation, and he's not sorry for this. Well, maybe a little. Either way, his take on the situation has nothing to do with the fact that he's currently harboring a fugitive from the law.

"Are they interviewing you about Liddy?" Marta asks, her face growing even paler. "She said Garrett was going to hit her, and she stepped aside when he came toward her. They cannot say she did this on purpose, yes?"

"That's what she told the police, and then they let her leave," Jason says. What he doesn't tell her is that an estranged wife who admits to arguing with her husband before his mysterious, possibly deadly, accident is a prime suspect. He's seen arrests made in far less plausible situations. "There had to be something wrong with the door. I'm guessing it's the building owner who's going to be in trouble. Not Liddy."

35

ROSE

"There's been an accident at Metropolis," Zach tells Rose over the phone.

"What kind of accident?" She's been up all night planning what to say, and she's worried she's not going to be able to pull off pretending that she has no idea what happened. It's seven in the morning and she's trying to get the girls fed and out the door without waking Vince, who's sleeping in his chair in the living room. It's easy for her to sound distracted and like it's just an ordinary day. "Hold on a sec."

She presses the phone to her chest. "Emma, leave your sister alone! If she doesn't want to eat her toast, that's her business. Finish up, both of you. Now. Get your backpacks ready and your coats and boots on. We're leaving in ten." She raises the phone to her ear, swallows hard. "Is everything okay?"

"No."

"What is it? What kind of accident?"

"Can you get over here as soon as possible? We can talk then."

Get over here. Talk. "Is, is the building okay?" she asks because she's figured this would probably be the first thing she would think. Not a person but a fire or a flood or something like that.

"It's standing," he says. "If that's what you mean."

"Zach, please, what's going on?" She wants him to tell her as much as possible over the phone. That way when she sees him she won't have to look him in the eye and ask questions that she already knows the answers to.

"A man fell down the elevator shaft last night."

"A man fell? What does that mean? A renter?"

"I don't really want to discuss this over the phone."

"Who was it? Is he okay?"

Zach hesitates. "His name is Garrett Haines. The W. Garrett Haines the Third. You know him, of him. He's a big man around town. And, no, he's not okay."

Rose lets out a gasp and hopes it sounds like a real one. "Is he dead?"

"Just get over here, Rose."

THERE ARE TWO police cars in the lot when Rose arrives. She took a cab, which she's never done before, because she has to know if Garrett is dead, if Liddy has been arrested, if anyone is aware that she, Rose, was there when Garrett fell because she was covering up Michael's robbery. She also has to find out if Zach knows Liddy is living in a storage unit, if he's going to fire her and then have her arrested.

She isn't exactly sure what her crime is, but she's got to be breaking Cambridge building codes and maybe she's also guilty of some kind of insurance fraud. Even if it's not either of these, she's guilty of something. At least of not being loyal to a guy who's given her the chance to do things that hardly any other boss would for someone without much education or real skills. And of course she's guilty of taking money that's not hers to take.

Yellow police tape is stretched across the front of the elevator door, and Zach is standing in her office talking to a cop. The two men turn and look at her when she walks in. The cop's face is serious but normal-looking. Zach, who's so happy-go-lucky and cracking jokes all the time, almost doesn't look like the same person. He's slouched and pasty and his blood-shot eyes burn into hers. He always acts like such a kid and now he looks like an old man.

B. A. SHAPIRO

"This is Rose Gentilini," Zach tells the cop. "The office manager I was telling you about." He turns to Rose. "Officer Thomas."

Rose shakes his hand and tries to smile like it's just any other day. *The office manager I was telling you about.*

"We're going to need to speak to you, Ms. Gentilini," Officer Thomas says.

"Me?" Rose's voice squeaks, and she's sure she looks and sounds guilty. "I, uh, I wasn't even here."

"It's not about the accident, per se. I understand you're the one responsible for rentals, and we want to ask you some questions about this. Also about the elevator maintenance contract. The inspections."

"Of course, of course," Rose says. *Responsible for rentals.* "I know about those things. Be happy to talk to you. I'll be here all day." She glances at Zach, who doesn't correct her. "Just let me know when. Whenever. Just let me know."

"I'll be back in an hour or two," the cop says, and leaves her alone with Zach.

She turns to face him. He drops into one of the chairs and points to the other. Rose sits. Her legs are wobbly and she's glad for the chance to get off them. "Is the man who fell dead?"

Zach runs his hands through his hair, which make pieces of it stand up in clumps. "He's in bad shape, had to have surgery, but he's not dead. I'm guessing this could change at any moment. The cops said he was barely alive when they finally extracted him."

Extracted him. Rose thinks of the thud of Garrett's body against the door and how he dropped out of sight. Dropped right out of sight.

"I know," Zach says, although she's said nothing. "I have to go down to the police station in an hour."

She studies his ashen face, dotted with stubble, and the lines etched into his forehead, and she wonders if maybe he's just upset about what happened to Garrett and he doesn't know about any of the things she's done wrong. "There's, there's a renter here," she says because that's what an innocent person would say. "She has two units actually. Liddy Haines. Is she a relative? Was, was she involved?"

"She's his wife, and she was here. They were standing in front of the elevator on the fourth floor, apparently arguing and—"

"Was she hurt too?"

Zach gives her a strange look. "As far as I know, she's fine. The police said she's at the hospital with her husband. They're going over there to talk to her sometime later today."

Rose wants to ask more questions about Liddy but supposes that she should be the most interested in the details of the accident. "I don't get how this could've happened."

"Apparently, one of the elevator doors wasn't hinged properly." Another swipe through his hair. "Haines knocked up against it and fell through the bottom."

Rose acts like this is confusing. "Fell through the bottom of what?"

"The bottom of the door. It somehow slid inward, created a gaping space . . ." Zach shudders.

"So Garrett broke the door?" Rose asks and then worries that Zach might wonder why she's calling a man she doesn't know by his first name.

Zach doesn't notice. He stares over her shoulder and swallows hard. "The police have been all over the place. They seem to believe something was wrong with the elevator before this happened. That it wouldn't have been possible for Haines to break it on his own. They talked about the door's safety retainers, something about gibs. They think the elevator . . ." He stops and looks right into her eyes. "They think it might not have been properly maintained."

"But it has!" So this is why Zach is upset, and it has nothing to do with her or with Liddy or Marta or Serge. "It was last winter, I remember. Maybe March? The annual inspection had to be put off because of a snowstorm. But they came. Both the maintenance people and the city. I have the paperwork."

"The problem is that the certificate in the elevator expired two years ago, on December 20, 2015."

"No. That can't be right. I must have forgotten to replace it. Sorry, shouldn't have done that. But I know it's in here." She crosses to the wall of file cabinets, yanks open the top left drawer, and grabs a file from it. *Thank you, Jesus. Thank you, Jesus.* She and her family are saved. *Thank you, Jesus.*

"Are you sure?"

Rose sits down and flips through years of inspection applications and canceled checks and receipts from the maintenance company. She lifts up a certificate and grins. She screwed up, but it was a small screwup. Not posting it in the elevator isn't all that bad. She hands the certificate to Zach.

"Great." He takes it from her and smiles for the first time since she got here. "This could save my ass if Haines sues." His smile fades as he checks the date and then checks it again. When he looks up his face is all white like it was when she first got here. "This expired December 22, 2016. Over a year ago."

Rose takes the paper and runs her finger under the date. That isn't possible, but there it is, right in her hands. This isn't some small screwup after all. She searches through the file again, but there isn't a more recent certificate. She goes to her desk and pulls up last year's calendar on her computer. She's supposed to file an application for the elevator inspection a month before the last certificate expires, and she always marks the date to remind herself. Sure enough, there's a reminder to do just that on November 14, 2017, but apparently she never did it. She closes her eyes so she can't see the screen.

The middle of November was when Vince got fired and when he started drinking and not moving from his chair. She must have let the application fall through the cracks of her life. And now this is going to destroy Zach and herself. Even if no one ever finds out about Liddy and Serge and Marta, or Michael stealing from the renters, or her being at Metropolis when it happened. Garrett Haines would be a fool not to sue

Zach, and whatever else Liddy has said about him, she never said he was a fool.

"I'm so sorry, Zach. Oh dear God, I'm so, so sorry. I've been taking care of these inspections for ten years. I've always done it right before . . . I don't know, I don't know how this could have happened."

Zach is staring blankly at the certificate and doesn't say anything.

Rose walks over and touches his shoulder. "I'll do anything, everything, I can to make this right."

He startles at her touch and jerks away from her. "There isn't anything you can do," he says dully. "It's already done."

36

JASON

Jason sits next to the man who owns Metropolis as they both wait to speak to a detective. He knows this because he overhead the man's conversation with the receptionist when he came in. Zach Davidson is his name, and Jason is surprised that he's so young. He hadn't thought much about it, but now he realizes he always assumed whoever owned the building was some pudgy older guy, vaguely Italian. Even those who are stereotyped are guilty of stereotyping, for Davidson is fit, somehow clearly hip, and he's probably no more than ten years older than Jason.

As Jason stealthily checks him out, he realizes that Davidson's age is probably closer to his own, that it's the man's exhaustion and obvious anxiety that have added a decade. And who can blame the poor guy? Although Garrett Haines is still alive, his condition is critical and he could die at any time. If there's negligence involved, which seems more than likely, Davidson is sure to be facing some serious charges. A tough break. Really tough.

A woman in an unflattering beige uniform leans out the office door and calls, "Jason Franklin?"

Jason forgets all about Davidson's problems as he worries about possibly digging himself into an even deeper hole, risking both his law license and his freedom for hiding Marta's presence at Garrett's fall from the police. This is further complicated by the fact that, as far as the police are concerned, he's in the questionable position of being seen as both a witness and Liddy's lawyer, although he's neither.

Before the EMTs and police arrived, he had advised Liddy to say nothing to anyone. When she struggled to follow his advice, he interceded, which is how the police developed this impression. Jason didn't want her to say anything about Marta. Nor did he want her to incriminate herself if she had purposely pushed Haines, a question he didn't ask. No lawyer would.

They sit down, and the detective immediately begins the interrogation, his tone curt. "Describe what you saw when you went up to the fourth floor." He'd asked Jason to do this last night.

"Liddy Haines was sitting on the landing in front of the closed elevator. She was sobbing and almost incoherent, but she managed to tell me enough to call nine-one-one."

"What else did she say?" Also previously asked and answered.

"'It's Garrett. He fell in.'"

"And you knew who both Ms. Haines and Garrett were?"

"Yes."

"How did you know this?"

"Ms. Haines has a storage unit at Metropolis, where my office is."

"I've never heard of a lawyer with an office in a storage unit."

Jason wants to point out that he'd actually heard of a lawyer with an office in a storage unit at least three times last night, but he resists. "It's odd, but it works for me."

"And you claim you went to Harvard?"

"Yes." As annoyed as Jason is at the detective's unrelenting suspicion, he's relieved that there doesn't appear to be any speculation that Liddy might not have been alone. So Jason says nothing more. Finally, with a wave of frustration, the detective dismisses him.

Jason heads toward Metropolis to pick up the computer, files, and clothes Marta asked him to bring to her. Scattered snow showers were forecast, but it's coming down much more heavily than that, bringing the streets to a standstill. As he sits locked in traffic, he switches on the radio.

It's the top of the hour, and a meteorologist is talking about how little accumulation there will be. Jason watches the air turn thick with snow, the bushes and grassy areas hugging the sidewalks growing completely white. Then a news announcer comes on and begins reporting on Garrett Haines's accident.

"W. Garrett Haines the Third, the well-known Boston real estate executive and philanthropist, is in critical condition at Mass General after a two-story fall down an elevator shaft at the Metropolis Storage Warehouse on Mass Ave in Cambridge last night. Mr. Haines is currently undergoing surgery. As of now, the fall is being labeled an accident, but a person familiar with the investigation, who did not wish to be identified, indicated police are not ruling out foul play."

Jason switches off the radio. If they're talking about foul play, they have to be talking about Liddy.

JASON FLIPS OPEN his computer a little before six the next morning. The *Boston Globe* is reporting that Jason Franklin, attorney at law, accompanied Lidia Haines when she spoke to police at her husband's bedside at the hospital, where W. Garrett Haines III is in the ICU that's named after him. The article adds that Mr. Franklin, an attorney, was also with Ms. Haines at the time of Mr. Haines's accident, and goes on to mention that Franklin's office is located at the Metropolis Storage Warehouse in Cambridge, where the incident occurred.

Despite the fact that there are some inaccuracies and false insinuations in the article, like he hadn't been with Liddy at the hospital and he's not her attorney, shit is going to hit the fan. His cell begins to explode with the ding of emails, the tritone of texts, and the chime of calls, followed by the pulse of voicemails. He mutes all of the sounds and puts the phone in his pocket, but it vibrates, and he turns this feature off too. Not that he believes silencing his phone is going to change anything. It's just that he needs time to prepare for the onslaught.

He had explained to the police, both at Metropolis and at the station, that he wasn't representing Liddy, that he was just a friend helping her through a difficult time and that she'd be retaining another attorney for that job. He'd hoped this would keep his name out the papers, but clearly it had not.

Jason punches in his mother's number. He knows his parents are getting ready for a day of teaching, and that they'll be startled to see a call from him this early.

"Jason!" his mother cries. "Is everything all right? Are you okay?"

Jason would smile at her predictability, but smiling isn't a possibility when he knows how much his news is going to upset her. "I'm fine, Mom," he says. "Perfectly fine. Everyone is fine. There's nothing to worry about."

"Then why are you calling this early?" The suspicion and fear in her voice are palpable. "What's wrong?"

"There's one small thing I need to tell—"

"I knew it. Is it cancer?"

"No, Mom, I told you nobody's sick. It's nothing like that. It's about my job."

"Your job? What about your job?"

"It's about Spencer Uccello . . . I'm not working there anymore."

"What do you mean?"

"I mean that I've gone out on my own."

"On your own," she repeats, hesitates. "This doesn't seem to be enough of a reason for a six a.m. call. What aren't you telling me?"

There's no other alternative, so Jason dives in. "There was an incident at the firm, and we decided to part ways. I was working for one of our big corporate clients, defending the business against an immigration violation, when I discovered that two of the vice presidents in the company were involved in human trafficking. They were financing the people bringing in these migrant women and girls and then selling them off to—"

"What do you mean 'part ways'?"

"I anonymously leaked the information about the trafficking to a federal government official, who stepped in and stopped it."

"Well, then you did the right thing." His mother sniffs. "Are you saying Spencer Uccello would have just let them get away with it?"

"No one knew about it but me, and if I'd kept it to myself, no one at the firm would have known either. Which is what would have made me a team player and gotten me a partnership."

"I don't understand what you did that didn't make you a team player."

"It wasn't what I did so much as how I did it. I used materials protected by attorney-client privilege to back up my claim, which is illegal for a lawyer to do. When it all came down, it didn't take much to figure out who had given the feds the materials, which I admitted when they asked. In the end, the client—"

"It's good you told the truth. It makes me proud."

"In the end, the client never found out the firm was behind the arrests, which was exactly the way Spencer Uccello wanted it to stay. But they couldn't keep an attorney who had knowingly broken the law, especially one who had been disloyal to a client and, in their minds, to the firm."

"They fired you for that!" she cries, full of indignation. "I think that's just—"

"Mom, it's over. They didn't fire me. I walked away. We made a deal everyone could live with, and it was all very hush-hush. No one outside of a few of the higher-ups at the firm knew anything about it. Spencer Uccello had a reputation and a big client it wanted to keep. I had a reputation and a license I wanted to keep. It's been over a year, so there's no reason—"

"Over a year? This happened over a year ago, and you didn't tell us?"

Jason can hear her injured tone, and he wants to kick himself. He'd tried to convince himself he was keeping this a secret out of consideration for his family's feelings, that he didn't want to deprive them of the joy they took in his success. But now he understands he was ashamed of his fall from grace. It was all about him, not about them. "I'm sorry. I should have told you but I, I didn't want to upset everyone. Disappoint everyone."

"We're your family! It's okay to upset your family. That's what we're here for."

"I know. I was wrong. And it would have been—"

"Why are you telling me this now? Why this very moment?"

Jason sighs. "There was another incident. Happened a few days ago. I was—"

"Another incident related to human trafficking?"

"No, no. Completely different. Nothing to do with Spencer Uccello. It happened in the building where my new office is. And it's in the news. The *Globe*. A man fell down an elevator shaft. Horrible thing. But I'm mentioned in the article. And so is my office."

"That philanthropist? I heard about that. You're right—it was horrible, just horrible. But wasn't he in some kind of self-storage place? I thought it sounded odd that there was an elevator. Aren't those usually just garages lined up next to each other?"

"This is a building. The units are inside the building. It's big, and there are five floors, so—"

"Are you telling me your new office is in a storage unit?"

"That's what I'm telling you," Jason says miserably. "I'm sorry, Mom. I—"

"Oh, Jason, I thought I raised a smarter boy. Why would we care where your office is?"

37

LIDDY

Liddy doesn't recognize the doorman when she enters the lobby of The Tower. It's been a little over three months since she walked out of here on that crisp fall afternoon, and except for the unfamiliar face and the snow outside, it's exactly the same as when she left. Which feels odd, although it probably shouldn't. Why would it be different just because she is?

"Welcome home, Ms. Haines," the doorman says. Is there a Tower resident recognition test that potential employees have to pass in order to be hired? Either that or he saw her picture online or in the *Globe*.

"Thank you," she says, and quickly walks to the elevator. Normally, she would introduce herself, find out his name, a little about his life, but nothing is normal today. She hesitates before pushing the elevator button, shudders at the thought of climbing into the box. But what choice does she have? It's fifty floors up.

As she rises, Liddy's stomach slips. She can visualize Garrett sprawled on the top of the car, almost feel the weight of him over her head. Jason and the police made sure she didn't see his broken body at Metropolis, but her imagination is strong, and it's almost as if she had.

When she walks through the door and turns on the lights against the encroaching afternoon darkness, the condo is also exactly as it was. Blanca, who comes in twice a week, must have been here this morning.

Liddy catches the faint scent of lemon oil, and when she walks into the bedroom, there are vacuum marks on the carpet.

Liddy's mind careens as she tries not to think about Garrett. About the accident. About her culpability. What a thing to have happened. What a thing to have had a hand in. Fortunately, she'd never told anyone about discovering the PI or trying to figure out how to counter Garrett's next step. She'd purposely never mentioned this to Marta. And she's pretty sure she never discussed the girl's accident at Fenway with anyone but Garrett.

She was forced to show the police her unit, as they asked what she and Garrett were doing at Metropolis. When they saw it, she explained that she used it as a writer's retreat and sometimes slept there when she was working late. To say they were skeptical would be an understatement. The popcorn and marijuana didn't help. When they find out she's been hiding from Garrett for months, all bets are off. Many people, including friends, Burke colleagues, and the staff at The Tower will report they haven't seen her since September. And then there's Garrett. If he's able to tell his side of the story, she's screwed.

Robin and Scott are at the hospital with Garrett, have been for hours. Even though he's in the ICU in an induced coma and they only allow visitors in one at a time, every hour, for only five minutes. Until the swelling in his brain is reduced, he'll most likely remain in that state for days. If not weeks.

How will this mess with the twins' world? With their heads? Their futures? Liddy shudders. The rush of images, sounds, and the unpredictable forking outcomes are relentless. Earlier, as Liddy had scanned the faces of the arriving passengers at Logan, she almost hadn't recognized her own children. In the four months since they'd left for school, Robin had grown at least two inches and lost a cushion of baby fat that left her appearing more like a young woman than a child. Scott, on the other hand, could have been Robin's younger brother. He'd gained no height but had added on quite a few pounds.

When they caught sight of her, they hurled themselves at her, clutching her the way they had when they were small. Liddy wrapped her arms around them, pressed her nose to their hair, and drank in their slightly sour smell. Her babies. Her poor, poor babies. "It's going to be okay," she murmured over and over again. "It's going to be okay."

Robin, dark like her father, was the first to pull away, her long eyelashes clumped together with tears. "Is it? He's going to be okay?"

Scott, light like Liddy, raised his face to her.

"The doctors are hopeful," she told them. "He's in pretty bad shape now, but there are reasons to think this could turn around."

They accepted her words, but the fear didn't leave their eyes, and she took them directly to the hospital. Liddy begged the ICU nurse to let the three of them go in together, but she was allowed to take in only one at a time. Robin wanted to go first, but as soon as she stepped around the curtain, she backed away from the bandaged, bruised, and unconscious man, then fled to the waiting room. Scott was more stoic, but he didn't last much longer than his sister.

Neither of the kids is particularly close to Garrett, but huddling with her stricken children in the waiting room reminded Liddy that, despite his coolness to them and what he'd done to her, he was their father and always would be, that they loved him and needed him. It was Robin who insisted that she, Liddy, go home to shower and get a change of clothes. As reluctant as Liddy was to leave them alone, she was desperate to get out of the hospital. She promised to return in an hour and told them not to go in to see Garrett until she did.

Now she strips, throws the clothes she knows she'll never wear again into the hamper, and steps into the shower. She turns it as hot as she can tolerate, stands under the almost blistering water, and cries. At first, she was so shocked she couldn't cry, and since Robin and Scott arrived she hasn't let herself. Now she does. Wrenching, full-bodied sobs, wails—for what happened, for what might happen to Garrett, to Marta, to herself. But mostly for her children, whose lives will never be the same. And for the fault she bears in that.

When there are no tears left and her throat feels as if it's been stripped of its lining, she climbs out of the shower, overwhelmed by a torrent of conflicted feelings for Garrett. Her husband, the father of her children, is either going to die or remain severely incapacitated. She's been furious at him for years, even wished him dead at times, but now she remembers the other Garrett, the good Garrett.

How much fun they'd had together in the early years. The cross-country road trip, the trek through Greece, the sweet nights in her tiny apartment and even tinier bed, summer evenings in the company box at Fenway, the outfield grass an Ireland green. All the laughter, all the love and hope. How generous he'd always been to her and the kids, the millions of dollars he'd donated to charities every year, how he'd stepped in to help her mother.

Admittedly, she's wanted to be free of him, and there's no denying that his fall might hand her exactly that. Which gives her motive. She left him and lied about where she was going. There are people who can testify to her real feelings for him. She'd inherit many millions of dollars. The spouse is always the first to be suspected. A bolt of terror drives itself between her ribs.

The detectives asked her the same questions over and over and over again, both last night and this morning. From the details of the accident and their argument to how much money Garrett is worth. "So if the worst happens, you're going to be a very rich lady," one cop had remarked.

"I'm already a very rich lady," she told him.

And although Jason smiled at her statement, the cop did not.

She thinks she managed to give the same answer each time and knows she didn't mention Marta, but it was all so confusing she can't be sure. At Metropolis, Jason had patted her back when they finally let her go, so at least she'd convinced him. Unless he was just trying to show the police that he believed her. "No comment," was all she'd said to the media outside Metropolis, the hospital, and the police station. The same when they'd stormed her just now on the sidewalk in front of The Tower, three doormen forcing them into the street, the concierge promising police assistance to keep them from the building.

Liddy towels her hair dry and puts on her bathrobe, which hangs on the back of the door, as it always has. Her creams and cosmetics are on the counter, exactly where she left them, and she applies them by rote. She looks at herself in the mirror and would have been shocked by the swelling around her red-rimmed eyes, by her sunken cheeks and blotched skin, if she weren't so shocked by everything else.

She tries not to picture Garrett as he lay in the ICU, almost unrecognizable, intubated and hooked up to an impossible number of machines, tubes running in and out of his body, his face purple, eyes invisible under the swollen folds, curved metal tongs screwed into his skull. But she can't stop herself. Nor can she stop the overwhelming guilt for her role in this.

He suffered multiple bone fractures, including to the ribs, limbs, and face, contusions to the lungs and other internal organs, and an unspecified traumatic brain injury. But the greatest concern is the partial severing of his spine at C2, one of the highest cervical vertebrae. It wasn't completely cut through, which would have guaranteed quadriplegia, total paralysis from the neck down. Although that might be the case anyway.

The doctors decide to bring Garrett out of his coma. Although the brain swelling hasn't subsided as much as they would like, he has to be awake in order for them to determine the extent of his injuries. An unconscious man may not respond to a pinprick even if there's feeling in his limb. Robin is with Garrett when he begins to stir, and after alerting the nurses, she comes into the waiting room to tell them. For once, the staff allows all three of them into the ICU together.

"Dad," Robin whispers, tears running down her face. "It's me, Robin. We're all here."

"Hey, Pops," Scott says, choking back a sob.

Liddy remains silent.

"R-rrrr," Garrett says as he tries to speak through his swollen and cracked lips.

"Yes, it's me. It's Robin, your daughter."

Garrett tries to move his head, but it's immobilized by the tongs. "Wa-wa-wa," he stutters, then lets out a sound like the shriek of an injured and terrified animal.

The howl reverberates inside Liddy's skull, as it clearly does for the kids, and they all jump back from the bed. A nurse gently suggests it's best if they return to the waiting room. No one argues. When they get there, they collapse in a heap on the couch, holding on to each other.

Liddy presses the twins to her. Her babies are completely devastated, and her heart rips open. She hasn't fully explained what happened, just told them Garrett accidentally stumbled into the elevator door and described the Fenway Park incident. When Scott asked what they were doing at Metropolis, Liddy said they had a storage unit there and were bringing in some boxes.

"He tried to say Robin," Liddy says, trying to console them. "He recognized you. That's a good sign."

Scott wipes his face with a tissue from the box on the coffee table and stands at the window, hands shoved into his pockets. "I don't know what to wish for."

Liddy closes her eyes, hiding from the anguish on her son's face. A wish for Garrett to live might lead to a life of pain and paralysis. To wish him to die is, well, to wish him to die. "Let's wish for a full recovery," she says.

Scott turns. "And if that's not a possibility?"

"Don't say that!" Robin cries. "It is possible!"

Scott looks at his sister, his face set, then it softens. "Right. Right. Let's go with that."

Liddy knows if Garrett pulls through, he'll tell a different story. He'll accuse her of trying to kill him, counter her contention that she sidestepped his attack and claim it was she who pushed him. Although it would be his word against hers, his word might hold more sway, especially with the police's suspicions already raised. And if he recovers, he'll turn Marta into ICE. He's been cuckolded by her, a woman. A man scorned, particularly W. Garrett Haines III, is not a force to be underestimated.

FIVE DAYS LATER, Garrett is still heavily medicated and sleeps almost twenty-three hours out of twenty-four. He's strapped to a rotating bed, both his legs and one arm in casts. There are weights attached to the tongs in his head, stretching his neck. It's a horrible, wrenching state, bad for the twins to see every day.

He hasn't responded to the pinpricks, isn't able to move anything below his neck. Nor can he speak, his attempts a guttural mishmash of sound. The doctors say it's still early, that things might change, but as the days pass, that outcome is becoming difficult to believe in.

Robin and Scott insist they're going to stay until Garrett is stable, that they won't leave Liddy alone before there's a more definitive diagnosis, but it's clear to her that they have to return to school. There's nothing for them to do in Boston but stare at their paralyzed father. She supposes she could find a private school in the area, but it's halfway through the year and if they're in Zurich, they'll be distracted by their classes and friends and extracurriculars. Here, this is impossible.

Their presence as well as their company has been such a support, and Liddy doesn't want them to leave. She wants to beg them to stay with her forever, but she doesn't. Instead, she forces them to go.

38

MARTA

It has been over a week, and although she has spoken to Liddy on the phone, this will be the first time they have seen each other since the accident. Liddy is enduring the worst days of her life, and Marta assumes that the woman who will come through the door will be a very different Liddy than the one she has known.

Marta is different also. Isolation and fear and unbearable longing will do that to a person. There are only a dozen apartments in Jason's building, and they agreed that she should stay inside his place as much as possible. If ICE or the police come around, it will be best if the other tenants have no knowledge of her. This means she is a captive inside his small rooms.

The apartment is what Jason said is called railroad-style. There are three rooms back-to-back, and there is very little natural light. The front door opens into a small living room, filled with furniture too large for it, and there are two tiny windows facing an alley. The kitchen follows, with no windows at all. The bedroom is reached through the kitchen and has three windows, but they look onto the brick exterior of the building next door. Jason apologized for the lack of amenities, but Marta just laughed. She has been living in far worse conditions.

Jason leaves by six in the morning and often does not come home until ten at night. He is careful to stay out of her way. She tries to do the same, but this is difficult, as she has not been outside since she arrived that horrible night, and she works doggedly on her dissertation in his living room to muffle her fears. Her first draft is almost complete, and she is aware her time in Jason's apartment is limited. As are her options. Perhaps she should return to Metropolis. Or take her chances with a judge. She searches for a premonition to guide her, but *una hija* is not there. Nor is *una hija* available for Liddy, both their futures dark and unknowable.

The intercom beeps, and Marta hurries to push the button. She opens the door at Liddy's knock, but stays hidden until Liddy enters the room and she can close it behind her. Marta and Liddy lock eyes for a long moment, then they grab each other, press themselves together. They cry, then laugh, then cry again. Liddy's tears take longer to subside.

Marta leads her to the couch and then goes into the bathroom to wet a washcloth with cold water and grab a box of tissues. She has no idea how Liddy will bear this. Witnessing Garrett's fall. Feeling responsible for his condition. Being a mainstay for her children. Tolerating police suspicions and the media's devotion to dramatic speculation. Spending days at the hospital, pretending she cares about a man whom she despises.

"Please lie down, Lid." Marta gently tips Liddy so that her head rests on the soft arm of the couch and her legs are stretched out on the cushions. Marta presses the washcloth over Liddy's eyes. Liddy has been strong for everyone else, and now Marta must be strong so that Liddy does not have to be. "There," she murmurs. "This will make you feel better."

Liddy does not respond.

Marta is horrified by Liddy's appearance. She has lost at least ten pounds, and her beautiful cheekbones are so starkly defined under her pale skin that she appears otherworldly. "I will go make us some tea," she says. "I have asked Jason to buy a box of your lemon ginger."

"Good old Jason . . ." Liddy hiccups and tries to laugh, but it turns into a sob. "I'm sure I'm all cried out, but then it seems there's always more."

Marta kisses her on the forehead. "I am right here. I am with you." When her words make Liddy cry harder, Marta adds, "If this is the way you feel about it, then I am not here. I am leaving. I am going to the kitchen."

Liddy raises her arm and grabs Marta's hand. "Just make sure you don't go any farther."

When Marta returns with two steaming mugs in her hands, Liddy has removed the washcloth and stopped crying, although her eyes are still closed and her breathing is ragged. Marta puts the tea on the coffee table, sits, and then lifts Liddy's legs, placing them on her own lap. "You look like hell," she tells Liddy.

Liddy opens one eye. "You don't look so great yourself."

"I am still glad to see you."

"Me too."

When Liddy says nothing else, Marta asks, "Do you want to talk about it?"

"Do I have to?"

"No." Marta raises Liddy's hand, turns the palm upward, and kisses it. "We can be quiet, or you can talk about something else."

"Is there anything else to talk about?"

"There is always the weather."

"I haven't even noticed." Liddy pushes herself up on one arm and looks out the small window overlooking the alley. "Still winter," she says.

"Would you like to talk about the results of my multivariate regression analyses?"

"Maybe later," Liddy says with a small smile.

"How about my varimax rotation?" Marta asks, encouraged by Liddy's response.

"They're almost certain he's going to lose the use of the lower half of his body."

"Oh," is all Marta can say. "This is a terrible thing."

"It's also possible he may not be able to move anything below his shoulders." Liddy looks at Marta, her eyes beseeching. "Please don't hate me, but I think the worst thing about this is that it looks like he may regain almost all of his brain function."

"Oh," Marta says again as she takes in the implications of Liddy's words. "You think I will hate you because you are afraid of what Garrett will be like if he has a brain and no body?" She flinches at the image conjured by her words. "I would never feel this way about you. And especially not for this."

"I feel for him. I do." Liddy sits up. "It's the worst thing that can ever happen to a person, short of death. Maybe even worse. And it's terrible for the kids to see him like this. But if his brain recovers, he's going to lash out." She buries her head in Marta's chest. "And if he dies, how will I live with the guilt?"

"There is nothing to feel guilty about if he lives or if he dies." Marta strokes Liddy's hair gently and massages her scalp. "He was the one who turned ugly. He was trying to hurt you. When you stepped out of his way, you were protecting yourself. You did nothing wrong. And soon the police will recognize this as the truth."

"We don't know that!" Liddy's voice rises, and there is a note of hysteria in it. "No one does!" Liddy's eyes wildly scan the room, and her pupils are huge.

Marta thinks back to Liddy's restlessness and preoccupation in the days before Garrett appeared, her lack of surprise when she saw him standing in the open doorway, her warning about the elevator. "Please, please do not do this to yourself," Marta begs, and pulls Liddy back into her arms. "It was a terrible accident. Just because you were there does not make you responsible."

"He'll come after me. Punish me for all he believes I did and didn't do. And punish you." Liddy holds Marta fiercely. "He'll do everything he can to get you deported—and he's a man who can do more than most." She lets go and slumps into the couch. "He once told me he'd kill me before he'd let me be with anyone else."

Marta struggles not to physically react to the fear that spikes through her. "If he lives, I believe it is possible that this experience will change him. Even he will have to appreciate the gift he has been given. An over-do? A do-over, yes? It seems he will want to live every day to its fullest. He will want to let go of his old hostilities and enjoy what he has."

"One would think," Liddy says. They sit silently, holding each other.

"I was thinking I should return to Metropolis," Marta says, groping for a change of subject. "This is not nice for Jason. He has given up his home to me. But now I am not sure. Do you think this is not a good idea, because if Garrett recovers he will tell ICE where I am?"

Liddy pulls away. "Could you stick it out here a little longer? At least until we know what he's going to be capable of?"

"I am concerned this is not fair to Jason. As you can see, it is a very small apartment, and he insists that I sleep in his bed while he sleeps on the couch every night."

"Really?" Liddy raises an eyebrow, and she looks almost like herself for the first time since she walked through the door. "His bed?"

"Ah!" Marta is thrilled Liddy is able to joke. "So you are jealous?"

"Has he asked to join you in this bed?"

"He has always been a perfect gentleman." Marta adopts a coy look. "But who knows what might happen if I remain here? He is an appealing man."

"Does he know about us?" Liddy is suddenly serious. "He saw us in our bathrobes when, when . . . he saw us together."

"I do not think he noticed this."

"How does he feel about you moving back to Metropolis?"

"He does not think it is a good idea either. He said sometimes there are policemen there, even if they are not ICE. They are still checking the elevator. He says they are reviewing paperwork and information about the tenants." Marta sighs. "He told me Rose was fired."

"The owner found out we were living in the building? That's going to make things really rough. Her husband is out of work. And the issues with her son."

"That was not the reason. She forgot to get the elevator inspected, and Jason says this mistake opens the building owner to a negligence suit."

Liddy's eyes cloud. "And we know who's going to jump all over that."

"At least he will not be able to do any of this soon. Not in his condition."

"He's improving every day on the cognitive tests. His speech is much better. Some of the time he's even understandable."

"But if he cannot move, he will not be—"

"That's what assistants are for. All he has to do is ask Rochelle to call the feds and tell them where you are. He has lawyers in-house, so he'll just ask one of them to get all the suits moving forward against the building owner and whomever else he can sue. It's not like he has to do any of the work himself." Liddy's shoulders droop. "If it weren't for me, you wouldn't be in this mess."

"None of this is your fault," Marta assures her.

But is this correct? Liddy knew the elevator was broken. Liddy wanted more than anything to be free of him. He'd threatened to turn her, Marta, in to ICE, and Marta knows Liddy would do whatever she could to protect her.

Liddy shrugs and picks at the pills on the washcloth. "Still."

"Do not even think these things. Meeting you and being with you are worth any risk."

Liddy takes Marta's hand. "So you'll stay here?"

"I think I should not leave now." Marta does not mention that she and Jason have been considering an asylum hearing. Liddy doesn't need another thing to worry about. "Jason tells me that I can stay for as long as I wish. But how can he mean this?"

"From what you've told me, I think he's got a sweet spot for you," Liddy says with a faint smile. "Just don't tell him about us. That could screw your whole deal."

Before Liddy can slip back into sadness, Marta says, "And speaking of us . . ." She winks. "Jason's bed is very nice . . ."

Their lovemaking is rough. They bite and they yell and they twist, and they try to drive everything else away. This works for a while, and the world disappears. But as they lie tangled in the sheets, sweaty and breathing heavily, reality comes roaring back. There is no escape. They clasp each other tight, and then they both fall into a heavy sleep.

Marta wakes to the sound of Jason's voice, a singsong "Hi, Marta, I'm ho-o-me."

"Shit," Liddy says. "Guess we've screwed your deal."

39

JASON

The police have been in and out of Metropolis for the week and a half since the accident. But in recent days, instead of cops, most of them appear to be techies, taking photographs, measuring, climbing around in the elevator shaft, and they ask Jason no questions. This would seem to indicate the police have accepted his version of the events, and as he's spending at least twelve hours a day at his desk, it would be a real pain in the ass if they hadn't. If only he could say the same for Liddy.

Two people in his tiny apartment is less than ideal. Marta tries to make herself as unobtrusive as she can, and he does the same. But it's an impossible feat, given the square footage. It can't go on like this, especially as his attraction to her grows. And because she's right there, constantly thanking him and apologizing for her presence, he's even less comfortable with his feelings. Still, he's glad he forced her to leave Metropolis that night, offered to let her stay with him, glad he lied to the police to protect her. His family's acceptance of his departure from Spencer Uccello has given him a different perspective on what he chose to do there. And what he chose to do for Marta.

After she acknowledged that returning to Metropolis wasn't a good idea, they've been discussing taking her chances before a judge. He's confident he's devised a strong case for asylum, yet there are so many particularities he can't control: ICE officers, the judge, the police, laws that can change at a moment's notice. Not to mention the current administration's penchant for what can only be described as cruelty, which is especially perilous for Marta because she disregarded a deportation order. But now that it looks like Haines will make a full mental recovery and will most certainly report her to ICE, the courtroom may be the only remaining choice.

Tonight it's freezing outside, windy and predicted to plunge into single digits, but he walks into Central Square for dinner anyway. To Brick & Trowel, where the martinis are excellent and the burger with cheddar and bacon and some kind of magical sauce is, as far as he's concerned, the best in the city. After a couple of hours of eating and drinking and talking to an attractive woman who works in an MIT lab doing experiments on pig tendons, he wraps himself up and heads out. It's almost nine, late enough to go home.

He's looking forward to being with Marta, talking and watching that incredible smile flit across her face. Maybe she'll be up for a movie. Sometimes she is. Mostly romantic comedies, and who can blame her for wanting this escape? And then they'll sit together on the couch, mostly in silence, but a comfortable silence, watching the lovers who bend themselves into ridiculous contortions that tear them apart, but who almost always end up happily ever after.

He doesn't see her when he walks into the apartment, scans the living room and kitchen, and for a moment he's panicked that she might have left. But she wouldn't do that. She's either in the bathroom or the bedroom. "Hi, Marta, I'm ho-o-me," he says, imitating those 1960s husbands in the sitcom reruns his father thinks are hilarious.

He hears sounds from the bedroom and sits down on the couch to give her some privacy. It really is way too small in here for two people. Unless they're a couple.

"I'll be right out!" she calls from the other side of the bedroom door.

He picks up the remote and turns on the television, searches for romantic comedies. But before he can find anything he thinks Marta might like, she comes out of the bedroom. With Liddy. Both women are rumpled and have guilty looks on their faces.

Marta takes Liddy's hand. "Guess we should have told you before," she says with a flush and a broad smile on her face. She glances lovingly up at Liddy.

Liddy waves her fingers. "Hey, Jason."

He's speechless. How could he have not seen this? How could he not have suspected? The two of them in front of the elevator. Holding on to each other as if they would never let go. Marta refusing to leave Liddy. Liddy ordering her to do so. Both in bathrobes.

He stands and gives Liddy a hug. "Hey, you. Welcome to my castle." He smiles and insists she sit down, asks what he can get her. He winks at Marta, to show her he's okay with this. But he's not all that okay with it. He's actually, and stupidly, crushed.

40

ZACH

Five months later: June 2018

Now that he's moved from developing to printing, Zach is even more intrigued by the whole photography thing. It takes forever to get the prints to look right, but he relishes the challenge. He makes every rookie mistake and then finds ingenious new ways to screw up, which to him is part of the fun of learning a new skill: figuring out how to get better at it.

He spills chemicals on the floor because he rocks the trays too hard. He mixes up his tongs and contaminates the developer. He doesn't wrap the photographic paper tightly enough, rendering every expensive sheet in the pack useless. On Monday, when he removes a photo from the water, the paper is pink. On Tuesday, the paper is brown. And on Wednesday, it's covered with white specks. But every once in a while, he prints a decent one, and the previous mistakes become necessary stepping stones.

Some of the rolls Zach has developed are photos of Metropolis, and although he's determined from the negatives that they don't contain anything potentially damaging to him, he prints them anyway. It strikes him that Metropolis is a living organism comprised of hundreds of cells, a gestalt greater than its parts, and he's curious about how it worked when it was occupied.

A repository for memories and treasures and secrets and junk. Things to be honored. Things someone forgot about or was just too lazy or sentimental to throw away. And all these people. Did they know each another?

Were there friendships, love affairs? Even with his neophyte attempts, many of the prints glow with complexity and unexpectedness, although there's an aura of melancholy emanating from almost all of them.

Which, once again, raises questions about Serge, his state of mind, his state of being. The sadness in the photos seems to bear out Zach's notion that something happened to the man—and that it wasn't good. Maybe he should take a break from printing the gloomy Metropolis photos, even if they are extraordinary.

The film he shot that day at Downtown Crossing is still inside the Rolleiflex. He takes the camera from the linen closet and removes the roll, holds it in his hand, spins it between his palms. He doesn't really want to see his amateur efforts after working with Serge's, but he's curious, so he develops the negatives and prints the contact sheet.

He's surprised to find that one of his photos isn't half-bad: a rear shot of the tall woman in the billowing red cape—which, of course, isn't red in the black-and-white shot but somehow almost looks like it is—marching out of the lower right side of the picture. You can see the authority in the set of her shoulders, the defiance in her stride, almost sense her story. It has a touch of the intimacy Serge conjures, and the off-center composition lends it a touch of intrigue, as does the fact that she's slightly out of focus.

As soon as it's dry, Zach goes to the living room to show Lori. But the living room is dark, as are the grounds outside the windows. When he checks the clock and sees it's after eleven, he winces. Lori is going to give him some serious shit for letting the zone swallow another evening.

She's in bed, reading a decorating magazine. When he enters the room, she doesn't lift her head.

"Want to see something cool?" he asks her.

She holds up a finger, flips between two pages, and then folds down the corner of one. "Can it wait? I've got a showing first thing in the morning."

"But you're reading."

"I was just about to turn the light out." She places the magazine on the nightstand and raises her hand to the lamp.

"It'll be quick." Zach thrusts the photograph at her. "I shot it, developed it, and printed it. Not bad, huh?"

Lori takes the photo from him. "It's nice," she says. "Another picture you plan to sell to random suckers?"

Zach retrieves the photo and returns to his darkroom. He works there for another couple of hours, and as he hoped, she's asleep when he gets into bed. He breaks up with her the next day. So much for making it to a year.

ZACH DEVELOPS TWO rolls of Metropolis photos that are nothing like anything he's seen before. He prints the two contact sheets and then about half of the individual photographs. As he watches the images rise from the watery depths of his tray, he's completely bowled over. Each is of a single storage unit and has the same feel as Serge's photos depicting people, except there are no people in the shot.

Instead, there are scenes he saw at the auction: the fancy office, the austere bedroom, Liddy Haines's pied-à-terre, which, because of the light spilling through the windows, looks more like a hotel's luxury suite. Others are completely new to him: units filled with wine, doghouses, bicycles, and one that appears to hold hundreds of violins. There are children's toys and toilet seats and broken chairs, beat-up suitcases and mattresses, and a seemingly endless number of shoes. Although the photographs are devoid of people, they somehow still contain their owners, who hover, invisible and ghostlike.

Zach has no idea how Serge pulled this off, but the pictures are heart-stoppingly brilliant. The hoarders' units—filled with unopened Amazon boxes, broken-down machinery, racks of clothes with their tags still attached—cry out with unanswerable questions and untold stories. But the collectors are even more fascinating, as are the things they chose to accumulate. Wine and violins and books, even doghouses, he can understand, but what's with hundreds of elephant statues, cartons overflowing with campaign buttons, or three walls of shelves lined with Princess Diana dolls?

His awe soon morphs into rage, as he realizes how Serge got access to these shots. Rose. She knew it was both illegal and unethical to allow a stranger into a unit without the tenant's permission. She knew it was her responsibility to ensure the elevator was inspected every year. And she should have known Liddy Haines was living in her unit and, most likely, Serge was too. A dereliction of duty on so many fronts. Her actions vis-à-vis Serge and Liddy may technically have nothing to do with his own forfeiture of Metropolis, but Zach is unable to separate her felonies from her misdemeanors.

41

SERGE

"Hey, listen to this, Scarecrow!" Diamond yells even though she's sitting right next to him.

He lifts his head from the bench. He thought her name was Ruby but now he knows it's Diamond. This is good because she got mad at him and yelled whenever he called her Ruby and for the longest time he didn't understand why. But now he knows. Before he called her Ruby he called her Red Poncho in his head. He never said it out loud because he knew it wasn't really her name. But she does always wear the red poncho. Ruby red.

She waves a newspaper in front of his nose. "Look! Your old stomping grounds!"

He puts his head back on the bench.

"Sit up!" she commands. "This is important!"

He does what she asks. He usually does what she asks even though he's not exactly sure why. She brings him food, for one thing, like she just did. And she brings him places where someone else brings him food. But she's always talking in exclamation points. He prefers commas.

Diamond takes his plate off the bench and puts it underneath. She lays a crumpled-up newspaper between them, smooths it down. "Look!" she orders.

He looks but doesn't see anything but a bunch of scribbles and a photograph of a castle. Diamond never takes his plate away, especially not when there's still food on it because she's always screaming that he doesn't eat enough. So this must be important.

He looks again, blinks. He knows it isn't scribbles. He's not an idiot. It's words. They're sentences that will explain why Diamond took his plate away. He doesn't really care why she took it away, but it's sort of interesting that she did.

There's not that much interesting in his days anymore. He sits with Diamond and sometimes the others on the grass, except that it's all brown now and sometimes there aren't enough chairs and there's snow—so you can't sit without getting wet but he sits anyway. He likes it better when it's just the two of them. He also likes it if he can lie under the bench, but if Diamond sees him doing that she screams some more, so he only gets to do it when she's not around.

When it's dark Diamond takes him to where he slides his tray and people put food on it. It doesn't taste too bad. Sometimes he sleeps there but most of the time he doesn't. He likes to eat there but not to sleep there. Too bright. Too noisy. Too many people who talk too much. Lots of them yell just like Diamond.

She punches her finger at the picture of the castle. "Metropolis Storage Warehouse! Remember? You said you lived there!"

He thinks about this, but he's pretty sure he never lived in a castle. "I never lived in a castle."

Diamond throws her hands in the air. "It's not a fucking castle! It's a storage place, and you were living inside one of the storage units!"

"There are turrets."

"Scarecrow! It's just a building!"

He thinks about this and puts his head on the bench again. Now she's talking in lots of exclamation points and it makes him not want to talk to her anymore. But he says, "I never lived there either."

"You told me you did! A guy fell down the elevator shaft! Can you believe it? Fucking A. A real rich bastard too. What a way to go. I'd rather freeze to death or drown or anything else, but smashing two stories into concrete! Fucking A."

"I never lived anywhere where there was an elevator."

"You did! You told me you did!" She presses her face close to his and her breath smells like coffee and maybe a kind of rot. "Were you lying to me?"

"I don't lie, but sometimes I forget," he admits.

42

LIDDY

It's been two months since the accident, and Liddy no longer runs mental replays of "the good Garrett" or harbors illusions that he'll emerge from his trauma a kinder and gentler man. Suing the owner of Metropolis is one thing, informing ICE about Marta's whereabouts, although not unexpected, is quite another. Yet Liddy wrestles with guilt and a detached pity for the man. Her dreams resurrect that night in fractured and tilted ways that leave her confused and sweating. Her conflicting memories and even more conflicting emotions hollow out her soul.

Garrett is still in the metal halo, still strapped to the bed, and although the cast is off his arm, the two on his legs remain. It appears that he'll regain movement above his waist, and the swelling and bruising on his face are almost gone. But half his scalp remains heavily bandaged, and the rest is covered with a multitude of angry scars. The worst is the stillness of his lower body, his legs lifeless on the bed.

She visits him every other day, a task she detests but considers part of her penance. "You botched it, and I'm still alive," he hissed at her the last time she went, the raw fury in his eyes forcing her to step back. "I was there, and I remember, and I'm going to make sure you pay for what you did to me. Big-time."

•••

LIDDY AND MARTA are on the couch at Jason's apartment. "I'm so sorry Garrett did this to you, and I keep kicking myself for ever marrying such an ass," Liddy says.

"You were young and very much in love. This is not a good recipe for seeing clearly."

The truth is that Liddy had known but had deliberately chosen not to see—or, more precisely, had chosen to see only one side of the two-faced Janus she'd married. He'd been so crazy in love with her, probably still is in his demented, controlling way, and being adored is a drug that blurs your vision. It's also a tough drug to walk away from.

Marta interrupts Liddy's ruminations. "There is no point in worrying yourself with these questions. He may have tried to do a spiteful and cruel thing to me, but he did not succeed. I am fortunate that both you and Jason insisted I not move back to Metropolis, so I wasn't there for ICE to find."

Liddy gives Marta a light kiss, tries to take her advice. "What would we do without Jason?"

"I am concerned that there is—how do you say?—something going off with him."

"Because he's got the hots for you," Liddy teases.

"I believe it has to do with his old job. There was trouble there, and this is why a lawyer of his caliber is in an office at Metropolis and living in this tiny apartment. I think he might move away."

"He said that?" Liddy is surprised at how upsetting she finds this.

"He has not, but I am still concerned."

"His family is all here, and they're very close. He wouldn't leave them," Liddy says, then notices the expression on Marta's face. "Is this one of your premonitions?" She's not sure she believes in Marta's *una hija* abilities; it's an absurd notion. But Marta never lies, and she does seem to have a sense about things.

"I am not certain, but I feel trouble is around Jason. It is how I felt trouble around you the night Garrett came. I have tried to encourage him to talk, but this is not his way."

Before Liddy can answer, her phone rings. It's Jason. "Hey, you. Speak of the devil. I'm at your apartment. If you're coming home in time for dinner, I'll run out and pick us up some Mexican." Jason loves Mexican.

"Listen, Liddy, we need to talk."

She clutches the phone.

"I got a call from Garrett's lawyer, Gene Blalock. I told him I wasn't representing you, and that I didn't know who was, but he insisted I give you this message anyway."

Liddy throws Marta a desperate look and puts the phone on speaker.

"They're planning to tell the police you intentionally pushed him and that you knew the elevator was broken," Jason says.

Liddy's ears ring, and dots of black threaten to blot out her vision. "How, how could he even think of such a thing?" But she knows exactly how he could think of such a thing.

"Blalock insinuated there's evidence it was tampered with, that you messed with the elevator and plotted to kill him. They're going to claim it was premeditated."

Stay calm. Think. Think. Breathe. No one knows she discovered Garrett's PI. No one knows that she knew about the Red Sox elevator incident. No one but Marta knows she knew the elevator door was off its hinge, and Marta will never tell. "I was hiding from him," she finally says. "If I thought he was going to show up, why didn't I just leave? Why set up some inane trap?"

"You can make all the logical arguments you want about your state of mind, but if they go to the police, who already have their eye on you, the cops could believe there's enough evidence to—"

"But there isn't!" Liddy cries. "No evidence I pushed him. No evidence I was trying to kill him! What do I know about elevators?"

"True, but they maintain anyone standing in front of the elevator would have been able to see it was broken. Garrett is the injured party here, the sympathetic party, and he's ready to put everything he's got behind it. Which is why you have to get yourself a top-notch criminal lawyer. ASAP."

Liddy clutches Marta's hand more tightly. Panic closes her throat.

"The evidence shows there was a scuffle," Jason continues. "And even though you said you stepped aside when he lunged at you, they have medical proof he hit the door with his back, which they contend could only have happened if he were pushed. I'm sorry, Liddy, but this makes your statement suspect. Along with your credibility."

Liddy groans and crumples into herself. The twins. The police. A trial. The media. Marta.

"Liddy?" Jason asks. "Are you there? Are you okay? Put Marta on."

"No," Liddy says. "I mean, yes—yes, I'm here."

"Garrett is offering a deal."

A way out. A way out. A way out.

"He wants you to leave Marta, agree to never be involved with anyone else, man or woman, and move back in with him. To be a couple again."

"No."

"If you do this, he'll drop the suit, won't tell the kids that you tried to kill him, and won't pursue Marta. But if you don't, Garrett plans to take his evidence to the police, find Marta, and have her deported."

It's as if the whole room has disappeared: no couch, no table, no Marta. Just white. Pure-terror white.

"He's willing to give you a short waiting period to consider this before he goes to the police," Jason adds when Liddy doesn't respond.

Liddy blinks. The world returns, and she wishes it hadn't.

"This is a tough one." Jason pauses. "Blalock said Garrett wants you to know he loves you more than ever and that he wants to spend the rest of his life with you."

Despite her anguish, or maybe because of it, Liddy bursts out laughing. "He thinks I tried to kill him, and he wants to spend the rest of his life with me? He loves me so much he's blackmailing me in order to keep me?" What she doesn't say is that it isn't love; it's revenge.

"There's something else."

"Of course there is." Liddy's laugher becomes louder, raw, and Marta holds her tighter.

"I'm serious. Liddy, listen to me. You have to leave my apartment. Right now."

Her laughing ceases as rapidly as it started. "Why?"

"Think about it. If he's playing this kind of game, looking for ways to hurt you, it's logical to assume he's already in the process of finding Marta. He discovered where you both were before, and it's pretty easy pickings for him to follow you to her now."

LIDDY GETS A burner so her calls to Marta can't be traced, and although they talk to each other multiple times a day, it's a far cry from being together. When Marta first moved to Jason's, they attempted to reinstate their practice of not interfering with each other's work schedule. But Liddy hasn't been able to write since the accident, and Marta is such a workaholic she needs to be encouraged to take breaks. So the charade has been dropped, and although it's two in the afternoon and Liddy knows she'll be interrupting Marta, she calls anyway.

"Did you speak with the attorney Jason suggested to you?" Marta asks without saying hello.

"Dawn Kenner. Yeah, she's as tough as he said. Maybe too tough."

"Why is this?"

"She wants to play Garrett's game right back at him. Accuse him of tampering with the elevator and trying to kill me."

Marta doesn't respond immediately. "This is a reasonable legal tactic?"

"She seems to think so. Said if they try to use the rigged-elevator argument, even though they haven't provided any proof yet that it was tampered with, we can take this and turn it back on him. Which I have no intention of doing." Liddy doesn't tell her that Dawn was concerned about the evidence that Garrett hit the elevator door with his back. There's no reason to worry Marta more than she already has.

"There is some poetry in her idea."

"I get it, but if I follow her strategy, it'll kick off a media circus that will drag the kids in. Their parents accusing each other of attempted murder? Given Garrett's prominence and the gruesomeness of the accident, it's sure to be a huge story. I can't do that to them. I won't."

"It is a difficult position, but is it not—how do you say?—telling his bluff? And then nothing will come of it."

Liddy laughs. It's astonishing how just talking to Marta makes her feel better. "Calling his bluff."

"So it is possible this attorney has a better idea than you believe."

"Perhaps," Liddy says, to make Marta think she's considering it. But she knows that in this kind of situation, Garrett doesn't bluff. *I was there, and I remember, and I'm going to make sure you pay for what you did to me. Big-time.*

Marta hesitates. "There is something else we must discuss."

Liddy presses her fingers to her temple. "Something I'm not going to like?"

"It is true I have made a decision you may not like. But I believe it is the right one."

Liddy feels the same way she did when Jason told her they needed to talk. "What kind of decision?"

"I plan to move forward with my asylum appeal. I will go before a judge."

"It's too dangerous," Liddy cries. "This is no simple asylum case. You're in violation of a deportation order! It's not possible. You'll get arrested. No. I won't let you do it." She recognizes she has no right to interfere with Marta's decision, but this doesn't stop her. "There are too many things that could go wrong. You can't. Please don't do this!"

Marta waits patiently and, when Liddy is done, says, "Jason thinks I can win, and there is no other choice, which I know you understand. I cannot remain in hiding. I cannot be a burden to Jason. I want to live a normal life, to work, to be with you. It is the only way this can happen."

43

ROSE

Rose worked the 6:00 a.m. to 2:00 p.m. shift, and she comes home exhausted and stinking of grease. Of all the things she hates about this job, the grease is the worst. It sticks to her for hours after she's punched out and makes her feel like the place never leaves her. Grease in her hair and in her skin and in her clothes.

Vince is watching television from his chair when she walks in the door. He doesn't turn, but she says hello on her way to the shower. He's still mad at her, and even if he has the right to be, he also doesn't have the right to be. But all she can think about now is getting rid of the grease that reminds her of the job she now has and the better one she had before.

She started sending out résumés the day after Garrett Haines fell, even though Zach didn't fire her until the next day. She knew it was coming, and what with Vince and all, she had to get a jump on things. She applied for administrative assistant jobs everywhere, from an accountant around the corner to an engineering company in Cambridge to big corporations through Monster.com. Even a couple of staffing agencies. She got lots more interviews than she thought she would, but when her references were over ten years old and she had none from her last position, the employers lost interest real fast. So she took the job at Taco Bell.

She stands under the shower and tries not to get mad at Vince but she does anyway. He still isn't working and when she confessed everything to him about Metropolis he threw a fit. He got all furious over the money she took from Serge, Marta, and Liddy, and especially about her letting Serge into other units to take pictures. Vince said it was immoral and she was immoral and that she'd broken the law. He insisted she go to confession that very day.

But when she came home from church, he was still on the warpath and started in on her about how she had broken the law just so Michael could be on the football team that didn't do anything to stop him from screwing up. Vince claimed he was so deeply disappointed in her that he didn't want to even look at her. That's a laugh. How about how deeply disappointed she is in him—always being in his chair with his drink, and his dirty hair that's no picnic to look at or to smell.

And "immoral" is the wrong word anyways. She didn't hurt anyone and actually helped them by giving them a place to live when they didn't have anywhere else to go. She wasn't blackmailing anyone or threatening them, and they were all happy to pay her. Grateful even. She isn't saying that what she did wasn't wrong because Zach could have gotten into trouble if she got caught, but it wasn't immoral. And it isn't even why Zach is in trouble now. She didn't say any of this to Vince and just listened to him carry on. She doesn't like to argue and didn't want to start a fight that would upset the girls.

After her shower she starts dinner. They've been eating a lot of pasta since she got fired, which is what she's making when the doorbell rings. Vince doesn't move so she wipes her hands and goes down to the first floor. The young girl who's standing on the other side of the glass has skin the color of Marta's and is nicely dressed. Rose opens the door. "Can I help you?"

"I'm looking for Ms. Rose Gentilini," the girl says with a weak smile. When Rose says that's her, the girl pulls an envelope from her oversized bag and offers it to Rose. "This is for you."

Rose takes it from her. "What is it?"

"You've been served." She nods and walks back to the sidewalk.

Rose turns the envelope over and back. Very official-looking. She rips it open. A subpoena ordering her to appear at the law offices of Bernkopf Goodman on March 22, to be deposed in the personal injury lawsuit of W. Garrett Haines III, of Boston, Massachusetts, vs. Metropolis Storage Warehouse, of Cambridge, Massachusetts. Dear Jesus.

"I'M, I MEAN, I was, I was the office manager there," Rose answers Mr. Blalock, Garrett Haines's lawyer. Ms. Rubin, Zach's lawyer, told her to give short answers because if she kept talking she might admit to some important thing by mistake.

"Ms. Gentilini, could you please tell us exactly what your duties were at the Metropolis Storage Warehouse?"

Rose is nervous enough and being called Ms. Gentilini when she always thinks of herself as Mrs. Gentilini is making it worse. She also doesn't like how they keep saying Metropolis Storage Warehouse instead of just Metropolis. She tries to answer Mr. Blalock's question, but she stumbles and stutters and is sure she's repeating herself and leaving things out. She didn't know a deposition was so much like a trial and all official like this. She thought a lawyer was just going to ask her questions in his office.

Instead she's in a big conference room on the thirty-third floor with a huge table and walls on three sides that are all windows facing the water and the city. Mr. Blalock is here with two other people, and Ms. Rubin has one assistant. Then there's the stenographer and two other girls that seem to be just hanging around. The lawyers made Rose swear to tell the truth, and now both of them are asking her questions back and forth and back and forth. She's been afraid of this ever since the girl gave her the envelope, but it's even worse than she thought.

"So one of your duties was to oversee maintenance of the two elevators in the building?"

"Yes," she says, and it comes out almost like a whimper.

Mr. Blalock checks his notes. "And ensuring that annual inspections were completed in a timely fashion was also part of this responsibility?"

She closes her eyes and nods.

"Please speak up, Ms. Gentilini. The court reporter needs verbal responses."

"Yes."

"And when was the last time these inspections were done?"

Rose stares out to the harbor and watches the planes taking off and landing at Logan. She doesn't look at anyone in the room and just answers each question as quickly as she can. Except that no matter how fast she talks, each answer makes her sound like a bigger and bigger fool. And this makes it seem like Zach is a bad owner who cared so little about the safety of his building that he turned the responsibility for it over to a fool.

44

JASON

I t's still dark outside when Jason walks into his office. He slipped out of the apartment without breakfast or even checking his phone, trying not to disturb Marta, who's been having difficulty sleeping. He puts his coffee and muffin on the desk, flips open his computer, and runs his eyes down the voluminous number of emails that came in overnight. There's one from the Boston Immigration Court, and he clicks on it. Mercedes Bustamante is to present herself to Judge Susan Cohen at 10:00 a.m. on April 9, 2018, JFK Federal Building, 15 New Sudbury Street, room 320.

Two weeks ago, Marta had asked him to submit the forms necessary to set up an asylum screening interview, which he did. He's more than familiar with these laborious procedures, but now that his client is an individual rather than a large corporation, the degree of difficulty, not to mention the cost, rankles him.

EOIR-26, Notice of Appeal to the Board of Immigration Appeals from a Decision of a USCIS Officer, $110. EOIR-40, Application for Suspension of Deportation, $100. I-485, Application to Register Permanent Residence or to Adjust Status, $635. And on and on. No wonder there are so many undocumented immigrants in the country. Not for the first time, he thinks about all the people who wouldn't be able to complete all this paperwork. Or pay for it. Or even figure out how to get access to it. Cynic that he is, he has to wonder if this is the point.

He appeared before Judge Cohen a few times when he was at Spencer Uccello, and he respects her. She's smart and strict in a fair-minded way, but sometimes she can be a stickler for the letter of the law. It's this last trait that concerns him. Marta's violation of a deportation order might be enough for the judge to find her ineligible for asylum. But his case is strong, and he's counting on the judge's fair-mindedness and integrity to save Marta in the end.

He adds the hearing to his calendar and then clicks on an email from Metropolis Storage Warehouse: *Metropolis will close its doors on April 28th and all storage units must be vacated by April 20th. Failure to do so will result in forfeiture of all property remaining on the premises.*

Shit. Not unforeseen, but still, shit. He heard that Zach Davidson was forced to turn over the building to Garrett Haines without a penny of compensation. The poor bastard. Davidson, not Haines. Although Jason supposes that Haines is a poor bastard too. But in the case of W. Garrett Haines III, the bastard part is primary.

"So that's the deal," Jason tells Marta over Mexican take-out in his apartment that evening. "There's not much we can do about Metropolis closing down, but I just want to make sure one more time that you're comfortable moving forward with the hearing."

"I am sorry you will be losing your office."

"We knew it was coming." Jason shrugs. "And maybe it's for the best."

Marta puts down her taco, wipes her fingers on her napkin. "Why would this be for the best? Are you planning to find a nicer place to work?"

Jason hesitates. He isn't ready to discuss his still nebulous plan, although talking it over with Marta might be helpful. But then he notices the fearful look in her eyes. "I'll figure it out. Let's run through your options."

"There are no options. I will go to court. I have discussed it with Liddy. She does not want me to do this but understands that there is nothing else I can do. I talked to Dr. Ullman, and he feels the same. Liddy has agreed to bring my work materials from Metropolis to her condominium for safekeeping. If I do not return, she will give them to Dr. Ullman."

Refugee roulette. Jason pushes around the beans on his plate. "We might be able to come up with a different living arrangement for you. Something like what you had at Metropolis, or find a rental and I could sign the lease. A roommate situation through Craigslist. You could change your name again and move in with another grad student. Pay cash. Finish your dissertation."

"And then what am I to do? Even if I can receive my degree, which I think will be difficult, as I will not be able to defend my dissertation in person, I will not be able to look for a job. Or to be hired." Marta shakes her head. "I am finished with changing my name, and I am finished with pretending I am someone who I am not. There is no other course."

"Okay," he says. "Then that's what we'll do."

Marta smiles her beautiful smile. "Thank you."

As they eat in a companionable silence, Jason recalls how shocked he'd been when Marta and Liddy walked out of his bedroom that night in January. Just as he'd been shocked that Marta was living at Metropolis. In both instances, if he'd opened his eyes, he would have seen what was parading right in front of him. As he cares deeply for Marta and is quite fond of Liddy, he's made peace with the situation.

Watching them together made him think about Sabrina. She's invited him to come for a visit anytime, and he's thinking about a cross-country road trip. The early closing of Metropolis seems like the kick in the butt he needs. Without fully recognizing the magnitude of this decision, he makes up his mind to do it. And it may be more than just a trip—a new job, a new life, and maybe even the rekindling of old love. He'll stay in Boston until Marta's case is settled, refer his other clients, and then he'll head west.

"You still have not told me why closing down Metropolis is a good thing for you."

Jason laughs. The woman is a mind reader. "Let's focus on you. There are a boatload of materials we've got to collect before the hearing."

THEY SPEND THE next two weeks pulling together Marta's testimony and amassing the supporting evidence needed to substantiate her claims. Although Jason has his arguments outlined, filling in the details is a time-consuming task, and they proceed through the points one by one. There can be no inconsistencies. Every position must be fully supported and airtight.

A signed and notarized letter from the admin of the sociology department at Tufts, stating that she erroneously reported to USCIS that Mercedes wasn't a full-time student and that she had failed to inform them of Mercedes's change of address. A printout from Tufts showing that Mercedes is a full-time student in good standing at the university. Letters from her Cambridge landlord attesting to the dates Mercedes lived in his building and from her Boston landlord attesting to the dates she lived in his, also signed and notarized. A copy of the USCIS notice to appear addressed to the Cambridge address on a date she was living in Boston. A copy of the USCIS notice that her visa had been revoked in absentia, also sent to the Cambridge address after she moved. And these are just the materials necessary to demonstrate the legitimacy of their position that the deportation proceedings were based on miscommunications between the university and USCIS.

"You have been so helpful and wonderful to me," Marta says one night as Jason is scanning the English-language reports of Maduro and his henchmen's barbarities while she's looking through the Spanish. "I do not want to ask any more of you than I already have, but . . ." Her voice drifts off.

He raises his eyes and smiles at her. "But there's something else you want to ask."

"A favor. It is about my family."

He tries to work out a crick in his neck with his fingers. "Shoot."

"I have been trying to discover what has happened to my mother and sisters, but I have been unable to find any information. It is possible that they are still in Venezuela. Or perhaps they have fled to another country." She hesitates, and he guesses the additional possibility she doesn't want to say out loud. "If I am deported, this information will be valuable to me. And if I am granted asylum, perhaps I will be able to bring them here."

"You want me to try to find them?"

"As always, I will pay you for your time."

He cocks his head to the left and to the right, then presses a knuckle into the spot on the back of his right shoulder that feels as if a spike is being driven through it. "It's not my area of expertise, and I probably won't be able to find anything more than you did."

"But you will try?" Her dark eyes are full of pain and pleading.

"I will."

45

LIDDY

It's Saturday, and Marta's appointment at the Immigration Court is on Monday. Although Marta claims to be optimistic, Liddy can hear in her voice that's she's more concerned than she's letting on. As is Jason. Liddy finds it difficult to believe the United States would deport someone caught up in a technicality that has nothing to do with either her eligibility for a visa or, as ICE claims, her threat to the security of the country. But she's also worried.

Fortunately, the twins are coming for the weekend, flying in from Zurich this afternoon, the best kind of distraction. Liddy can't wait to be with them, but it's going to be tough for them to see Garrett. It's been two months since they were last here, and although Garrett is regaining his mental faculties at a rate that astonishes his doctors, it remains difficult to look at him.

She calls Marta, and they say encouraging things that are more hope-based than fact-based. When Liddy hangs up, she checks her email and sees a message from Garrett's lawyer. Blalock reiterates their offer, reminding her, as if she weren't aware, that she has six days to accept or reject the proposal.

If she doesn't respond by 5:00 p.m. on that date, they will bring their evidence to the police, who Liddy fears are amassing evidence against her on their own. She imagines Garrett grinning as he dangles his own version of the sword of Damocles over her head. If only he had died. As soon as this thought crosses her mind, she's overwhelmed by guilt. He may be a petty and vindictive man, but he wouldn't be strapped down to that hospital bed if it weren't for her.

She's been stalling about retaining an attorney, which is clearly a mistake. Especially as the media keep insisting there might have been foul play, and a number of her friends as well as a colleague at the Burke told her detectives had come around asking questions about her. Dawn Kenner, the lawyer Jason suggested, scared her off with her aggressive advice to fight Garrett at his own game, and Liddy never called her back. Nor has she called anyone else. Some kind of magical thinking, she supposes: if she doesn't have a lawyer, there won't be a suit. Idiotic thinking is more like it. Even though it's Saturday, she calls Kenner's office and leaves a message.

The twins insist on taking a cab to save her the hassle of airport traffic, and it's a little after two when the concierge calls to tell her they're on their way up. Liddy rushes down the hall to the elevator. When Robin steps out, she runs into her mother's arms. Scott puts his arms around both of them. The new man of the family.

Liddy settles them in the kitchen, grabs a Sprite for Scott and brews a pot of tea for Robin and herself. When the tea is ready, she brings the drinks and the kids' favorite cookies—Tate's double chocolate-chip—to the table.

She pulls her chair close to Robin's and gently pushes a lock of hair off her forehead. "Lemon ginger," she says. "Our favorite."

"How is he, Mom?" Scott asks. There's a waver in his voice.

"Mentally, much better every day," she tells them. "Moving forward physically. He's sitting up a lot of the time, sometimes even using a wheelchair. You'll be pleased."

They both look skeptical but don't ask for more particulars. Liddy doesn't offer any. "I love you both more than the trees," she says instead, an inside joke from when they were toddlers. Neither laughs or even smiles.

Robin presses the mug between her hands, holds it against her chest. "Like, why is it so cold here? It's April."

Liddy forces a laugh. "You're a New England girl, born and bred. You know very well what April is like. It sucks."

Robin's smile is weak, but at least it's there. "What about the rest of him?"

"Looking good for his arms, hands, and chest. Very good."

"Nothing below that?" Scott takes a long swig of his soda and doesn't meet her eyes.

"That doesn't look as good."

"How will he stand it?" Robin cries. "He's always been active. Rushing everywhere . . ." She covers her face with her hands.

Liddy hugs Robin tight, tries to take the girl's pain and pull it into herself. She rocks her just as she did when Robin was a small child with child-size problems. Even though she's well aware that now Robin's problems are adult-size and rocking isn't going to do anything to solve them.

Robin pulls away. "So he'll be, like, in a wheelchair for the rest of his life?" She frames the sentence as a question. "He'll never be able to play golf or go to a Red Sox game?"

"The world is a much more accommodating place for handicapped people than it used to be," Liddy tries to reassure her. "He'll probably be able to do lots of things. Get around much better than we think."

"Maybe Scott was right," Robin says. "Maybe it would have been better if he'd, if he'd—"

"I didn't mean it," Scott interrupts. "Don't say that."

"Right," Liddy says quickly. "You need to think positively. It's no help to him if you're upset when you see him."

"Should we go to the hospital now?" Scott asks, although he doesn't seem all that keen on the idea.

"Why don't you both go put your things away and wash up. Then you can go."

The twins don't seem to notice her use of "you" rather than "we." They haul themselves up and head toward the bedrooms. While Liddy waits, she stares out at the denuded Common, fifty floors below. Spring comes late to Boston, always much later than anyone thinks or hopes it will, and the city is still brown, dull, and barren. She watches the rivulets of rain streak down the glass, sips her tea. It isn't just April that sucks. And the kids aren't going to like it when she doesn't go to the hospital with them. After Garrett's vindictive lawsuit and pending deadline, not to mention his vicious words the last time she visited, her plan is to never see him again.

When the kids come back into the kitchen, Liddy says, "I think I'm going to stay here. Why don't you go on by yourselves? Call an Uber. We'll go out for dinner when you get back."

"What do you mean you're staying here?" Robin demands.

Scott frowns and glances at his sister. "We thought you'd come with us."

"Aren't you both a bit old to need your mother to hold your hands?" she tries to tease, but it falls flat.

Scott rolls his eyes—the same eye roll she's been the recipient of since he was seven. "You know that's not what it's about."

"Yeah," Robin says. "You know."

"You were at the hospital alone the last time. Remember? You insisted I go home to shower."

"That was different," Robin counters. "You were a wreck, and had been there all night—and you came back right away."

Liddy tries again. "It's better for him to have only one visitor at a time. I want you both to have all the time with him you can. He tires easily, and just the two of you will be a lot for him to handle."

"I don't care," Robin says. "I mean, I care that he gets tired, and we don't want to wear him out, but if it's a short visit, it's a short visit."

Scott nods. "That's cool with me."

"You'll do fine. You have each other, and at least now you can communicate with him, understand what he's saying. And he'll probably be sitting up, most likely in a wheelchair, not in the bed."

Scott considers this, but Robin sticks her chin out and shakes her head. Once a stubborn child, always a stubborn child.

"He also looks a lot better than when you were here in January," Liddy says in as upbeat a voice as she can muster. "The bruising has gone down, and his arm and one leg aren't in casts anymore. You'll see—it will be fine."

"We just flew thousands of miles to see our paralyzed father, and we need you to be with us," Robin says. "Maybe Scott is strong enough, but I'm not. You have to come." Her face crumbles. "I need you to keep me from freaking out."

Liddy goes to the closet and gets her raincoat.

GARRETT IS PLEASED to see the twins, but he ignores Liddy. Which is fine with her. She has no interest in fake chitchat. She's here for Robin and Scott, not for him. He's in a large private room now, and unfortunately this means all three of them can be with him at the same time. While he and the kids talk awkwardly, Liddy pretends to read the news on her phone.

He's in bed, rather than the wheelchair she promised, but Scott is stoic and gives Garrett two pen-and-ink drawings he made for him; Garrett actually looks at them, which is surprising, as he's never shown any interest in Scott's artwork before. At first, Robin stares at a spot above her father's head, holding Liddy's arm so tightly Liddy wonders if it might bruise. But after a few minutes, she loosens her grip and her breathing grows more regular. Until Garrett begins to seize.

His eyes suddenly roll up, and his head begins to ricochet against the pillow, snapping his chin into his chest and then snapping the back of his head into the pillow, his legs completely flaccid. Liddy and the twins jump from their chairs, all shouting. Liddy runs to get a doctor, leaving Robin with her hands covering her eyes and Scott staring at Garrett in terror. As soon as the team arrives, Liddy pulls them from the room.

They sit on chairs outside the nurses' station, mutely holding hands and watching the flow of doctors and nurses and carts rushing in and out of Garrett's room. Robin whispers, "I shouldn't have said what I did."

At first, Liddy doesn't understand what she's talking about. Then she remembers their earlier conversation. "What you said has nothing to do with this. You know that. He's had seizures before. It's part of his condition. I'm sure he'll be fine."

Finally, the doctor comes out and tells them the seizure is over, that they gave Garrett a sedative and he's resting comfortably. Robin and Scott thank the doctor. Liddy says nothing.

WHEN LIDDY PULLS into a parking spot in the Metropolis lot and looks up at the building, she experiences a full flashback to that night: the shadowy hallway, the terry cloth of her bathrobe, the familiar scent of Garrett's aftershave, the wild panic as she watched his flailing hands disappear down the elevator shaft. She tries to stifle her response to keep from scaring the kids, but her heart is racing and a veneer of sweat covers her face. This structure, once a source of pleasure and refuge, now looms hulking and medieval, the rain and heavy cloud cover enhancing the gloom.

She takes a deep breath and turns off the motor. The three of them sit in silence. "You're sure you're up for this?" she asks them.

The Tower condo was still being renovated when the kids left for Switzerland in August. The first time they saw it completed was right after the accident, and given the circumstances, it's not surprising that neither noticed much about it. This trip they've been more observant, and as they roamed through the rooms noting the amazing views, they couldn't help but see that, aside from a few photos, it looked like the home of a couple, not a family.

"What happened to all our stuff?" Robin had demanded. "Like my pictures and trophies? Where are all my clothes?" Her face was red, and her eyes were wet. "It's, it's like we've been erased."

"Yeah," Scott seconded, also close to tears. "Like just because we're going to school in Switzerland we don't live here anymore? Where are my sketchbooks? My drawings? You threw out my sketchbooks?"

"No, no," Liddy quickly assured them. "I have all your things. They're in storage. I saved them for you. We can go over there anytime if you want to see them." As soon as this last was out of her mouth, she realized her mistake.

They had immediately clamored for their possessions, not yet connecting "in storage" to Garrett's accident. Their distress had rattled her, and she'd spoken without thinking, only meaning to comfort them, to let them know they hadn't been wiped out by the move, that she loved them and thought about them all the time. But offering to take them to the scene of Garrett's accident? It had just slipped out, and after proposing it, she didn't feel she could renege.

Now with the hulking building casting its long shadow over the car, and the kids clear on the connection to Metropolis, it's obvious she should have taken a stronger stand. What was she thinking, bringing them here? Bringing herself here? "We don't have to go in," she says into the quiet car. "I can put it all in storage somewhere else. You can go through it later. Some other time."

"No," Scott says from the back seat. "I want my sketchbooks to show Mr. Templeton." Mr. Templeton is his art teacher, whom he adores.

Liddy turns to Robin, who's staring at her lap. "What do you think, sweet stuff? You can stay in the car. It shouldn't take that long."

Robin slowly shakes her head. "No," she says softly. "I want my pink straw hat. And some of the pictures you said are in there."

Blood pounds in Liddy's ears as they cross the parking lot, pounds even more as she punches in the code and they enter the building. She finds herself surprised that the elevator is still crisscrossed with yellow police tape. She'd somehow imagined that it would be fixed by now. But then she realizes that the old owner isn't going to put any money into a property he's going to lose. And the new owner, W. G. Haines Companies, hasn't taken it over yet.

"Here?" Robin croaks as they walk past Rose's office and stand in front of the elevator.

"Upstairs," Liddy says. "The unit's on the fourth floor."

The twins think there's only one unit, the one where their belongings are stored. There's no way she's going to tell them about the second. Nor is she going to tell them anything more about the accident. As far as Robin and Scott know, Garrett slipped and accidentally fell through a broken elevator door. There's been no discussion of fighting or pushing or rigging or attempted murder, which is exactly how Liddy wants it to stay. But she has to acknowledge that, given the police, the media, and Garrett's fast-approaching deadline, this may not be how it remains.

When they climb the stairs to the fourth-floor landing, the kids freeze in front of the elevator. It, too, is taped up, and the door is still askew, angled behind and away from the track at the bottom.

Robin moans, and Scott catches her as she starts to slump to the floor. "I'm okay," she tells him, and struggles to her feet.

"We can leave anytime either of you wants," Liddy reminds them.

"Let's go in there," Scott says, his voice tight. "Right now."

Liddy sweeps them away from the elevator and walks quickly toward #454. She, too, needs to get away. When she slides the door open, the kids stand in the threshold and take it in. Neither moves. Neither says a word.

"I thought it was going to be a bunch of boxes," Scott finally says. "This is, uh, like a room. A real room, like someone could almost live here."

Robin can't stop staring. "Like out of some old-fashioned novel. Like we're dead and you're some kind of crazy old lady trying to keep us alive."

"That Miss Havisham person," Scott says.

"There wasn't room in the apartment," Liddy explains. "I thought you might want this stuff someday."

Scott stares at his posters, at his desk, at his sketchbooks.

"My dollhouse!" Robin cries. "You saved my dollhouse. I love this."

The twins wander around the room, touching their things, opening books, reading papers, looking at photos on the bulletin boards, and, in Robin's case, moving tiny pieces of furniture.

Scott presses two thick sketchbooks to his chest. "Thanks, Mom."

Robin puts the pink straw hat on her head. "And sometimes you came here?" She points to the chair and the reading lamp. "Like you came here to kind of hang out with us?"

Liddy nods, unable to speak. Robin and Scott come to her and hug her again. "We love you more than the trees," Robin says into Liddy's shoulder.

46

JASON

On Monday morning, Jason and Marta take a cab to the JFK Federal Building. Marta is quiet and contained, although she hadn't been able to eat any breakfast. Jason can't imagine what must be going through her mind. There's a large construction project underway at Government Center, and when they arrive, many of the surrounding roads are closed. The driver asks if he can drop them on Cambridge Street. It's a rainy day, windy and cool, and this will entail a hike across City Hall Plaza, but they reluctantly agree.

The plaza is one of the most despised places in Boston, called out by an international group of architects as the worst public space in the world. Hyperbole aside, Jason agrees with that assessment. It's a wide-open expanse of brick, edged by hulking concrete buildings that look like the Soviets designed them rather than the highly praised modernist architects who did. And don't get him started on City Hall itself.

The plaza is not only ugly; its design sends the wind cutting in all directions, and huge puddles cover the bricks due to poor drainage. Jason lowers his head and pulls his hood down over his face. He'd like to put his arm around Marta, who looks so small and forlorn, but instead he links his arm through hers. Why hadn't he thought to bring an umbrella?

Like rain on a wedding day, he's going to take this stormy April weather as a good omen. Of course it had rained on his own wedding day, and look at how that turned out.

The JFK building—two offset towers connected by a glass walkway and an atrium—isn't as bad as some of the others surrounding the plaza. There are terraces and even a patio, but its flat facade is concrete and reeks of stark functionality. Again, Jason thinks of the Soviets.

When they get inside, the only people in uniforms are those checking IDs and manning the metal detector. No ICE. So far, so good. They find the correct elevator, exit at the third floor, and enter the offices of the Boston Immigration Court. Jason gives Marta an encouraging smile and goes to the desk.

"We have a screening interview today with Judge Susan Cohen at ten o'clock. Mercedes Bustamante. I'm her attorney, Jason Franklin."

The man checks his computer, then a handwritten log. He grunts and starts typing. "Courtroom Five," he finally says, pointing down a hallway to his right. "Take a seat outside, and someone will be with you soon."

They make their way down the corridor, find the correct room, and wait on the wooden bench across from the closed door. Jason feels as if he should give Marta a pep talk, or at least a few words of comfort, but everything he thinks of feels trite. So he says nothing. The man claimed someone would be with them soon, but it's been fifteen minutes, which in Jason's book, isn't the definition of "soon."

And then someone is there. Two men dressed in black vests stamped with large white letters: ICE FEDERAL AGENT. They approach the bench, guns hanging from their belts.

Jason jumps to his feet. "Is there something I can do for you, agents?"

They station themselves in front of Marta, legs wide. "Mercedes Bustamante?" the older one asks.

"I'm her attorney," Jason says. "Ms. Bustamante is here for an asylum screening interview. What is it that you want?" He glances at his watch. "We're already late for our hearing."

Marta stands and throws a desperate look in Jason's direction. "I am Mercedes Bustamante."

The younger agent pulls out a pair of handcuffs.

"There's no need to detain her," Jason says. "She came here of her own free will."

The agent ignores him, pulls Marta's hands behind her back, locking her tiny wrists. "Ms. Bustamante, you're in violation of a deportation order. Please come with us."

"Don't say anything to anybody," Jason calls after her. "Don't answer any questions. Tell them you won't talk without your attorney present. This won't take long." But the last part is a lie.

JASON STORMS INTO Judge Cohen's courtroom, which is small and unimposing, and heads down the aisle toward the front. A Latina in tears, accompanied by a woman who appears to be her mother, nearly knocks him over as they rush past, clearly distressed by the ruling just issued. The judge is behind the bench, taking a file folder from the top of a towering pile.

"Your Honor!" he calls loudly. "My client was just arrested outside in the hallway. While we were waiting to come speak to you!"

"And you are?" The judge raises an eyebrow.

"Jason Franklin. I represent Mercedes Bustamante. We had a ten o'clock credible-fear screening. And two ICE agents took her away before we could enter your courtroom!" Another lawyer might be faking outrage at this moment, but Jason has no need for pretense.

"Please come forward, Mr. Franklin," the judge says, which he does. "And what was the officers' stated reason for the arrest?"

"They claimed Ms. Bustamante is in violation of a deportation order. However, we have submitted all the necessary forms, applications, and backup materials and were granted this hearing by the Department of Justice. She came here of her own free will to plead her case, and before she had the opportunity to—"

"Is Ms. Bustamante in violation of a deportation order?"

Jason hands her the thick file. "Technically, yes, Your Honor. But her removal and deportation proceedings were based on a miscommunication between her university and the United States Citizenship and Immigration

Services. There was also a mistake regarding Ms. Bustamante's place of residence, and she was ordered deported in absentia before she was even aware there was a violation!"

The judge studies the materials in front of her. "Why didn't Ms. Bustamante contact us as soon as she became aware of the violation? This deportation notice is from ten months ago."

"She contacted me when she discovered it, which was only recently due to the mistakes and miscommunications I just described. And given the current immigration situation, I believe it would have been foolish for her to contact the government without an attorney."

Judge Cohen examines Marta's visa, then skims the supporting materials. There are over seventy-five pages, and Jason had been pleased by their heft, certain that the extent of his due diligence would improve Marta's chances of success. But from the frown on the judge's face, he now understands this might work against them.

"Her visa is valid, and she's never missed a single mandated check-in," Jason continues. "And, as you can see—"

"This is a complicated application, Mr. Franklin, and I need more time to study it. I'll take what you have told me under advisement and rule at a later date."

"But, Your Honor, Ms. Bustamante has done nothing wrong," Jason protests. "It's a question of due process, the foundation of which is the opportunity to be heard. She wasn't properly notified and therefore didn't have the chance to defend herself."

The judge reviews the pages for about five minutes before Jason is compelled to add, "If you don't adjudicate her case today, she'll be locked up and housed with the general prison population. For who knows how long. She's young and fragile, and it's a grave injustice for her to be treated like a common criminal. She's a doctoral candidate at one of the finest universities in the country, has been a model student and visa holder."

The judge raises her eyes. "Perhaps she's a model student, but these documents indicate she's far from a model visa holder."

"That's only because of a series of clerical errors, and it was also my understanding that agents in Boston were not arresting undocumented immigrants who entered government offices seeking asylum."

"That applies to undocumented immigrants who are not in violation of a deportation order."

"At the very least, she deserves to be considered for bail," he says, a last-ditch effort in what he now recognizes is a lost argument.

"I'm not insensitive to the situation, Mr. Franklin. But unfortunately my docket is more than full today," Judge Cohen says. "It would be unethical for me to rule on this case until I've reviewed all aspects of her request." The judge pauses, looks him in the eye. "Your client entered a federal building while in violation of a deportation order, and the law is the law. Which is what the ICE agents were following when they made the arrest."

"Thank you, Your Honor," is all he can say, his hopes that Judge Cohen's fair-mindedness would overcome her inclination to follow the letter of the law now dashed.

JASON IS FAMILIAR with the procedures following an ICE arrest. Marta will be processed at the JFK Building and then taken to the Suffolk County jail, which is located in an iffy part of the city, where the South End bleeds into Dorchester. There, as he unnecessarily explained to the judge, Marta will be treated the same way as someone arrested for a much more serious crime, like assault or rape. As a criminal.

At least Marta has him. A person with a private immigration attorney is twice as likely to receive asylum and four times as likely to receive bail, Jason's primary objectives at the moment. He checks his watch, unable to believe it's only been half an hour since they entered the courthouse. He won't be able to see her until midafternoon at the earliest. He calls the jail to find out their time estimate, but the woman says there's no record of a Mercedes Bustamante and there's no way to determine when the detainee will arrive.

He takes the T to Kendall Square and slogs through the rain to Metropolis. The sky has grown blacker, and the rain is heavier, a perfect mirror to his mood. He thinks about calling Liddy but decides to wait until he's got something positive to report. Liddy had advised Marta not to go to court, and apparently Liddy, rather than he, offered the better guidance.

Jason calls the ICE Enforcement and Removal Operations field office to ascertain if, by some wild chance, Marta has been granted bail. He calls Judge Cohen's office to determine how long it will be until she's able to review Marta's file. He calls the jail to see if Marta has arrived yet. He calls the Evercom Correctional Billing Services to find out if he can put money in an account so she can make phone calls from inside the jail. He fails in every circumstance.

Marta asked him to try to find her family a few days ago, and it seems, now, this is the only thing he can do to help her. He flips open his laptop and types Marta's mother's name, Amparo Bustamante, into a number of data broker websites that claim to be able to find anybody. He fails once again. It would have been a real long shot for her to be sitting on the internet waiting to be discovered. He tries to find the Venezuelan equivalent of a data broker, but his Spanish isn't up to the task, and given Maduro's affinity for tyranny, there probably aren't any sites.

So he texts his childhood friend Tovar Ticas. Var is a hacker, who sells his services on the dark web, a constellation of hidden sites that aren't accessible to standard search engines. These digital black markets hawk everything from child pornography to hit men to information not available to the general public. In addition to Var's regular business, xBlkOnion, he performs dark web searches for a limited number of customers, a group that includes Jason. In fact, Var is how Jason verified the child trafficking by his Spencer Uccello client. If anyone can find Amparo Bustamante, Var can. Jason types, *Pizza tomorrow*, which will elicit the phone number of one of Var's many burners.

Jason leans back in his chair, looks at the furniture, the office equipment, the books, and the stuffed file cabinets. He eyes his backup office supplies, the refrigerator, coffee machine, and all the other accouterments he's managed to acquire over the last year, and he wonders what the hell he's going to do with it all. It occurs to him that, except for the files, he could just leave it all behind. Maybe take the law books for his niece Tawney. Head to California. There's not much left for him here, except his family, and the idea of a fresh start has a lot of appeal. He could become a public defender, maybe an immigration lawyer for a nonprofit, or perhaps something not related to the law at all. His family won't be happy, but that's what airplanes are for.

His phone rings. It's Liddy. She knew the time of the hearing, probably tried to reach Marta, and, failing that, turned to him. "Hey," he says.

"How did it go? Marta didn't answer. What's going on?"

WHEN HE CHECKS in with Suffolk County jail at one o'clock, they still claim they have no record of Marta's arrest. At two, it's the same. And at three. Not until three thirty is he told that Mercedes Bustamante has been "received." Her attorney can meet with her if he or she arrives at the jail before five. Jason calls an Uber and rushes outside to meet it.

The driver chooses the city route, heading over to Mass Ave instead of jumping on I-93, and they're immediately caught in rush hour traffic, which incenses Jason. But it's probably the same on the highway. As they inch over the bridge between Cambridge and Boston, he stares at the rear of the stately houses of Back Bay, which look pretty good even if they are the B sides.

As a kid, he'd fantasized about living in Back Bay, but when he had the chance, he chose the Ink Block in the South End instead. It was a good choice, but he still has a longing for the wide tree-lined streets and handsome town houses, especially on Comm Ave. If he stays in California, he'll never have the chance to live here.

The rain has let up, but it's still miserable, windy and cold. The sun hasn't set, which is a bonus, but the cloud cover is so thick it's almost as if it has. Jason drums his fingers on the armrest. Almost four, and they haven't reached Huntington Ave. Miraculously, the traffic thins when they hit Columbus, and they move quickly until it jams again right past Boston Medical.

It's a particularly dreary part of town, colloquially referred to as Methadone Mile, overrun with victims of the triple epidemics of opioids, poverty, and homelessness. Garbage, picked up by the wind, smashes into lampposts, wire fencing, and sleeping men who appear unaffected by the impact. All the lights in the hospital are on, illuminating the driver's head from behind, but this brightness is also grim, given the desperation that must be going on inside the Level I trauma center. The best place in the city to be treated for a gunshot wound.

Finally, they pull onto Bradston Street, where the jail, a four-story concrete building, sits amidst warehouses and auto body shops, the elevated highway looming behind. Jason leaps from the car. It's four thirty.

The guard behind the glass partition takes his ID. "You need to wait for a room to open."

"How long will that be?" Jason asks. "I was told I only had until five."

"That's correct, sir. You can return at nine tomorrow morning."

"That's not possible. I have to see my client today. Now. Right now."

The guard, a boy with dull-blond hair, a dull-blond beard, and dull-brown eyes, blinks. "You need to wait for a room to open."

Jason realizes there's no point in pursuing this, and he sits in one of the fifty or so hard plastic chairs set in rows, as if in a small theater. But there's no stage, no screen, just a concrete wall to stare at as you wait to see an incarcerated loved one. At least the waiting area is empty. He's been here during visiting hours when it's noisy and smelly and crowded, arguments and fights breaking out every few minutes. Women and children sobbing. Sometimes grown men too.

It's now after four forty-five, and Jason approaches the partition again. Before he can say anything, the guard holds up his hands, an apologetic smile on his dull face. Jason spends the next fifteen minutes pacing the linoleum floor, worn smooth by countless feet doing the same over countless years. At five o'clock, another guard, this one old and overweight with a ruddy complexion, tells him that he has to leave. They're locking up for the night.

47

LIDDY

As Liddy listens to Jason, her stomach cramps so violently that she has to bend in half to ease the pain. She wants to scream that she had told them so, that if they had listened to her none of this would have happened. But she knows it's not that simple, even if it's true. "When can I see her?"

"Probably not for a couple of days," Jason says. "They should let me speak with her this afternoon, but because you're technically just a friend, you have to be preapproved. If you go over to the jail after three o'clock tomorrow afternoon with three forms of ID, they'll give you a visitation application."

This is unbelievable. Unbearable. "But I can talk to her on the phone?"

Jason sighs. "The jail won't connect you. Marta has to call you from inside. I've put in a request—"

"When can she do that?"

"Liddy, listen to me. There are lots of crazy rules and regulations. They don't allow free calls out. I'll deposit money to her phone account, and then she'll be able to call you collect."

"Collect?" Liddy explodes, her rage erupting at anything in its path, even the least significant. "If she has to call collect, why the hell does there need to be money in her account?"

"It's a pay phone. We have to be—"

"But she's all alone!" Liddy wails. "She's got to be terrified, and there's no one to help her . . ." She dissolves into sobs. "She didn't do anything. It's a goddamn clerical error!"

"I'm going to get her out of there. I've presented our case to the judge, and she seemed inclined toward us. She just needs more time to go through all the details. Judge Cohen also said she was sympathetic to the fact that Marta shouldn't be in a county jail, so she's more than likely to allow Marta to post bond while she goes through the paperwork."

Liddy tries to focus on Jason's words, his optimistic words. But he was optimistic ICE wouldn't arrest Marta in a Boston courtroom. "Then she'll be able to come here? Stay with me?"

"Once she's released on bail, she should be able to do pretty much anything while awaiting trial—with the exception of leaving the state. Even start running outside again."

"She'll love that." Liddy swipes at her eyes and blows her nose. If Jason can get Marta out quickly, maybe this won't be as bad as it appears.

"Okay, good. Just try to relax. I'm going down there as soon as I can, and I'll call you after I've talked to her. Okay? You all right?"

"Yes, no, but I guess I'm as okay as I can be. Thank you. Don't know what we'd do without you."

"All in a day's work," Jason says.

Liddy doesn't contradict him, but it's not all in a day's work. He's a kind man who's putting a positive spin on a bad situation to keep her from completely freaking out. As soon as she clicks off from Jason, the phone rings in her hand, startling her.

It's her friend Sandy, calling to invite her to Rockport for a few days. "A little getaway," Sandy says. "I've got something you might enjoy."

It's tempting, but there's no way Liddy is leaving town with Marta in jail. "Thanks, that would be lovely. But I, I need to stay with Garrett . . ."

"How's he doing?" Sandy asks in the hesitant voice everyone uses when they ask her this question.

"It's hard," Liddy admits. "But he's slowly improving."

"Look, how about I drive down to you right now, bring you a couple of grams to lift your spirits? I've got a few hours before my painting class."

This offer Liddy accepts. It's mind-boggling how many people are anxious to come to your aid when your husband is suddenly paralyzed: Sandy, who is more aware than most of Liddy's true feelings toward Garrett; her doctor, who gave her a three-month prescription for Ambien; everyone she knows, even those she doesn't know but who seem to know her. It's as if she's wearing a neon sign declaring she's a trauma victim, handle with care. Which she supposes is true.

Although she would never have wished it, the power of Garrett's blackmail has been seriously weakened by Marta's arrest, his threat to have her deported now moot. Liddy calls Dawn Kenner to get her take on the situation. Despite Liddy's despair over Marta, when they hang up she feels almost hopeful.

It's been over three months since the accident, and the detectives who had been hounding her and her circle appear to have finally eased up, as has the media. According to Dawn, this would seem to indicate that the police don't have any substantive evidence against her and most likely won't take Garrett's accusations seriously. There are no witnesses, so his claim that Liddy pushed him is a he-said/she-said proposition, and the fact he hit the elevator with his back can be mooted by an expert who testifies he could have lost his balance and turned himself around. Therefore his threat to tell the kids she tried to kill him will come to nothing, because there won't be anything to tell.

Dawn pointed out, to Liddy's great relief, that there's probably no proof the elevator was tampered with either. If there were, Garrett's lawyer would have shown it to her weeks ago. She also suggested that, now that the Marta blackmail is off the table, they present their countersuit to Garrett as soon as possible, to which Liddy heartily agreed.

Robin and Scott left last night, and Blanca came in this morning, fully erasing any sign of their visit: the beds have been changed, the bathrooms scrubbed clean, the towels washed. They're gone, but they'll be back. Just as Marta will be back. And as soon as Marta is released on bail, she'll move in here temporarily. Then after she's granted asylum, they'll find a new home with room for the twins. They'll be able to be together just like any other ordinary couple, no longer two women forced to hide in a storage unit.

When the concierge rings to tell her Sandy is on her way up, Liddy grabs her coat and purse and puts them out on the table in the entryway, along with an envelope filled with cash. She slips on her shoes and throws a scarf around her neck. She tells Sandy that she's on her way to visit Garrett. She's already late. Wishes she could stay and do a few lines with her, but she can't. They'll have to do it some other time. When things calm down. She'll come to Rockport. Thanks so much for bringing the coke over. So unnecessary, so kind. Kiss. Long hug. Kiss. Goodbye.

An hour after Sandy leaves, Liddy has snorted about a quarter of a gram and is completely immersed in the process of reorganizing and emptying her bureau to make room for Marta's things, bagging clothes she doesn't wear anymore to give to Blanca. She could also give Garrett's clothes to Blanca, as he's lost over twenty pounds and is unlikely to ever wear them.

Now that he's improving, he'll probably return here. It's on one floor, and there's room for the 24/7 aides he's going to need, especially because he won't have a wife to take care of him. So Liddy decides not to touch the clothes; the aides will be more than capable of disposing of his unneeded belongings.

The cocaine is as good as the last gram she got from Sandy. Although Liddy doesn't want to get ahead of herself, the coke pushes her there, and she also decides that after Marta's status is straightened out, she's going to file for divorce. It'll look bad, but so be it. Garrett will throw everything he's got at her, and it will cost her a fortune in legal fees, but she'll end up with more than enough to live very comfortably. Most importantly, she'll be free.

While she works, she checks her phone constantly, fretting that Jason hasn't called back. He promised this morning that he'd get in touch as soon as he talked with Marta. Does this mean there's another problem? That he didn't get to see her? Liddy can't stand the thought of Marta all alone in that horrible place. It's after five when Jason finally calls. "How is she?" Liddy demands. "What did she say?"

"We're going to have to wait until tomorrow." Jason's voice is laden with weariness. "The jail closed before I had a chance to see her."

Liddy sits down on the floor in front of the closet. "So she's been all by herself all day?"

"I'm sorry. I'll go back first thing in the morning. I'm sure I'll be able to talk to her then."

Liddy takes in the clothes and shoes strewn on the bed and floor, the empty drawers waiting to be filled with Marta's possessions, and her spirits completely deflate.

"Liddy? Liddy?" Jason is saying. "Are you there?"

"Y-yeah," she manages to stammer. "Yeah, I'm here. Just trying to take it all in."

"Look, we'll know a lot more tomorrow, so try to relax as much as you can. Hopefully, I'll have some better news for you then. Why don't you have a couple of drinks? Call for takeout. Try to sleep."

Liddy almost laughs. The coke has nullified any hunger or fatigue she might have, and she has no desire for alcohol. "That's a good idea," she says. "I think I'll do just that."

After the conversation ends, she goes over to the trivet, where four lines are neatly arranged. She picks up the straw and snorts two of them. Then she shakes out two pills from her Ambien bottle and downs them. She'll finish packing up her things, then she'll do the other two lines and get ready for bed. When the Ambien hits, she'll conk out, and then it will be morning.

THE NEXT DAY, Jason's better news doesn't materialize. He saw Marta for only a few minutes, and although he tried once again to spin it, Liddy can tell that Marta is a mess. The judge hasn't reviewed the credible-fear and deportation materials yet, nor has she ruled on bail, and the assistant at the immigration court refused to guess when she might do so.

Liddy has trouble dredging up either the fury or the optimism she felt yesterday; she's just nauseated and depressed by Jason's report. She feels horrible and contemplates doing a few lines to beat back the hangover. It's tempting, but she has to go to the jail this afternoon, and she can't be high when she does. Who knows, she might end up in jail too.

Instead she takes another Ambien and sleeps through her alarm. When she wakes up, it's six and the jail is closed.

48

MARTA

There is no Liddy. There is no Jason. There is no work. There is no running. What there is are four other women in a roughly ten-by-twelve-foot cell meant to accommodate two. There is also the harsh light from the huge fixture mounted on the ceiling outside the cell, focused directly on her pillow. And there is her mattress squeezed between two sets of what she thinks are called bed bunks.

Marta burrows her head into the pillow, but the foam is thin and smells of things she doesn't want to think about, and she turns on her back. The humiliations of the day fill her head: the handcuffs; the strip-down; the cavity search; the shirt and pants too big and rough against her skin, holding the odor of chlorine and someone else's sweat.

Perhaps more distressing than any of these were the hate-filled glares she received from her four cellmates when she followed the mattress into the cage.

The "Fuck off, rich bitch" from a white woman with greasy hair.

The "No fucking room for you here" from a Black girl with a heavy southern accent.

The "Can't build that wall soon enough" from a large lump on a mattress with her head facing the wall.

They know nothing about her, but they hate her nonetheless.

The Latina on one of the top bunks is crying softly, but Marta will not do the same. If she starts, there will be no stopping. Jason will get her out.

He will get her asylum. He is an excellent attorney with many years of experience, and he will do anything and everything necessary to save her.

She thinks she may have managed to sleep for a few minutes, because an explosion of light and the buzz of hundreds of fluorescent bulbs bursting on jolt her out of a semiconscious state. This is followed by the smashing of metal.

"Turn off the fucking lights!" the Black girl screams, and slams her pillow over her eyes.

"Shut up, Tanya," the white woman says with little enthusiasm.

Marta does not know what to do or where to look or how to be. She is afraid she is going to vomit, but she is even more afraid of the viciousness of her cellmates if she does. She pulls into herself and tries to push the nausea down. She counts the bars.

Eighteen across by eleven high. She tries to think of happy things, as Mamá used to counsel her when she was a little girl and had a bugbite or bruised knuckle. Liddy, Jason, sunshine, running, multiple regressions, Dr. Ullman. But fear overwhelms her nonetheless.

A guard kneels in front of the bars and unlocks a gate at the bottom. Four trays come flying through, and then the gate is locked shut. "Chow!" he yells. "Come and get it, ladies!"

Her cellmates scramble for the trays, but Marta does not move. "Don't even think about it, Miss Richy Rich," says the heavyset woman, whose surprisingly pretty face Marta wasn't able to see last night. Then they all climb on their mattresses and begin to eat.

Given the current state of her stomach, Marta is happy the guard didn't bring her breakfast. There is something watered-down and red, which might have once been tomato juice. And something that looks a little like French toast, but it is so undercooked it flops on the plate and swims in a thin yellow liquid. Her stomach rebels at the sight, and she gags.

The woman with the greasy hair breaks into loud laughter. "Can't take it, fancy girl? You ain't seen nothing yet."

After the trays are collected, two female guards take all of them to the shower, along with the women from other cells. There are at least twenty-five women and some girls so young they look prepubescent. They are all goaded down a hallway littered with chunks of paint and who knows what else. Marta's pants and slippers are too big, and she stumbles twice. Curses follow in her wake.

Hand signs flash. Shoulders rub. Whispers are shared. A woman is kneed in the small of her back and falls to the floor. No one helps her up. It is immediately apparent who is powerful and who is not, who is in the right clique and who is not. Not cliques, gangs. Marta tries to make herself as small as possible.

The Latina from her cell steps next to her. "*Mi nombre es Beatriz,*" she whispers. "*No hables con nadie.*" Do not talk to anyone.

"Mercedes," she whispers back.

"*¿Detenida?*" Detainee?

"*Sí.*"

"Speak fucking English!" someone behind Marta yells, and jabs her with an elbow. "You're in America now. But probably not for long!" Then she begins to cackle as if what she said was the funniest thing ever spoken. At least a dozen women join her.

Marta glances at the woman. This one is powerful. Dangerous. She nods and does not say any more. Beatriz steps away.

They are told to strip and hang their underwear and clothes on numbered hooks. Marta follows orders. She is handed a washcloth covered with rust spots and led, along with the rest, into an open stall lined with showerheads dribbling water. The cement is caked with mildew, which stretches across the floor and up the walls. The shampoo dispensers are empty, and the slivers of soap are barely capable of washing a body, let alone hair. The place smells like rot and urine and body odor. Marta again prays she will not throw up.

49

ROSE

Michael has been staying out later and later, and lots of times he doesn't come home at all. Any scare he got from being arrested has disappeared, and Rose has her hands full with Taco Bell and the girls and deciding which bills to pay and which she can hold out on for another month. What with trying to keep everything else going, she doesn't have time to figure out what to do about Michael. Vince just sits in his chair and drinks his beer and continues to ignore her, so he isn't any help at all.

Sometimes she thinks about calling Liddy and asking to borrow the money she once offered. But Rose has got her pride and they're not that desperate. Other times she thinks about contacting Garrett. Jason said Garrett is threatening to tell the police that Liddy pushed him, and Rose bets Garrett would be thrilled to know there was an eyewitness to back up his claim—and pay her handsomely for the information. It wouldn't be a very nice thing to do to Liddy. But even though Liddy hasn't been much of a friend to her lately, Rose can't bring herself to do this.

When she finally gets up the energy to confront Michael about the stealing, he acts like it's no big deal. It breaks her heart that her own son can think like this, can be like this. "Michael," she pleads, "your six months isn't up yet and if you get into trouble again you're going to have to go back to court. And then it's juvie, like the judge warned you about."

As usual, Michael's eyes are slits, and from what she can see of them they're all bloodshot. He leans against the wall as if he needs it to keep him standing up. Which he probably does.

"You can't go around stealing other people's things, and you can't do any drugs, like I know you're doing and—"

"All my drug screens have come up clean," he interrupts.

"I'm not a fool and I know that doesn't mean anything. It's obvious to me and to anyone who looks at you that you're high all the time. So don't add lying to your mother to the rest of your sins."

"You're making a big thing over nothing. Like always."

"It is a big thing! Stealing is a big thing. Getting sent up is a big thing. It's like jail in there. It is jail. If you don't do everything the judge told you you've got to do, they could make you stay there for years."

"Not gonna happen."

"What's not going to happen? You're not going do what the judge says or you're not going to go to detention?"

"Ma, stop trippin'," he says. "I'm cool."

"You aren't cool—not even close—and you're only fourteen, and you're going to destroy your life before you're old enough to even have one. And you'll destroy mine and your father's along the way!" Rose wants to slap his face like she did when he was little and mouthed off to her. But she doesn't dare. He's not that boy anymore, and even though she doesn't think he'd hit her back, she's not sure he wouldn't. And what good would a slap do anyways? In his condition he probably wouldn't even feel it.

THIS TIME WHEN her phone rings in the middle of the night, Rose doesn't think it's a wrong number and she knows that Michael isn't asleep in his room. She doesn't want to answer it because she doesn't want to hear what the man on the other end is going to tell her. But she has no choice. If it's something bad like Michael has been arrested again, she's going to have to do something about it.

It's a woman cop this time, and Michael hasn't been arrested. He's been shot.

WHEN ROSE GETS to the hospital, she's not sure how she managed to find it, seeing that it's all the way into the city and in an area she's never been to before. The lady cop told her they took Michael to the ER at Boston Medical Center because they were the best equipped to handle gunshot wounds. Gunshot wounds. Her boy has a gunshot wound. *Dear Jesus, dear Jesus, dear Jesus, please make him be okay.* She wishes Vince were with her, but she didn't want to tell her mother about Michael until she knew more, so Vince had to stay with the girls.

She pushes through the ER doors and skids into the room, which is packed. There are three people already lined up at the desk. "Michael Gentilini!" she yells as she races forward. "Michael Gentilini! Is he here? Where is he? Is he alive?"

"There are people ahead of you," the woman behind the desk says. "Please wait your turn."

"I can't. It's my boy. He's been shot. I don't know if he's—"

"I'm sorry. You still have to wait your turn."

"He's only fourteen!" Rose cries. "I need to know what's happened to him!"

A Black man with a white beard looks at the two women in line behind him. They nod and the man waves Rose ahead.

"Bless you, sir, bless you," Rose says, and turns to the receptionist. "Michael Gentilini."

"Are you immediate family?"

"I just told you I'm his mother! Where is he?"

"The receptionist stares at her screen. "Michael Gentilini, you say?"

"Yes. Yes. That's what I say!"

The woman raises her eyes. "And you are . . . ?"

"Rose Gentilini. His mother!" She knows her voice is shrill and demanding and if she makes this woman mad it will just make things worse. She tries to calm down. But how can she calm down? "Can you please, please find him?"

"Do you have ID?" the receptionist asks.

Rose digs into her pocketbook and hopes she didn't leave her wallet at home. She didn't, but she has trouble pulling her license out. When she frees it, she just about throws it at the woman. "Please," she says. "Please, he's only fourteen."

The receptionist stares at the photo, gives it back, and says, "Your son is in surgery right now. Take a seat, and the doctor will be with you as soon as she's finished."

"What kind of surgery? How bad is it? Was he shot? Where? Does he need blood?"

"We have plenty of blood, and I'm not authorized to give information on a patient's condition. Just take a seat, Ms. Gentilini."

"How long will it be until I can see the doctor?"

The old man with the white beard makes a noise that sounds kind of like a bark. Rose steps to the side and looks around, but there aren't any seats. She's got to ask more questions and get more answers, but the receptionist is already talking to the man. There's no one else to ask so she sits on the floor in an empty corner and drops her head into her hands.

She prays like she's never prayed before. Offering Jesus everything, anything, if he'll only save Michael's life. *Please, Jesus, please let him live.* Her sweet baby boy with his pudgy cheeks, grinning his grin with no teeth, and his shiny dark eyes seeing only her and wanting only her, her precious firstborn. It was her job to keep him safe, and she let him down. So far down.

More people pour into the waiting room, and it's almost like she's watching one of her television shows. There's a child with skin so black he's almost blue sitting all by himself and bleeding from a gash at the back of his head. There's a man with a broken leg, crying like a baby, and a teenager who's so skinny his ribs show through his T-shirt, throwing up into a pail. There's a shriveled-up woman whose face is covered with an oxygen mask, and a girl screaming that she's going into labor but it doesn't even look like she's pregnant. And then there are two junkies with eyes that are a lot like Michael's. Someone finally leaves, and Rose grabs a chair that has a different view. But it doesn't matter because it's the same show.

Doctors come into the waiting room all the time and yell out names. Thompson. Tang. Washington. Qaock. Josephs. Laghari. Clark. Reddy. No Gentilini. Rose calls Vince but has nothing to tell him. When she hangs up she bows her head, waits, and prays some more.

"Gentilini!" a girl in bloody scrubs calls out, a face mask hanging crooked off her ear. "Gentilini. Michael Gentilini!"

Rose doesn't figure out that this is Michael's doctor right away because she looks like a kid and Rose expected the doctor to be a man. She jumps up, rushes over. "Me!" she says. "Me. Michael's my son. I'm Rose Gentilini. How is he?"

"I'm Dr. Hale. It's nice to meet you, Ms. Gentilini." The doctor takes her arm and leads her to the side of the room. "I just operated on your son, and the surgery went well."

"Thank you. Oh, thank you, doctor. I can't thank you enough." Rose thinks she's going to faint. "So he's okay? He's going to be all right?"

"We'll need to take it day by day."

Rose blinks. "But you just said it went well."

"The surgery went well," Dr. Hale says. "Michael has a perforating wound to the abdomen, which means the bullet went completely through. It nicked a number of organs, and there's a nasty exit wound. He also lost a lot of blood at the scene."

Rose's knees start to buckle, and the doctor grabs her by the arm. The doctor waves two young men off a couple of chairs, puts Rose into one, and takes the other for herself. "He has a good chance," she says. "He's young and healthy, and those are very strong indicators."

"A, a good chance?" Rose says. "A good chance to, to . . ."

"To pull through. Yes, Ms. Gentilini, he has a good chance."

Rose doesn't know how she's sitting here talking just like she's some kind of normal person when Michael got shot and he could be dying right now. It feels like she isn't here at all, like she's watching herself on that television show she was watching before. Like she's some actress sitting and talking. "You, you're saying he might not, might not . . . ?"

"Let's not go there, okay? Michael is in recovery right now, and they'll bring him down to intensive care in a couple of hours. He has a substantial intra-abdominal injury, and I expect he'll stay in the ICU for at least a week. Maybe more."

"ICU," the Rose actress repeats. "That sounds bad. Does he really need that?"

The doctor stands. "I'm sorry, Ms. Gentilini, but for now he does."

PART FOUR

50

ZACH

Three months later: July 2018

Serge's shots are so flawlessly framed that Zach has never dared to mess with the compositions, and from day one, he's done no cropping. But now that his skills are improving, he does spend time working out the right exposures, the density and contrasts, the tones and shadows, how to dodge and burn to get the values just right.

At each step, he wonders how Serge would have handled it. He scrutinizes the pictures Serge printed himself, tries to learn from the man's choices, stay true to his eye. Which is near impossible. Zach pulls his latest print from the water and hangs it on the line, a Metropolis ghost photo. Clearly an artist's studio, another tenant using his or her space in ways Zach hadn't imagined.

He squints and manages to distinguish a roller coaster made of glued-together dominos undulating on the floor, a triangular cascade of fishing line supporting a waterfall of plastic, thousands of straws pasted to the wall and carved into a cityscape. Each piece is completely arresting, but, as always, Serge's photo goes beyond just capturing the contents of the room. For Zach understands that he's also looking at the person who shaped them.

A number of images that Serge printed himself lie on the counter, and Zach tries to figure out how he did what he did. Zach guesses the man must have been self-taught, responding to each photograph as it displayed itself to him. From his gut rather than from a class critique in art school. Which is what makes Serge so difficult to emulate. And so damn good.

It's time to take these photographs out into the world. A different type of person might start with Facebook groups or internet sites or blogs or magazines, but that's not Zach's style. Galleries and museums. No reason to go anywhere but directly to the top to introduce a new talent, especially one discovered in an abandoned storage unit. Which he's learned is exactly how Vivian Maier's photographs were found—you can't make this shit up. The media will be all over it. And hopefully the money will be too.

He can feel the champagne bubbles on his tongue, the tiny round bits of caviar too. There are fawning critics from New York, Paris, and Tokyo; galleries begging to put on one-man shows; collectors begging to purchase. All are astonished at Serge's eye, appreciative of Zach's. Accolades rain down, cash flows in, the future is full of promise.

He sits on the edge of the tub and contemplates the other three Metropolis photographs he just printed: a rear shot of a workman carrying a ladder, wearing jeans and a Red Sox T-shirt; a teenage couple kissing along the railroad tracks in the hulking shadow of the building; a janitor mopping the floor with fierce concentration.

Serge had framed the workman so the top of the ladder is out of the shot, leading the viewer's eye to the parallel shadows the rungs throw on his completely bald head. Would Serge have shaded the shadows as deeply as Zach had? Zach lit the teenage boy's face and darkened the girl's. Would Serge have done it the other way around, highlighting her long lashes and the smoothness of her skin?

He could sell only the photos Serge printed himself, which will surely generate interest. But Serge's shots of the storage units, the ghost photos, are the most unusual and remarkable, and unfortunately these are the ones, with the exception of the kids' room, that the man never got around to printing.

Zach is game to print the negatives. It will obviously take him time to get the photos to the necessary level, but he's made great strides in just the last few weeks. He'll buckle down on fine-tuning his skills and find a pathway into Serge's head, a way to see how he sees.

IT TAKES ALMOST a week for Zach to select a group of photographs that highlights Serge's talent. They're mostly shots Serge printed himself, but also a number of the ghost interiors Zach printed. This curating is tricky, as so many of the pictures are brilliant, and he can include only a fraction of them. He learned a long time ago that you can't overwhelm buyers with choices; if too many are offered, confusion results and the impact is reduced. As are the sales. He settles on twenty-three and then spends a shitload for a portfolio case worthy of its contents. Extravagant, maybe, but necessary. He's also learned that presentation is crucial.

With this folder under his arm, he heads to SoWa, South of Washington, in Boston's South End, where dozens of galleries line Harrison Ave. For decades, maybe more, Newbury Street was home to the best galleries in the city, but high rents and collectors' desire for the less traditional shook everything up. This area used to be full of neglected buildings, its most famous landmark a homeless shelter, and is now the trendy place to be.

The streets are teeming with summer tourists, and there's a festive air. Although he's aware that the proper procedure is to email the portfolio prior to an in-person solicitation, this isn't his style either. Successful sales are the result of face-to-face interactions. He visits gallery after gallery— Bromfield, Abigail Ogilvy, L'Attitude, Matter & Light—and quickly discovers that most don't show photography, and the ones that do are booked a year ahead.

But he's not about to accept this as the last word on the subject. With the persistence that transformed his dorm-room marijuana dealing into a multimillion-dollar business, he persuades several proprietors to take a look at the photos anyway. He generates the interest and positive responses he expects, and drums up three promises to get in touch if a scheduled show falls through. He also receives an equal number of invitations to return in six months. Not bad, but not what he needs.

Undaunted, he moves down the brick pathway and enters the

Nickerson & Hagan Gallery. When he explains his mission to the woman behind the desk, she calls for the owner. Zach introduces himself to Nathaniel Nickerson, who studies the photos with deep interest. "Do you have more of these?"

"Many more," Zach tells him enthusiastically. "Some even better."

Nathaniel goes back to the beginning, turns the pages, returns to the interior Metropolis pictures again and again. "Love the squares. A Rolleiflex, yes? Also the compositions. I'm particularly drawn to the inside shots of this old warehouse. These rooms filled with random items." He raises his head. "What kind of warehouse is it anyway?"

"It's not. It's a self-storage facility in Cambridge, near MIT. Built around the turn of the twentieth century."

Nathaniel looks again. "Ah, yes, of course. How unusual." He pauses at a photograph that took days for Zach to print. It's a shot of a small man tenderly placing a cello onto a stand in the middle of a unit filled with hundreds of violins. He's holding the instrument as if it's a beloved child.

"I like that one too." Zach looks Nathaniel in the eye, projecting how impressed he is with Nathaniel's discernment. "One of Laurent's best, I think."

Zach's first attempt at printing this photograph was a total bust. He couldn't get the lighting right, and the shot is all about illumination. It took him dozens of tries, but in the end he believes he got into Serge's head. Over and over, Zach had burned to darken the edges of the racks of violins, bringing the shadow lines forward. Then he dodged the spaces between the man's body and his cherished cello, burnishing the wood and leading the viewer into the photo, into an understanding of this particular man's love of music, of humankind's love of music.

"The use of light here is extraordinary," Nathaniel says. "As it is in so many of these."

"Serge Laurent uses light like a musician uses his instrument," Zach tells Nathaniel. "To create wonder and emotion."

"Exactly." Nathaniel smiles at him, then returns to the portfolio. "I'm also captivated by the photographs of the rooms of possessions. The things someone obviously couldn't part with. Highly personal and revealing, and yet there's nobody there."

"I call them 'ghost photos.' The invisible owners hovering out of sight."

Nathaniel gives Zach a long, appreciative look, then flips between the kids' room and the artist's studio. He pulls at his earlobe. "If you have more of these, maybe we could do a show that's half photographs of people inside the building and half just the stashed property. We could call it 'There and Not There.'"

Zach promises to return in two weeks with more photos. *So much for your stinging insights, Lori.*

51

JASON

Jason is hoping for a longer visit with Marta today than the fifteen minutes he had yesterday. Clearly in shock, she didn't even look like herself, smaller somehow, her eyes unfocused. And she kept rhythmically, almost ritualistically, picking at a thread on the leg of her ill-fitting pants. She hardly spoke, and when she did, it was in a whisper. He tried to be as encouraging as possible, more encouraging than he had any right to be. When he told her Liddy sent her love, she broke down. Before he could console her, a guard took her away.

He has an hour-long appointment scheduled with her this morning, and he hopes, given the additional time, they'll be able to have an actual conversation. But when he calls to verify, he's informed the jail is on lockdown: no phone calls or visitors, including attorneys. It's rare for a county jail to go on lockdown, so he's suspicious. But when he checks Boston.com, he sees it's true. Three women tried to stab a guard using toothbrushes they whittled down to sharp points. An investigation to find the perpetrators and their accomplices is ongoing.

Things have changed at Suffolk, as they have at most city and county jails. These used to be places where people stayed a few days, maybe a week: those awaiting bail or a trial, some ready to be transferred to prison, maybe one or two serving out a short sentence. But now that arrests and convictions are up, the prisons are bursting, and this causes clogged county jails, which means a convicted murderer can be in a cell with a person who can't pay bail on a shoplifting charge. Or with a legal visa holder whose paperwork got screwed up. The overcrowding increases the wrath of those forced to live in these inhumane conditions, as well as the type of attacks that caused the lockdown.

He's got to get Marta out of there. First, he calls the local ICE office where bail is processed. He punches Marta's alien number into the automated system. *"There is no record of that number at this ICE ERO location."* He tries again, taking more care when pressing the buttons. *"There is no record of that number at this ICE ERO location."* He calls the main number again and doesn't choose any of the offered options, hoping that eventually an actual person will come on the line. After about five minutes on hold, just as he's about to hang up, someone does. "ICE ERO field office, Burlington," a belligerent voice booms.

Jason explains his predicament and then waits another five minutes before Belligerent Voice returns and says, "You've got the wrong alien number for Mercedes Bustamante."

Jason grabs a pen to write it down, but Belligerent Voice offers no additional information. "May I please have the correct number?" Jason asks as pleasantly as he can, given that he wants to smash the phone into his desk. Or better, into the guy's face. There's a grunt and then a spew of numbers.

"Would it be possible for you to tell me if Ms. Bustamante has been granted bail?"

"No. That's what the automated system is for. Got to start over and go through the system."

When Jason puts in the correct number, the system reports that no bail has been approved. Next he calls Judge Cohen's office, and again he strikes out. The judge is in court. He leaves a message. Then he checks on the status of the lockdown at Suffolk, but there haven't been any updates.

His phone rings, and he sees it's Liddy. He's less than eager to recount the details of his morning and tries to convince himself that she'll be better off not knowing. But that's not fair to her. "Hey," he says. "How are you?"

"You tell me."

"Holding steady."

"I didn't have a chance to pick up the visitation application yesterday, so I'm on my way over there now. Is there any chance they'll let me see her today?"

Jason wonders what could have kept Liddy from going to Suffolk yesterday, but he doesn't ask. "There's a glitch. A lockdown at the jail."

"A lockdown? Was there a riot? Is Marta okay? What does—"

"No, nothing like a riot," he interrupts, before she can work herself up even more. "It's not that big a deal. A few desperate women tried to stab a guard using sharpened toothbrushes." He sighs. "I'm sure Marta is fine."

"But you don't know?"

"I do. If there were a problem involving her, they would have contacted me. I called to double-check, but no one's allowed in today. Not even lawyers. I'll call again later and see if I can get more information."

"Can I still get the application?"

"Not today. I'm sorry, Liddy. It's a bad break. But hopefully everything will be up and running tomorrow. Just check to make sure they're open before you go." He doesn't tell her it could be days, that actually there's no telling how long the lockdown could go on.

52

ROSE

Rose has asked the receptionist twice when she'll be able to see Michael, even though she knows the receptionist doesn't have this information. But she has to do something. Sitting around in this waiting room of horrors is driving her crazy. As is not knowing. She's not leaving until she gets to see Michael and is sure he's going to live. After she spoke with the doctor, she called Vince. He promised he'd get the girls to school as early as possible and then come to the hospital to be with Michael because Rose has to be at work at six. He actually sounded like his old self, but a worried old self, and he didn't even blame her for Michael getting shot.

There's a nurse here named Dave who says she should try to sleep and that he'll come wake her when she's cleared to see Michael. Boys who are nurses and girls who are doctors and Michael fighting for his life. The world turned upside down.

She isn't asleep when Dave finally shows up. He leads her behind the curtain and stands right next to her as she stares at the bed. It's like there's just a lump under a sheet with tubes going in and out and screens and lights and a whole bunch of machines that sound like they're going to break apart. It doesn't seem like there could be anything human there. She hears a cry like someone's strangling and thinks it's Michael but then realizes the noise is coming from her. She rushes to the bed.

Dave stops her before she can get there. "You have to be careful," he says. Then he lifts Michael's hand from under the sheet. It's covered with needles. And there are all kinds of other things taped to his skin. Dave puts the dead-looking hand on the bed. It doesn't seem like it could be Michael's hand, but she knows it is. "You can touch him, Ms. Gentilini. Just make sure not to dislodge any of the equipment. You can talk to him, too, if you like."

"Can, can he hear me?" This can't be Michael all bandaged up with his face the color of ash, not moving and barely breathing. Someone shot her baby.

"We don't know for sure, but it's possible. And if he does, it'll help him get better faster," Dave squeezes her arm and leaves them alone.

Rose drops to her knees, touches Michael's hand. "Michael, it's Mommy and you're going to be fine so don't be afraid. I'm here. I'm here, right here, and I'll always be here for you. They're taking good care of you, and I love you, and you've got to stay with me."

Michael doesn't move. His hand is too cold to belong to a living person. When another nurse tells her the time is up, Rose stumbles out of the ICU. *Dear Jesus, please don't let him die.*

She doesn't think she can sleep, but she sort of does for a little while. A bunch of doctors show up when it's still dark, and Rose bolts out of her chair. But the doctors go into the ICU before she gets a chance to ask them anything. She's all groggy and scared and just stares at the white jackets walking away from her. She's not sure she wants to hear what they're going to say. They could say Michael has passed or that he's never going to wake up or that he's going to be paralyzed for the rest of his life like Garrett Haines.

She needs a cup of coffee, but she has to talk to the doctors no matter how scared she is of what they're going to tell her. She needs to go to the bathroom, but she can't leave to do that either. So she starts to make deals with God. All the things she's going to stop and start doing if he lets Michael live. But she has trouble because each promise seems to float away before she can even think it, and all that's left inside her is fear.

Someone touches her shoulder, and Rose jumps up. "Is he dead?" she cries.

The doctor has tons of wrinkles around his eyes, and when he smiles at her there's even more. "He's alive, Ms. Gentilini. And although there's still a long way to go, if I were to guess, I'd guess he's going to stay that way."

"Stay what way?" she demands. "Like the way he is now? He, he didn't hear me or anything. And he's so cold . . ."

"Please sit," the doctor says and then takes the chair next to hers. "The news is hopeful. He's a strong boy, young, healthy. His injuries are bad, and though it may not seem like it at the moment, he caught some luck. No major organs struck. A seeing-eye hit."

"Seeing-eye what?"

"I'm sorry. Bad baseball analogy. Drives my wife nuts. But the important thing for you to understand is that it looks like Michael is going to pull through."

She stares at the doctor. "He's not going to die?" she finally whispers. Her prayers, her prayers. "Thank you, Jesus, thank you, Jesus, thank you, Jesus."

The doctor stands and puts his hand on her shoulder. "He may be in the hospital for a couple of weeks, but I'm thinking he'll be walking out of here under his own steam."

Rose knows she should thank the man—kiss his feet even—but her legs are so weak that he's gone before she can get out of the chair. She can't stay either. She's got to get to work because she can't afford to lose a day's pay. Her insurance is nowhere near as good as it was at Metropolis, and it's not going to come close to covering everything Michael is going need.

The ICU nurses promise they'll take good care of him until Vince comes, and that they'll call her if there's anything important she needs to know. She doesn't want to leave Michael alone even if it's only for a little while, but she's got no choice.

53

JASON

Jason walks to the Starbucks in Central Square. There are two Starbucks closer to Metropolis, and he has a pretty good coffee maker in his office, but after talking with Liddy about the lockdown, he needs the air. Even if it's cool, damp air. The problem with spring in New England is that it doesn't really exist. It goes from winter to cold rain, and then suddenly it's ninety degrees. Everyone forgets this. Winter-weary Bostonians who have been looking forward to the blue skies and balmy breezes of spring are, year after year, sorely disappointed. This includes Jason.

When he gets to the Starbucks, it's crowded, as always. Also noisy, and it reeks of too much sugar and yesterday's pastries, the bitter bite of coffee beans overwhelmed by the chemical odor of the unnecessary air-conditioning. It takes ten minutes to get his cappuccino. He spies a vacant seat along the bar facing the street and squeezes into it. He's packed between a teenager yelling into her phone and two women with crying babies on their laps. He grabs a messed-up *Boston Globe* someone left behind. No front section, but there's Sports and Metro. He should have stayed in the office.

He's happy to read that the Red Sox are having their best ten-game start in franchise history, 9–1, with a whopping win against the Yankees last night, 14–1. Benintendi looks like an All-Star, and Price could lead the pitching staff in wins. But it stresses him out that everyone in Red Sox Nation is already predicting, in April, that the Sox are going to win the World Series. Especially after what happened last season. It's like believing in a Boston spring.

Fortunately, the mothers and crying babies leave, but a large elderly man quickly takes one of the spots and reverently places down a plate holding a blueberry scone, two croissants, and a thick slab of caramelized pound cake. Then he elbows his way into Jason's personal space. The other chair is just as quickly filled by a scruffy millennial with a laptop the size of a suitcase.

Jason's phone dings. It's a text from Var: an encrypted website address followed by a letter/number password that runs over fifteen digits. When he follows the instructions, a message flashes on the screen: *Possible info on family. Two to three days.* Then both the message and the site disappear—similar to Snapchat but much more sophisticated. The first encouraging news of his discouraging morning.

He picks up the Metro section, skims the headlines: UMass budget problems, a pastor charged with child rape, a car crash involving a pregnant woman. Then he sees one that really bums him out. Two 14-year-old boys shot in Revere, one dead.

Fourteen. Fourteen years old.

Two boys were shot in Revere on Tuesday night, Revere Police reported, and three men were arrested after a chase. The shooting took place in Fredericks Park, 15 Everard Street, just before 11:45 p.m., and the victims have been identified as Michael Gentilini, 14, and Reginald Green, 14. Green was declared dead at the scene, and Gentilini was taken to Boston Medical Center, with a gunshot wound to the abdomen. The three men arrested, all believed to be in their early 20s, are expected to be charged with one count of murder and two counts of assault with intent to murder. The motive for the incident is still under investigation, but a neighbor said there has been a recent increase in gang activity in the neighborhood.

Jason reads the article three times, and as much as he wants to have misread it, it's the same each time. He's surprised the paper identified the boys by name, given their age, but at least Michael is still alive. Although it sounds as if that could change at any minute. He checks with Boston Medical, but they won't tell him anything. He could go over there, give Rose some support. But that seems presumptuous, as does calling her. He decides on a text of condolence and concern.

His phone immediately rings, but when he answers, all he hears is sobbing. Jason stands, throws his half-full cup in the trash, and walks outside. "How's he doing?"

"He's, he's in bad shape," she gasps. "Really bad, and they keep telling me he's young and strong and that's a good thing but they hardly let us see him. Only once an hour for five minutes."

"It's an ICU rule—that's how they do it. But Boston Medical is a Level One trauma center. Best place for him to be."

"Yeah, so I heard."

Jason hesitates. "Did they tell you if he's going to be okay?"

"This doctor this morning said that if everything goes well he should be okay. Something about a seeing-eye hit that I didn't understand. I think about the bullet missing stuff. But, oh, a bullet. In my boy!"

"That's good news, Rose," Jason says, hoping to steer her to the positive. "They wouldn't say that if it weren't true. Very encouraging."

"But if you saw him . . ." Crying overtakes her words.

"Tell me what can I do to help."

"If, if . . . When he gets better, do you think that judge is going to send him to juvie? Because he got into trouble?"

Jason hasn't thought that far out yet, but of course they will. "Don't get ahead of yourself. It's all about getting him healthy, getting him out of there."

"But will they?"

Jason hesitates again, then says carefully, "We can ask the court to take the fact that he's been hurt into consideration."

"Will that work?"

"I'll do everything I can to make it happen."

Before Marta was arrested, Jason had been spinning pleasant visions of a leisurely road trip to California in the near future, wending his way across the country, perhaps ending up in Sabrina's bed. And now another complication: Michael Gentilini in the ICU and facing criminal charges. There's little chance Jason will be able to keep the boy from being shipped off to juvie, most likely Carbone Hall in Framingham, where it will be difficult for Rose to visit, but he's got to stick around and try.

"He can't go there!" Rose's voice rises, thin and reedy. "I was talking to this girl in the waiting room and she told me that everyone who gets sent there comes out worse than they were before. They're all in gangs and have these new criminal friends and lots more criminal enemies. She said if he doesn't die now he'll probably die when he comes back!"

Jason can only imagine the conversation. "Rose, listen to me, this girl doesn't know what she's talking about, doesn't know what's going to happen to Michael. She's just shooting her mouth off. I'm your lawyer, so let me—"

"You're not hearing me! He. Can. Not. Go!"

"Okay, okay. I get it. He can't go. But you can't let this rattle you like this. You've got to focus on praying, and holding Michael's hand, being there for him. I'll start looking into the legal aspects of this right away. This afternoon."

"We don't have any money and I don't have any—"

"We'll deal with that later. Michael is the only thing you've got to think about now—and taking care of yourself so you can take care of him."

"Thank, thank you," she stammers, and then begins to weep again. "You're a good man. May God bless."

When he hangs up, he thinks about all the thanks he's been getting lately. From Rose, from Liddy, from Marta. These women are thanking him because he's telling them what they want to hear, not necessarily what's true or what's going to happen or what he's actually going to be able to accomplish. It starts to spit a cold rain, and he thinks again of California, which is suddenly very far away.

54

ROSE

The whole day feels weird as Rose takes orders, buses tables, and wipes down counters just like it's any old shift. She's so busy that for a second here and there she actually forgets that last night Michael got shot and he's lying in a hospital bed because a bullet went clear through his body. It makes her feel guilty to forget but it's also a relief.

Jason said he's going to do his best to keep Michael out of juvenile detention, but Rose could tell from his voice that he doesn't think his best will do the trick. She's sure Michael is going to get arrested as soon as he can leave the hospital. That girl in the waiting room said she'd seen way too many boys go up as good kids and come back as bad men who end up dead or in prison right after they get home. This will not happen to her boy. It will not. Her mind spins with possible ways to make sure it doesn't.

She and Michael could take off and try their luck in some other city. But this obviously won't work. There's the girls and Vince and no money. She could send Michael on a bus to her cousin Helene in New Jersey and tell the police he ran away. This would work better but won't really work either. Rose isn't going to be able to pay Helene anything and Michael isn't the easiest kid. Plus he eats a lot. How long will someone who isn't his mother be able to put up with that—or the trouble he's probably going to get himself into?

What she needs is someone who's got enough power and money to make the judge think again about what to do with Michael. Liddy is a possibility. But now with the television saying that the police are investigating if someone might have pushed Garrett on purpose—and it's got to be Liddy they're talking about—Liddy probably won't be able to do anything. The only person she sort of knows who might be able to help is Garrett Haines. He's as important as they come and must have lots of pull in the right places.

She bets ol' Garrett would be more than willing to swap a little of that pull for an eyewitness who can place the blame for his accident on Liddy. There's no doubt in her mind that Liddy pushed him, and must have pushed him hard. Rose went to the fourth floor the morning after it happened, and there's no way Liddy wouldn't have seen that the elevator door was hanging open. It was right there. Plus from everything Liddy told her about Garrett, Liddy had reasons to want him dead.

It would be a mean thing to do to Liddy and that's what stopped Rose the first time she thought about this. But now it's not money she wants. It's Michael's life. And she figures that being considerate of someone who hasn't been that nice to her isn't all that important anymore.

THE NEXT DAY, Rose goes to Mass General to talk to Garrett. This hospital has got it all over Boston Medical. Everything is cleaner, outside and inside. Even the people are cleaner. It's prettier and smells much better. Rose buys flowers she can't afford at the store in the lobby, figuring they'll make her seem more visitor-like and proper. She's wearing her best dress. When she asks for Mr. Haines they send her to a room where she's got to show ID and then sit around and wait for someone to come and interview her.

The woman who comes looks more like an admin than a nurse and Rose knows this is going to be the hardest part. "I don't know Mr. Haines personally," she says the way she planned out. "But I've always admired him and what he's done for so many people—especially my kids. Because of him, through one of his charities, Boston Partners in Education, my three children got to go to a really good preschool program and now they're all on the honor roll. And this is because of what he did, and I'd like to tell him this," she lies.

"That's very nice . . ."

"So I just wanted to tell him how sorry I am about what happened to him. And to thank him personally for everything he's done for my family." Rose holds up the flowers like the admin can't see them.

"If you give me your name, I'd be happy to bring him the flowers and tell him what you've told me."

"I'd like to give them to him myself."

"I'm sorry, Ms. Gentilini, but as you know, Mr. Haines isn't well. His doctors restrict visitors to family and close friends."

Rose grips the flowers so tightly she feels a stem break. "I was at Metropolis the night of his accident, and I saw what happened. I'd like to tell him about that too."

The admin acts unimpressed, but she nods and asks Rose to please wait for her to check with Mr. Haines. In a few minutes she comes back and says Mr. Haines will be happy to see her, and then she takes Rose to his room.

The whole hospital might be nice, but where they're walking is some supernice part that must be just for rich people. It's quiet and there's pretty tile on the floor and wood halfway up the walls. There's lots of paintings and they might even be the real thing. When they get to his room it looks like it should be in some fancy hotel.

Mr. Haines is sitting in a wheelchair behind a big desk that's covered with files and papers and a huge computer monitor. He takes off his glasses and his eyes are suspicious and cold when she walks over to him. "I understand you have something you'd like to tell me," he says.

Rose lays the flowers down on the desk. "I saw her push you," she says quickly. "Liddy, Mrs. Haines, I mean. I work there and was just leaving the building and I heard arguing and climbed down the stairs to see what was going on. I didn't mean to be nosy but I was worried that something bad—"

Mr. Haines holds up his hands. "Tell me what you saw. Second by second, if you can remember."

Rose does, except that she leaves out the part where she didn't actually see Liddy push him. She doesn't need to because it's obvious that's what happened. When she finishes he asks if she's willing to sign some papers that say just what she told him. When she says she will, his voice and his eyes get all friendly and he wants to know what he can do to repay her.

She presses her fingernails into her palm so hard there are little red marks all over them when she gets home. "I've got a son . . ."

AFTER SHE EXPLAINED the situation, Mr. Haines said he would take care of it, and in a few days Michael's arrest disappears. Poof, it's gone. "Expunged" is what she thinks Mr. Haines called it. Whatever's the right word, it's just the same as if the whole thing never happened in the first place. So now there's no reason for Michael to have to go to juvie. He's got another chance to get it right and so does she.

Jason is surprised when Rose tells him Michael's record got wiped clean, and he's even more surprised when she says it was because she knew someone who knew someone. He doesn't ask who and she gets the feeling that maybe he doesn't want to hear the answer. And even though she feels a little bad about ratting out Liddy, it saved her child's life, so how bad can she feel?

55

LIDDY

Jason had said he hoped the lockdown at the jail would be lifted by this morning, but either way, Marta is still behind bars. As Liddy waits for the movers in the Metropolis parking lot, she tries not to obsess over those guard attacks. Instead, she focuses on the fact that once she shows the movers what to take, she'll never have to step foot inside this building again. And this afternoon she should be able to fill out her visitor application and maybe even see Marta.

After the kids left, she took the cash she and Marta had stashed in their units, but Marta's unit is still packed with dozens of cartons holding all the work product she's completed over the past four years. The twins took the things they wanted, and Liddy has decided to just leave the furniture in both units. She knows she should donate it, but she's exhausted and can't take on anything else right now. Most likely it will be auctioned off and someone who needs it will eventually get to use it anyway.

So it's just Marta's things plus the dollhouse Robin claims she wants to save for her own children—but Liddy suspects she wants for herself—that will go into the storage room at The Tower. This is only temporary, as she doesn't expect to be in the condo for long, but it's the simplest solution for now.

When the moving truck pulls in, Liddy climbs out of the car and motions for the men to follow her through the front door. She punches in the code and avoids looking at Rose's empty office as well as the police tape still guarding the elevator. So much lost. Rose lost her job. Marta lost a place to live. The owner will lose his business. Jason will lose his office. And everyone else will be forced to leave too.

It infuriates her that Garrett will end up with Metropolis, but so be it. She's finally going to be free of him, although she's a little troubled that she hasn't heard from Dawn since the attorney submitted the countersuit to Garrett's lawyer. Liddy has been so distracted by Marta's situation she almost forgot about it. She calls Dawn's office, but Dawn is in court, so she leaves a message with her paralegal . The day is warm, but a shiver crawls up Liddy's spine.

When the movers finish unloading at The Tower, Liddy heads across the Common to the Public Garden to cheer herself up. The spring has been rainy and dreary so far, but the last two days of sun have transformed the city. The reddish buds on the trees are opening into shiny green leaves, tulips line the walkways, cherry trees on the Esplanade are flowering, and crocuses thrust their yellow stamens upward. Even a group of homeless people on the Common are smiling: two men play Frisbee with a woman in a red cape; a skinny redheaded man is sprawled out on a bench, his heavily bearded face tilted toward the sun.

THE NEXT MORNING she wakes to a text from Jason: *Lockdown is over. Heading to Suffolk.*

Liddy knows she can't get her visitor application until three, but she rushes into the shower to make sure she'll be ready. After she towels dry, she puts up water for tea and pops a piece of bread in the toaster. Still no word from Dawn, which is troubling, but it's early, and surely she'll call with news soon. Today is the thirteenth, the day Garrett has to respond to her countersuit, the day she turns his scheme back at him, the day he's going to fail.

"Good morning, my friend," she says when Jason calls.

"And a very good morning to you too."

"I got your text. How's she doing?"

"I haven't been there yet. I'm on my way to the ICE office in Burlington."

"Marta hasn't seen anyone in days!" Liddy cries, astonished that Jason would make this decision. "You have to go see her first. She must be out of her mind!"

Jason chuckles. "It's just that I've got to fill out some paperwork to make sure everything goes smoothly"—he pauses dramatically—"when she gets released."

Liddy presses the phone to her ear. "Released?"

"Bail! Marta is getting out on bail!"

"Bail," she repeats slowly, not quite comprehending. But as the word flows through her body, her muscles liquefy and she understands. "Bail!"

"That's why I'm going up to Burlington," Jason is saying. "When I'm done, I'll head right over to Suffolk. Just have to pay the fee, and then—"

"How did this happen?"

"I annoyed the hell out of Judge Cohen's assistant. The judge read through the materials and decided Marta is a good candidate for bail. And even better, she set—"

"When? When will this—"

"Hold on, Liddy. Don't you want to hear the best part?"

"Best part?" Liddy knows she keeps repeating Jason's words, but she's having trouble taking it all in.

Jason laughs. "The judge set a date for Marta's asylum hearing. A week from next Monday."

"Thank you, thank you, thank you," Liddy cries. "Will she be out today? Can I meet you at Suffolk so—"

"Be patient," Jason warns. "You know how bureaucracies work. Slow and tortuous. Plus she has to be discharged from Suffolk and then sent to the Burlington office for the official release. So I'm—"

"Why can't she just leave from Suffolk? That doesn't make any sense."

"Procedure, procedure, procedure," Jason reminds her. "So I'm guessing Monday. Too bad it's a Friday, because nothing can happen over the weekend. Probably in the afternoon. Will that work for you?"

"Yes, yes, that works for me. Absolutely. We'll go together then."

Liddy spins happily around the apartment for the rest of the morning. After Marta's arrest, Jason brought over the clothes Marta had left at his apartment, along with her computer and files. But Liddy had been too superstitious to unpack them, wary it might jinx Marta's chances. Now she hangs Marta's clothes in the closet she cleaned out earlier and places the rest into bureau drawers. She sets Marta's laptop on Garrett's desk, clears room for the papers, and stacks the files. She stands back and surveys her work, pleased. Again, temporary, but Liddy can't wait to see Marta's face when she sees her new office.

The phone rings while she's eating lunch. Dawn. "Did he agree?" Liddy asks. Of course he did. Today everything works out.

There's a pause. "It didn't go the way we hoped."

Dawn reads a draft witness statement Garrett's lawyer sent, asserting that Liddy pushed Garrett into the clearly broken door. Liddy starts shaking so badly that her phone falls to the floor. She scrambles to pick it up and drops it again. When she finally retrieves it, she sees that the glass has shattered. "This, this can't be right." She knows that it can be but tries anyway. "There wasn't anyone else in the building. Who's this so-called witness?"

"His attorney didn't say, but he's sending me the signed affidavit in a day or two, so we'll know then. He did say that their original offer has been extended, and you have forty-eight hours to agree or they're taking the statement and their other evidence to the police."

Liddy stares at the half-eaten yogurt in front of her, tipped sideways on the place mat, the empty cup of tea. "So if I don't go back to him, I'll be arrested?"

"Not right away. At least not until after they do more investigating, make sure they have enough evidence. And I'm sure I can slow down the—"

"But I'll have to go to the police station for questioning," Liddy says, amazed that she's thinking so clearly, speaking so lucidly. "And the media will find out."

"We don't know that for sure either." Dawn hesitates. "But, yes, that's likely to be the next step."

Liddy watches the tiny sailboats on the Charles River catching the wind, tacking this way and that. "Tell them if Garrett agrees no one will ever see that statement, especially the media and the kids, and there won't ever be a trial, I'll live with him and pretend to be his loving wife. I'll give up Marta, do whatever else he wants. But it needs to be in writing. Ironclad."

"Don't jump to a decision right now," Dawn advises. "Give it some time. I'll email a PDF of the draft statement over to you. We can still fight this. Still win, or at least get it down to simple assault. Eyewitness accounts are notoriously suspect, and—"

"This will destroy my children. I'm not going to do that."

"Listen to me," Dawn says sternly. "There's no evidence you tampered with the elevator or that you were aware it was broken. And there's no way they can prove you knew Garrett was coming that night. Also, battered woman's syndrome is a viable defense, which both Marta Arvelo and Rose Gentilini can testify to."

"No, you listen to me. I will not put my kids through a trial where their mother is accused of trying to kill their father. Or the media circus that's going to accompany it. There are no choices here."

"Please, do me a favor and take some time with this." Dawn's voice is softer, more conciliatory. "Maybe we can avoid a trial, come to some kind of compromise."

"If I don't go back to him, he'll take it to trial. He's not the compromising type."

"How about you sleep on it? We'll talk in the morning. Things might look different then."

"Do you have children?"

Dawn hesitates. "No, I don't."

"That's why you think if I sleep on it, things will look different tomorrow."

Liddy hangs up and goes to her computer to read the statement. As much as she would like to deny its content, she can't. For it describes exactly what happened that night.

Yes, she and Garrett were standing in front of the elevator, close together and yelling in each other's faces.

Yes, it was easy to see that the elevator door was off its track.

No, she hadn't sidestepped his advance, as she'd told Marta, Jason, and the police, because Garrett had made no advance.

And, yes, she had pushed him into that broken door as hard as she could.

56

MARTA

Fifteen empty seats surround her, and to an outside observer it would appear that Marta is the only passenger in the police van. Yet this outside observer would be wrong. Hundreds of phantoms, whose fear and sweat she can smell, ride along with her. Despair rises from the rows behind her and hovers like an amputated limb that throbs long after it's been cut off. She is haunted by their stories, alive and pulsing.

The guards came for her when it was still dark, and now the sun is rising behind the glass buildings of the Seaport. It is Monday, and Jason had told her that on Monday morning she would be taken to a town north of the city that starts with a *B* and released on bail. He promised he would be waiting for her. Her knight in bright armor. Despite these promises and the van and the fact that she is on I-93 North, dressed in the slightly musty clothes she wore to court a week ago, it does not feel as if she is moving toward anything good.

The driver cracks his window, and Marta greedily inhales the air infused with car and truck exhausts. Not particularly fresh, but it is better than what she has been breathing. The air at Suffolk was thick and hot and suffocating, and the single hour a day outdoors in the yard was canceled more often than not.

When she did go outside, she stayed close to the building's facade, afraid to catch the attention of the guards or the angry women arguing and whispering and casting the evil eye in every direction. Now the sun is hot on her right shoulder. Traffic encases them. A horn honks. She presses her hand into the metal edge of her seat until it hurts and there's a red line running across her palm. All of her senses confirm that she is here, so she must be.

In less than an hour, Marta sits in a holding cell while her paperwork is being processed. So much paperwork and so much processing, and yet no one has confirmed she will be free when it is complete. She examines the room with its hard bench and its cinder-block walls and its green metal door without a knob. Bars crisscross a two-foot square window set at eye level in the door. Do they really believe a person could climb through such a tiny rectangle? They do not. If she has learned anything in the past week, it is that bars are a symbol. A symbol of power and a symbol of submission.

Marta is not certain if she slept more than a few minutes at a time while she lived within all those bars. But she knows that she hardly ate and she was only allowed two showers with hardly any soap. She cannot imagine what she looks like or what she smells like, and she is ashamed.

Finally, a woman in street clothes enters and indicates that she should stand. Marta uncoils, and the woman leads her into a brightly lit waiting room. Jason jumps from a chair, rushes toward her, and gives her a hug. They have never hugged before, and Marta is moved. "Thank you," she says. "I'll never be able to thank you enough." Her eyes scan the room. No Liddy.

Jason grabs her arm. "Let's get you out of here."

Marta follows him through the door. She is filled with dread because of Liddy's absence, but when the sun hits her, she stops and raises her face to meet it. Here she is, walking outdoors. Here she is, crossing a parking lot. Here she is with Jason, her savior, her protector. No handcuffs. No guards. No enraged women. She stretches her arms above her head and wiggles her fingers at the sky. Then she drops them. Where is Liddy?

They climb into his car, and when Jason clicks his seat belt, he says, "Why don't we go to my place? All of your things are there, and you can shower and get a change of clothes. Take a nap. What do you say?"

"I would very much like a shower. And a nap. Thank you." Maybe Liddy is waiting for her at Jason's apartment. But Liddy promised to bring the clothes and the work materials that she left at Jason's to her condo at The Tower. Why has she not done so? Marta's chest tightens.

They are silent as Jason pulls out of the office park and enters the highway. "I can see you're a bit shell-shocked," he finally says. "And who wouldn't be after what you've been through? But I have some good news for you, something very surprising that might come as an additional shock . . . And, uh, I just want you to be prepared." He glances over at her.

Marta meets his eyes, and he turns quickly back to the road. What he wants is to prepare her for the bad news that is coming right after whatever this good news is. And the bad news is about Liddy. *Una hija.*

"Would it be better if we waited until we get to the apartment?" he asks when she does not respond. "Maybe after you've showered and had something to eat?"

She leans her head against the headrest and closes her eyes. She is so very tired. "I am ready to hear it now."

Jason exits the highway and pulls into a shopping center. He turns off the car, touches her hand. "Your mother and sisters are alive and safe. They're in Spain."

This is so unexpected that it takes a few seconds for her to understand his words. Her mother and sisters? They are in Spain? This is not possible. She stares out the windshield at the row of scrawny trees on the grass median separating the slanted rows of yellow lines. Maduro and his men are everywhere. After what they did to Papí and Juan, they would never have allowed the rest of the Bustamantes to leave Venezuela alive. She turns to him, incredulous.

Jason's smile is kind. "I checked and double-checked. I'm sure. I have their contact information. There's been no mistake."

JASON'S BATHROOM IS cramped and could have used improvements years ago, but the shower is strong and hot. She is in a shower by herself. There is soap. There is shampoo. The naked bodies of dozens of other women do not surround her. She shivers, despite the warm steam, and remembers how she had to push against those bodies to get to the rusty water. All that sad skin, doughy and slippery. All those angry words.

But she is not there anymore. She is free. She raises her face to the water. Her mother and sisters are alive. She will be able to talk to them soon, and perhaps be able to see them. A miracle. She washes herself and her hair three times. She still does not feel completely clean, yet she does not feel quite as dirty. This is the same for her joy and relief. She is afraid to ask Jason about Liddy, because what he's going to tell her will surely undercut those feelings.

Marta dries herself, changes into fresh clothes, and steps into the kitchen. Jason is making chocolate-chip pancakes, her favorite breakfast. There is a place mat and a napkin on the little table. Also a cup of coffee, a glass of orange juice, and a vase filled with spring flowers. She is overwhelmed by the sweetness of the tableau. Jason places her full plate on the table and bows like a waiter in an elegant restaurant. A voracious hunger grips her, and she attacks the food. He leans against the counter and watches her with a pleased smile on his face. Then he turns to make another batch.

When she finishes the second helping, she pushes her plate away and takes a sip of coffee. Dark and strong, with a tiny dab of cream, exactly as she likes it. "This was lovely. Thank you."

Jason pours himself a cup of coffee and sits across from her. "Guess you were hungry."

"I probably should not have eaten so fast. It is a long time since my stomach has held so much food." She pats her midsection, which feels far too thin. "So much good food," she adds with a feeble smile.

Jason does not meet her eyes and then clears his throat. Neither is a good sign. "Marta . . ."

She forces herself to look at him and feels a rush of empathy. This is no easier for him than it is for her. "Please, Jason, please say what you have to say."

He clears his throat again. "This isn't as good as my last news."

"I do not expect it to be," she says, and to make it easier on him she adds, "It is about Liddy."

He inspects his coffee cup and then raises his eyes. "Yes."

And suddenly Marta sees it all. "Garrett," she says. "He has won."

Jason nods.

"Tell me."

After Jason describes the details of the agreement, he says, "I'm sorry, Marta, but when Garrett comes home from the hospital, they'll move back to the condo together—which is why I picked up all your things and brought them here. And if Liddy defaults on any of his conditions, the witness statement will be sent to the police."

Move back to the condo together. How will Liddy stand it? How will she?

"It would be difficult to prove premeditation," Jason continues, and it sounds as if his voice is coming from far away. "But now that an eyewitness has corroborated Haines's story, plus some of the physical peculiarities, this could be enough for a judge or jury to find her guilty of felony assault and battery, maybe more."

"This would result in many years in jail?" she whispers.

"Yes."

Marta cannot speak.

Jason begins to back up his chair, but then he remains seated. "Haines gave her no choice. Just like he did with the owner of Metropolis, he threatened to come to the courtroom in a hospital bed and testify that she tried to kill him. As you can imagine, she's heartbroken, devastated, and furious. But she can't put her kids through a trial. Or the media frenzy."

Marta's chest is so tight she can only take small breaths. "I will never be able to see her again."

Jason closes his eyes and nods.

Marta stands abruptly. "I think I would like to take the nap that you suggested. I am very tired, so I will be able to use the couch. I hope this will not bother you."

"No couch for you." Jason stands also. "I made up the bed. It's all yours."

She thinks about protesting, but she is so bone-weary and heartbroken that staging any kind of argument is beyond her strength. "Thank you," she says again, and stumbles off into the bedroom. She collapses on the bed and sleeps through to the next day.

AFTER THREE DAYS of eating and sleeping and showering, Marta feels more like the person she was before her arrest. She has not left the apartment, although she is free to do so. She is exchanging her grief over losing her family for grief over losing Liddy, and finds she is incapable of doing more than sitting on the couch and pretending to watch television. It is a newer bereavement, more visceral. Often it becomes unbearable, and she can do nothing but submit.

She is unable to stop thinking about the witness statement. This explains the terrible guilt Liddy was feeling. Why she yielded to Garrett's threats. But because Liddy knew the elevator was broken, this does not mean she was responsible for tampering with it. Marta is infuriated that Garrett would propose such a falsehood to the police.

Yet there is also lightness. Her mother and sisters are alive. She has not contacted them, and will not do so until she knows if she will be granted asylum. She does not want to raise false hopes, theirs or her own. If it goes well, she will find a small apartment, finish her dissertation, receive her degree, and begin her career. Perhaps she will move to Spain, or perhaps her mother and sisters will move here.

Jason warns her that even after asylum is granted—if asylum is granted—their family reunion might take some time. She cannot travel on her Venezuelan passport and will need to secure a refugee travel document. He says that many asylees travel abroad without problems, and it is just a matter of paperwork. If her family is in possession of Spanish passports, they may be able to come here right away.

On Saturday night, they go to a French restaurant in the South End for dinner. She has been cowering inside Metropolis and Jason's apartment for almost a year, and it is strange to be able to go out with no fear of arrest. They order a bottle of wine, raise their glasses. It is an unseasonably warm night, and the sidewalks are full of dogs and babies and happy couples, both straight and gay. It should be Liddy and she who are walking along with them, hand in hand. But this is not to be.

"Have you made a decision about what is next for you?" she asks Jason. Since they met, he has been reticent about himself, and she does not like that their conversations are always about her. She is surprised when he actually answers her question.

"I'm out of here as soon as you're all set, and are no longer in need of the services of a top-notch immigration lawyer," he says with a grin.

Although not unexpected, Marta is stunned by his revelation. "Where will you go?"

"A cross-country road trip, to clear my head and figure out what I want to be when I grow up. Maybe live in California for a while." He shrugs. "I'm going to stash my work files in my parents' basement, save the law books for my niece, and leave all the office furniture at Metropolis. What else am I going to do with it? Move it to another storage facility? I'll do the same with the furniture in the apartment. Which means you're welcome to stay there until the lease runs out in September."

"It seems I am always thanking you," Marta says, her eyes filling with tears at the prospect of losing him too. "You are a good friend, and I will miss you."

57

ZACH

The four images Zach printed this morning hang from clothespins suspended on the line above the tub. He walks back and forth in front of the pictures and confirms his suspicion that none of them will work. Damn. Serge's unruly organizational skills are making it extremely difficult to find the interior Metropolis photographs Nathaniel asked for.

To make matters worse, it appears from the various subjects, locations, and weather conditions that Serge took his photographs in spurts, shooting two or three rolls at the same time, and then, days or weeks or even months later, turning to a completely different place and focus. It also seems that he developed and printed the pictures in the same way. That this is who the man is: two settings, on and off.

Zach is starting to develop, pun intended, an image of Serge Laurent, the man. Granted, it's just a fantasy he's spinning, but it cheers him to conjure Serge, to give him form. He's tall and lanky, probably middle-age, and something bad must have happened to him: a screwed-up family, extreme poverty, sexual abuse, the battlefield, some other traumatic event. He's troubled, possibly seriously. Maybe he has PTSD or he's bipolar.

A lonely genius using his camera in an effort to make sense of a world that doesn't make sense to him. Zach hasn't personally experienced war or tragedy—his own measly difficulties pale in comparison—and he feels for Serge, who clearly didn't enjoy these advantages. He wishes he could meet him, help him get back on his feet. Maybe when he has enough photos for the show, he'll try to find him again.

Zach has printed all the shots from the rolls he developed, and there are only a few that might work for Nickerson & Hagan. One of a wine cellar with built-in shelving, another of rows upon rows of Princess Diana dolls, and one of a unit that looks like a store, with women's clothes neatly hanging on long racks, most with their original tags still attached.

He's pleased with his handiwork but needs far more than these three photographs. So it's back to developing the rest of the rolls Serge shot and left in their canisters, which, of course, lack any kind of identification. The only way to determine what's on each one is to blindly pick one and go through the whole pouring-and-shaking routine. He'd much rather be printing.

By late afternoon, he's developed five rolls, and none of them contain anything he can use. Zach threads another into the tank, figuring it's time for his luck to change. And it does, for when he gets to the final rinse and holds the strip of negatives up to the light, he lets out a whoop. Twelve inside shots.

He quickly prints a contact sheet and inspects the photographs with his jeweler's loupe. Two are of the janitor he saw earlier, but in these the janitor is emptying trash instead of mopping floors. Seven are of Rose, sitting at her desk. Serge shot the photos through the window in the office door, warping the image while also, in some indeterminable way, clarifying it. A woman at work, tired but focused on her task, a sense of purpose tinged with despair. A sad, overburdened everywoman.

One of Serge's gifts is his ability to send the viewer on a journey in his subject's footsteps, transferring his own empathy for the subject to the viewer. In this case, the journey punches Zach in the gut, and he's forced to admit that he's probably been too hard on Rose. It's not as if he's never made a mistake. Although in this case, she made more than one.

There are also three photos of that workman in a Red Sox shirt, who Zach recognizes from a previous roll. In all three, the guy is standing toward the top of his ladder, fiddling with something on the side of an elevator door. He appears to be in his twenties, white, with a dark beard and a shaved head. Not a big man, but strong and wiry, and clearly agile, from his obvious comfort with his precarious perch.

Zach does a quick print of the three workman photographs—he'll do more iterations if, on closer inspection, they turn out to be as good as he thinks—and hangs them on the line. In one, a stream of light emphasizes a battered work belt filled with tools and reflects off the wrench he's using to pull something from the top of the elevator door. Zach wonders if it's the one Haines fell through and looks more closely. He can just make out the faded image of the number 4 above the buttons. The sound of rushing blood fills his ears.

Could the man be messing with the elevator doors? Could this be related to the accident? For that to be possible, the photo would have had to have been taken in early January of this year, right before Haines fell, as there were no reports of any problems before that night. Zach checks the contact sheet with the loupe. Rose is wearing a sweater, and the janitor is in long sleeves, which would point to winter, but which winter? Rose didn't say anything about elevator repairs at the deposition, so this photo couldn't have been taken this year. Unless . . .

His mind starts diving in multiple directions. What if it was this winter, and Rose lied about not hiring the workman because the two of them were up to something nefarious? But that doesn't make any sense—what could they possibly have been doing? It's more likely that she didn't mention the workman because she didn't know about him. And if this is so, then maybe the elevator was purposely tampered with and the accident wasn't an accident at all.

Whoa. If he could prove this, it would clear him of wrongdoing. Then he would get Metropolis back, he wouldn't be broke, and he wouldn't have to involve the IRS in any of the particulars of the purchase or sale. His world would return to its normal axis.

There are cartons of Rose's office materials, including her computer, piled in the third bedroom, along with the rest of the castoffs Zach brought from Metropolis. He leaves the bathroom and grabs her laptop.

It's dead, and he roots around in the cartons before he finds the power cord. As it boots up, he sits on the floor and balances the laptop on his knees.

Zach goes to her calendar, enters "elevator" into the search bar, winces when a pane appears on the right side of the screen listing ten years' worth of "elevator" entries. Almost all reference inspections or reminders to set up inspections. There are a number of entries that mention appointments for repairs, and he enters "elevator repair" into the search bar. There are seven, but none later than 2016.

He returns to the bathroom and pores over the prints. He hadn't noticed that the back of the workman's shirt says DEVERS 11, and this makes him smile. Rafael Devers, the promising Red Sox third baseman, is one of his favorite new players. The kid had a bang-up rookie year, but he came up in the middle of last summer, halfway through the season, so his numbers weren't good enough for a Rookie of the Year candidacy, which Zach believes he deserved.

Devers was smacking game-winning home runs and initiated a triple play during the regular season, but it was his playoff feats that made him a household name in Red Sox Nation. And those feats didn't happen until the end of the season. The 2017 season. Holy shit.

A Devers shirt wouldn't have been on sale until after last year's playoffs, late October. This means the photo was taken between then and the night Haines fell. There are no entries on Rose's calendar for elevator repairs during that time.

ZACH HAS AN ex-girlfriend who's a lawyer at a big firm in Boston, and he phones her. After they exchange pleasantries, Naomi says, "I'm guessing you're not calling me at the office because you've repented your evil ways and want to get back together."

"True that," Zach confirms. Naomi is only vaguely aware of the whole Metropolis calamity, as he never gave her more than the cursory details, but he does now. He also tells her what he found. She listens carefully, asks a few questions, reminds him that she's a trust attorney, with no expertise in this area, but promises to get back to him after she talks to one of her partners, who does handle this type of case.

An hour later, Naomi calls. "If these pictures are what you think they are, Brad says they might be enough evidence to countersue Haines. Maybe even get your building back. But it's not going to be easy, and you need lots more to back the photos up. As Brad put it, you've got 'miles to go before you sleep.'"

"Tell me what to do."

"First, he says you have to make sure your assistant didn't hire him. Second, talk to someone at the company that made the elevator and find out exactly what happened that night and why. Third, if you can, find more photos of the workman and the elevator, preferably doing something more directly incriminating. And those are the easy parts."

"Can't wait to hear the hard parts."

"After you've done all that, someone has to figure out who he is. He could be an unsavory type, dangerous even, so you can't do it yourself. You're going to have to either hire a detective or convince the police a crime has been committed. Then they, or your detective, have to find your Red Sox guy, confront him, and get him to corroborate your suspicions."

58

SERGE

Diamond is staying in the place just for ladies. She can stay all day and that's different from the place for men. She gets three meals there and she doesn't have to stand in line. He has to stand in line for everything in the place for men. She says she sits at a table and they bring her food to her. No one ever brings him anything in the place for men. He only goes to the place for men when Diamond makes him. When she tells him he smells like a horse.

He doesn't blame her for staying in a nice place. He wishes he could. Well, not really but maybe if people brought food to him at a table. But then he's not all that hungry anymore so it probably wouldn't be worth it. He likes to sleep outside and if you stay in that nice place you have to sleep inside. That's what Diamond says anyway. And he'd have to be a lady, which is also a problem.

It's been hot and stormy but if he crawls under the bench it's not as wet as it is on the grass. It's muddy and smells funky but that's okay. He can't take deep breaths anyway so he doesn't smell much. He coughs a lot and if he coughs into the mud no one cares.

He knows he's sick. Sicker than sick. He's got a pain that's always in his stomach. Sometimes it goes into his chest and makes him cough even more. And sometimes it even goes across his back. He doesn't know what that's about. There's something in his stomach but it's not in his chest or in his back. The thing is hard and kind of round and seems to be getting harder and rounder. Reminds him of a basketball. Or at least half of one. It makes him not want to eat.

He wears his coat all the time to cover it up even though it's been very hot. He doesn't want anyone to see it and he especially doesn't want Diamond to see it because she'll make him go back to the place for men and see a nurse. He doesn't want to see a nurse who's going to make him sleep inside and make him eat because that will hurt too much. There isn't much room in his stomach for food. It's too full of the hard thing that keeps getting bigger.

It's boring without Diamond. Even if she's always talking in exclamation marks. No one calls him Scarecrow anymore. No one says anything to him at all. That's okay. He thinks it's been a long time since he's said anything. He clears his throat. It feels thick and scratchy.

"Hello," he says to two pigeons on the grass in front of his face. It doesn't sound like "hello." It sounds more like he's rubbing pieces of sandpaper together, saying nothing at all. The pigeons fly away. He wants to fly away like the pigeons.

He closes his eyes and sees himself flying above his own head. Above the whole Common. Swooping and diving and then just hanging in the air, the wind under his wings. So peaceful. It feels even better than he thought it would. He sees himself lying under the bench but he knows he's not really there. He's flying.

PART FIVE

59

MERCEDES

Marta is Mercedes again, and this is almost as disconcerting as when Mercedes became Marta. Although she was Marta for less than a year, that time was so potent it feels almost equal to her thirty-one years as Mercedes. Yet here she is, lying on a couch in a grand apartment in Madrid. She is free to do as she likes. There will be no more looking over her shoulder. There will be no more handcuffs and no more guards.

Her feet are pressed to those of her sister Abril, just as they so often were when they were children. Voracious readers both, they often spent afternoons with their noses in their books and their feet toe-to-toe. Mercedes softly presses her big toe to Abril's, and her eyes fill with tears of gratitude. She is indebted to the judge, but mostly it is Jason Franklin who made her new life possible.

He researched every possible avenue to prove her worthy of asylum and presented her case to the judge in such a logical and methodical manner that it did not seem possible anyone could disagree. Yet the judge asked both of them so many questions that Mercedes feared she did not believe the evidence. As Judge Cohen slowly reread Jason's brief, Mercedes had begun to sweat and was certain she was going to faint. Her hands clenched the seat of her chair in an attempt to stay upright. Then, suddenly, it was over. Asylum was granted. She was free.

Her family had never expected to survive Maduro's wrath, nor escape from Venezuela, nor ever see Mercedes again. They had tried to find her last summer, but even with the aid of detectives, they failed, because by then she had become Marta. It took a little over three months for the US government to give Mercedes permission to go to Spain. And when they finally did, it was a wondrous reunion. At the airport in Madrid, the four Bustamante women cried and clung to each other. Heaven.

With assistance from Papí's cousin Lucía, who had immigrated to Spain ten years earlier, and the equivalent of roughly two million US dollars in bribes, Mamá, Abril, and Sofía were smuggled out of the country. After a harrowing journey, they arrived in Madrid and settled into the Salamanca district, which is home to many Venezuelan expats. Lucía also helped Mamá bring out almost all of their money, some of which she and Abril invested in two apartment buildings. Mamá goes to Iglesia de la Purísima Concepción every day to give thanks to Jesús for their many blessings. Her daughters do not accompany her to the church, for their thankfulness is of a harder and more tarnished type.

Mercedes can't stop wondering what goes on in the heads of men like Maduro, Hitler, Pol Pot, Ivan the Terrible, and Caligula. Men without empathy or conscience, who have destroyed others just because they could. *Why?* she keeps asking herself. *Why?* She places the book she is reading on the coffee table and tries to stifle a sob, which comes out as a wet, strangled sound.

Abril looks up and closes her own book. She is three years younger than Mercedes, taller with lighter eyes and skin, and they look nothing alike. Yet they are the most alike of the Bustamante children in temperament. They are both intellectual and soft-spoken, both intensely driven. "Do you want to talk about it?" Abril asks gently.

"There is nothing to say."

"And there is everything to say. When you are ready."

Abril was at home when Papí was disappeared and when Juan was murdered. With Mercedes and Juan gone, she became the eldest. She was Mamá's main support and the mastermind of their getaway. So it is not surprising that Abril is more solemn and even less talkative than she was before. Mercedes supposes this is true of all four of them. Sofía, the once happy-go-lucky baby of the family, is the most somber of all. Theirs may not be the most cheerful of households, but it is a loving one.

Mercedes stands and kisses her sister's forehead. "I think I will go out for a run."

"Do you want company?"

Mercedes shakes her head. She needs to be alone so she is able to mourn. She misses Liddy even more now that they are thousands of miles apart. She is aware that this makes no difference, as they would be unable to be together if they lived on the same block, but somehow the distance intensifies her longing. The simultaneity of her own arrest and Garrett's victory had torn them apart, not even allowing for a proper goodbye. Now, cruelty upon cruelty, they cannot even speak to each other on the telephone. Liddy is as unreachable to her as are Papí and Juan.

"*Te amo,*" Abril says. She understands the need to be alone.

Mercedes blows her a kiss. "*Te amo.*"

The Salamanca district of Madrid is quieter than most of the city, its wide streets lined with ornate buildings from the nineteenth century. Mercedes heads for El Retiro, one of the city's largest parks. She likes to run there because she can lose herself in the beauty of its ponds and sculptures, its rose gardens and palaces.

Yet this does not occur today. She cannot wrench her thoughts away from Liddy, whose life must be constant torture. Mercedes does not blame Liddy for her decision, even as she wishes it could have been otherwise, but she is horrified by the depravity of Garrett's revenge: forcing Liddy to live with him when he knows nothing will make her more miserable. She speeds up in an attempt to leave these useless thoughts behind. She covers much ground, but no matter how fast she runs, they keep up with her.

She exits the park and runs along the fashionable Calles de Serrano and de Goya and de Velázquez, home to some of the most exclusive stores and homes in Madrid, dodging shoppers and tourists. After Jason left Boston, he was kind enough to allow her to stay in his apartment while she awaited permission to leave the United States. It was convenient that she did not have to search for a new place to live, but it also made her sad. She and Liddy had spent some happy, and, yes, some not-so-happy times there. But at least they had been together and were able to dream of a shared future.

Dr. Ullman, dear man, was as delighted about her asylum as he would have been if she were his own daughter. And he was impressed with her dissertation, particularly the strength of the combined effects of childhood zip code, maternal education, and the number of books in the household, which together explained almost 80 percent of the variance in later-life outcomes. Fortunately, her committee had agreed with him. As she runs, she thinks about the people at Metropolis and wonders if her results would have predicted where each is at this moment.

Liddy, who would have been among those closest to the finish line when the race started, has an advanced degree, is working on a novel, and, however miserable she might be, is safely ensconced in the one percent, which is where she began. Jason, who would be midway among the runners, has an advanced degree but is living a middle-class life, also where he began. Rose, who would be hovering closer to the starting line, is currently standing in the same place. And even Mercedes herself fits the projection: wealthy to wealthy. The only one she can think of whose position would not have been predicted by her data is the owner of Metropolis, who must have started toward the front of the runners and now lags behind with Rose. Still, even given the owner, this admittedly small sample would seem to confirm her findings.

She is allegedly working on an article based on these findings, which she and Dr. Ullman plan to submit to the *American Sociological Review*. This possibility should spur her into action, but it does not. She is also supposed to be looking for a job. And although she's made a few meager attempts, running and grieving and getting reacquainted with her family take most of her time, and she does not imagine this will change in the near future.

Her mother and sisters, obviously, want her to stay in Madrid, or at least in Spain. But her preliminary job inquiries indicate that universities in Britain or the United States would be a better match. There is a tenured position in the UK, in the sociology department at her alma mater, Cambridge. And there is a postdoc at Harvard, where she would be able to pursue her research.

Mercedes is thinking she would prefer to begin her career in research, but returning to Boston might prove too difficult for her. She is eligible for US citizenship, but without Liddy, she doesn't believe she can live in a place so filled with Marta's memories.

60

LIDDY

"I'm not happy with the look of these handrails around the toilet," Hillary tells Liddy as she eyes the special-order bars that are supposed to look more like towel racks than supports for the disabled. Hillary is an interior accessibility designer. They've been working together to remodel the condo so it's a place where, as Hillary puts it, a person with disabilities will find it easy to live and expand his potentials. It seems that no one uses the word "handicapped" anymore.

"They're thicker than I'd like," Hillary continues, frowning at the bars. "That's better for Mr. Haines but not as attractive. Do you want me to have them refabricated? Or should I try to find thinner ones?"

"Not worth the bother," Liddy assures her. "Looks great, like a bath you'd find in a high-end hotel." Which is true. With its half walls, multilevel cabinetry, and marble shower enclosure flush to the marble floor, not to mention towel-rack grab bars, it's barely recognizable as an accessible bathroom.

"I'm so glad you think so." Hillary is clearly pleased. "I hope it's working out for Mr. Haines as well?"

"Absolutely," Liddy says. "Although he mentioned that the opening under his desk in his bedroom is a little too low."

The main bedroom now belongs to Garrett, and Liddy sleeps in the smaller bedroom off the foyer, which is at the other end of the condo.

This makes it easy for her to avoid him when they're both at home and leaves the guest room, next to him, open for his aides. He has a rotation of four aides helping him every hour of every day, which ensures that he and she are never alone. As perfect as being in a maximum-security gilded prison can be.

Hillary inspects the desk, pulls out a tape measure, mutters to herself as she gauges the space. "I'll get Stephan back here tomorrow to do the modification." She consults the list on her phone. "All we have left are a few small issues in the kitchen and the leaky faucet in the powder room."

They review the kitchen problems as Hillary double-thumbs notes into her phone and promises to get everything taken care of within the week. "This is the end of my punch list," Hillary says. "So if there's nothing else, I'd like to close down the job as soon as we've knocked off these last items. Sound good to you?"

Liddy agrees that it does and walks Hillary to the door, relieved to have the renovation behind her. In addition to Garrett's bathroom, the entire apartment had to be retrofitted: kitchen gutted, walls taken down and doorways widened, carpeted floors removed and replaced with hardwood, light switches and thermostats lowered to wheelchair level. Garrett was in the hospital, and Liddy stayed at a hotel down the street for three months while the work was being done.

Garrett goes into the office every day, runs Haines Companies as he always did, gets to Fenway Park to take in as many Red Sox games as he can. He even started playing golf again with the help of an accessibility golf pro, but this doesn't seem to be going as well as he hoped.

It's August, ten months since she moved into Metropolis, over five months since she last saw Marta. The many whiplashes of the past year have deeply shaken her. The pain of losing Marta relentlessly claws at her, and she still can't believe Garrett played her so successfully or that she's back living with him at The Tower. He won, and as he promised, he's making her pay. The agreement she signed allows him access to all of her devices, her car's GPS, credit cards, and bank accounts. It also stipulates that Robin and Scott remain at the boarding school in Zurich and go to overnight camp every summer, which is where they are now.

Dawn counseled her not to sign the agreement, but Liddy did anyway, and she hasn't talked to the attorney since. Not even to discover the witness's identity. She made her choice, and the details don't matter anymore. She hid her cash before the renovation, but she's afraid Garrett has secretly installed hidden cameras, so she hasn't gone near it. It's consoling to know it's there, her mythical life raft, even if she doesn't know if she'll ever be able to sail.

When she snorted her last gram of coke a couple of weeks ago, her heart started racing as if she'd just run a marathon, and she realized how horrible it would be for Robin and Scott to have a paraplegic father and a mother who died of a drug overdose. It's been easier to quit than she would have thought. Three-day hangovers and no cash are a strong deterrent, as is the fear of her children's heartbreak.

Sometimes Liddy thinks she'd rather be an actual prisoner, to serve her time for an assault conviction and then walk out with the rest of her life to herself. Probably five years, maybe only three, as she has a clean record and no proof has turned up that the elevator was tampered with— or that she had anything to do with it. She'd be forty-eight, forty-nine, even fifty, none of which are too old to start over. Except for the reality of being locked up in a real prison, of confessing. A mother who tried to kill her children's father would be even worse than a mother who ODed on cocaine.

SHE AND GARRETT are having dinner at Mistral, an elegant restaurant in the South End. An aide sits discreetly at a small table to their left. Garrett likes to be in bed by eight, so it's early and the restaurant is quiet, the waitstaff attentive to the point of obsequiousness. Garrett is a big tipper, and, as always in public, an extremely charming man. Every so often, she finds herself almost forgetting what he's done to her. Although she rarely forgets what she's done to him.

"So how did the writing go today?" he asks after they've had a few sips of their drinks: his, ice water; hers, vodka on the rocks. "Did you manage to get Clementine out of Vermont?"

Liddy savors the cold viscosity warming her esophagus. It was a good writing day, five new pages, but stubborn Clementine hasn't gone anywhere. "She's still there," she says ruefully.

"Not going to leave anytime soon?"

Liddy has to smile at the thought of her rascally protagonist. "Can't say for sure, but sometimes I think I'm having trouble getting her out of Vermont because I'm always a little homesick for it. When I write about Vermont, I get to pretend I'm there."

Garrett places his hand over hers. "We can go up this weekend. Stay in a nice inn. What do you think?"

She pulls her hand away, but not too quickly, as there's a game to be played here. "I'm on a bit of a roll with the book, and I think I'm better off spending the time working."

He stares deeply into her eyes. "If you change your mind, we can do it at the last minute. Just say the word."

This from a man who believes she tried to kill him, who takes her acquiescence to his blackmail as proof of her guilt. Which makes no sense. If he just wanted arm candy, he could easily find a much fresher bonbon than her forty-four-year-old self. There has to be something else he's after, a bigger and bolder plan to extract even further revenge. She must remain vigilant. He is not to be trusted.

Liddy grabs the large menu and stands it upright in front of her face. According to their agreement, she is to accompany him at least twice a week to a public place, to portray themselves as a happily married couple. She despises every minute of this forced congeniality, of this production they're staging, but he's made it clear that if she fails to perform, he will be more than willing to show the witness statement to the police. Checkmate.

So far, her performance appears to be acceptable, as their friends and acquaintances, even the media and Garrett's aides who are with them every day, believe the Haineses are a happy, if tragic, couple. As do Robin and Scott.

"What are you going to order, hon?" she asks when the waiter is within hearing range. "I think I'm going for the Dover sole."

For the rest of the evening, Garrett appears so interested in her book that Liddy wonders if at some point he might begin to loosen her reins. It's her fault he's in a wheelchair, and although his demands are outrageous, there's no denying he has reason to be furious. Perhaps she should try to be more sympathetic, both for his sake and, ultimately, for her own.

This attempt lasts until the next afternoon, when Liddy returns from a meeting at the Burke and goes into her bedroom to change her clothes. As she reaches for the shorts and T-shirt she hung on the hook in the bathroom, she hesitates. Something is off. She scans the countertop, takes in the placement of her creams and cosmetics. She's an admittedly compulsive person, who likes her things in a certain order, and she's positive she left her daytime moisturizer to the left of her eye cream, as she always does. Now it's on the right. Blanca didn't come in today, but even if she had, Blanca is well aware of Liddy's preferences and is careful to return everything to its rightful place.

Liddy carefully inspects the drawers and the cabinets, the shampoos and conditioners lined up in the shower. She walks into her closet, which appears the same as always; nothing stands out as being altered. But something has been.

She whirls around and yanks out the top drawer of her bureau. She flips it over, and nightgowns spill over her feet. She stares numbly at the smooth bottom of the drawer. The envelopes she'd pasted there are gone. As are the envelopes she'd pasted on the next one and the next one and the next one. Her clothes litter the floor in colorful piles, but she barely notices. All the cash she brought with her from Metropolis is gone.

Liddy drops onto the bench at the foot of the bed. Her guess is that Garrett will never mention the money or the fact that he had his detective search her room while she was out. Once again, she had underestimated

Garrett's ruthlessness, as well as his level of distrust. To her peril. She won't make this mistake again, her determination to be on high alert now magnified. But her error was costly. Her life raft is gone, and now she has absolutely nothing of her own, only what he chooses to give. And not to give.

THAT NIGHT, LIDDY dreams she and Jason are frantically searching for Marta in the Public Garden. They run around the duck pond, rush over the footbridge, race along the pathways edging the water, but Marta isn't there. Liddy knows this is her last chance to see her. She dives under the weeping willows. Nothing. Then Jason disappears. Pop, and he's gone. Liddy turns in a circle and all the other people pop out of sight too. Like a series of lights being extinguished one by one. Pop. Pop. Pop. And she's alone.

When she wakes, the strong summer sun edges the curtains, and it's almost eight thirty, which means Garrett is long gone. The nightmare was boringly predictable but, nonetheless, pummels her. She never did get to say goodbye to Marta in person. They'd managed a few tearful conversations over Jason's phone, but when he left for California there was no longer a way for them to directly communicate.

Jason is in touch with Marta and texts Liddy coded updates, so she knows that Marta, now officially Mercedes again, is in Spain. Liddy is thrilled for her, free from ICE and reunited with her family, but she wishes they could share this happiness together. Enraged at the truss in which Garrett has bound her, she flings off the covers and stomps into the bathroom to take a shower.

As the water pours down on her head, she tries to tamp down her fury. She lives in a beautiful apartment, in a city she loves, unencumbered by financial concerns. A place where she can write. A place just about anyone in the world could only dream of being. But she's not big enough to get past her own self. Golden chains are still chains.

When she steps out of the bathroom, her phone is ringing. It's Jason, which is unusual. "Everything okay?" she asks.

"And hello to you too."

"Sorry, but is everything okay?"

"It probably is. I'm going to be quick so the call doesn't register as long and spook Garrett." Jason pauses. "Rose told me the building owner might have evidence that the elevator was tampered with."

Liddy's stomach clutches. "The elevator?"

"He wanted to know if she'd hired anyone to fix it in the months before, uh, before the accident. Which she hadn't."

"And this means . . . ?"

"Apparently, Davidson found photographs of a workman standing on a ladder and messing with the top of the elevator door. He thinks the pictures might clear him on the negligence suit if he can prove it was rigged, so he's trying to get more evidence."

Liddy's heart is pounding so hard she's having trouble hearing Jason. "And you, you think this could be bad for me?"

"It shouldn't be, because you didn't do it. I just figured you'd want to know what's going on. The ultimate outcome depends on what Davidson finds and how Garrett decides to interpret it."

61

ZACH

The first thing Zach does after talking to Naomi is call Rose. The conversation is awkward, to say the least, but she gives him what he needs: she didn't hire anyone to work on the elevator in the months preceding the accident. When he hangs up, he pulls the strip that contains Serge's photos of Rose out of its celluloid sleeve. He holds it up to the light, takes in her purpose and despair, her resolution to do what she must. Resentment stirs, but mostly what he feels is sadness.

Now that he has Rose's confirmation, Zach is determined to develop every roll Serge ever shot. He's going to find more condemning photos of, as Naomi calls him, Red Sox Guy. And when he has proof that the elevator was tampered with, he's going to Humpty-Dumpty his life back together. Maybe another bad analogy, but he's hopeful he'll have a much better ending than poor Humpty did.

He's already submitted two 2018 estimated tax payments from cash in his money market account, and he has enough left to cover the September installment. But his funds are running low, and the fourth is due next January. Not to mention what he's going to owe in April.

The next morning, he talks to an engineer at Otis Elevator, who explains that if the safety retainers and gibs—which are what hold the door in place—are improperly hinged, the bottom door can move inward, which is exactly what happened to Garrett Haines and also to the girl at Fenway Park. It seems backward to Zach—but the engineer insists that, in a case like this, if someone hits the door with even a small amount of force, the bottom will open into the shaft, creating a "fall hazard."

The engineer adds that this kind of unhinging would most likely be caused by either improper installation or a lack of maintenance, which gives Zach pause. But when he presses, the man acknowledges that it could also be the result of someone purposely manipulating the retainers and gibs.

Zach settles himself for the long haul. A bin with roughly a hundred canisters of undeveloped film sits next to him on the floor, and a half dozen negative strips he developed yesterday wave on the line as a fan stirs the acrid air.

62

LIDDY

After Jason tells her about Zach Davidson's search, Liddy hangs up and stares at the home screen on her phone. It's a photo of Robin and Scott at about eight in bright ski outfits against the cobalt-blue sky of Vail. She remembers that family trip well. The twins had gone to ski school every day, and by the end of the vacation they were bombing down the green runs with such glee that she and Garrett could only watch and laugh. Garrett was in a good mood that week, mostly because the kids were occupied all day and he had her to himself. And, truth be told, she also had a great time. They took the high-speed lift to the top of the mountain and did the black diamonds all the way to the bottom, skied back to the hotel room for some sweaty sex, then snapped on their boots and went back up again. Another lifetime ago.

And now there's the elevator. Liddy understands why Davidson is doing this, but it's yet another sword over her head. If the man finds evidence the elevator was tampered with, Garrett will conclude he has confirmation not only that she pushed him but that it was premeditated. It would be difficult to prove she was behind this, but the mere fact of it would add to Garrett's arsenal against her, making his threat to turn her in to the police at the smallest infraction even more ominous.

She turns the phone facedown on the table, not able to look at her children's shining faces. How will they survive this? How will she survive this? Because now the charge wouldn't be assault; it would be attempted murder. Not three to five years. Twenty or thirty. Maybe more.

FOR THE FIRST few weeks after Jason's call, Liddy was a wreck, losing weight, barely sleeping, on high alert for a phone call or a text or a visitor announcement from the concierge. More frightened of Garrett than ever, she flinched every time he came home or wheeled himself to where she sat, afraid to look at him, for fear of seeing that knowing sneer on his face. But six weeks have now passed without any evidence emerging, and Liddy is starting to relax her vigilance.

It's her birthday, and Garrett's driver brings him home early to make her a special dinner with the assistance of his favorite aide, Penelope. He's being very secretive and wants Liddy to leave the condo for the rest of the afternoon. She resists, arguing that it's her birthday and she should be able to do what she wants, which is to write. He grudgingly agrees but with the condition that she stay in her room until he calls for her.

Who cares what he makes for her special dinner? The gesture is as infantilizing as he has made her life. Even more annoying, he's sure to present her with a lavish gift, as if he were a returning conqueror offering up riches from vanquished lands. Penelope will be helping him serve, so Liddy will be forced to gush over it, thank him, even kiss him, which makes her want to vomit.

Although Garrett has done things far worse than having her room searched and taking her hidden cash, that event pushed her over the edge, and weeks later she still isn't able to control her fury. There's the reprehensible invasion of her privacy, but the loss of the money eats at her even more. Although she had no idea how she would have used it, its existence was a metaphor for a potential escape. And now, no more metaphor. No more escape.

Liddy has started drinking earlier, taking more Ambien, and going to sleep earlier too, wandering around fuzzy-headed and unmotivated during the day, bailing on Clementine to watch old movies. She's discovered a fondness for Humphrey Bogart and queues up *Sahara*, which Bogie made right after *Casablanca*, and settles in.

An hour into the movie, there's a soft knock on her door. "Ms. Haines?" Penelope calls. "I'm sorry to disturb you, but Theo from downstairs says there are two men who want to speak to both you and Mr. Haines. Mr. Haines is taking a nap. What should I say?"

Liddy smirks. And here she thought Garrett was busy preparing her special birthday dinner. Must have delegated this loving effort to Penelope. Liddy pauses the movie so she can return to it, although she's pretty confident Bogie and his Brits are going to beat back the Germans.

"Did he say who they are?"

"I didn't think it was my business to ask."

Liddy goes into the spotless kitchen, notes a pot simmering on the stove and a pan covered with aluminum foil ready to be popped in the oven. From the spicy tang in the air, it's Indian. Although Indian is one her favorites, the thought of eating it with Garrett makes her stomach clench shut. She picks up the receiver. "Hey, Theo, who's down there?"

"They're detectives, Ms. Haines." Theo's voice is low and uncertain. "Cambridge Police."

"Send them up, please," she says with a composure she doesn't feel.

She paces across the broad entryway. *Calm. Calm. Stay calm.* She had assumed Davidson had given up. That it had come to nothing. But it's come to something. To assume, as the twins say, makes an ass of you and me.

63

ZACH

After three more weeks of feverish work, Zach still hasn't found any more Red Sox Guy pictures. It's mostly his fault, as negatives that might be good for Nathaniel's gallery show, especially the ghost photos, keep snagging his attention from his primary search. Zach is itching to print them but manages to stay away from the enlarger. Again and again, he shakes and fills and rinses. No printing allowed unless it's Red Sox Guy or until every roll is developed. This has the unfortunate effect of forcing him to reschedule the meeting with Nathaniel again, as he still only has three new prints to show.

He's in the darkroom for as many hours as his body will allow. The bin is slowly emptying, and soon all of Serge's photos will be developed. But No Red Sox Guy. Zach would be crushed, but he's not the crushed type and he's determined to land on his feet. Given the quality of the negatives, he has no doubt that when Nathaniel sees the photographs, it will be the beginning of an illustrious career for Serge Laurent and Zach's retreading as a talent manager.

His meeting at Nickerson & Hagan is next week. He's been putting aside the negatives that might work for the show, and he's got to get cracking on printing them. There's no doubt that representing Serge's photos has a far greater chance of success than finding some workman in a T-shirt, and that he should do this first. Instead, he pulls a marathon session to complete the developing. It's still his best hope.

When, with seven rolls remaining in the bin, Zach finds half a dozen shots of Red Sox Guy, he laughs so hard he almost cries. It's better than he could have imagined.

64

LIDDY

The policemen introduce themselves as Detective Chris Lundberg and Detective Brian Eakin. Even though one is tall and blond and the other is shorter with a dark beard, Liddy immediately forgets which is which. They refuse coffee or tea. Accept the offer to sit down. She trips over the edge of the coffee table, motions to two chairs. At least they're not wearing uniforms. Or maybe this is worse.

"P-please, please sit," she stutters. *Don't look guilty. Act normal. Stay cool.* She's terrified. Could Davidson and Garrett have been in on this together? Maybe they made some kind of deal to entrap her? Metropolis in exchange for the evidence, which Garrett then took to the police along with the witness statement? But that's crazy. Maybe Garrett never wanted her to be here with him. Maybe this was all a prologue to the "something else" she's feared all along. Whatever the explanation, she's screwed, screwed, screwed.

The detectives settle into the chairs. Liddy's only option is to sit on the couch across from them. Facing the windows. Like a naughty child waiting to receive a lecture from her parents. The sun forces her to squint to see their faces. Stupid move. She should have made them squint.

Liddy doesn't know what to do with her hands. With her eyes. If she doesn't look at the men, they'll think she's guilty. If she does, they'll see the panic. She puts her hands under her thighs to hide their tremble.

That looks guilty too. She places them on her lap, wills them to remain motionless. It's come to this.

"I'm, uh, I'm sorry, officers . . . ," she begins, stops. Has she insulted them by calling them officers? "I mean, detectives. But my husband, you know, Garrett Haines, he's resting at the moment. He's not well, but you probably know that too." She's a butterfly pinned to a board by their cool stares. A guilty butterfly. "He, uh, he recently had a bad accident."

They nod solemnly. "Would it be possible for him to join us, Ms. Haines?" the blond one asks. "We would like to speak with both of you at the same time, if we can. That way, we won't have to repeat ourselves." He flashes a lopsided grin. "Just lazy, I guess." This must be the good cop.

Liddy jumps up. An excuse to leave the room. "Of course, of course. No problem. I'll get him up. It might take a few minutes, though. He's in a wheelchair."

"That's quite all right," the good cop says. "We'll wait here."

Where else would they wait? Liddy walks down the hall, stops, and presses her forehead to the wall. They're Cambridge detectives, where Metropolis is located. Not Boston. It's clear to her now why she never turned herself into the police. No matter how confined she feels with Garrett as her jailer, it's going to be nothing compared with having a real one. No more golden bars. Actual bars.

She pounds on the door of the aides' room. "Penelope!" she calls. "Please wake Garrett and bring him to the living room right away."

Penelope is in the hall in an instant, and she looks at Liddy oddly. "Give me ten, and he'll be there."

Liddy isn't going back into the living room until she has to, so she steps into the aides' room and eyes the floor-to-ceiling windows. They're made of double panes of plate glass with only a small crank window at the bottom. Not nearly big enough to jump out of. Are these her last moments of freedom? She slumps on the bed. *The twins.*

In less time than Liddy hoped, Penelope is navigating Garrett's wheelchair down the hall. Garrett's querulous voice demands to know who these men are, complains that they've ruined his special dinner. Liddy pushes herself to a stand and slowly follows the wheelchair.

Penelope locks Garrett's chair in his spot alongside the couch and excuses herself. Liddy has no choice but to sit where she was before. The detectives introduce themselves to Garrett. This time, Liddy notes that Lundberg is the good cop. If right now there can be such a thing.

Eakin gets right to the point. "We have some photographs we'd like to show both of you. We need you to help us identify the people in the pictures."

"Will that be all right with you, Mr. Haines?" Lundberg asks. "With you, Ms. Haines?"

Garrett tries to turn on his charisma. "We'd be happy to accommodate you, detectives," he says with a wavering smile. "But, as I'm sure you can appreciate, I would prefer to wait until our attorneys are present."

"Oh, that won't be necessary." Lundberg's smile is wider and more authentic-looking than Garrett's. Although probably just as fake. "This is only about giving us a hand figuring out who's in the pictures. It's no big deal."

"I'm sorry, gentlemen, but I must insist." Garrett releases the brake on his chair, turns himself toward the foyer, and waves graciously for them to follow. A cordial host leading his guests to the door at the end of a pleasant visit. "Please feel free to contact Gene Blalock at Bernkopf Goodman in the morning," he says. "I'm sure he'll be happy to set up a mutually convenient appointment."

Liddy looks from Garrett to the detectives. And back. No answers on the impassive faces.

The detectives remain seated. "Questions have been raised about the legitimacy of your accident," Eakin calls out to Garrett.

Liddy presses her hands together. Hard. Bites her lip. Forces herself to stop.

Garrett spins his chair around and glares at the detective. "Legitimacy?" His laugh is harsh. "You're actually going to sit in my living room and tell me the accident that made me a paraplegic, that keeps me confined to this chair, isn't legitimate?"

Eakin meets Garrett's glare. "Perhaps 'legitimate' isn't the right word." He whips a manila envelope from his briefcase and dumps six black-and-white photographs onto the coffee table. "Maybe 'questionable' would be more accurate."

Liddy leans toward the photos as Garrett yells, "Don't look at them!"

But she does. Just as Detective Eakin knew she would. The pictures were taken at Metropolis. Square. Old-fashioned but obviously recent. They're all photos of the same young man, wearing a Red Sox shirt, atop a ladder working on an elevator door. In three of the photographs, Garrett stands beside the workman, clearly speaking with him. In one, Garrett points to the top of the door.

Garrett inside Metropolis. Garrett talking to a man working on an elevator door. A man whom Rose told Zach Davidson she never hired. Liddy turns to Garrett.

"This is unwarranted," Garrett declares, with such certainty that Liddy questions what she's just seen. "Please let yourselves out, officers. I'm calling my attorney right now, and neither my wife nor I will answer any of your questions or respond to your innuendos." He whips his wheelchair around and heads out of the living room, gripping his cell phone.

"Where are you going, Mr. Haines?" Eakin calls after him, but it's clear from his tone that the detective isn't particularly interested. Garrett doesn't answer.

Lundberg stands and follows him. "Can I help you with anything, sir?" he asks. Garrett again doesn't respond, just turns the corner toward his room. Lundberg lets him go.

Liddy's brain feels as if it's saturated with glue, working far too slowly, groping to comprehend what everyone else seems to already know.

"Have you ever heard of a man named Todd Lewis?" Eakin asks her.

"No, no. I, uh, I don't think so. Should I have?"

"This workman." The detective points to the pictures spread on the coffee table.

"You, you know his name?" Liddy asks, even as she recognizes the question is nonsensical.

"He's well-known to us," Detective Lundberg says. "Has been for years. Long rap sheet. A convicted felon out on probation. Seems he wasn't anxious to go back to prison, so he gave it all up, hoping that snitching on the bigger fish would help his cause."

"All up?" she croaks. "All what up?"

"Lewis claims he was hired by your husband and paid ten thousand dollars to mess with the elevator at the Metropolis Storage Warehouse." Eakin pulls a notebook from his briefcase. "Gave us the dates he was there, his exact instructions, the payment schedule. A third up front, a third after the preliminary adjustments were complete, final third due after he removed the gibs, early evening January seventh. The night of your husband's accident."

Hired by Garrett? Removed gibs? Ten thousand dollars? Liddy picks up the photographs, and they flap in her trembling hands. *No, it's not possible. No.* "So, so are you saying that this, these photos, prove Garrett tampered with the elevator? That he hired this man to do it for him?" Then her head snaps up as if she's been punched, and perhaps she has. "That he was going to . . . Going to . . . To me?"

"That's for the courts to decide," Lundberg says. "But these photographs, along with Mr. Lewis's confession and assertions, have serious implications. I'm sorry, Ms. Haines, but we're going to have to take your husband down to the station for questioning."

65

JASON

His mother wasn't happy. Neither was his father or his niece Tawney. But Jason is. Although he's got some guilt around his family's distress, he recognizes that he needs to do what's right for him. He doesn't want to get too ahead of himself, but he's pretty sure Sabrina is pleased with his decision too.

He's been in San Francisco for almost four months now, and although the weather is cooler and rainier than he imagined, in almost all other ways, the move has been a boon. Through a friend of a friend he snared a sublet that runs until the end of the year. It's not in the greatest location, but it sure beats his Allston apartment. There are two bedrooms, a reasonably sized living room, and although the kitchen is dated, it easily holds a table for four. Plus it's furnished. The perfect place to figure out what's next, and that's beginning to fall into place.

He may be finished with corporate law, but his corporate law credentials have come in handy, as did his old boss's recommendation. Those years at Spencer Uccello advising companies hiring foreign nationals, as well as his smaller pro bono immigration cases there and the ones he was involved with on his own, turned out to be the exact prerequisites for a job at the ACLU. And now he's helping immigrants get visas and green cards, as well as supporting them through asylum petitions.

He landed the job three months ago. It's better than he expected it to be, and he's better at it than he would have thought. He'll never get rich like his cronies at the firm, but Jason now recognizes that, just as Sabrina said, the whole big-condo, fancy-dinner, and expensive-suit crap wasn't him. He finally appreciates that the fat, nerdy kid with glasses doesn't have to prove himself to anyone.

The ACLU office is above a Walgreens on Drumm Street, and this is just fine with him also. As is his cubicle in a noisy room with no lofty view of the harbor. But there are windows—a step up from Metropolis— even if they look out on an alley. He unplugs his laptop and puts it and a few files into his backpack, then says goodbye to his colleagues, one of whom is becoming a friend. He saunters down the street toward Olé, his favorite Mexican restaurant, to meet Sabrina for dinner.

He likes San Francisco, which in some ways reminds him of Boston. It's newer and hillier, but the politics are similar and it has the same big-city, small-town feel. It, too, has an ocean—different from the Atlantic, but just as salty and alluring and unruly. Of course he misses his home-town and his family, and even after everything that happened, he misses Marta and Liddy and those crazy days at Metropolis.

Things worked out for most of his clients in Boston, especially Marta. Kimberlyn Bell got the price she wanted for her house in Roxbury, and although the whole Rose/Michael case was basically a fiasco, somehow they ended up on their feet. He's still not certain how Rose got Michael's arrest expunged, and he doesn't want to know. Liddy isn't faring as well, but he holds out hope that someday Garrett will relent and let her resume a more normal life.

Sabrina, as always, is late. When they were married, this drove him nuts, but now he just expects and accepts. He doesn't know if this new attitude is due to his increasing maturity or because he is, once again, completely smitten with her. Jason orders two margaritas with extra salt and some guacamole, chats with the server as she prepares the guac at the table. The margaritas arrive, and he sips as he watches the door.

When Sabrina dashes in, her long braids flying away from her face, he's struck by how beautiful she is. She glows. He stands, and Sabrina kisses him lightly on the cheek, pushes him playfully back into the booth, and then slides into the seat across from him.

It's warm and damp outside, and she gracefully lifts her hair to the top of her head to cool off. This motion reveals her long neck and makes her cheekbones even more prominent. Her coppery skin shines. "Ain't you the gallant brother," she says in a teasing voice. "Standing up when a lady arrives."

"You got that right." Jason doesn't tell her there was nothing gallant about it, that it was the sight of her that caused him to jump to his feet, that he wasn't even aware of what he was doing. He's wary of coming on too strong. There's a lot of history between them, and she'll bolt if she feels any pressure to commit to being more than they are until she's ready.

Exactly what they are isn't clear. They've progressed from the initial awkward lunches to dinners and then to actual dates. From no touching to quick, dry kisses and then to longer and wetter ones. But there's been no sex and no talk of a future together. Jason was married to Sabrina for eight years, and he recognizes that she's starting to respond to him. But he's also aware he still has a lot to prove to her.

She grabs a handful of chips and starts scooping the guacamole. "Hungry as all get-out."

"Go for it," he encourages. Sabrina is always "hungry as all get-out," and he's always liked this about her. She's tall and full-bodied, and he likes that about her too. At the moment, there isn't much he doesn't like about her.

"Spent half the day sitting on my ass at the courthouse," Sabrina grouses. "That fucker Grinnell. Just loves to lord his judgeship over us peons. Especially if we're from Safe Horizon."

Jason has had his own run-ins with the Honorable Frank Grinnell. "Babe, you ain't seen nothing till you've seen how he treats you if you're from the ACLU."

"True that," she says, and takes a long draw on her margarita.

Jason's phone rings, and when he sees it's Liddy he lets it ring through. He'll return it later. But then she calls again, and then again. "Sorry," he says to Sabrina. "Something's up with Liddy."

"Jason," Liddy cries into his ear. "It's over! I'm free!"

66

ROSE

Rose is making yet another variation of tomato sauce for dinner, this time with onions and green peppers and tofu. No one much likes the tofu but it's way cheaper than meat and has almost as much protein and it really stretches the sauce. When she gets back from Walmart she'll make a big batch of garlic bread, which everyone likes and will take their attention off the tofu.

Public school in Boston started three weeks ago, and the kids are getting into the groove. Rose is kind of too, but climbing in and out of it every day is wearing her down. Emma started middle school and it has a different schedule and bus stop than the school Charlotte goes to. She complains that she can't stand it there but if she's so miserable why does she come home all happy after soccer? Charlotte and her fifth-grade classmates are the big boys and girls of the elementary school and she likes being the top dog almost as much as not having her older sister there bossing her around all day.

Michael is home and on the mend but he's had to have four more surgeries since he got shot and it looks like there'll be at least two more. The school sends over a tutor two days a week and they gave Michael a laptop, but he's not interested in either one. The only thing he does is complain about the pain and how he's sick of doctors and hospitals. Even with it all, she still believes she did the right thing. What any mother would do to save her child. Well, most of the time she believes this.

Rose has benefits from Taco Bell but they're not good ones. And the medical bills come in all the time and mostly she doesn't even open the envelopes, just pushes them into an already stuffed drawer. There's her paycheck and Vince's disability but the disability is way less than they thought it would be and his VA insurance doesn't cover much of anything. At least Vince mostly stopped drinking and gets himself out of bed in the morning to feed the kids and get them on the bus. After that it's all on her.

She still works the 6:00 a.m. to 2:00 p.m. shift and then rushes home to meet the elementary school bus. She gets a free lunch that she doesn't eat so she can bring it home for Charlotte's snack. Emma gets her snack at soccer practice and Michael eats way less than he used to. Her mother invites them downstairs for dinner a couple nights a week so at least no one is starving.

It drives her nuts that Vince won't take the pills the doctor says he needs because he's depressed. She tries to get him to because he needs them even more now that he's not drinking so much. But no, all he wants to do is take naps and sit in front of the TV. She gets that taking the medicine messes with his macho idea of himself and she tries to make him understand that this isn't his fault. War and what the doctor said was brain chemistry and bad luck and mistakes—hers more than his—are the reason they're where they are. But he just gets mad and clams up, and she knows she shouldn't bother.

After Charlotte settles down to do her homework and the sauce is finished, Rose grabs all the returnable cans and bottles and heads to Walmart. She waits at the bus stop, grocery bags and empty bottles stuffed awkwardly under her arms. The bus takes forever to come and the traffic is terrible and the late afternoon rush at the store has already started when she gets there. The narrow aisles are crowded with grumpy customers who growl at her when she tries to get past their carts or grab something from a shelf they're standing in front of.

She's always been a big coupon clipper and good at finding bargains, but now she's also got to figure out how much everything she buys weighs.

Vince and her used to shop together on Saturdays and they'd both carry the bags to and from the bus stops. But now he can't walk more than a couple of blocks, let alone carry any bags.

Rose tries not to be bitter and to thank God for all that she has. Even though depression is a real sickness Vince isn't actually sick and Michael is getting better and the girls are healthy. They may not have a lot of money but there's a roof over their heads, and because her parents own the house this can't be taken away.

There are all of those refugees running from wars that have to leave all their possessions and try to get to countries that won't let them come in. Look at what happened to Marta. Rose knows she has it way better than all of them.

67

ZACH

Zach thinks back to the day of the auction, only five months ago. The first time he saw the deserted storage units. The first time he saw Serge's photos. The first time he wondered about the lives of the tenants. So many questions—some now answered, others never to be. Incredible how it came down, how quickly it turned back on itself. For him, for Liddy Haines, for Garrett Haines, and maybe for Serge. If they can find him.

Zach and Rose are walking toward the Common and the Public Garden after having searched Downtown Crossing. It's one of those October days when the sky is an impossible shade of translucent blue, the sun is strong, and a crisp breeze flutters the multicolored leaves still clinging to the trees. He has Serge's Rolleiflex, and he can't stop himself from taking a few shots, even as he recognizes they're all going to be clichéd. It would be difficult to take such a photograph on such an afternoon and not have it be clichéd. But if Serge were behind the camera, he'd find a way to make the scene his own.

With Rose's help, Zach is trying to find Serge again, which is more promising than the last time because Rose actually knows what the man looks like. Who could have guessed he had red hair? Or a beard? Although Serge obviously could be anywhere, or nowhere, Zach still has a strong sense that this is the spot he would choose to be.

"He's not easy to miss," Rose says for the second time, clearly nervous around Zach. "I haven't seen him since last Christmas, but how much could he have changed?" She laughs awkwardly. "He couldn't have gotten any shorter, and I doubt he's gained weight wherever he is."

"That's good," Zach says. "Keep your eyes open." He'd like to make Rose more comfortable, but even though things worked out in the end, there's a part of him that still holds a grudge. He keeps wondering if she knew Liddy and Serge—and who knows how many others—were living at Metropolis. This question remains unasked, because he's pretty sure she'd tell him the truth.

He's still astonished he found those photographs of Garrett Haines, and that the police were so quick to recognize and locate Todd Lewis, aka Red Sox Guy, who immediately confessed. Even more amazing is that he'll soon own Metropolis again. Haines's attorney called Brad Berger, Naomi's partner, and offered a deal: if Zach signed an affidavit testifying he would never mention what he discovered and he destroyed all relevant photos and negatives, the lawsuit against him would be nullified, his property promptly returned.

When Zach first heard the proposal, he was outraged. Who did this arrogant asshole think he was, trying to buy his way out of an attempted murder charge? How dare the man demand he destroy Serge's photographs? Order him to sign an affidavit procuring his silence? Haines was trying to kill his wife. He'd planned and plotted and messed with Zach's building and all the people involved with it.

"Absolutely not," he told Brad. "I'll sue him and get the building back on my own. No way I'm buying into his blackmail. If the lawsuit is moot, that means it's nullified already. Right? Why would I do any of those things?"

Brad quickly apprised Zach of the facts undermining his righteous stand. If he didn't take Haines's deal, there would be years of litigation, followed by additional years before the property was returned to him. There would be hefty attorney fees, and if it went to trial, Zach probably wouldn't get his hands on any money for another few years, depending on whether he revived the business or put it up for sale.

Zach pointed out that this might be a baseless threat, that Haines would probably back down before dragging himself through the dirt, and suggested they call his bluff. Brad smiled the smile you give a small child who claims she's going to grow up to be the Queen of England. "Sure," he said. "It's possible. And as much I'd be thrilled to take your money, is it really worth the chance that he doesn't back down?"

So after careful consideration, Zach caved. Lofty principles are one thing; moving ahead with his reclaimed life and putting this whole annus horribilis behind him is quite another. When he told Sheldon the news, the accountant promised to immediately request a return of his estimated tax payments. When he told Katrina, she said she was proud of him, impressed by his perseverance, and indicated a possible willingness to reconsider her claim that he was the worst boyfriend ever.

Haines was in the process of selling Metropolis to MIT for dormitories, and once the particulars are finalized, Zach will offer MIT the same deal. The lawyers on both sides believe it will be quickly accepted. This will obviously produce the same capital gains that have been stalking him, but now he'll actually be receiving the gains, and therefore will have the cash to pay the taxes. It's all been very hush-hush, with no mention in the media of the transfer of properties or what precipitated these moves. If he were less of a cynic, he'd be puzzled over how such a major transaction was being kept secret.

Nickerson & Hagan is putting on *There and Not There*, a one-man show of Serge's interior Metropolis photographs in December, which is why Zach is trying to find him now. Nathaniel concurred it wasn't necessary for Serge to sign a release, as Zach is the legal owner of the artwork, but Zach wants Serge to see his photographs admired and appreciated, to return the camera so Serge can take more, to return the negatives so he can print more.

And he wants Serge to get the money he deserves from the sales, no cut taken. Zach is aware that being this charitable isn't the burden it might have been before he was back on his financial feet, but he truly believes in the effort. And he wants to meet the man who produced such remarkable work. Maybe find out why he left it behind.

Rose scans the Tremont-Boylston corner of the Common as Zach thrusts the Rolleiflex out in front of him, hoping, as he had when he was here in June, that Serge will see the camera and approach them. She shakes her head, and they walk on toward Beacon Street. He sees a group of people he thinks he recognizes from last time, although they could be a completely different bunch, also dressed in tattered clothes, presumably homeless, sitting in a circle of short-legged beach chairs.

"How about over there?" he asks Rose, gesturing toward them.

She looks carefully, shakes her head again. "I'm sorry I'm not being more help." Her eyes are sad and beseeching, slightly damp. "It seems like I'm always saying 'I'm sorry' to you. And you probably don't want to hear it, but—"

He holds up his hands to stop her. He doesn't know if it's the expression on her face or if it's just time. "Look, Rose," he says, "it's over, it's done, and things worked out in the end. So let's just close that all down, okay?"

"Really?" she asks breathlessly. "You're willing to forgive me?"

He looks her in the eye for the first time all day. He's not sure he's willing to forgive her, but he is willing to put it behind them. "How about if I give you a job recommendation to prove it?"

"For real?"

Zach is embarrassed by the relief that floods Rose's face. "For real."

Before Rose can respond, a woman in a long and dirty red cape stands, separates herself from the group on the grass, and marches toward them, glaring. Zach definitely recognizes her from June. He had taken a photograph of her as she strode away from him, down the slope of the Common toward the Public Garden. If he remembers correctly, she was pissed off then too.

The woman moves closer and points her finger at him. "Where'd you get that camera?"

He cups the Rolleiflex in his hands. "It belongs to a man named Serge Laurent."

"So what the fuck are you doing with it?"

"Do you know him?" he asks as Rose takes a couple of steps back.

"Like hell I do."

Does this mean she does or she doesn't? "Do you know where he is?" he tries. "I've got good news for him."

She squints. "What kind of good news?"

"You know him?"

She reaches out and tries to grab the camera from around his neck. "Let me see that."

Zach holds it to his chest. "I'll give it to Serge when you tell me where I can find him."

"What's this good news?"

There's no reason to tell her anything, but from her demands and questions he's pretty sure she knows Serge and probably knows where he is. "There's an art gallery in the South End that's going to have a show of his photographs, and I want to tell him about it."

The woman sneers. "Right. We all believe that."

"It's true," Rose adds. "Lots of his pictures. If they sell them, he could make some real money."

"And you came here because you want to give him money?" She looks from one to the other, clearly incredulous. "Why would you do that?"

"I'm Zach Davidson." He holds out his hand.

The woman doesn't take it. "How did you get his camera?"

Zach drops his hand. "He left it in his storage unit."

"At the castle?"

He's confused, but Rose says, "Yes, Metropolis."

She ponders this. "I'll give it to him."

"He's the only one I'm giving it to," Zach tells her.

"Keep your stupid camera." She spits on the ground. "I don't need it, and Serge sure as hell doesn't need it. He doesn't need any money either."

"Why not?" Zach's stomach turns.

"You figure it out," she says defiantly.

Zach and Rose share a glance. Rose's eyes fill with tears, and surprisingly, or maybe not so surprisingly, Zach's do too. He hopes Serge didn't die alone.

"Where were you with your tears and money when he needed it?" The woman storms down the slope of the Common toward Charles Street, just as she had the last time Zach saw her. Then she stops and comes toward them again, her face hollow with sorrow. "When's his show?" she asks.

"December tenth to January ninth. Nickerson and Hagan Gallery on Harrison Ave."

"Don't know that he'd of liked that, but I kind of do," she says, and heads back to her circle.

"Me too," Zach calls after her, his voice catching on the words.

68

LIDDY

Liddy sits on her balcony, staring out over the roofs of the South End's stately town houses to the harbor beyond. She's currently renting an apartment at the Colonnade, an upscale hotel/apartment building on Huntington Ave. She sips her vodka and shivers slightly in the evening air, watching the purple clouds skim across the sky, pushed by the autumn breeze. Random church steeples jut above the houses. Random islands jut above the water.

Her change of fortune was as swift as Garrett's fall, and just as life-altering. A slash in time. Before, she was a hostage to a despot and a charade of a marriage, a woman preening for the crowds with the proverbial gun to her back. Now, she's her own person, one who just signed divorce papers that will leave her free to do whatever she wishes.

Her independence makes her giddy. She's going to finish *Leaving Vermont*, add to her tutoring hours at the Burke, increase her philanthropy, and, if all goes well, spend the rest of her life with Marta, who will be in Boston in nine days. Marta has a number of job interviews set up, and Liddy has been looking at houses in the area for the two of them and the twins. Robin and Scott are coming back home for good after the fall semester, and if Marta gets the job at Harvard, maybe they'll live in Cambridge, which seems fitting.

Liddy takes another sip of vodka, pulls her jacket tighter around her shoulders. She supposes she should be angrier with Garrett, but there's no reason to muck up her good mood. True, he did manage to save himself from the fallout of his actions: no trial, no media circus, no prison time, no arrest. But his underhanded dealings kept the debacle hidden from the kids. And this makes everything worth it.

She isn't privy to the specifics of his finagling, but there's no doubt it was the result of his money and influence. Expensive and unscrupulous lawyers. Calling in favors from his prominent friends: some in the police department, others in the court system, the district attorney's office, the media. According to Marta's Race of Life, this is a completely predictable outcome.

She could have filed a civil suit against him, but her desire to shield the twins precluded this. In exchange for her lack of legal action, he agreed to destroy the witness statement, allow Robin and Scott to go to high school here, and grant her a divorce with a generous settlement. She could have pushed for more money, but she'll lack for nothing.

Liddy finishes off her vodka and stands. Apparently, just as he'd threatened when he'd twisted his arm around her throat, Garrett wanted to kill her because he couldn't bear for her to be with anyone but him. The logic of a classic batterer. A narcissist intent on controlling everything in his world.

As she steps into the warmth of the apartment, she basks in its silence, in the fact that there's no Garrett and no aides, no one's mandate to fulfill but her own. She glances at the clock. Well past Garrett's dinnertime. But she's not particularly hungry, and now would be a good time to finish the chapter she's been working on for the last few days.

She'd left Clementine sitting in her van with the key in the ignition, unsure whether to turn it. But now Liddy sees that Clementine is going to push ahead and finally get her butt out of Vermont. She puts her glass in the sink and heads for her study.

EPILOGUE

Zach is more upset by Serge's death than he would have expected, both at the loss of a great talent and at his own loss for never getting a chance to meet the man. He's also troubled by the homeless woman's accusation. *Where were you with your tears and money when he needed it?* Zach reminds himself he had no idea who Serge was or that the man needed help until months after he disappeared from Metropolis. Still.

But the biggest blow comes when he gets a call from Nathaniel Nickerson. "I'm really sorry to tell you this," Nathaniel says. "More than you can know."

Zach is working on the final touches to one of Serge's ghost photos for the show. He stops what he's doing and sits down on the closed toilet seat.

"We're closing the gallery."

"Oh man, that sucks."

"Yes it does." Nathaniel's voice is strained. "It's complicated, unexpected, and I won't bore you with the details, but we're not going to be able to put on the Laurent show."

"That soon?" Zach feels bad for Nathaniel, but even worse for Serge. The poor guy can't get a break, alive or dead.

"We have no choice."

"I'm really sorry. What a loss. For you and for everyone else."

"People are always talking about starving artists and how tough being a creative is, but it's also tough trying to support the creatives."

"Can't argue with that." Zach doesn't know what to say that might console Nathaniel. Not to mention himself. He doesn't need the money the photo sales would have brought, but that's not the point. All of Serge's hard work—and all of his own. He wanted to share Serge's genius with the world, and now this might not be possible.

"You can come by and pick up the photographs I have," Nathaniel says. "We'll be here until the end of the month."

ZACH GOES BACK into sales mode, approaching more galleries, contacting museums and photography websites. It doesn't go well. Everyone is inundated. No one has the time or the inclination. All of Serge's photographs are framed and ready, a well-dressed and impressive collection, but the ball has been canceled.

When Katrina comes over for dinner one night in mid-November they brainstorm the options. She's at the counter watching him cook and drinking a glass of wine. "I've still got some contacts from my photographer days. I can hit them up, but it's tough out there. Worse than it's ever been."

"Isn't that what everyone says? And then the next year they say the same thing. It's always worse than it's ever been." He dresses the salad and gives it a toss.

"Because it is."

"I've been thinking about doing it myself."

"I've always been impressed by your overconfidence." Katrina smiles at him to soften her words. "Where are you thinking?"

"Metropolis."

She tilts her head. "And the fact that you've never done anything like this before isn't a problem?"

"Why would it be?"

ZACH SPENDS THE next month publicizing *There and Not There*. He's all over Instagram, Facebook, and Twitter with posts and photos and ads. Katrina designs the graphics, and Nathaniel helps with logistics,

local media, and pricing. The three of them email and text everyone in
their contacts lists. Zach arranges for a junk company to take the furniture from Rose's office and paints the walls and floors a pure white. After
hours of moving, hanging, and rehanging photographs, he and Nathaniel
are satisfied. Then Zach hires a caterer and a bartender, and, except for
nervous anticipation, the preparation for the show is complete.

The afternoon of the opening, it snows. There's little accumulation, but
the roads are slushy, and the first snowfall of the year is always met with
a hesitation to travel that isn't in evidence by midwinter. But Metropolis
is a short walk from the Kendall Square T stop and the major arteries are
clear, so Zach isn't worried.

Nathaniel is. "Weather can kill an opening. A traffic accident can kill
an opening. A big news event can kill an opening."

"Your optimism is overwhelming me," Zach says.

"If a fraction of the thousands of people we've reached out to show up,
we'll be fine," Katrina reminds them.

Nathaniel walks in circles around Rose's office, muttering to himself.

"It's going to be great," Katrina adds.

"Right," Zach agrees.

But they're wrong and Nathaniel is right. The opening is scheduled
from six to eight, and by seven fifteen only about thirty people have come
through and only two remain. Worse than the numbers, most of those
who bothered to make the trip didn't appear particularly impressed. No
sales. Zach stands in front of the ghost image of Liddy's pied-à-terre,
floored by the lack of interest.

Kristina puts her arm through Zach's. "This sucks."

"Yup."

"I'm proud of what you tried to do for him—and you should be too."

"Thanks," Zach mumbles. It's hard to be proud of himself for failing.
He'd been so sure of success.

Nathaniel and Kristina leave at seven thirty, as they both have to work
in the morning, and now one of the two remaining patrons does also. A
lone man scrutinizes the ghost photo of the lawyer's office. He's stayed in

front of it for quite a while, and now that Zach thinks about it, the guy has probably been at the opening longer than anyone else. A potential sale?

Zach walks over to him. "Hey, isn't that terrific? It's one of my favorites."

The man's eyes are locked onto the photo, and he doesn't respond right away. "What I like most about these photographs is that they each contain a story," he finally says. "A mystery you want to figure out."

Zach is impressed. "I feel that too. Who are these people? Why these things? Why this place?"

The man turns around and faces Zach. From afar, Zach had thought he was much older, but he sees now that they're probably around the same age. The completely white beard had thrown him off. "Who is this Serge Laurent?" the man asks. "Was he here tonight?"

"He died recently. It's a terrible loss."

"Did you know him?"

"Unfortunately not, but through a series of strange twists and turns, I came to own his photographs—as well as thousands of unprinted negatives." He holds out his hand. "Zach Davidson."

"Matt Lever." They shake.

"Are you an artist?" Zach asks him.

Matt laughs. "Far from it. I'm an appreciator, a minor collector."

"I found all of these in an abandoned storage unit in the building. Just like the way they discovered Vivian Maier's photos."

Matt's eyes light up. "You've got to be kidding me."

"Nope. Serge printed most of them, and I printed the rest."

"So you're a photographer too?"

"Nope. Just an appreciator like you."

"Did you put up this show?"

"With some help from my friends. Nathaniel Nickerson, in particular."

"It's awful what happened to their gallery. If landlords don't stop raising rents, there won't be any small businesses left."

Zach is surprised that Matt knows about this, and it occurs to him that maybe Matt is a bigger collector than he claims. "Nickerson and Hagan was going to do this show, but then it was forced to close. I'm in such awe of Serge's work that I felt people needed to see it and appreciate it—to be as bowled over by his gift as I am. And this was the only way I could think of to make it happen." Zach looks around the empty room and shrugs. "Which apparently didn't work. Frankly, I'm disappointed. Maybe even a little crushed."

Matt nods. "Tell me about him."

Zach explains the little he knows, obviously omitting the role Serge's photos played in his newly regained ownership to Metropolis. "I tried to find him a couple of times but couldn't. I wanted to meet him. To have him tell me what he was thinking, what he was going for, how he mastered the light—and how the hell he managed to create so much emotion and power."

"It's remarkable work. Do you have more?"

"Lots." Zach is so relieved to hear Matt say this that he almost forgets he's trying to persuade him to buy some photos, but his salesman persona quickly kicks in. "Obviously, these are only photos of Metropolis, but Serge was a master of street photography. On par with—if not better than—Diane Arbus or Robert Frank or even Vivian Maier."

"That's saying a lot."

"It's true. I'd be happy to show you some of the others. They're not here, but I could bring them to you. Wherever and whenever is convenient."

Matt's smile is strangely enigmatic. "How about tomorrow morning at my office?"

"Sure," Zach says, thrilled to finally have some confirmation of his feelings—and perhaps a sale. "Where are you located?"

"You know where the *Boston Globe* is?"

"Exchange Place, right? You're in that building?"

"Yes," Matt says. "I'm the *Globe*'s art critic. And if the other photos are as good as these, I want to help you bring Serge Laurent's work to people who will value it as much as you and I do."

ACKNOWLEDGMENTS

WHEN YOU BEGIN to write a novel, it feels as if you're setting off on a voyage alone into the great unknown. But that isn't true—although the great unknown part is—as there are so many others who accompany and assist you along the way. For *Metropolis*, there is one person who aided and abetted me like no other: Dan Fleishman. My husband, my first reader, my brainstorming buddy. He was there through all my struggles and doubts, cheering me on. Thanks, honey.

And then there are my writing buddies. Who could ever survive this grueling, multiyear process without the support of those who are doing the same? Jan Brogan, of course, Gary Goshgarian Braver, Scott Fleishman, Jessica Keener, Caroline Leavitt, Lyn Millner, and Dawn Tripp. You are my community, the ones who always have my back. Many thanks to my experts, who checked my facts and steered me in directions I wouldn't have known to take: Susan Cohen, Landon Davis, Vicki Konover, Kathy Kreuger, Tracy Prebish, and Karen Stebbins.

Amy Gash is every writer's dream editor: patient, exacting, thoughtful, funny, and respectful—and also a good friend. The incredible team at Algonquin is also a gift, with a special thanks to Chuck Adams. And to Ann Collette, the agent who never gave up, I will always be grateful.